圖解

生活實用**英語**

舉目所及
的人事物

檸檬樹

出版前言

無邊無際的英文單字，如何有效歸納記憶？

【圖解生活實用英語】全系列三冊，
系統化整合龐雜大量的英文單字，分類為：

「眼睛所見」（具體事物）
「大腦所想」（抽象概念）
「種類構造」（生活經驗）

透過全版面的圖像元素，對應的單字具體呈現眼前；
達成「圖像化、視覺性、眼到、心到」的無負擔學習。

第 1 冊【舉目所及的人事物】：眼睛所見人事物的具體單字對應
第 2 冊【腦中延伸的人事物】：大腦所想人事物的具體單字對應
第 3 冊【人事物的種類構造】：生活所知人事物的具體單字對應

「各種場面」的「小群組單字」與「生活場景」實境呼應，
將英語學習導入日常生活，體驗眼前蘊藏的英文風景，

適合「循序自學」、「從情境反查單字」、「群組式串連記憶」。

生活場景中，「常見人事物」的英文說法。

觀賞「馬戲團表演」，你會看到……

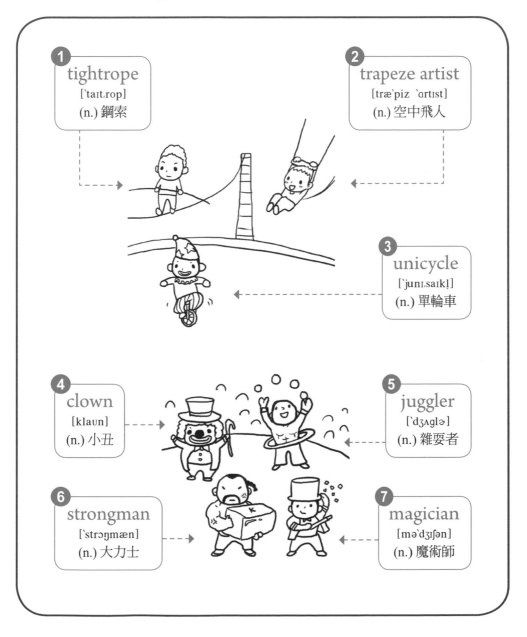

1 tightrope
[ˈtaɪt.rop]
(n.) 鋼索

2 trapeze artist
[træˈpiz ˈɑrtɪst]
(n.) 空中飛人

3 unicycle
[ˈjunɪ.saɪkl̩]
(n.) 單輪車

4 clown
[klaʊn]
(n.) 小丑

5 juggler
[ˈdʒʌglə]
(n.) 雜耍者

6 strongman
[ˈstrɔŋmæn]
(n.) 大力士

7 magician
[məˈdʒɪʃən]
(n.) 魔術師

從「學生百態」，可能連想到⋯⋯

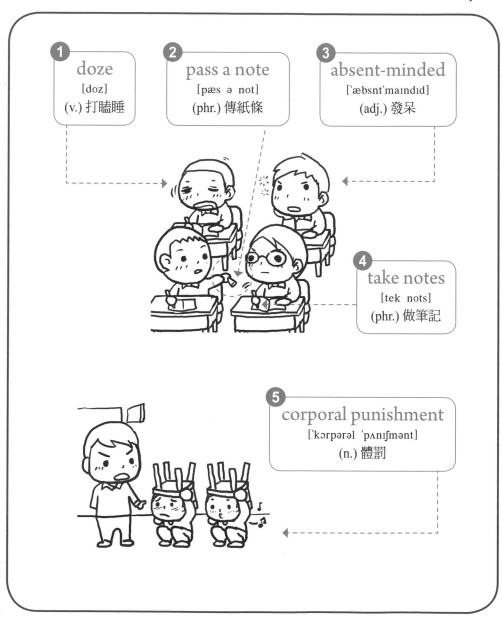

1 doze
[doz]
(v.) 打瞌睡

2 pass a note
[pæs ə not]
(phr.) 傳紙條

3 absent-minded
[ˋæbsntˋmaɪndɪd]
(adj.) 發呆

4 take notes
[tek nots]
(phr.) 做筆記

5 corporal punishment
[ˋkɔrpərəl ˋpʌnɪʃmənt]
(n.) 體罰

第 3 冊：人事物的種類構造

〔種類〕彙整「同種類、同類型事物」英文說法。

「奧運項目」的種類有……

1 fencing
[ˈfɛnsɪŋ]
(n.) 擊劍

2 equestrianism
[ɪˈkwɛstrɪənɪzm̩]
(n.) 馬術

3 archery
[ˈɑrtʃərɪ]
(n.) 射箭

4 boxing
[ˈbɑksɪŋ]
(n.) 拳擊

5 weightlifting
[ˈwetlɪftɪŋ]
(n.) 舉重

6 wrestling
[ˈrɛslɪŋ]
(n.) 角力

〔構造〕細究「事物組成結構」英文說法。

「腳踏車」的構造有……

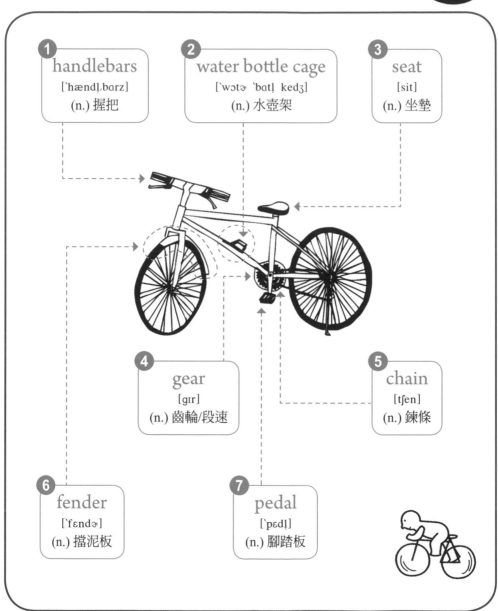

1 handlebars
[ˈhændl͵bɑrz]
(n.) 握把

2 water bottle cage
[ˈwɔtɚ ˈbɑtl͵ kedʒ]
(n.) 水壺架

3 seat
[sit]
(n.) 坐墊

4 gear
[gɪr]
(n.) 齒輪/段速

5 chain
[tʃen]
(n.) 鍊條

6 fender
[ˈfɛndɚ]
(n.) 擋泥板

7 pedal
[ˈpɛdl͵]
(n.) 腳踏板

本書特色

【舉目所及的人事物】：
「眼睛所見各種場面」的「小群組單字」，與生活場景實境呼應！

◎ 以插圖【十字路口周遭】（單元 001）對應學習單字：
交通警察（traffic police）、行人（pedestrian）、斑馬線（zebra crossing）、
紅綠燈（traffic light）、人行道（sidewalk）、地下道（underpass）。

◎ 以插圖【平面停車格】（單元 009）對應學習單字：
監視器（security camera）、高度限制（height limit）、速度限制（speed
limit）、電梯（elevator）、停車格（parking space）。

◎ 以插圖【碼頭邊】（單元 010、011）對應學習單字：
燈塔（lighthouse）、海鷗（seagull）、碼頭（marina）、救生圈（life preserver）、
起重機（crane）、堆高機（forklift）、貨櫃（cargo container）。

各單元有「4 區域學習板塊」，點線面延伸完備的「生活單字＋生活例句」！
「透過圖像」對應單字，「透過例句」掌握單字用法，就能將英文運用自如。
安排「4 區域學習板塊」達成上述功能：

1. 【單字圖解區】：
   各單元約安排 5～7 個「具相關性的小群組單字」，以「全版面情境插圖」
   解說單字。

2. 【單字例句區】：
   各單字列舉例句，可掌握單字用法、培養閱讀力，並強化單字印象。

3. 【延伸學習區】：
   詳列例句「新單字、時態變化、重要片語」。

4. 【中文釋義區】：
   安排在頁面最下方，扮演「輔助學習角色」，如不明瞭英文句義，再參考
   中譯。

採「全版面情境圖像」解說單字：
插圖清晰易懂，舉目所及的人事物，留下具體英文印象！

【單字圖解區】

全版面情境插圖，對應的「人、事、物」單字具體呈現眼前。

【學習單字框】

包含「單字、KK音標、詞性、中譯」；並用虛線指引至插圖，不妨礙閱讀舒
適度。

2 pedestrian
[pəˋdɛstrɪən]
(n.) 行人

← （單字）
← （KK音標）
← （詞性、中譯）

【小圖示另安排放大圖】

讓圖像構造清楚呈現。

 （單元 010：船錨放大圖）

4 anchor
[ˋæŋkə]
(n.) 船錨

【情境式畫面學習】

透過插圖強化視覺記憶，能減輕學習負擔，加深單字印象。

可以「從情境主題查詢單字」，任意發想的單字疑問，都能找到答案！
全書「202 個生活情境」，「蘊藏 202 種英文風景」。生活中看到、想到的
場景，都能透過查詢主題，「呈現該場景蘊藏的英文風景」。
最熟悉的生活百態，成為最實用的英語資源。

適合親子共讀，利用插圖誘發學習興趣，將英語導入日常生活。
本書「以圖像對應英語」，「用英語認識生活中舉目所見的人事物」，也適
合親子共讀。可透過圖像誘發學習興趣，藉由「圖像英語」認識生活周遭，
探索未接觸的世界，並增長英語知識。

單字加註背景知識，同步累積生活知識，提升英語力，豐富知識庫！

受限於生活經驗，許多生活中隨處可見的人事物，可能「只知名稱、不知背景知識與內涵」。本書透過圖解指引英文單字，對於常聽聞、卻未必了解本質的單字，加註背景知識，有助於閱讀時加深單字印象。同步累積生活知識，對於聽說讀寫，更有助力。

◎ 單元 010【碼頭邊】的【anchor】（船錨）：

用於穩定船舶的鐵製倒鉤，一端以鐵鏈和船身相連，將另一端拋至水底或岸上，可使船停住。

◎ 單元 012【郵輪上】的【first mate】（大副）：

負責駕駛輪船的人，地位僅次於船長。

◎ 單元 125【宇宙中】的【black hole】（黑洞）：

恆星於核心燃料耗盡後，所產生的重力塌縮現象。

書末增列【全書單字附錄】：
詞性分類 × 字母排序，清楚知道「從這本書學到了哪些單字」！

依循「詞性分類＋字母排序」原則，將全書單字製作成「單字附錄總整理」。有別於本文的「情境式圖解」，「單字附錄」採取「規則性整理」，有助於學習者具體掌握「學了哪些單字、記住了哪些單字」。

<u>讓所經歷的學習過程並非蜻蜓點水，而是務實與確實的學習紀錄。</u>

目錄 Contents

※ 本書各單元 MP3 音軌 = 各單元序號

交通

單元

164	電梯 (2)	elevator (2)
165	花店 (1)	flower shop (1)
166	花店 (2)	flower shop (2)
167	美容院 (1)	beauty salon (1)
168	美容院 (2)	beauty salon (2)
169	戶外廣場 (1)	outdoor plaza (1)
170	戶外廣場 (2)	outdoor plaza (2)
171	戶外廣場 (3)	outdoor plaza (3)
172	行李箱內 (1)	in a suitcase (1)
173	行李箱內 (2)	in a suitcase (2)

特殊場合

174	車禍現場 (1)	car accident scene (1)
175	車禍現場 (2)	car accident scene (2)
176	火災現場 (1)	fire spot (1)
177	火災現場 (2)	fire spot (2)
178	警察局 (1)	police station (1)
179	警察局 (2)	police station (2)
180	加護病房 (1)	ICU (= intensive care unit) (1)
181	加護病房 (2)	ICU (= intensive care unit) (2)
182	電視節目現場 (1)	live television show (1)
183	電視節目現場 (2)	live television show (2)
184	動物醫院 (1)	animal hospital (1)
185	動物醫院 (2)	animal hospital (2)

186	軍事堡壘 (1)	military fortress (1)
187	軍事堡壘 (2)	military fortress (2)
188	命案現場 (1)	crime scene (1)
189	命案現場 (2)	crime scene (2)
190	教堂裡 (1)	in a church (1)
191	教堂裡 (2)	in a church (2)
192	教堂裡 (3)	in a church (3)
193	寺廟裡 (1)	in a temple (1)
194	寺廟裡 (2)	in a temple (2)
195	溫室裡	in a greenhouse
196	建築工地 (1)	construction site (1)
197	建築工地 (2)	construction site (2)
198	記者會 (1)	press conference (1)
199	記者會 (2)	press conference (2)
200	記者會 (3)	press conference (3)
201	法庭上 (1)	in court (1)
202	法庭上 (2)	in court (2)

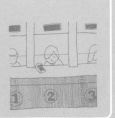

001

十字路口周遭

MP3 001

1 traffic police
[ˈtræfɪk pəˈlis]
(n.) 交通警察

2 pedestrian
[pəˈdɛstrɪən]
(n.) 行人

4 traffic light
[ˈtræfɪk laɪt]
(n.) 紅綠燈

3 zebra crossing
[ˈzibrə ˈkrɔsɪŋ]
(n.) 斑馬線

5 sidewalk
[ˈsaɪdˌwɔk]
(n.) 人行道

2 pedestrian
[pəˈdɛstrɪən]
(n.) 行人

6 underpass
[ˈʌndɚˌpæs]
(n.) 地下道

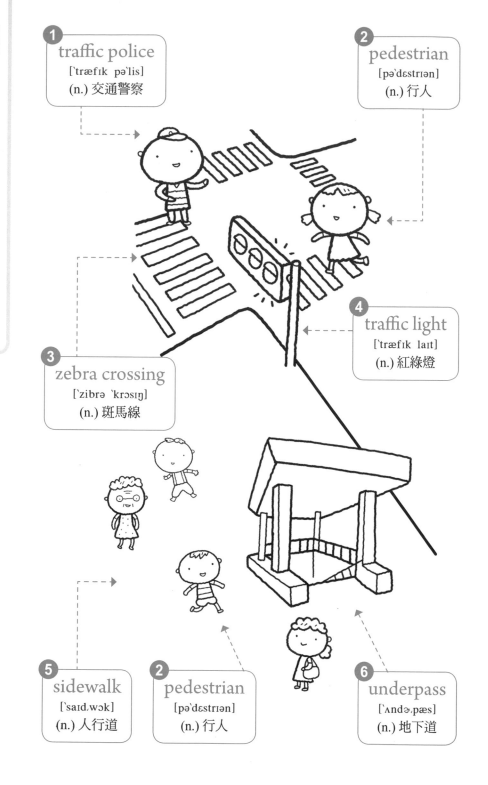

❶ 交通警察

Frank always follows the instructions of the traffic police when he is
driving.　　　　　　　　遵循指示

❷ 行人

The driver accidentally crashed into a pedestrian because he was
distracted.　　　　　不小心撞上　　　　　　　　　　　　他不專心

❸ 斑馬線

Be careful! You should not cross here because there is no zebra crossing.
　　　　　　　　　不該穿越這裡

❹ 紅綠燈

You must remember to stop the car when the traffic light turns red.
　　　　　　　　　　　　　　　　　　　　　　變紅燈

❺ 人行道

I ran into an old friend on the sidewalk.
　偶然遇見

❻ 地下道

It's raining now. Let's use the underpass so we won't get wet.
　　　　　　　　　行走地下道　　　　　　　被淋濕

學更多

❶ follow〈遵守〉· instruction〈指示〉· driving〈drive（駕駛）的 ing 型態〉
❷ accidentally〈意外地〉· crashed into〈crash into（撞到）的過去式〉· distracted〈分心的〉
❸ careful〈小心的〉· cross〈穿越〉· there is no...〈沒有…〉· zebra〈有斑紋的〉
❹ remember〈記得〉· stop〈暫停〉· turn〈轉變〉
❺ ran into〈run into（偶然遇見）的過去式〉· friend〈朋友〉
❻ raining〈rain（下雨）的 ing 型態〉· wet〈濕透的〉

中譯

❶ Frank 在開車時，總會遵循交通警察的指示。
❷ 那名駕駛因為分心，不小心撞上了一名行人。
❸ 小心！你不應該在這裡穿越馬路，因為這裡沒有斑馬線。
❹ 當紅綠燈轉為紅燈時，你必須記得要停車。
❺ 我在人行道上巧遇一位老朋友。
❻ 目前在下雨，我們走地下道才不會被淋濕。

1 overpass
[ˋovɚˌpæs]
(n.) 天橋

2 car
[kɑr]
(n.) 車輛

3 street sign
[strit saɪn]
(n.) 路標

4 stop line
[stɑp laɪn]
(n.) 停車線

5 lane
[len]
(n.) 車道

5 lane
[len]
(n.) 車道

6 traffic island
[ˋtræfɪk ˋaɪlənd]
(n.) 分隔島

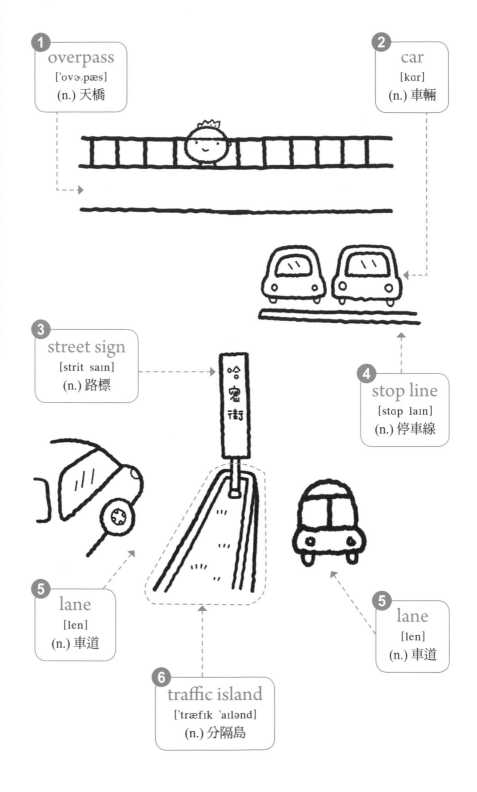

❶ 天橋

Using the overpass is the safest way to cross the road.
　　　　　　行走天橋　　　　　　　　　　　　　過馬路

❷ 車輛

My parents bought a new car last week.

❸ 路標

Can you see the street sign? I forgot to bring my glasses.

❹ 停車線

Don't go past the stop line; you might get a fine.
　　　　　　超越　　　　　　　　　　被開罰單

❺ 車道

This lane is for buses only, let's not drive on it.
　　　　　　　　　公車專用

❻ 分隔島

There is a man directing traffic on the traffic island.
　　　　　　　指揮交通

學更多

❶ safest〈最安全的，safe（安全）的最高級〉‧ way〈方式〉‧ cross〈穿越〉
❷ parents〈父母〉‧ bought〈buy（買）的過去式〉‧ last〈上一個的〉
❸ forgot〈forget（忘記）的過去式〉‧ bring〈攜帶〉‧ glasses〈眼鏡〉
❹ past〈通過〉‧ fine〈罰款〉
❺ bus〈公車〉‧ drive〈行駛〉
❻ there is...〈有…〉‧ directing〈direct（指揮）的 ing 型態〉‧ traffic〈交通〉‧
island〈島狀物〉

中譯

❶ 走天橋是過馬路最安全的方法。
❷ 我父母上週買了一輛新車。
❸ 你能看清楚路標嗎？我忘記帶眼鏡了。
❹ 不要超越停車線，你可能會被開單受罰。
❺ 這個車道是公車專用的，我們不要開（車）到上面。
❻ 分隔島上有一名男子在指揮交通。

003

汽車內部

MP3 003

1 car window
[kɑr ˈwɪndo]
(n.) 車窗

2 sunroof
[ˈsʌnˌruf]
(n.) 天窗

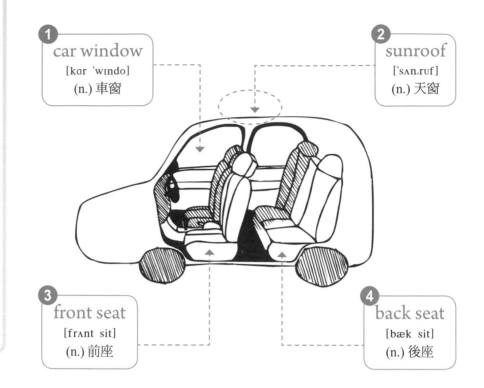

3 front seat
[frʌnt sit]
(n.) 前座

4 back seat
[bæk sit]
(n.) 後座

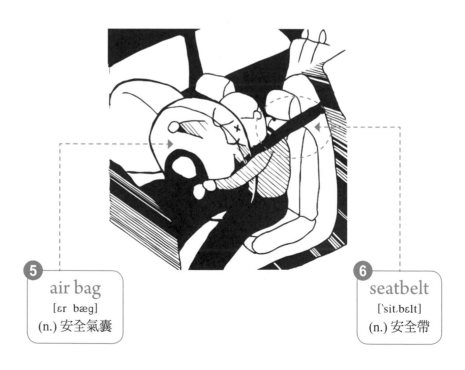

5 air bag
[ɛr bæg]
(n.) 安全氣囊

6 seatbelt
[ˈsitˌbɛlt]
(n.) 安全帶

❶ 車窗

Please roll up the car window, honey. It's hot outside.
搖上車窗

❷ 天窗

I love your sunroof! It's great to have it open on a nice spring day!
使它打開

❸ 前座

Sally loves to sit on the front seat with her daddy and go for rides in the country.
去兜風

❹ 後座

There is no back seat at all in some fancy sports cars.
根本沒有後座

❺ 安全氣囊

Air bags have saved many people's lives in crashes.
救了許多人命

❻ 安全帶

You must fasten your seatbelt when you're riding in a taxi.
搭計程車

學更多

❶ roll〈捲動〉‧ up〈往上〉‧ outside〈外面〉
❷ great〈極好的〉‧ nice〈美好的〉‧ spring〈春季〉
❸ sit on〈坐於…〉‧ front〈前面的〉‧ ride〈乘車兜風〉‧ country〈鄉間〉
❹ there is no...〈沒有…〉‧ back〈後面的〉‧ at all〈根本〉‧ fancy〈奢華的〉‧ sports car〈跑車〉
❺ saved〈save（拯救）的過去分詞〉‧ lives〈life（性命）的複數〉‧ crash〈車禍〉
❻ fasten〈繫上〉‧ riding〈ride（搭乘）的 ing 型態〉‧ taxi〈計程車〉

中譯

❶ 親愛的，請搖上車窗。外面很熱。
❷ 我好愛你的天窗！在美好的春日打開來很舒服！
❸ Sally 最愛跟她父親坐在前座，去鄉間兜風。
❹ 有些奢華的跑車根本沒有後座。
❺ 許多遭遇車禍的人都是靠安全氣囊得救。
❻ 搭乘計程車時，你必須繫上安全帶。

004

汽車駕駛座

MP3 004

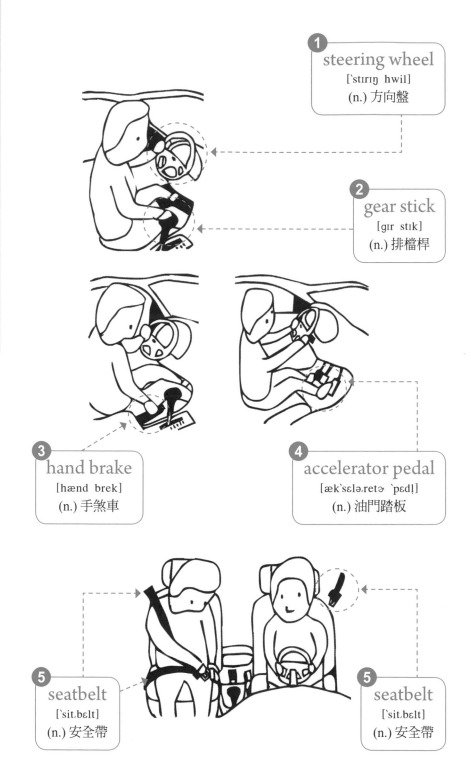

1 steering wheel
[ˈstɪrɪŋ hwil]
(n.) 方向盤

2 gear stick
[gɪr stɪk]
(n.) 排檔桿

3 hand brake
[hænd brek]
(n.) 手煞車

4 accelerator pedal
[ækˈsɛləˌretɚ ˈpɛdl̩]
(n.) 油門踏板

5 seatbelt
[ˈsitˌbɛlt]
(n.) 安全帶

5 seatbelt
[ˈsitˌbɛlt]
(n.) 安全帶

❶ 方向盤

Keep your hands on the steering wheel at all times when driving.
<u>保持雙手在方向盤上</u>

❷ 排檔桿

Use the gear stick and the clutch to shift gears.
<u>切換排檔</u>

❸ 手煞車

The hand brake should be used whenever you park on a hill.
<u>每當你在斜坡上停車</u>

❹ 油門踏板

Be very careful not to step down too hard on the accelerator pedal.
<u>太過用力向下踩踏</u>

❺ 安全帶

Please fasten your seatbelt.

學更多

❶ keep〈保持〉‧ steering〈操縱〉‧ wheel〈輪盤〉‧ at all times〈隨時〉‧ driving〈drive（開車）的 ing 型態〉

❷ gear〈汽車排檔〉‧ stick〈棒狀物〉‧ clutch〈離合器〉‧ shift〈切換〉

❸ brake〈煞車〉‧ whenever〈每當〉‧ park〈停車〉‧ hill〈斜坡〉

❹ careful〈小心的〉‧ step〈踩踏〉‧ down〈向下〉‧ hard〈用力地〉‧ accelerator〈油門〉‧ pedal〈踏板〉

❺ fasten〈繫上〉

中譯

❶ 開車時，要隨時保持雙手操控方向盤。

❷ 使用排檔桿及離合器換檔。

❸ 每當在斜坡上停車時，都要使用手煞車。

❹ 要非常小心避免太過用力地踩下油門踏板。

❺ 請繫上你的安全帶。

005

公車內 (1)

MP3 005

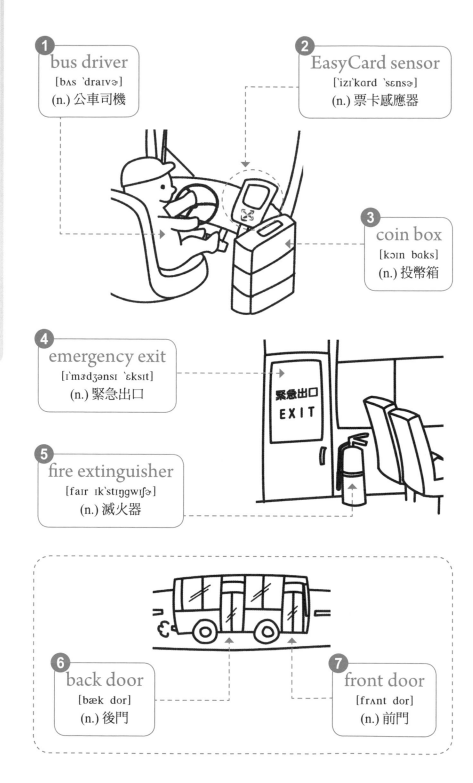

1 bus driver
[bʌs `draɪvə]
(n.) 公車司機

2 EasyCard sensor
[`izɪ`kɑrd `sɛnsə]
(n.) 票卡感應器

3 coin box
[kɔɪn bɑks]
(n.) 投幣箱

4 emergency exit
[ɪ`mɝdʒənsɪ `ɛksɪt]
(n.) 緊急出口

5 fire extinguisher
[faɪr ɪk`stɪŋgwɪʃə]
(n.) 滅火器

緊急出口
EXIT

6 back door
[bæk dor]
(n.) 後門

7 front door
[frʌnt dor]
(n.) 前門

❶ 公車司機

Ask the bus driver where the next stop is.
<u>下一站</u>

❷ 票卡感應器

Passengers can use the EasyCard sensor to pay.

❸ 投幣箱

If you don't have an EasyCard, just drop some coins into the coin box.
<u>丟一些零錢</u>

❹ 緊急出口

In case of emergency, everyone should know where the emergency exit
<u>萬一有緊急狀況</u>　　　　　　　　　　　　　　　　<u>緊急出口被設置於哪裡</u>
is located.

❺ 滅火器

Get the fire extinguisher, quick! There's a fire at the back of the bus.
<u>有火災</u>

❻ 後門

Please exit using the back door, please.

❼ 前門

On this bus, you need to exit through the front door.
<u>由前門下車</u>

學更多

❶ next〈下一個的〉‧ stop〈停車站〉
❷ passenger〈乘客〉‧ sensor〈感應器〉‧ pay〈付款〉
❸ drop〈丟入〉‧ coin〈錢幣〉‧ into〈到…裡〉
❹ in case of...〈如果發生…〉‧ located〈locate（設置於…）的過去分詞〉
❺ extinguisher〈消滅者〉‧ quick〈迅速的〉‧ fire〈火災〉
❻ exit〈離開〉‧ using〈use（使用）的 ing 型態〉‧ back〈後面的〉
❼ bus〈公車〉‧ through〈經由〉‧ front〈前面的〉

中譯

❶ 問一下公車司機下一站是哪裡。
❷ 乘客可以使用票卡感應器付款。
❸ 如果你沒有悠遊卡，就丟一些零錢到投幣箱裡。
❹ 發生緊急狀況時，每個人都必須知道緊急出口在哪裡。
❺ 去拿滅火器，快！公車後方起火了。
❻ 請由後門下車。
❼ 搭乘本公車，請由前門下車。

006

公車內(2)

MP3 006

1 support ring
[sə`port rɪŋ]
(n.) 拉環

2 passenger
[`pæsṇdʒɚ]
(n.) 乘客

3 seat
[sit]
(n.) 座位

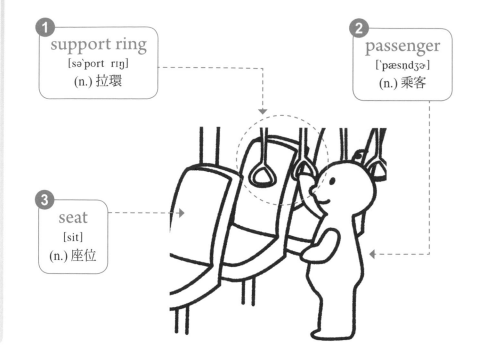

4 buzzer
[`bʌzɚ]
(n.) 下車鈴

5 priority seat
[praɪˋɔrətɪ sit]
(n.) 博愛座

3 seat
[sit]
(n.) 座位

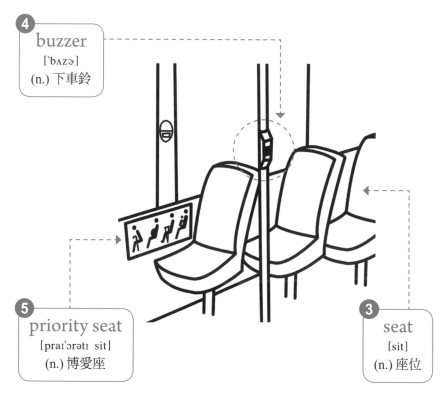

❶ 拉環

Grab onto the support ring or you may fall inside the bus.
　　　　　　抓住拉環

❷ 乘客

Some passengers choose to ride the bus to work, rather than the MRT.
　　　　　　　　　　　　搭公車

❸ 座位

Do you see any empty seats? I guess we'll have to stand.
　　　　　　　　　　　　　　我們必須站立

❹ 下車鈴

You forgot to press the buzzer! Now the bus isn't stopping at our stop!
　　　　　　　　按下車鈴

❺ 博愛座

Priority seats should be reserved for those who are elderly, pregnant or disabled.
　　　　　　　　　　　　　　　　　　年長者、孕婦、殘障人士

學更多

❶ grab onto〈緊抓…不放〉‧ or〈否則〉‧ fall〈跌倒〉‧ inside〈在…的裡面〉

❷ choose〈選擇〉‧ ride〈搭乘〉‧ rather than...〈而不是…〉

❸ empty〈未占用的〉‧ guess〈猜測〉‧ have to...〈必須…〉

❹ forgot〈forget（忘記）的過去式〉‧ press〈按壓〉‧ stopping〈stop（停止）的 ing 型態〉‧ stop〈停車站〉

❺ priority〈優先〉‧ be reserved for...〈留給…〉‧ elderly〈年長的〉‧ pregnant〈懷孕的〉‧ disabled〈殘缺的〉

中譯

❶ 在公車內要抓住拉環，否則你可能會跌倒。

❷ 有些乘客選擇搭公車上班，而不是搭捷運。

❸ 你有看到空位嗎？看來我們只好站著（搭車）。

❹ 你忘記按下車鈴了！現在公車不會停在我們要下（車）的站！

❺ 博愛座應該留給年長者、孕婦、或是殘障人士。

007

停車場出入口

🔊 MP3 007

1 car park ticket machine
[kɑr pɑrk ˋtɪkɪt məˋʃin]
(n.) 停車收費機

2 toll collector
[tol kəˋlɛktə]
(n.) 收費員

3 boom gate
[bʊm get]
(n.) 收費閘門

4 exit
[ˋɛksɪt]
(n.) 出口

5 ticket
[ˋtɪkɪt]
(n.) 停車收費單

6 entrance
[ˋɛntrəns]
(n.) 入口

❶ 停車收費機

There are automatic car park ticket machines at many small lots.

小型停車場

❷ 收費員

The toll collector can give you change back after you pay the fee.

找零錢給你

❸ 收費閘門

You can't drive in until the boom gate has been lifted.

❹ 出口

There is a long line at the exit, so we'll have to wait for a while.

排隊排很長

❺ 停車收費單

You need a ticket if you park at a parking lot.

❻ 入口

Sir, you'll find the entrance to the parking lot around the corner.

停車場的入口

學更多

❶ there are...〈有…〉．automatic〈自動的〉．lot〈作特地用處的一塊地〉
❷ give...back〈返還…〉．change〈零錢〉．pay〈支付〉．fee〈費用〉
❸ drive〈行駛〉．in〈朝向…〉．until〈在…之前〉．lifted〈lift（舉起）的過去分詞〉
❹ line〈排隊隊伍〉．wait〈等候〉．for a while〈一會兒〉
❺ park〈停車〉．parking lot〈停車場〉
❻ around〈在…附近〉．corner〈轉角〉

中譯

❶ 許多小型停車場設有自動的停車收費機。
❷ 你付費後，收費員會找零（錢）給你。
❸ 收費閘門升起之前，你不能朝著它開（車）過去。
❹ 出口排了很長的隊伍，所以我們必須等一下子。
❺ 如果在停車場停車，你會有一張停車收費單。
❻ 先生，在轉角附近你會看到停車場的入口。

008

機械停車格

MP3 008

1 mechanical parking
[məˈkænɪkḷ ˈpɑrkɪŋ]
(n.) 機械式停車

2 upper level
[ˈʌpə ˈlɛvḷ]
(n.) 上層

3 vehicle
[ˈviɪkḷ]
(n.) 車輛

4 handicapped space
[ˈhændɪˌkæpt spes]
(n.) 殘障停車格

5 parking space
[ˈpɑrkɪŋ spes]
(n.) 停車格

6 lower level
[ˈloə ˈlɛvḷ]
(n.) 下層

❶ 機械式停車

Mechanical parking is very popular in countries where space is limited.
空間有限的國家

❷ 上層

The upper level of the parking lot has more parking spaces available on the weekend.
有更多可以用的停車格

❸ 車輛

Don't worry, miss. Your vehicle is safe here.

❹ 殘障停車格

You may not park in any handicapped space if you do not have a permit.
停任何殘障車位

❺ 停車格

I can't find a parking space anywhere! I'm going to be late for my appointment.
我的約會要遲到

❻ 下層

I can't remember where we parked exactly, but I think our car's on the lower level.
我們在哪裡停車

學更多

❶ parking〈停車、停車處〉・popular〈受歡迎的〉・country〈國家〉・space〈空間〉・limited〈有限的〉

❷ upper〈上面的〉・level〈層〉・parking lot〈停車場〉・available〈可用的〉

❸ worry〈擔心〉・safe〈安全的〉

❹ handicapped〈殘障的〉・permit〈許可證〉

❺ late〈遲到的〉・appointment〈約會〉

❻ remember〈記得〉・parked〈park（停車）的過去式〉・exactly〈確切地〉・lower〈較低的〉

中譯

❶ 機械式停車在空間有限的國家很受歡迎。
❷ 在週末時，（機械式）停車場的上層有更多車位可以使用。
❸ 小姐，別擔心。您的車輛在這裡很安全。
❹ 沒有許可證的人，不能停在任何一個殘障停車位。
❺ 我到處都找不到停車格！我的約會要遲到了。
❻ 我記不太清楚我們把車停在哪裡，但我想我們的車是停在下層。

009

平面停車格

MP3 009

1 security camera
[sɪˈkjʊrətɪ ˈkæmərə]
(n.) 監視器

2 height limit
[haɪt ˈlɪmɪt]
(n.) 高度限制

3 speed limit
[spid ˈlɪmɪt]
(n.) 速度限制

限高 3.5 m

3.5m

30

P

004

4 elevator
[ˈɛləˌvetɚ]
(n.) 電梯

5 parking space
[ˈpɑrkɪŋ spes]
(n.) 停車格

❶ 監視器

Don't even think about stealing a car from this parking lot! There are
別想偷車

security cameras all over.

❷ 高度限制

That truck has surpassed the height limit and won't be able to enter.

❸ 速度限制

Obey the speed limit; otherwise, you'll likely get a speeding ticket.
被開超速罰單

❹ 電梯

There is an elevator to take you upstairs.
帶你到樓上

❺ 停車格

Parking space is always at a premium in big cities.
總是非常稀罕

學更多

❶ think about〈考慮〉・stealing〈steal（偷竊）的 ing 型態〉・parking lot〈停車場〉・
security〈保安、防備〉・all over〈到處〉

❷ truck〈卡車〉・surpassed〈surpass（超出）的過去分詞〉・enter〈進入〉

❸ obey〈遵守〉・otherwise〈不然〉・likely〈可能地〉・speeding ticket〈超速罰單〉

❹ there is...〈有…〉・take〈帶領〉・upstairs〈往樓上〉

❺ premium〈加價、附加的金錢〉・at a premium〈非常缺乏、稀罕〉

中譯

❶ 別想從這個停車場偷走車輛！這裡到處都有監視器。

❷ 那輛卡車超出高度限制，所以無法進入。

❸ 要遵守速限，不然你可能會被開超速罰單。

❹ 有電梯可以讓你搭到樓上。

❺ 停車位（格）在大城市總是一位難求。

010

碼頭邊(1)

MP3 010

1 ferryboat
[ˈfɛrɪ͵bot]
(n.) 渡輪

2 sailor
[ˈselə]
(n.) 水手

3 fishing boat
[ˈfɪʃɪŋ bot]
(n.) 漁船

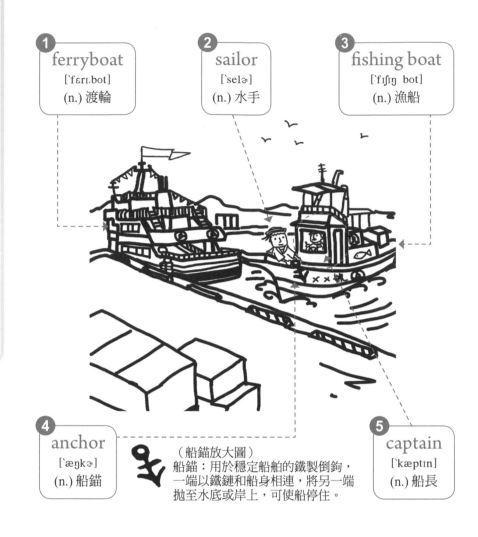

4 anchor
[ˈæŋkə]
(n.) 船錨

（船錨放大圖）
船錨：用於穩定船舶的鐵製倒鉤，一端以鐵鏈和船身相連，將另一端拋至水底或岸上，可使船停住。

5 captain
[ˈkæptɪn]
(n.) 船長

6 fish stand
[fɪʃ stænd]
(n.) 魚貨攤

7 seafood
[ˈsi͵fud]
(n.) 海鮮

❶ 渡輪

Let's take the ferryboat from Staten Island, New York to Manhattan.
紐約的史泰登島

❷ 水手

Tim's decided to become a sailor in the military when he grows up.

❸ 漁船

My cousin works on a fishing boat in the summer for his dad.

❹ 船錨

A heavy anchor will keep the ship from moving.
避免船隻移動

❺ 船長

Did you see the captain at the harbor? He's quite handsome.

❻ 魚貨攤

Let's buy some fresh fish at that fish stand over there!
新鮮的魚

❼ 海鮮

I love seafood and it's healthy, too!

學更多

❶ take〈搭乘〉・from...to...〈從…到…〉・Manhattan〈曼哈頓〉
❷ decided〈decide（決定）的過去分詞〉・military〈軍隊〉・grow up〈成年〉
❸ cousin〈堂兄弟姊妹、表兄弟姊妹〉
❹ heavy〈重的〉・keep... from...〈避免〉・moving〈move（移動）的 ing 型態〉
❺ harbor〈港口〉・quite〈頗為…〉・handsome〈英俊的〉
❻ fresh〈新鮮的〉・stand〈攤子〉・over there〈在那裡〉
❼ healthy〈健康的〉

中譯

❶ 我們搭乘渡輪從紐約的史泰登島到曼哈頓吧。
❷ Tim 決定長大後要在軍隊當水手。
❸ 夏天時，我表哥會到漁船上幫忙他父親做事。
❹ 沉重的船錨能避免船隻移動。
❺ 你有看到港口的那個船長嗎？他挺帥的。
❻ 我們去那邊的那間魚貨攤買些新鮮的魚吧！
❼ 我愛吃海鮮，而且它也很健康！

碼頭邊(2)

MP3 011

1 lighthouse
['laɪt،haʊs]
(n.) 燈塔

2 seagull
['si،gʌl]
(n.) 海鷗

3 marina
[mə'rɪnə]
(n.) 碼頭

4 life preserver
[laɪf prɪ'zɝvɚ]
(n.) 救生圈

（救生圈放大圖）

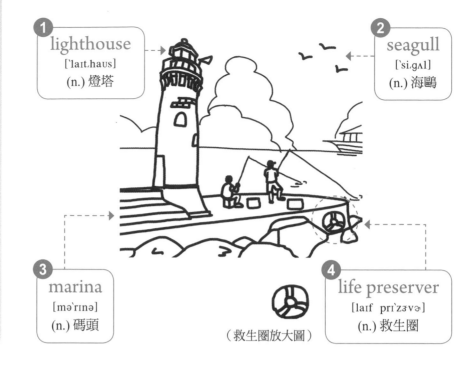

5 crane
[kren]
(n.) 起重機

6 forklift
['fɔrk،lɪft]
(n.) 堆高機

7 cargo container
['kɑrgo kən'tenɚ]
(n.) 貨櫃

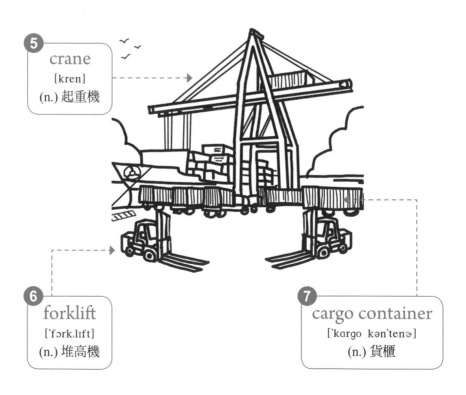

❶ 燈塔

The lighthouse helps boats avoid crashing into the shore.
<u>避免撞到岸邊</u>

❷ 海鷗

If you go to the beach, you'll see lots of seagulls.

❸ 碼頭

Our boat is docked at the marina year-round.

❹ 救生圈

You need a life preserver if you want to go sailing.
<u>航海</u>

❺ 起重機

In order to lift some of the heavy containers, the workers must use a crane.

❻ 堆高機

Jason operates a forklift at work, moving around heavy boxes for his boss.

❼ 貨櫃

Cargo containers are unloaded at the harbor all day and all night.
<u>整天整夜</u>

學更多

❶ boat〈船〉．avoid〈避免〉．crashing into〈crash into（撞到）的 ing 型態〉．
shore〈海岸〉
❷ beach〈海邊〉．lots of〈大量的〉
❸ docked〈dock（停靠碼頭）的過去分詞〉．year-round〈一整年地〉
❹ sailing〈sail（航海）的 ing 型態〉
❺ in order to...〈為了…〉．lift〈抬起〉．container〈貨櫃〉．worker〈工人〉
❻ operate〈操作〉．at work〈在工作〉．around〈四處〉．box〈箱子〉
❼ unloaded〈unload（卸貨）的過去分詞〉．harbor〈港口〉

中譯

❶ 燈塔會幫助船隻避免撞到岸邊。
❷ 如果你去海邊，你會看到許多海鷗。
❸ 我們的船整年都停靠在碼頭。
❹ 要出海航行時，你必須有救生圈。
❺ 為了抬起某些沉重的貨櫃，工人一定得用起重機。
❻ Jason 工作時要操作堆高機，替他的老闆四處移動沉重的箱子。
❼ 貨櫃不分日夜在港口卸貨。

012

郵輪上 (1)

1 pilothouse
[`paɪlət.haʊs]
wheelhouse
[`hwil.haʊs]
(n.) 駕駛艙

兩個單字都是「駕駛艙」。

2 first mate
[fɝst met]
(n.) 大副

負責駕駛輪船的人，
地位僅次於船長。

3 captain
[`kæptɪn]
(n.) 船長

總管全船事務
的人。

4 deck
[dɛk]
(n.) 甲板

5 cabin
[`kæbɪn]
(n.) 船艙

船內部可容納
客貨的地方。

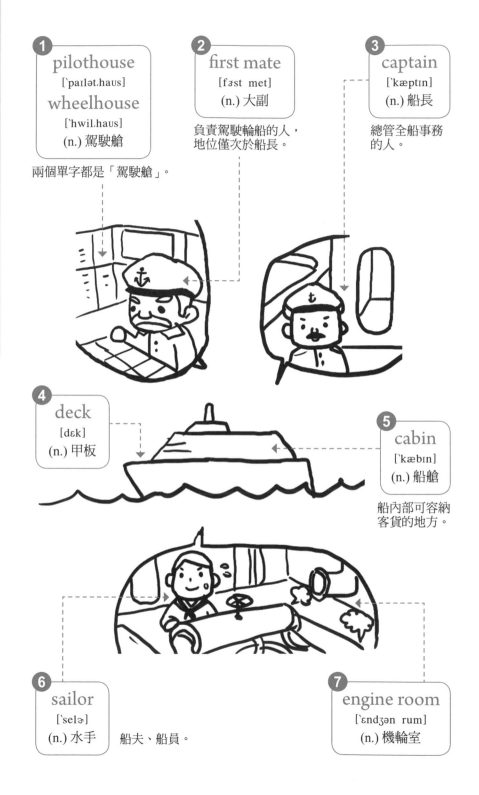

6 sailor
[`selɚ]
(n.) 水手

船夫、船員。

7 engine room
[`ɛndʒən rum]
(n.) 機輪室

❶ 駕駛艙
The pilothouse is where the ship's captain controls the ship.

❷ 大副
The first mate is second in command to the captain.
指揮權僅次於船長

❸ 船長
When I went on a cruise last year, the captain took me on a tour.
帶我參觀

❹ 甲板
Let's go below deck and find our cabins.

❺ 船艙
These 1ˢᵗ class cabins are worth the extra money.

❻ 水手
There are some really sexy sailors walking around the marina today.
在碼頭附近走動

❼ 機輪室
The engine room is usually off-limits to passengers.
禁止乘客進入

學更多

❶ captain〈船長〉‧control〈控制〉
❷ mate〈助手〉‧second in command to...〈指揮權僅次於…〉‧second〈第二的〉‧command〈統率、指揮權〉
❸ went〈go（去）的過去式〉‧cruise〈乘船旅行〉‧tour〈遊覽〉
❹ below〈到…下方〉
❺ class〈等級〉‧worth〈有…的價值〉‧extra〈額外的〉
❻ sexy〈迷人的〉‧around〈在…附近〉‧marina〈碼頭〉
❼ engine〈發動機、引擎〉‧off-limits〈禁止進入的〉‧passenger〈乘客〉

中譯

❶ 駕駛艙是船長操控船隻的地方。
❷ 大副的指揮權僅次於船長。
❸ 去年我搭船旅行時，船長帶我四處參觀。
❹ 我們一起下去甲板，找我們的船艙吧。
❺ 這些頭等船艙值得額外的收費。
❻ 今天碼頭上有許多迷人的水手走來走去。
❼ 機輪室通常禁止乘客進入。

013

郵輪上 (2)

🔘 MP3 013

1 movie theater
[ˈmuvɪ ˈθɪətə]
(n.) 電影院

2 casino
[kəˈsino]
(n.) 賭場

3 restaurant
[ˈrɛstərənt]
(n.) 餐廳

4 ballroom
[ˈbɔlˌrum]
(n.) 宴會廳

5 passenger
[ˈpæsn̩dʒə]
(n.) 乘客

6 club
[klʌb]
(n.) 俱樂部

7 swimming pool
[ˈswɪmɪŋ pul]
(n.) 游泳池

❶ 電影院

Is it true that this ship has two movie theaters?

❷ 賭場

Hey, do you want to try a few hands of poker down at the casino?

試玩幾局撲克牌

❸ 餐廳

The restaurants on the ship are really good because of their talented chefs.

❹ 宴會廳

There's a formal ball being held tonight for all the passengers in the ballroom.

今晚會舉辦正式舞會

❺ 乘客

Some of the cruise lines can accommodate as many as 2,000 passengers.

多達 2000 名乘客

❻ 俱樂部

Let's go dancing at the club tonight. The DJ there is terrific!

去跳舞

❼ 游泳池

This cruise ship is huge—it has three different swimming pools!

學更多

❶ true〈真實的〉
❷ a few〈一些〉・hand〈牌卡遊戲的一局〉・poker〈撲克牌遊戲〉・down〈到某地〉
❸ talented〈有才華的〉・chef〈主廚〉
❹ formal〈正式的〉・ball〈舞會〉・held〈hold（舉辦）的過去分詞〉
❺ cruise line〈郵輪〉・accommodate〈可搭載…乘客〉・as many as…〈和…一樣多〉
❻ dancing〈dance（跳舞）的 ing 型態〉・terrific〈非常好的〉
❼ cruise ship〈郵輪〉・huge〈龐大的〉・different〈不同的〉

中譯

❶ 這艘船有兩間電影院是真的嗎？
❷ 嘿，要不要到賭場試玩幾局撲克牌？
❸ 船上的餐廳真的非常棒，因為那裡有出色的廚師。
❹ 今晚將在宴會廳為全體乘客舉辦正式舞會。
❺ 有些郵輪可以搭載多達兩千名乘客。
❻ 我們晚上到俱樂部跳舞吧。那裡的 DJ 很棒！
❼ 這艘郵輪非常大，它有三座不同的游泳池！

014

捷運站 (1)

MP3 014

1 entrance
[ˈɛntrəns]
(n.) 入口

2 exit
[ˈɛksɪt]
(n.) 出口

3 information center
[ˌɪnfəˈmeʃən ˈsɛntə]
(n.) 服務處

4 gate
[get]
(n.) 閘門

5 AVM (add value machine)
[ˈeˈviˈɛm] [æd ˈvælju məˈʃin]
(n.) 加值機

6 route map
[rut mæp]
(n.) 路線圖

7 ticket machine
[ˈtɪkɪt məˈʃin]
(n.) 售票機

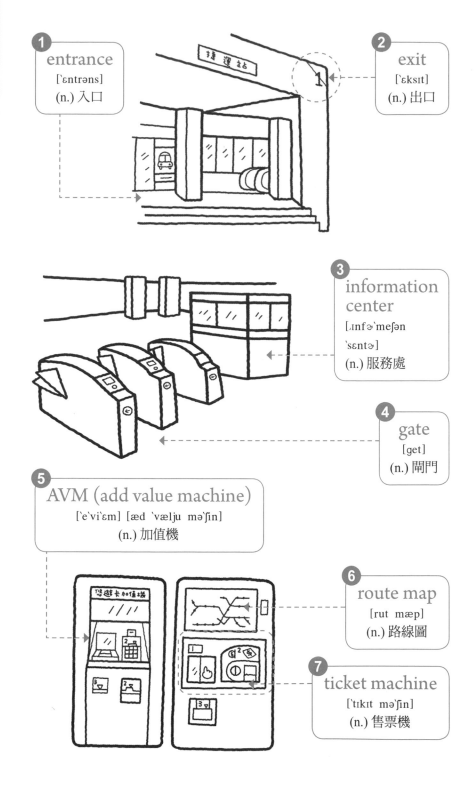

❶ 入口

I think the <u>entrance</u> to the MRT station is around the corner.
　　　　　　　捷運站入口

❷ 出口

Miss, you just need to <u>turn left ahead</u> for Exit #2.
　　　　　　　　　　　在前面左轉

❸ 服務處

If you need <u>some directions</u>, just ask the MRT workers in the information center.
　　　　　需要路線指引

❹ 閘門

Once you pay the fare, you can go through the gate.
<u>一旦支付車資</u>

❺ 加值機

The AVMs allow users to <u>add money to their EasyCards</u>.
　　　　　　　　　　　　加值他們的悠遊卡

❻ 路線圖

I <u>always carry around</u> a small route map with me when I'm traveling <u>around the city</u>.
　　總會隨身攜帶　　　　　　　　　　　　　　　　　　環遊市區

❼ 售票機

The ticket machines are very handy for buying tokens to use on the MRT.

學更多

❶ MRT station〈捷運站〉‧ around〈在…附近〉‧ corner〈轉角〉
❷ turn〈轉彎〉‧ left〈左側的〉‧ ahead〈在前面〉
❸ directions〈交通路線指引〉‧ worker〈工作人員〉‧ information〈資訊〉‧ center〈中心〉
❹ once〈一旦〉‧ pay〈支付〉‧ fare〈車資〉‧ through〈通過〉
❺ allow〈提供〉‧ user〈使用者〉‧ add〈增加〉
❻ carry around〈隨身攜帶〉‧ route〈路線〉‧ travel around〈環遊〉‧
　 traveling〈travel（旅行）的 ing 型態〉
❼ handy〈便利的〉‧ token〈代幣〉

中譯

❶ 我覺得捷運站入口是在轉角處。
❷ 小姐，前面左轉就是二號出口。
❸ 如果需要路線指引，可直接詢問捷運服務處的工作人員。
❹ 一旦支付車資，你就能通過閘門。
❺ 加值機提供使用者儲值悠遊卡。
❻ 當我在市區四處旅行時，都會隨身攜帶小型路線圖。
❼ 可以很方便的利用售票機購買代幣搭乘捷運。

015

捷運站(2)

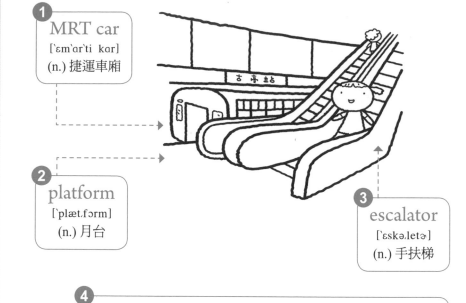

1 MRT car
[ˈɛmˈɑrˈti kɑr]
(n.) 捷運車廂

2 platform
[ˈplætˌfɔrm]
(n.) 月台

3 escalator
[ˈɛskəˌletə]
(n.) 手扶梯

MP3 015

4 Waiting Zone for Female Passengers at Night
[ˈwetɪŋ zon fɔr ˈfimel ˈpæsndʒə æt naɪt]
(n.) 夜間婦女候車區

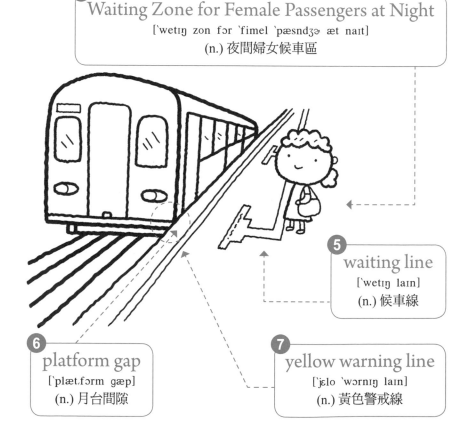

5 waiting line
[ˈwetɪŋ laɪn]
(n.) 候車線

6 platform gap
[ˈplætˌfɔrm gæp]
(n.) 月台間隙

7 yellow warning line
[ˈjɛlo ˈwɔrnɪŋ laɪn]
(n.) 黃色警戒線

❶ 捷運車廂
Which MRT car will you be riding in? I'll try to sit in the same one.
　　　　　　　　　　　　　　　　　　　　我會盡量坐相同車廂

❷ 月台
For safety reasons, you should stand back from the train platforms
while you wait.　　　　　　　站在月台邊緣後方

❸ 手扶梯
Hold onto the rail on the escalator as you ride up or down.
　　　　　　　　　　　　　　　　當你往上搭乘或往下搭乘時

❹ 夜間婦女候車區
There is a special Waiting Zone for Female Passengers at Night for the MRT.

❺ 候車線
Please stand behind the waiting line.

❻ 月台間隙
You must be careful to avoid the platform gap.
　　　　　　　要小心避開

❼ 黃色警戒線
You must always stand behind the yellow warning line.

學更多

❶ riding〈ride（搭乘）的 ing 型態〉・try〈試圖〉・same〈同樣的〉
❷ safety〈安全〉・reason〈理由〉・stand back from...〈站在距離…稍遠的地方〉
❸ hold onto...〈握住…〉・rail〈扶手〉・ride〈搭乘〉
❹ special〈專用的、特別的〉
❺ stand behind...〈站在…後面〉
❻ careful〈小心的〉・avoid〈避開〉・gap〈縫隙〉
❼ always〈總是〉・warning〈警戒〉

中譯

❶ 你會坐哪一節捷運車廂？我盡量和你坐相同車廂。
❷ 為了安全考量，候車時應站立於月台邊緣後方。
❸ 上下手扶梯時，請握緊扶手。
❹ 捷運設有專屬的夜間婦女候車區。
❺ 請站在候車線後方。
❻ 要小心月台間隙。
❼ 請務必站立於黃色警戒線後方。

016 捷運車廂 (1)

MP3 016

1 support ring
[sə`port rɪŋ]
(n.) 吊環

2 advertisement
[͵ædvɚ`taɪzmənt]
(n.) 廣告看板

3 window
[`wɪndo]
(n.) 窗戶

4 priority seat
[praɪ`ɔrətɪ sit]
(n.) 博愛座

5 passenger
[`pæsṇdʒɚ]
(n.) 乘客

兩個單字都是「車廂」。

6 car / carriage
[kɑr] / [`kærɪdʒ]
(n.) 車廂

7 seat
[sit]
(n.) 座位

❶ 吊環

For your safety, you should grab a support ring to hold onto as you stand inside the moving train.
在行進中的列車裡

❷ 廣告看板

There are advertisements posted inside the subway cars.

❸ 窗戶

Little kids love to look out the windows as they ride on the MRT.
看窗外

❹ 博愛座

The priority seats are reserved for pregnant women, the handicapped, and the elderly.
孕婦、殘障人士及年長者

❺ 乘客

Wow! There are so many passengers during morning rush hour.

❻ 車廂

Kids love riding in the first MRT car on the way to the Taipei Zoo.
在前往木柵動物園的路上

❼ 座位

Jessie would really like to sit down, but there aren't any seats available.
沒有位子可坐

學更多

❶ safety〈安全〉‧ grab〈抓住〉‧ hold onto...〈握緊…〉‧ moving〈移動中的〉
❷ posted〈post（張貼）的過去分詞〉‧ inside〈在…的裡面〉‧ subway〈地下鐵〉
❸ little〈年幼的〉‧ kid〈小孩〉‧ look out〈向外看〉‧ ride〈搭乘〉
❹ be reserved for...〈保留給…〉‧ pregnant〈懷孕的〉‧ handicapped〈殘缺的〉
❺ during〈在…期間〉‧ rush hour〈尖峰時間〉
❻ riding〈ride（搭乘）的 ing 型態〉‧ way〈路程〉
❼ sit down〈坐下來〉‧ available〈可取得的〉

中譯

❶ 為了您的安全，站立於行進中的列車時，應握緊吊環。
❷ 地鐵車廂內張貼著廣告看板。
❸ 小朋友坐捷運時，最愛看窗戶外的景色。
❹ 博愛座是保留給孕婦、殘障人士和年長者的。
❺ 哇！早上尖峰時間的乘客好多。
❻ 小孩子很愛在去木柵動物園時，坐在捷運第一節車廂。
❼ Jessie 很想要坐下來，可是沒有座位可坐。

捷運車廂 (2)

MP3 017

1 LCD display board / LCD display
[ˈɛlˈsiˈdi dɪˈsple bord] / [ˈɛlˈsiˈdi dɪˈsple]
(n.) 液晶顯示螢幕

兩個單字都是「液晶顯示螢幕」。

2 route map
[rut mæp]
(n.) 路線圖

3 door
[dor]
(n.) 車門

4 emergency intercom
[ɪˈmɝdʒənsɪ ˈɪntɚˌkɑm]
(n.) 緊急對講機

5 emergency handle
[ɪˈmɝdʒənsɪ ˈhændl̩]
(n.) 緊急逃生把手

❶ 液晶顯示螢幕
The LCD display board says the next train arrives in three minutes.

❷ 路線圖
Let's check the route map before we hop on.

❸ 車門
Watch out, sir! The doors are closing.

❹ 緊急對講機
Use the emergency intercom if you need to communicate with the driver
in an emergency.
_{聯絡司機}

❺ 緊急逃生把手
Never pull the emergency handle unless there is a real emergency.
Otherwise, you will be fined.
_{除非真的發生緊急狀況}

學更多

❶ next〈下一班的〉・arrive〈到達〉・minute〈分鐘〉
❷ check〈檢查、查核〉・before〈在…之前〉・hop on〈跳上車〉
❸ watch out〈小心〉・closing〈close（關閉）的 ing 型態〉
❹ intercom〈對講機〉・communicate with〈聯絡某人〉・driver〈司機〉・
  emergency〈緊急情況〉
❺ pull〈拉〉・unless〈除非〉・otherwise〈否則〉・fined〈fine（罰款）的過去分詞〉

中譯

❶ 液晶顯示螢幕顯示下一班列車三分鐘後抵達。
❷ 在上車前，我們來確認一下路線圖吧。
❸ 先生，請小心！門要關了。
❹ 若有緊急狀況需與司機聯絡，請使用緊急對講機。
❺ 除非真的發生緊急狀況，請勿拉起緊急逃生把手。違者將遭受罰款。

018

機場大廳

MP3 018

1 check-in counter
[ˈtʃɛkˌɪn ˈkaʊntə]
(n.) 登機報到櫃檯

2 flight attendant
[flaɪt əˈtɛndənt]
(n.) 地勤人員

3 carry-on luggage
[ˈkærˌɑn ˈlʌgɪdʒ]
(n.) 隨身行李

4 passenger
[ˈpæsn̩dʒə]
(n.) 乘客

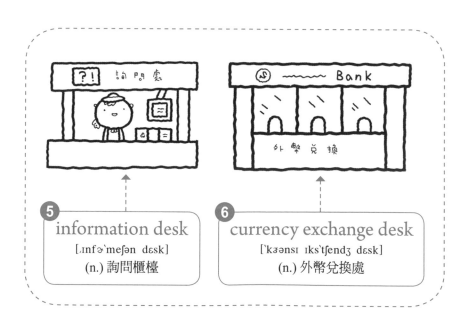

5 information desk
[ˌɪnfəˈmeʃən dɛsk]
(n.) 詢問櫃檯

6 currency exchange desk
[ˈkɝənsɪ ɪksˈtʃendʒ dɛsk]
(n.) 外幣兌換處

❶ 登機報到櫃檯

With luggage to check in, I'll need to go to the check-in counter first.

因為行李要託運

❷ 地勤人員

Are there any flight attendants who can speak Chinese?

❸ 隨身行李

My carry-on luggage is too heavy to lift into the luggage bin onboard by myself.

重到無法抬入

❹ 乘客

When it's time to board, passengers line up to present their tickets and ID.

登機時

❺ 詢問櫃檯

The information desk is very helpful if you need directions.

❻ 外幣兌換處

On his way to Macau, Gary goes to the currency exchange desk to change

在他到…的途中

some money.

學更多

❶ with〈因為〉．luggage〈行李〉．check-in〈登記報到〉．counter〈櫃檯〉．first〈首先〉

❷ flight〈飛行〉．attendant〈服務員〉．speak〈說〉．Chinese〈中文〉

❸ too...to...〈太…而無法…〉．lift〈抬起〉．luggage bin〈行李架〉．onboard〈機上的〉．
　by myself〈靠我自己〉

❹ board〈登機〉．line up〈排隊〉．present〈出示〉．ticket〈票券〉．ID〈身分證明〉

❺ helpful〈有幫助的〉．directions〈指示〉

❻ way〈路途〉．Macau〈澳門〉．currency〈貨幣〉．exchange〈兌換〉．change〈兌換〉

中譯

❶ 因為有行李要託運，我需要先去登機報到櫃檯。

❷ 有沒有會說中文的地勤人員？

❸ 我的隨身行李太重了，我無法自己把它抬到機上的行李架。

❹ 登機時，乘客要排隊出示機票和身分證明。

❺ 如果你需要指引，詢問櫃檯會對你很有幫助。

❻ 在 Gary 去澳門的途中，他會到外幣兌換處換一些錢。

019

登機文件與手續

MP3 019

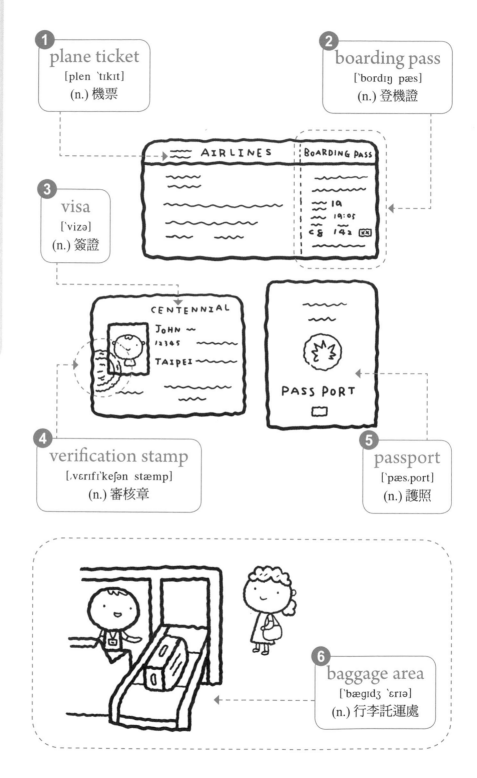

1 plane ticket
[plen `tɪkɪt]
(n.) 機票

2 boarding pass
[`bordɪŋ pæs]
(n.) 登機證

3 visa
[`vizə]
(n.) 簽證

4 verification stamp
[ˌvɛrɪfɪ`keʃən stæmp]
(n.) 審核章

5 passport
[`pæs‚port]
(n.) 護照

6 baggage area
[`bægɪdʒ `ɛrɪə]
(n.) 行李託運處

❶ 機票

Oh no! I forgot my plane ticket at home.

❷ 登機證

Your boarding pass will tell you what seat you have.
你要坐的座位

❸ 簽證

Some countries require visas before you can enter them.

❹ 審核章

An immigration officer will put a verification stamp in your passport
蓋審核章

once he's verified the information.

❺ 護照

My passport is expiring soon, so I'll need to get it renewed.
即將過期

❻ 行李託運處

Take your baggage to the baggage area for handling.

學更多

❶ forgot〈forget（忘記）的過去式〉‧at home〈在家〉

❷ tell〈告知訊息〉‧seat〈座位〉

❸ country〈國家〉‧require〈需要〉‧enter〈進入〉

❹ immigration〈移民〉‧officer〈官員〉‧once〈一旦〉‧verified〈verify（核對）的過去分詞〉‧information〈資料〉

❺ expiring〈expire（過期）的 ing 型態〉‧renewed〈renew（更新）的過去分詞〉

❻ baggage〈行李〉‧handling〈運送〉

中譯

❶ 喔不！我把機票忘在家裡了。

❷ 您的登機證將寫著您的座位號碼。

❸ 有些國家需要簽證才能入境。

❹ 移民局官員會在核對資料之後，在你的護照蓋審核章。

❺ 我的護照快過期了，我需要重新辦理。

❻ 把你的行李拿去行李託運處託運。

機場安檢處 (1)

1 passport
[`pæs,port]
(n.) 護照

2 basket
[`bæskɪt]
(n.) 置物籃

3 carry-on luggage
[`kærɪɑn `lʌgɪdʒ]
(n.) 隨身行李

4 security guard
[sɪ`kjʊrətɪ gɑrd]
(n.) 安檢人員

5 X-ray machine
[`ɛks`re məʃɪn]
(n.) X光檢測機

6 metal detector
[`mɛtl dɪ`tɛktɚ]
(n.) 金屬探測器

7 baggage screening monitor
[`bægɪdʒ `skrinɪŋ `mɑnətɚ]
(n.) 行李檢測螢幕

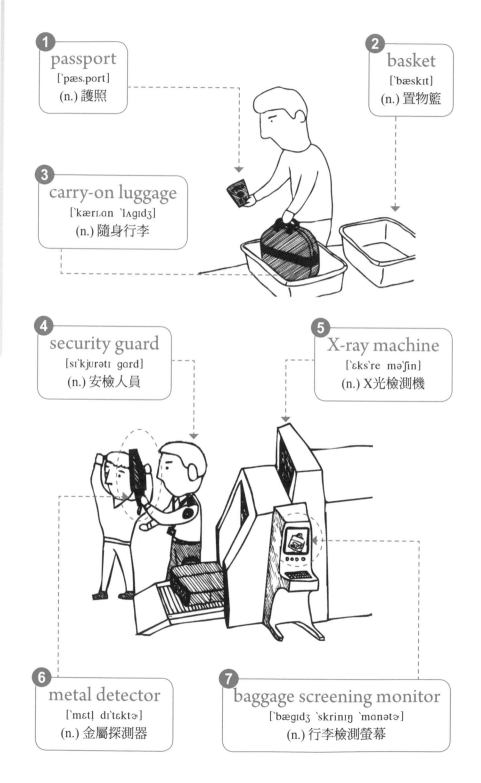

❶ 護照
Sir, don't forget your passport. It's still here in this basket!

❷ 置物籃
Use a basket to put your wallet and keys in as you go through security.
　　　　　　　　　　　　　　　　　　　　　　　　當你通過安檢時

❸ 隨身行李
Carry-on luggage must not exceed a certain size.

❹ 安檢人員
There are several security guards stationed inside the airport.
　　　　　　　　駐有多位安檢人員

❺ X光檢測機
The X-ray machines check luggage for any dangerous items.

❻ 金屬探測器
Please go through the metal detector now, miss.

❼ 行李檢測螢幕
There are many baggage screening monitors used at the airport.

學更多

❶ forget〈忘記〉‧ still〈仍然〉
❷ wallet〈皮夾〉‧ key〈鑰匙〉‧ security〈安全檢查〉
❸ exceed〈超過〉‧ certain〈特定的〉‧ size〈尺寸〉
❹ several〈多個的〉‧ guard〈看守員〉‧ stationed〈station（派駐）的過去分詞〉
❺ dangerous〈危險的〉‧ item〈物品〉
❻ go through...〈通過…〉
❼ baggage〈行李〉‧ screening〈審查〉‧ monitor〈顯示器〉‧ used〈use（使用）的過去分詞〉

中譯

❶ 先生，不要忘了你的護照。它還在籃子裡！
❷ 通過安檢時，要把皮夾和鑰匙放進置物籃。
❸ 隨身行李不能超過特定大小。
❹ 機場內駐有多位安檢人員。
❺ X 光檢測機會檢查行李是否裝有危險物品。
❻ 小姐，現在請妳走過金屬探測器。
❼ 機場使用許多行李檢測螢幕。

021

機場安檢處(2)

MP3 021

1 billboard for banned items
[ˈbɪlˌbord fɔr bænd ˈaɪtəms]
(n.) 違禁物品告示

2 banned item
[bænd ˈaɪtəm]
(n.) 違禁品

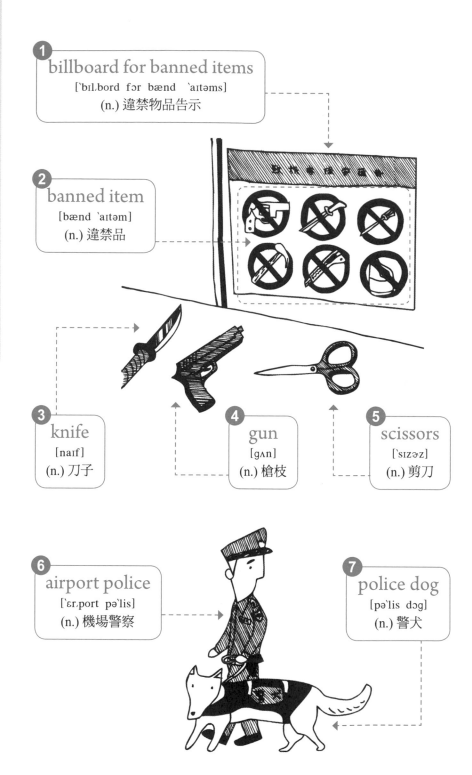

3 knife
[naɪf]
(n.) 刀子

4 gun
[gʌn]
(n.) 槍枝

5 scissors
[ˈsɪzɚz]
(n.) 剪刀

6 airport police
[ˈɛrˌport pəˈlis]
(n.) 機場警察

7 police dog
[pəˈlis dɔg]
(n.) 警犬

❶ 違禁物品告示

As you go through security at the Taoyuan International Airport, you
<u>在通過安檢時</u>
will see a billboard for banned items posted.

❷ 違禁品

Knives and guns are both banned items on planes.

❸ 刀子

Be careful with your knife or you might cut yourself.

❹ 槍枝

Rob has several guns because he's very interested in shooting.

❺ 剪刀

A few seconds after the baby girl was born, a nurse cut her umbilical cord
with a pair of scissors.　　　　　　　　　　　　　　<u>剪斷她的臍帶</u>

❻ 機場警察

When the man tried to flee, the airport police arrested him.

❼ 警犬

Police dogs are used to sniff out illegal drugs.
　　　　　　　<u>用嗅覺找出違法毒品</u>

學更多

❶ billboard〈廣告牌〉・banned〈被取締的〉・item〈項目〉・posted〈post（張貼）的過去分詞〉
❷ knives〈knife（刀子）的複數〉・plane〈飛機〉
❸ be careful with...〈小心…〉・or〈否則〉・cut〈割〉
❹ be interested in...〈對…感興趣〉・shooting〈射擊〉
❺ a few〈少量的〉・second〈秒〉・umbilical cord〈臍帶〉・a pair of scissors〈一把剪刀〉
❻ tried〈try（試圖）的過去式〉・flee〈逃跑〉・arrested〈arrest（逮捕）的過去式〉
❼ sniff out...〈以嗅覺找出…〉・illegal〈違法的〉・drug〈毒品〉

中譯

❶ 在桃園國際機場通過安檢時，你會看到那裡貼有違禁物品告示牌。
❷ 刀子和槍械是搭飛機的違禁品。
❸ 你拿刀子要小心，否則你可能割傷自己。
❹ Rob 有很多把槍枝，因為他對射擊很有興趣。
❺ 在小女嬰出生幾秒後，一名護士用剪刀剪斷她的臍帶。
❻ 在那個男人想要逃跑時，機場警察將他逮捕了。
❼ 警犬被用來以嗅覺查緝違法毒品。

022

候機時間

MP3 022

1 duty-free shop
[ˈdjutɪˈfri ʃɑp]
(n.) 免稅商店

2 VIP lounge
[ˈviaɪpi laʊndʒ]
(n.) 航空公司貴賓室

3 waiting room
[ˈwetɪŋ rum]

waiting area
[ˈwetɪŋ ˈɛrɪə]
(n.) 候機室

兩個單字都是「候機室」。

4 flight information board
[flaɪt ˌɪnfəˈmeʃən bord]
(n.) 航班顯示表

5 boarding area
[ˈbordɪŋ ˈɛrɪə]
(n.) 登機區

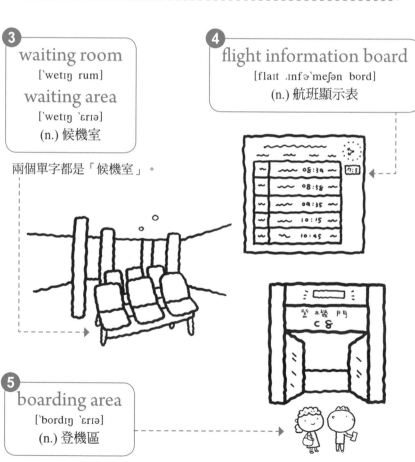

❶ 免稅商店

There are some beautiful gifts for friends and family available in the duty-free shops.

可以在免稅店買到

❷ 航空公司貴賓室

Most business travelers have access to VIP lounges due to their frequent flyer miles.

有權利進入　　　　　　　　　　　飛行常客里程數

❸ 候機室

There are waiting rooms all over an airport for passengers to relax in.

機場到處都有候機室

❹ 航班顯示表

John wants to know what gate he leaves from, so he checks the flight information board.

從哪一個登機門搭機離境

❺ 登機區

The boarding area is off-limits to those without tickets.

沒有機票的人

學更多

❶ there are...〈有…〉‧ beautiful〈美麗的〉‧ gift〈禮品〉‧ available〈可買到的〉
❷ business traveler〈商務旅客〉‧ access〈進入的權利〉‧ lounge〈休息室〉‧
　 due to...〈由於…〉‧ frequent flyer〈飛行常客〉‧ mile〈里程〉
❸ all over〈到處〉‧ airport〈機場〉‧ passenger〈乘客〉‧ relax〈休息〉‧ in〈在…裡〉
❹ gate〈登機門〉‧ leave〈離開〉‧ check〈查看〉‧ board〈告示牌〉
❺ off-limits〈禁止進入的〉‧ without〈沒有〉‧ ticket〈票券〉

中譯

❶ 可以在免稅店買到一些能送親朋好友的美麗禮物。
❷ 多數的商務旅客由於累積了許多飛行常客里程數，而得以使用航空公司貴賓室。
❸ 機場到處都有候機室提供旅客在裡面休息。
❹ John 想知道要從哪一個登機門搭機離境，所以他去看航班顯示表。
❺ 沒有機票的旅客禁止進入登機區。

023

飛機上 (1)

MP3 023

1 captain
['kæptɪn]
(n.) 機長

2 cockpit
['kak.pɪt]
(n.) 駕駛艙

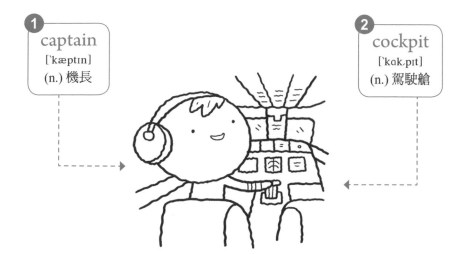

3 economy class
[ɪ'kanəmɪ klæs]
(n.) 經濟艙

4 business class
['bɪznɪs klæs]
(n.) 商務艙

5 first class
[fɝst klæs]
(n.) 頭等艙

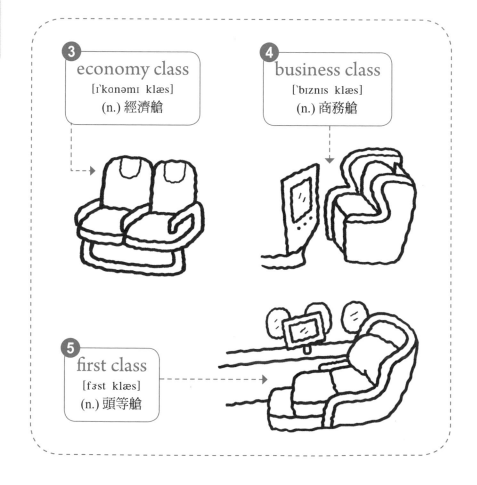

❶ 機長

I think our captain on this flight is a woman. That's cool.

❷ 駕駛艙

The cockpit now has a bullet-proof door to protect the pilots from terrorists.
保護駕駛員免受恐怖份子傷害

❸ 經濟艙

Economy class is all I can afford to fly right now.
我只買得起經濟艙座位

❹ 商務艙

Holly flies internationally a lot for her job, so her company buys her
因為工作經常飛國際線

business class tickets.

❺ 頭等艙

I love flying first class, but it's really expensive.

學更多

❶ think〈認為〉‧flight〈班機〉
❷ bullet-proof〈防彈的〉‧protect A from B〈保護 A 免於 B 的危害〉‧pilot〈駕駛員〉‧
terrorist〈恐怖份子〉
❸ afford〈買得起〉‧right now〈現在〉‧class〈等級〉
❹ internationally〈國際地〉‧company〈公司〉
❺ flying〈fly（搭飛機）的 ing 型態〉‧expensive〈昂貴的〉

中譯

❶ 我們這班飛機的機長似乎是位女性。好酷。
❷ 現在駕駛艙有防彈門，保護駕駛員免於恐怖份子的傷害。
❸ 我現在只買得起經濟艙的座位。
❹ Holly 因為工作經常飛國際線，所以她公司都幫她買商務艙的票。
❺ 我很愛坐頭等艙，不過那真的很貴。

024

飛機上(2)

MP3 024

1 overhead compartment
[ˋovəˋhɛd kəmˋpɑrtmənt]
(n.) 頭頂置物櫃

2 blanket
[ˋblæŋkɪt]
(n.) 毛毯

3 window seat
[ˋwɪndo sit]
(n.) 靠窗座位

4 aisle seat
[aɪl sit]
(n.) 走道座位

5 flight attendant
[flaɪt əˋtɛndənt]
(n.) 空服員

6 tray
[tre]
(n.) 折疊桌

7 seatbelt
[ˋsit.bɛlt]
(n.) 安全帶

❶ 頭頂置物櫃

There's no more room in the overhead compartment for my carry-on luggage.
沒有多餘的空間

❷ 毛毯

May I please have a blanket? It's quite cold in here.

❸ 靠窗座位

Miss, may I please have a window seat?

❹ 走道座位

David demands an aisle seat so that he can get up and walk around a lot.
經常起身並四處走動

❺ 空服員

Charlie thinks the flight attendants on Eva Air are gorgeous.

❻ 折疊桌

If you want a meal, you'll need to put your tray down.

❼ 安全帶

Ladies and gentlemen, please keep your seatbelts fastened while you're in your seats.
繫好您的安全帶

學更多

❶ room〈空間〉• overhead〈在上頭的、高架的〉• compartment〈隔間〉• carry-on luggage〈隨身行李〉

❷ may I please have...?〈可以給我…嗎？〉• have〈擁有〉• quite〈很…〉

❸ window〈窗戶〉

❹ demand〈需要〉• aisle〈通道〉• get up〈起身〉• walk around〈到處走〉

❺ flight〈飛行〉• attendant〈服務員〉• gorgeous〈美麗的〉

❻ meal〈餐點〉• put...down〈把…放下來〉

❼ keep〈維持某狀態〉• fastened〈fasten（繫上）的過去分詞〉

中譯

❶ 頭頂置物櫃已經沒有空間放我的隨身行李了。

❷ 可以給我毛毯嗎？這裡面相當冷。

❸ 小姐，可以給我靠窗的座位嗎？

❹ David 需要走道的座位，好讓他能經常起來走動。

❺ Charlie 認為長榮航空的空服人員都很美。

❻ 如果您想要餐點，您需要放下折疊桌。

❼ 各位女士和先生，當您在座位上時請繫好您的安全帶。

025

準備通關

MP3 025

1 immigration form
[ˌɪməˈgreʃən fɔrm]
(n.) 入境表

2 passport
[ˈpæsˌport]
(n.) 護照

3 visa
[ˈvizə]
(n.) 簽證

海關

4 passenger
[ˈpæsn̩dʒɚ]
(n.) 旅客

5 plane ticket
[plen ˈtɪkɪt]
(n.) 機票

❶ 入境表

Miss, can you please give me an immigration form?

❷ 護照

In order to renew a passport, you must fill out the paperwork and provide some photos.
　　　　　　　　　　　　　　　　　　　　　　　　填寫文件

❸ 簽證

Hey, France doesn't require a visa for tourists, right?

❹ 旅客

This morning's flight to Tokyo is packed full of passengers going to the US.
　　　　　　　　　　　　　　　　　　　　擠滿了要往美國的旅客

❺ 機票

Nowadays, buying a plane ticket online requires ID.

學更多

❶ give〈給予〉‧immigration〈移民〉‧form〈表格〉

❷ in order to〈為了…〉‧renew〈換新〉‧fill out〈填寫〉‧paperwork〈文件〉‧
provide〈提供〉

❸ require〈需要〉‧tourist〈觀光客〉

❹ flight〈班機〉‧packed〈pack（擠滿）的過去分詞〉‧full of〈充滿…的〉

❺ nowadays〈現在〉‧online〈線上的〉‧ID〈身分證明〉

中譯

❶ 小姐，可以請妳給我入境表嗎？

❷ 要更新護照，你需要填寫表單並提供一些照片。

❸ 嘿，去法國旅遊不需要簽證，對吧？

❹ 今天早上往東京的班機載滿了要前往美國的旅客。

❺ 現在，在網路上買機票需要身分證明。

026

出入境處

MP3 026

1 immigration officer
[ˌɪməˈɡreʃən ˈɔfəsɚ]
(n.) 移民局官員

2 departure
[dɪˈpɑrtʃɚ]
(n.) 出境

3 arrival
[əˈraɪvl̩]
(n.) 入境

4 immigration
[ˌɪməˈɡreʃən]
(n.) 出入境處

5 outbound gate
[ˈaʊtˈbaʊnd ɡet]
(n.) 出境閘門

6 inbound gate
[ˈɪnˈbaʊnd ɡet]
(n.) 入境閘門

❶ 移民局官員

The immigration officer asked to see my passport and visa.

❷ 出境

You can buy a bus ticket at the ticket counter around the departure hall.

在出境大廳附近

❸ 入境

My favorite airport arrival lobby in the world is the one where my family lives!

機場入境大廳

❹ 出入境處

Before leaving or entering a foreign country, you must go through immigration.

❺ 出境閘門

Sir, the outbound gate is around the corner.

在轉角附近

❻ 入境閘門

Wow, look at the crowd at the inbound gate. This is going to take a while.

花一些時間

學更多

❶ officer〈官員〉・passport〈護照〉・visa〈簽證〉
❷ ticket counter〈售票處〉・around〈在…附近〉・hall〈大廳〉
❸ favorite〈最喜歡的〉・lobby〈大廳〉
❹ foreign〈外國的〉・country〈國家〉・go through〈通過〉
❺ outbound〈向外國去的〉・corner〈轉角處〉
❻ crowd〈人群〉・inbound〈回本國的〉・while〈一會兒〉

中譯

❶ 移民局官員要求看我的護照跟簽證。
❷ 在出境大廳附近的售票處，你可以買到巴士車票。
❸ 全世界我最喜歡的機場入境大廳，就是我家人住的地方！
❹ 離開或進入其他國家之前，你必須通過出入境處。
❺ 先生，出境閘門就在前面轉角。
❻ 哇，你看入境閘門的人群。看來（入境）要花點時間。

1 health declaration form
[hɛlθ ˌdɛkləˈreʃən fɔrm]
(n.) 健康證明表

2 customs declaration
[ˈkʌstəmz ˌdɛkləˈreʃən]
(n.) 海關申報單

3 customs
[ˈkʌstəmz]
(n.) 海關

4 customs officer
[ˈkʌstəmz ˈɔfəsə]
(n.) 海關人員

5 verification stamp
[ˌvɛrɪfɪˈkeʃən stæmp]
(n.) 審核章

6 quarantine
[ˈkwɔrənˌtin]
(n.) 檢疫處

7 waiting line
[ˈwetɪŋ laɪn]
(n.) 等候線

❶ 健康證明表

Hong Kong requires all passengers entering the country to complete a health declaration form. _{所有要進入這個國家的旅客}

❷ 海關申報單

Since I didn't buy anything special at home, I don't have any customs declarations. _{在自己的國家裡}

❸ 海關

One of the areas you will need to pass through on your way in or out of a country is customs. _{在你進出一個國家的途中}

❹ 海關人員

Tim is training to become a customs officer.

❺ 審核章

The customs officer put a verification stamp in my passport. _{蓋了審核章}

❻ 檢疫處

That guy has a high fever. I think officials may put him in quarantine. _{發高燒}

❼ 等候線

Please stand behind the yellow waiting line.

學更多

❶ require〈需要〉‧country〈國家〉‧complete〈完成〉‧declaration〈聲明、申報〉‧form〈表格〉
❷ since〈因為〉‧special〈特別的〉‧at home〈在自己的國家裡〉
❸ area〈區域〉‧pass through〈通過〉
❹ training〈train（訓練）的 ing 型態〉‧become〈成為〉
❺ put〈put（放下）的過去式〉‧verification〈核實〉‧stamp〈戳記〉‧passport〈護照〉
❻ guy〈男性〉‧fever〈發燒〉‧official〈官方人員〉‧put＋某人〈使某人處於某種狀態〉
❼ stand〈站立〉‧behind〈在…的後面〉

中譯

❶ 香港政府要求所有入境的旅客填寫健康證明表。
❷ 因為我在國內沒買什麼特別的東西，所以不需要填寫海關申報單。
❸ 當你進出一個國家時，必須通過的一個地方是海關。
❹ Tim 正在受訓要成為海關人員。
❺ 海關人員在我的護照蓋了審核章。
❻ 那名男子在發高燒。我想機場人員會把他安置在檢疫處。
❼ 請站在黃色等候線後方。

028

提領行李

MP3 028

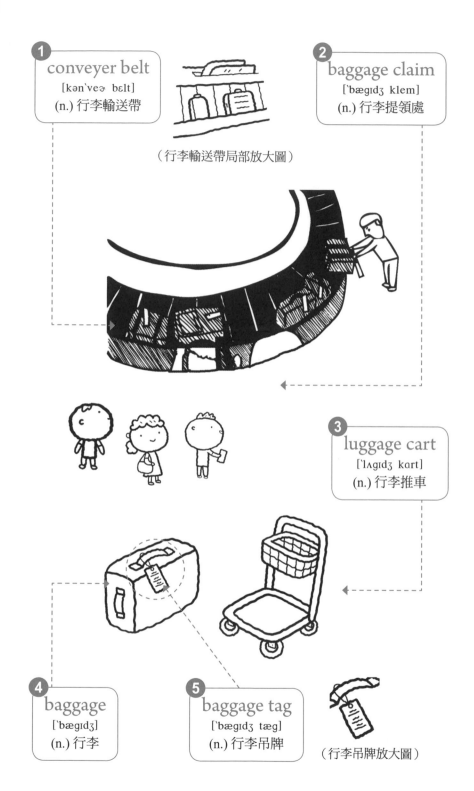

1 conveyer belt
[kən`veɚ bɛlt]
(n.) 行李輸送帶

（行李輸送帶局部放大圖）

2 baggage claim
[`bægɪdʒ klem]
(n.) 行李提領處

3 luggage cart
[`lʌgɪdʒ kɑrt]
(n.) 行李推車

4 baggage
[`bægɪdʒ]
(n.) 行李

5 baggage tag
[`bægɪdʒ tæg]
(n.) 行李吊牌

（行李吊牌放大圖）

❶ 行李輸送帶

The conveyer belt has stopped. I guess they've finished unloading the plane's
luggage.
卸除飛機的行李

❷ 行李提領處

If your baggage is delayed, you'll need to check with baggage claim
attendants to see when it will arrive.

❸ 行李推車

Miss, would you like a luggage cart for all your bags?

❹ 行李

Could you weigh my baggage?

❺ 行李吊牌

Can I borrow a pen? I want to fill out a baggage tag.
填寫行李吊牌

學更多

❶ conveyer〈運輸裝置〉．belt〈帶狀物〉．stopped〈stop（停止）的過去分詞〉．
finished〈finish（完成）的過去分詞〉．unloading〈unload（卸貨）的 ing 型態〉．
luggage〈行李〉

❷ delayed〈delay（延誤）的過去分詞〉．claim〈要求、認領〉．attendant〈服務員〉．
see〈了解〉．arrive〈抵達〉

❸ would you like...?〈你想要…嗎〉．cart〈手推車〉．bag〈旅行袋〉

❹ weigh〈秤…的重量〉

❺ borrow〈借用〉．fill out〈填寫〉．tag〈標籤〉

中譯

❶ 行李輸送帶停止了，我猜他們已經卸除完這架飛機的行李。

❷ 如果您的行李延遲，您需要向行李提領處的服務人員確認行李何時抵達。

❸ 小姐，妳需要行李推車放妳所有的行李嗎？

❹ 可以幫我秤重行李嗎？

❺ 我可以借一支筆嗎？我要寫行李吊牌。

029

高速公路上

MP3 029

1 rest area
[rɛst `ɛrɪə]
(n.) 休息站

2 road sign
[rod saɪn]
(n.) 路標

3 interchange
[`ɪntətʃendʒ]
(n.) 交流道

4 lane
[len]
(n.) 車道

5 ramp
[ræmp]
(n.) 匝道

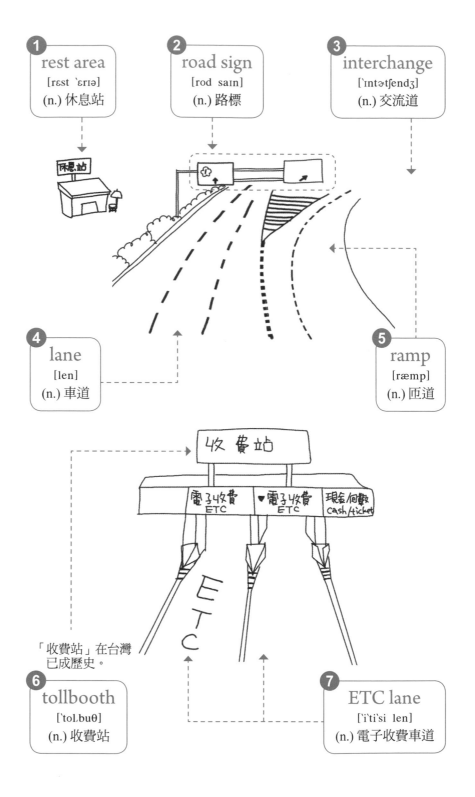

「收費站」在台灣已成歷史。

6 tollbooth
[`tol.buθ]
(n.) 收費站

7 ETC lane
[`ɪ`ti`si len]
(n.) 電子收費車道

❶ 休息站
Let's stop at that rest area ahead.

❷ 路標
Give me my glasses, honey, I can't read the road signs.
　　　　　　　　　　　　看不清楚

❸ 交流道
Interchanges link different highways together.

❹ 車道
Stop switching lanes! You're driving me crazy.
　　　　　　　　　　你正迫使我瘋狂

❺ 匝道
Take the ramp up to the highway.
　　　行駛匝道

❻ 收費站
There's a tollbooth ahead on the road. You'd better slow down to pay.
　　　　　　　　　　　　　　　　　你最好…

❼ 電子收費車道
ETC lanes are used to collect tolls electronically.
　　　　被運用於

學更多

❶ stop〈停車〉・rest〈休息〉・area〈區〉・ahead〈在前面〉
❷ glasses〈眼鏡〉・road〈道路〉・sign〈標誌〉
❸ link〈連結〉・different〈不同的〉・highway〈公路、幹道〉・together〈一起〉
❹ switching〈switch（切換）的 ing 型態〉・driving...crazy〈drive…carzy（迫使某人瘋狂）的 ing 型態〉
❺ take〈利用…道路〉・up〈到…〉
❻ slow down〈降低速度〉・pay〈付款〉
❼ lane〈車道〉・collect〈收取〉・toll〈過路費〉・electronically〈透過電子式地〉

中譯

❶ 我們在前面那個休息站停一下吧。
❷ 親愛的，把我的眼鏡給我，我看不清楚路標。
❸ 交流道連結不同的交通幹道。
❹ 別再切換車道了！你快把我弄瘋了！
❺ 請走匝道上公路。
❻ 這條路的前方有一個收費站，你最好降低速度以便付款。
❼ 電子收費車道是以電子化的方式收取過路費。

030

路肩拋錨車

MP3 030

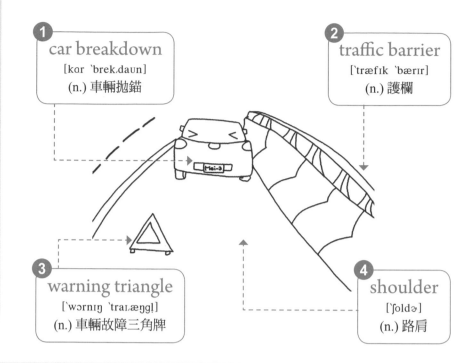

❶
car breakdown
[kɑr `brek.daʊn]
(n.) 車輛拋錨

❷
traffic barrier
[`træfɪk `bærɪr]
(n.) 護欄

❸
warning triangle
[`wɔrnɪŋ `traɪæŋgḷ]
(n.) 車輛故障三角牌

❹
shoulder
[`ʃoldɚ]
(n.) 路肩

---

❶ 車輛拋錨
Car breakdowns are awful—especially during rush hour.

❷ 護欄
Traffic barriers are used to keep vehicles from colliding into dangerous obstacles.
　　　　　　　　　　　　　　　　　避免車輛撞上危險的障礙物

❸ 車輛故障三角牌
Watch out for the warning triangle! You need to avoid that area.

❹ 路肩
After Tom's engine started smoking, he moved over to the shoulder of the road.

學更多

❶ breakdown〈故障〉・awful〈討人厭的〉・especially〈尤其〉・rush hour〈尖峰時間〉
❷ barrier〈柵欄〉・vehicle〈車輛〉・colliding〈collide（碰撞）的 ing 型態〉・obstacle〈障礙物〉
❸ watch out〈小心〉・warning〈警告〉・triangle〈三角形的物品〉・avoid〈避開〉
❹ engine〈引擎〉・smoking〈smoke（冒煙）的 ing 型態〉

中譯

❶ 車輛拋錨很討厭，尤其是在尖峰時刻。
❷ 護欄是用來避免車輛撞上危險的障礙物。
❸ 小心車輛故障三角牌！你要避開那附近。
❹ Tom 的汽車引擎開始冒煙之後，他把車子改開到路肩。

警車臨停

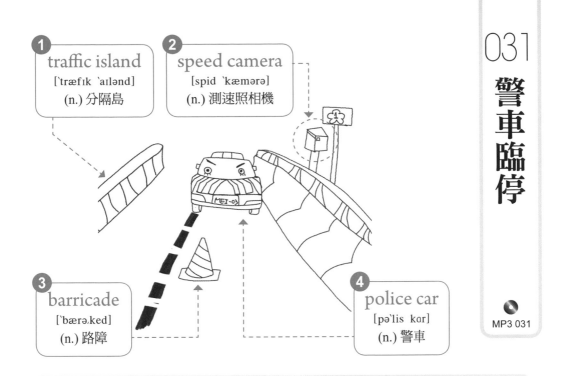

1 traffic island
[ˋtræfɪk ˋaɪlənd]
(n.) 分隔島

2 speed camera
[spid ˋkæmərə]
(n.) 測速照相機

3 barricade
[ˋbærəˌked]
(n.) 路障

4 police car
[pəˋlis kɑr]
(n.) 警車

---

1 分隔島
The truck crashed into the traffic island in the middle of the road.
　　　　　　　　　　　　　　　　　　　　　　　　馬路中間的

2 測速照相機
Hey, isn't there a speed camera on this road? Slow down!

3 路障
That barricade is there to prevent cars from driving over a hole in the road.
　　　　　　　　　　　　　　　　　防止車輛行駛過馬路上的凹洞

4 警車
Oh no! That police car wants us to pull over.
　　　　　　　　　　　　　　靠邊停車

學更多

1 truck〈卡車〉・crashed〈crash（碰撞）的過去式〉・traffic〈交通〉・island〈島狀物〉・middle〈中間〉
2 speed〈速度〉・camera〈照相機〉・road〈道路〉・slow down〈減速〉
3 prevent A from B〈防止 A 避免 B〉・over〈越過〉・hole〈凹洞〉
4 police〈警察〉・pull over〈靠邊停車〉

中譯

1 卡車撞到馬路中間的分隔島。
2 嘿,這條路不是有測速照相機嗎?開慢一點!
3 那個路障是要防止車輛駛過馬路上的凹洞。
4 喔不!那台警車要我們靠邊停車。

032

餐具擺放 (1)

MP3 032

1 fork
[fɔrk]
(n.) 叉子

2 napkin
[ˋnæpkɪn]
(n.) 餐巾

3 knife
[naɪf]
(n.) 餐刀

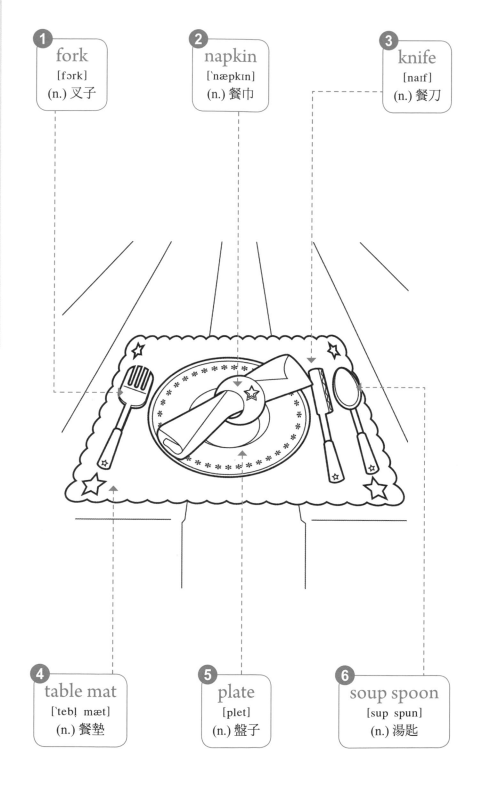

4 table mat
[ˋtebḷ mæt]
(n.) 餐墊

5 plate
[plet]
(n.) 盤子

6 soup spoon
[sup spun]
(n.) 湯匙

❶ 叉子

Miss, I dropped my fork on the floor. Can I have another one?
我的叉子掉到地上

❷ 餐巾

Zoe dropped her napkin on the floor when she got up to go to the ladies room.
起身去化妝室

❸ 餐刀

Be careful with your knife or you might cut yourself.

❹ 餐墊

Using table mats is an easy way to keep the table clean, especially when kids are eating.
保持桌面乾淨的簡便方式

❺ 盤子

One very traditional wedding gift is a set of beautiful china plates.
瓷盤

❻ 湯匙

Soup spoons are larger than regular spoons.

學更多

❶ dropped〈drop（掉落）的過去式〉‧floor〈地板〉
❷ got up〈get up（起身）的過去式〉‧ladies room〈女用化妝室〉
❸ careful〈小心的〉‧cut〈割〉‧yourself〈你自己〉
❹ table〈餐桌〉‧mat〈墊子〉‧way〈方式〉‧clean〈乾淨的〉‧especially〈尤其〉
❺ traditional〈傳統的〉‧wedding gift〈結婚禮物〉‧china〈瓷器、陶瓷器〉
❻ soup〈湯〉‧spoon〈湯匙〉‧regular〈一般的〉

中譯

❶ 小姐，我的叉子掉到地上了。可以再給我一支嗎？
❷ Zoe 起身要去化妝室時，把餐巾掉到地上了。
❸ 你拿刀子要小心，不然可能會割到自己。
❹ 使用餐墊便於保持桌面乾淨，尤其是在小孩子吃飯時。
❺ 有項非常傳統的結婚禮物，就是整組的美麗瓷盤。
❻ 喝湯用的湯匙比一般湯匙大。

033

餐具擺放(2)

MP3 033

1 chopsticks
[ˈtʃɑp.stɪks]
(n.) 筷子

2 bowl
[bol]
(n.) 碗

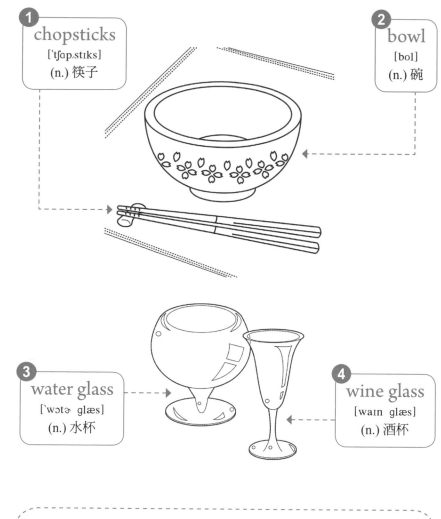

3 water glass
[ˈwɔtɚ glæs]
(n.) 水杯

4 wine glass
[waɪn glæs]
(n.) 酒杯

5 pepper mill
[ˈpɛpɚ mɪl]
(n.) 胡椒研磨器

6 salt shaker
[sɔlt ˈʃekɚ]
(n.) 鹽罐

❶ 筷子
Using chopsticks is not easy for some foreigners.

❷ 碗
I would just love a bowl of delicious noodles right now!
　　　我很想要…

❸ 水杯
I'd like a water glass with some water, please.
　　　　　　　　　　　　裝有一些水

❹ 酒杯
Christine received a set of expensive wine glasses for her wedding anniversary.

❺ 胡椒研磨器
If you turn the pepper mill back and forth, it will grind fresh pepper for you.
　　　　　　　來回轉動胡椒研磨器

❻ 鹽罐
Pass me the salt shaker. This spaghetti definitely needs some more salt.
　　遞給我…

學更多

❶ easy〈容易的〉‧ foreigner〈外國人〉
❷ just〈真的〉‧ a bowl of...〈一碗…〉‧ delicious〈美味的〉‧ noodles〈麵〉
❸ glass〈玻璃杯〉‧ some〈一些〉
❹ received〈receive（得到）的過去式〉‧ a set of...〈一組…〉‧ anniversary〈週年紀念日〉
❺ pepper〈胡椒〉‧ mill〈磨粉機〉‧ back and forth〈來回地〉‧ grind〈研磨〉
❻ pass〈傳遞〉‧ salt〈鹽〉‧ shaker〈有孔的佐料瓶〉‧ spaghetti〈義大利麵〉‧
　definitely〈肯定地〉

中譯

❶ 使用筷子對於一些外國人而言很不容易。
❷ 我現在很想要吃一碗好吃的麵！
❸ 請給我一個水杯，並裝一些水。
❹ Christine 在結婚紀念日收到一組昂貴的酒杯。
❺ 只要來回轉動胡椒研磨器，它就會幫你研磨出新鮮胡椒。
❻ 把鹽罐遞給我。這義大利麵絕對需要再加點鹽。

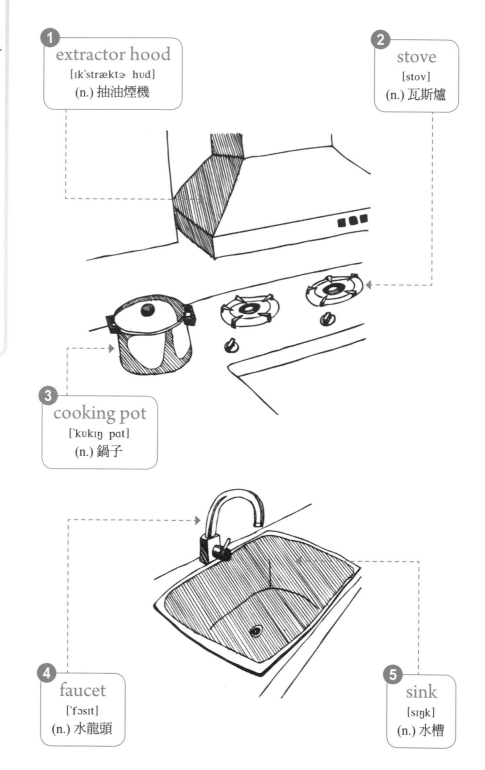

廚房流理臺

MP3 034

1 extractor hood
[ɪkˋstræktə hʊd]
(n.) 抽油煙機

2 stove
[stov]
(n.) 瓦斯爐

3 cooking pot
[ˋkʊkɪŋ pɑt]
(n.) 鍋子

4 faucet
[ˋfɔsɪt]
(n.) 水龍頭

5 sink
[sɪŋk]
(n.) 水槽

❶ 抽油煙機

The extractor hood is covered with grease that we need to clean off.

蓋著一層油

❷ 瓦斯爐

After you finish cooking, Sue, you need to scrub down the stove.

徹底洗淨瓦斯爐

❸ 鍋子

When Roger makes soup, he pulls out a big cooking pot and starts

拿出一個大湯鍋

throwing vegetables and meat in.

❹ 水龍頭

What's that sound, dear? Oh, the faucet is dripping in the kitchen.

❺ 水槽

The sink is plugged up. Can you call the plumber, please?

學更多

❶ extractor〈提取器〉・hood〈罩子〉・be covered with...〈覆蓋著…〉・grease〈油脂〉・
clean〈弄乾淨〉・off〈去除〉

❷ scrub〈擦洗〉・down〈徹底〉

❸ soup〈湯〉・cooking〈烹飪〉・pot〈鍋子〉・throwing〈throw（扔）的 ing 型態〉・
vegetable〈蔬菜〉・meat〈肉〉

❹ sound〈聲音〉・dear〈親愛的〉・dripping〈drip（滴水）的 ing 型態〉

❺ plugged up〈plug up（堵塞）的過去分詞〉・plumber〈水管工人〉

中譯

❶ 抽油煙機上都是油，我們需要清潔它。

❷ Sue，在妳煮完菜後，妳必須把瓦斯爐刷洗乾淨。

❸ 當 Roger 要煮湯時，他會拿出一個很大的鍋子，然後開始放入蔬菜和肉。

❹ 親愛的，那是什麼聲音？喔，廚房的水龍頭正在滴水。

❺ 水槽塞住了。你能幫忙叫水管工人來嗎？

廚具與設備

MP3 035

1 kitchen knife
[`kɪtʃɪn naɪf]
(n.) 菜刀

2 measuring spoon
[`mɛʒrɪŋ spun]
(n.) 量匙

3 spatula
[`spætjələ]
(n.) 鍋鏟

4 refrigerator
[rɪ`frɪdʒəˌretɚ]
(n.) 冰箱

5 oven
[`ʌvən]
(n.) 烤箱

6 cabinet
[`kæbənɪt]
(n.) 廚具櫃

7 microwave oven
[`maɪkroˌwev `ʌvən]
(n.) 微波爐

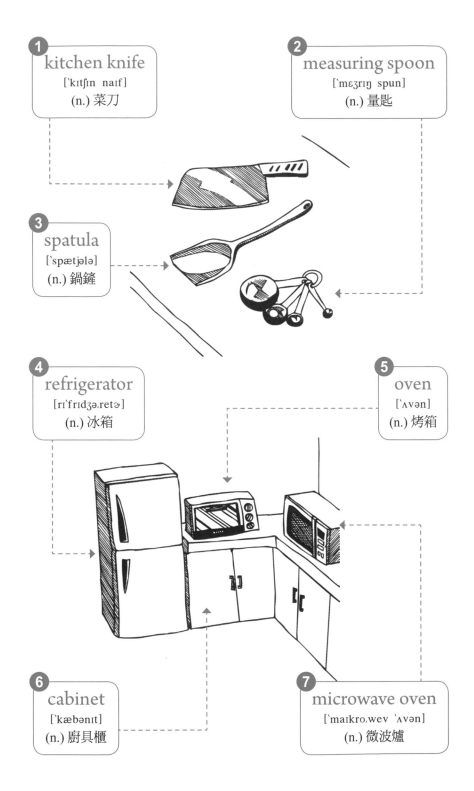

❶ 菜刀

This kitchen knife is so dull. I need to sharpen it before I start cutting.
我需要磨利它

❷ 量匙

I just bought a set of measuring spoons because baking requires very accurate measurements.

❸ 鍋鏟

Spatulas are made using a soft plastic material.
軟膠材質

❹ 冰箱

Oliver, your job today is to clean out the refrigerator.

❺ 烤箱

I'm saving to buy an oven for my apartment so I can make cookies!
我正在存錢要買…

❻ 廚具櫃

Just put the cereal box back into the cabinet when you've finished eating.

❼ 微波爐

I use the microwave oven to reheat food all the time.

學更多

❶ kitchen〈廚房〉・dull〈鈍的〉・sharpen〈磨利〉・cutting〈cut（切）的 ing 型態〉
❷ measuring〈測量〉・baking〈烘焙〉・accurate〈精準的〉・measurement〈測量〉
❸ made〈make（製作）的過去分詞〉・plastic〈塑膠的〉・material〈材料〉
❹ clean out〈清除不需要的東西〉
❺ saving〈save（儲蓄）的 ing 型態〉・apartment〈公寓〉・make cookies〈烤餅乾〉
❻ cereal〈穀片〉・finished〈finish（結束）的過去分詞〉
❼ microwave〈微波〉・reheat〈加熱〉・all the time〈總是〉

中譯

❶ 這把菜刀太鈍了，在切菜之前我必須先把它磨利。
❷ 我剛買了一套量匙，因為烘培需要非常精準的測量。
❸ 鍋鏟是用軟塑膠材質製作的。
❹ Oliver，你今天的工作是清掉冰箱裡不需要的東西。
❺ 我正在存錢替家裡添購烤箱，這樣我就能烤餅乾了！
❻ 你吃完穀片後，就把盒子放回廚具櫃。
❼ 我都用微波爐加熱食物。

036 窗台盆栽

MP3 036

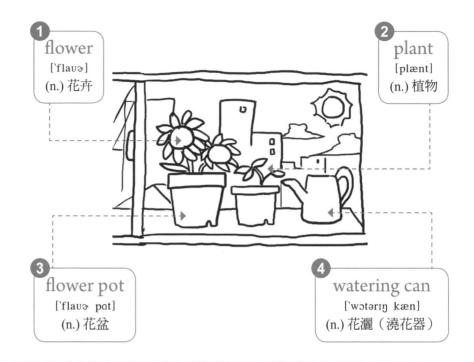

1 flower
[ˈflaʊɚ]
(n.) 花卉

2 plant
[plænt]
(n.) 植物

3 flower pot
[ˈflaʊɚ pɑt]
(n.) 花盆

4 watering can
[ˈwɔtərɪŋ kæn]
(n.) 花灑（澆花器）

❶ 花卉
Nancy picks up a bunch of fresh flowers every Monday on her way to work.
　　　　　　　　　　　　　　　　　　　　　　　在她的上班途中

❷ 植物
How long does it take you to water all the plants on your balcony?
要花你多少時間

❸ 花盆
I think a stray dog broke the flower pot outside our door.

❹ 花灑（澆花器）
Can you hand me the watering can? I want to water these wilting plants.

學更多

❶ pick up〈挑選〉．bunch〈束〉．every〈每個〉．Monday〈星期一〉
❷ water〈給…澆水〉．balcony〈陽台〉
❸ stray〈流浪的〉．broke〈break（毀壞）的過去式〉．pot〈罐、壺〉．outside〈在…外〉
❹ hand〈傳遞〉．wilting〈枯萎的〉

中譯

❶ Nancy 每週一上班途中都會買一束新鮮的花卉。
❷ 你幫你陽台上的植物澆水需要花多少時間？
❸ 我覺得我們門外的花盆是野狗弄破的。
❹ 你可以把花灑遞過來嗎？我想給這些枯萎的植物澆水。

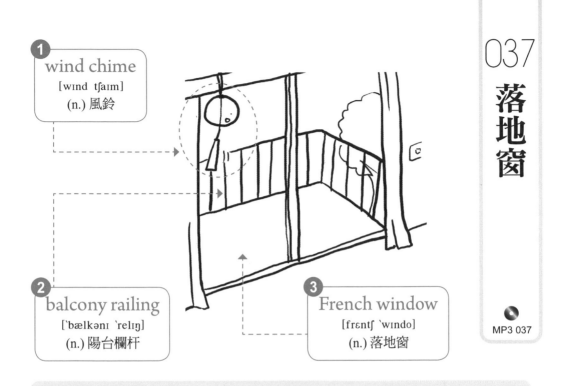

1 wind chime
[wɪnd tʃaɪm]
(n.) 風鈴

2 balcony railing
[ˋbælkənɪ ˋrelɪŋ]
(n.) 陽台欄杆

3 French window
[frɛntʃ ˋwɪndo]
(n.) 落地窗

037
落地窗

🔊 MP3 037

---

❶ 風鈴
Wind chimes **sound so peaceful** on a nice breezy day.
　　　　　　　　　　　　　　晴朗而微風吹拂的日子

❷ 陽台欄杆
This balcony railing **isn't high enough** for families with children.
　　　　　　　　　　　　　　　　　對於有孩子的家庭而言

❸ 落地窗
French windows **add so much style to a room.**

學更多

❶ sound〈聽起來〉‧ peaceful〈平靜的〉‧ breezy〈有微風的〉
❷ railing〈欄杆〉‧ enough〈足夠的〉‧ children〈child（小孩）的複數〉
❸ add〈添加〉‧ style〈風格〉

中譯

❶ 風鈴在晴朗、微風吹拂的日子裡聽起來很舒服。
❷ 這陽台欄杆對於有孩子的家庭而言不夠高。
❸ 落地窗會為一間房間添加許多設計感。

家門口

MP3 038

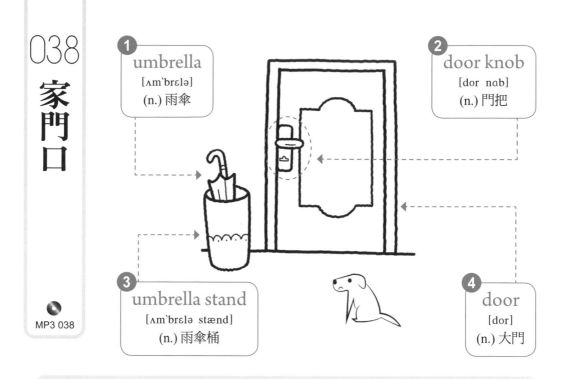

1 umbrella
[ʌmˋbrɛlə]
(n.) 雨傘

2 door knob
[dor nɑb]
(n.) 門把

3 umbrella stand
[ʌmˋbrɛlə stænd]
(n.) 雨傘桶

4 door
[dor]
(n.) 大門

---

1 雨傘
The best umbrella you can buy won't collapse in the wind and rain.

2 門把
Vince grabbed the door knob so hard that he pulled it off the door.
太用力　　　　　　　扯下門

3 雨傘桶
I know I put my umbrella in the umbrella stand earlier, but I don't see it now.

4 大門
Please close the door on your way out. I want to do some studying.
當你出去時　　　　　　　讀一下書

學更多

1 best〈最好的〉・collapse〈瓦解〉・wind〈風〉

2 grabbed〈grab（抓住）的過去式〉・knob〈球形的把手〉・pulled off〈pull off（扯下）的過去式〉

3 put〈put（放）的過去式〉・stand〈架子〉・earlier〈早先的時候〉

4 close〈關閉〉・studying〈study（讀書）的 ing 型態〉

中譯

1 你能買到最好的傘，就是那種不會在風雨中解體的傘。

2 Vince 太用力地抓住門把，結果把門都扯掉了。

3 我知道我先前把雨傘放在傘桶裡，可是現在卻沒看到。

4 你出去的時候請將門關上。我想要讀一下書。

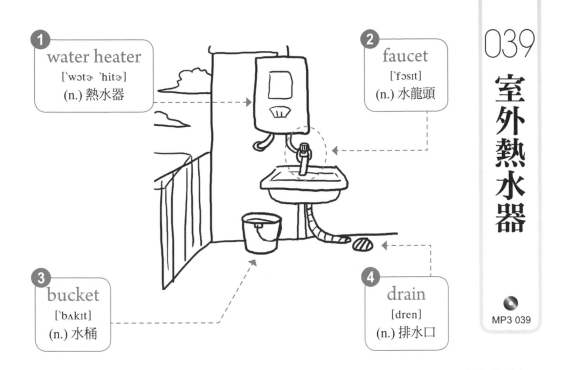

① water heater
[ˈwɔtɚ ˈhitɚ]
(n.) 熱水器

② faucet
[ˈfɔsɪt]
(n.) 水龍頭

③ bucket
[ˈbʌkɪt]
(n.) 水桶

④ drain
[dren]
(n.) 排水口

MP3 039

❶ 熱水器
Tony checked the water heater after he noticed the water wouldn't heat up for his shower.
他發現水溫不熱
❷ 水龍頭
I can't turn the faucet on. Can you try, please?
❸ 水桶
When Paula washes the floor, she uses a bucket of water.
❹ 排水口
After a lot of rain, the drains are filled up and flooding occurs.
被填滿

學更多

❶ noticed〈notice（察覺）的過去式〉・heat up〈把…加熱〉・shower〈淋浴〉
❷ turn...on〈打開…〉
❸ wash〈洗〉・floor〈地板〉
❹ a lot of〈大量〉・filled〈fill（填滿）的過去分詞〉・flooding〈洪水泛濫〉・occur〈發生〉

中譯

❶ Tony 淋浴時發現水溫不熱，後來他檢查了熱水器。
❷ 我無法打開水龍頭。可以拜託你試試看嗎？
❸ Paula 洗地板時，她都用一桶水。
❹ 大雨過後，排水口常堵塞並釀成水災。

087

衛浴設備 (1)

MP3 040

1 mirror
[`mɪrɚ]
(n.) 鏡子

2 toothbrush
[`tuθ,brʌʃ]
(n.) 牙刷

3 toothpaste
[`tuθ,pest]
(n.) 牙膏

4 soap
[sop]
(n.) 肥皂

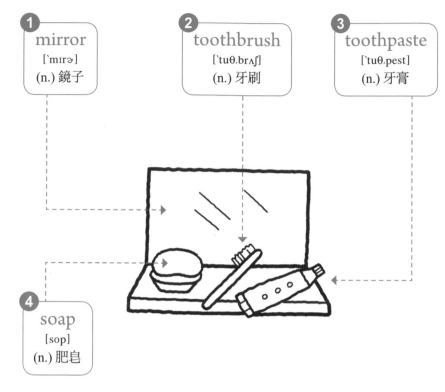

5 sink
[sɪŋk]
(n.) 洗手台/水槽

6 toilet paper
[`tɔɪlɪt `pepɚ]
(n.) 衛生紙

7 flush the toilet
[flʌʃ ðə `tɔɪlɪt]
(phr.) 沖馬桶

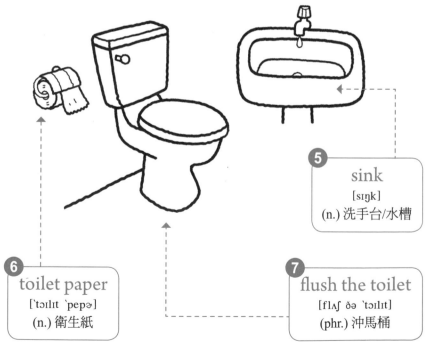

❶ 鏡子

Before Mike leaves for the day, he takes a look in the mirror to see if his
<u>Mike 每天離開公司前</u>
hair looks good.

❷ 牙刷

My dentist insists that I replace my toothbrush every three months.

❸ 牙膏

Bobby, you squeezed all the toothpaste out on the floor. You're in big trouble!
<u>你有大麻煩了</u>

❹ 肥皂

Where's all the soap? I thought we had three bars of soap in the cabinet.

❺ 洗手台 / 水槽

Fill the sink with some hot water and put your lingerie in there to soak.

❻ 衛生紙

Have we really run out of all the toilet paper?

❼ 沖馬桶

Sammy, Mom said not to forget to flush the toilet after you're finished in there.

學更多

❶ leave〈離開〉・take a look〈看一下〉
❷ dentist〈牙醫〉・insist〈堅持〉・replace〈取代〉
❸ squeezed〈squeeze（擠）的過去式〉・in trouble〈在危險的處境中〉
❹ thought〈think（以為）的過去式〉・bar〈條狀物〉・cabinet〈櫃子〉
❺ fill〈裝滿〉・lingerie〈女用內衣〉・soak〈浸泡〉
❻ run out of〈run out of（用完）的過去分詞〉
❼ forget〈忘記〉・flush〈用水沖洗〉・finished〈完成的、結束了的〉

中譯

❶ Mike 每天下班之前，他都會照鏡子看一下自己的頭髮是否很好看。
❷ 我的牙醫堅持要我每三個月換一把牙刷。
❸ Bobby，你把牙膏全部擠在地板上了。你闖大禍了！
❹ 肥皂呢？我以為我們置物櫃裡有三塊。
❺ 在水槽裝滿熱水，再將妳的內衣放進去浸泡。
❻ 我們真的沒有衛生紙了嗎？
❼ Sammy，媽媽說你上完廁所後，不要忘記沖馬桶。

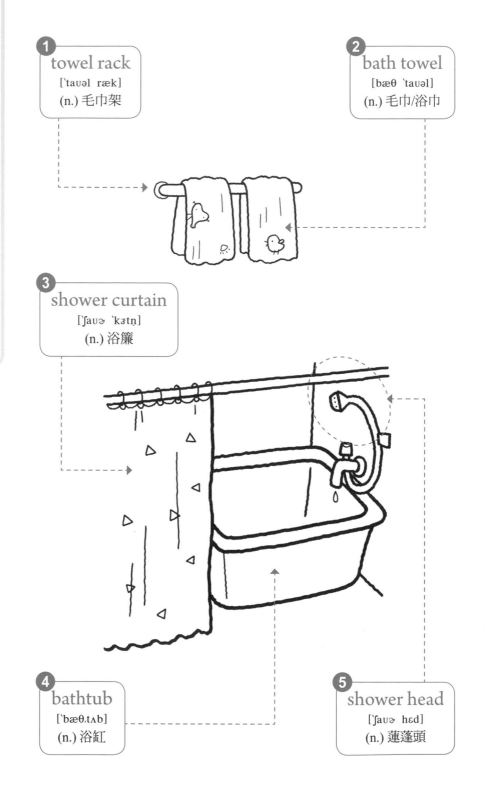

1 towel rack
[ˋtauəl ræk]
(n.) 毛巾架

2 bath towel
[bæθ ˋtauəl]
(n.) 毛巾/浴巾

3 shower curtain
[ˋʃauɚ ˋkɝtn̩]
(n.) 浴簾

4 bathtub
[ˋbæθˏtʌb]
(n.) 浴缸

5 shower head
[ˋʃauɚ hɛd]
(n.) 蓮蓬頭

❶ 毛巾架

Just hang up your damp towel on the towel rack in the bathroom.

只要掛你的濕毛巾

❷ 毛巾 / 浴巾

What a nice, fluffy bath towel. You must have paid quite a bit for it.

花了不少錢

❸ 浴簾

This shower curtain is so fun with all these cartoon figures on it.

上面有許多卡通圖案

❹ 浴缸

My sister doesn't like to take showers; she prefers to sit and relax in the bathtub instead.

她寧可坐著並放鬆

❺ 蓮蓬頭

I need to replace the shower head because it's spraying water all over the place.

學更多

❶ hang up〈掛起〉・damp〈潮濕的〉・towel〈毛巾〉・rack〈掛物架〉
❷ fluffy〈蓬鬆的〉・paid〈pay（付）的過去分詞〉・a bit〈一點〉・quite a bit〈相當不少的〉
❸ fun〈有趣的〉・cartoon〈卡通〉・figure〈圖案〉
❹ take showers〈淋浴〉・prefer〈寧可〉・relax〈放鬆〉・instead〈作為替代〉
❺ replace〈取代〉・spraying〈spray（噴灑）的 ing 型態〉・all over〈到處〉

中譯

❶ 把你的濕毛巾掛在浴室的毛巾架上就好了。
❷ 好蓬鬆的浴巾。你應該付了不少錢買的吧。
❸ 這浴簾上面很多卡通圖案好有趣。
❹ 我妹妹不喜歡淋浴，她寧可坐在浴缸裡放鬆。
❺ 我需要更換蓮蓬頭，因為它會把水噴得到處都是。

042

臥室

MP3 042

1 headboard cabinet
[ˈhɛd.bord ˈkæbənɪt]
(n.) 床頭櫃

2 alarm clock
[əˈlɑrm klɑk]
(n.) 鬧鐘

3 pillow
[ˈpɪlo]
(n.) 枕頭

4 quilt
[kwɪlt]
(n.) 棉被

5 bed
[bɛd]
(n.) 床

6 throw pillow
[θro ˈpɪlo]
(n.) 抱枕

7 bed sheet
[bɛd ʃit]
(n.) 床單

092

❶ 床頭櫃

Wow, that's convenient to have a headboard cabinet included with your bed.
那很方便

❷ 鬧鐘

Jonathon needs to buy an alarm clock because he's always late for work.

❸ 枕頭

Soft down pillows are to die for, aren't they?
令人渴望

❹ 棉被

Grandma made this quilt so it has special significance to me.

❺ 床

My apartment isn't furnished so I'll need to go buy a bed before moving in.

❻ 抱枕

Honey, you can't wash those throw pillows. They need to be dry-cleaned.

❼ 床單

It's Saturday. Let's get all the bed sheets washed and hung out to dry.

學更多

❶ headboard〈頂端的板〉‧cabinet〈櫃子〉‧included〈include（包含）的過去分詞〉

❷ alarm〈鬧鐘〉‧clock〈時鐘〉‧always〈總是〉

❸ soft〈柔軟的〉‧down〈羽絨〉‧die〈渴望〉

❹ made〈make（製作）的過去式〉‧special〈特殊的〉‧significance〈意義〉

❺ furnished〈furnish（裝潢）的過去分詞〉‧moving in〈move in（搬進新家）的 ing 型態〉

❻ throw〈投擲〉‧pillow〈枕頭〉‧dry-cleaned〈dry-clean（乾洗）的過去分詞〉

❼ sheet〈床單〉‧washed〈wash（洗）的過去分詞〉‧hung out〈hang out（掛出）的過去分詞〉

中譯

❶ 哇，你的床鋪還包含一個床頭櫃，很方便。

❷ Jonathon 需要買一個鬧鐘，因為他上班老是遲到。

❸ 柔軟的羽絨枕頭非常誘人，不是嗎？

❹ 這條棉被是祖母做的，所以它對我而言有特殊意義。

❺ 我的公寓沒有裝潢，所以我搬進去之前需要先去買一張床。

❻ 親愛的，你不能水洗那些抱枕。它們需要乾洗。

❼ 今天是星期六。我們把所有的床單洗好並掛起來曬乾。

043
衣櫥

MP3 043

1 mirror
[`mɪrə]
(n.) 鏡子

2 hanger
[`hæŋə]
(n.) 衣架

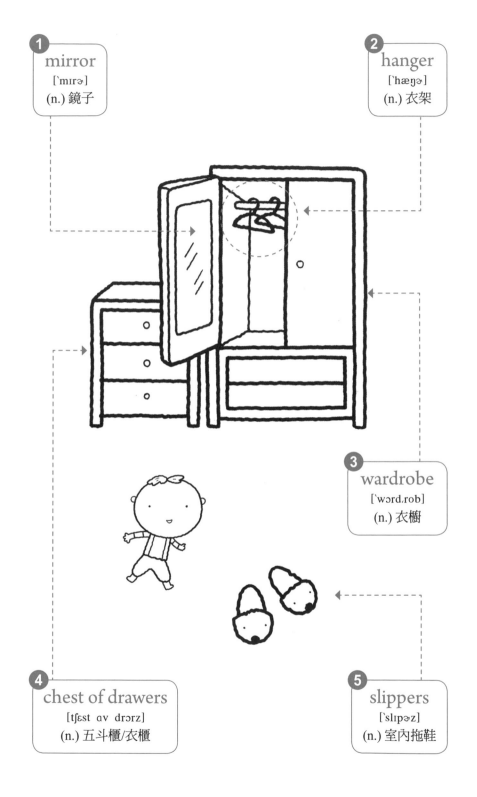

3 wardrobe
[`wɔrd͵rob]
(n.) 衣櫥

4 chest of drawers
[tʃɛst ɑv drɔrz]
(n.) 五斗櫃/衣櫃

5 slippers
[`slɪpəz]
(n.) 室內拖鞋

❶ 鏡子

Do you have a mirror with you? I think I have some food in my teeth.
<u>有食物塞在我的牙縫</u>

❷ 衣架

I have plenty of hangers in my room for all my clothes.

❸ 衣櫥

Brenda has way too many clothes for her wardrobe. She may need to
<u>有過多的衣服</u>
buy another one.

❹ 五斗櫃 / 衣櫃

A chest of drawers is great for storing pants, lingerie and casual shirts in.

❺ 室內拖鞋

You can't wear your shoes inside the house, but slippers are fine.
<u>但是室內拖鞋是沒問題的</u>

學更多

❶ teeth〈tooth（牙齒）的複數〉

❷ plenty of〈大量〉

❸ way too many〈太多的〉・another〈另一個〉

❹ chest〈衣櫃〉・drawer〈抽屜〉・storing〈store（收納）的 ing 型態〉・pants〈褲子〉・
lingerie〈女用內衣褲〉・casual〈非正式的〉

❺ wear〈穿著〉・inside〈在…的裡面〉・fine〈可以〉

中譯

❶ 你有帶鏡子嗎？好像有食物塞在我的牙縫。

❷ 我的房間裡有足夠的衣架掛我所有的衣服。

❸ Brenda 的衣服多到她的衣櫥裝不下。她可能需要再買一個。

❹ 五斗櫃很適合用來收納褲子、內衣褲和休閒襯衫。

❺ 你不能穿鞋在屋裡走來走去，不過室內拖鞋沒關係。

044

書桌上

MP3 044

1 reading glasses
[ˈridɪŋ ˈglæsɪz]
(n.) 老花眼鏡

2 penholder
[ˈpɛn.holdə]
(n.) 筆筒

3 reading lamp
[ˈridɪŋ læmp]
(n.) 檯燈

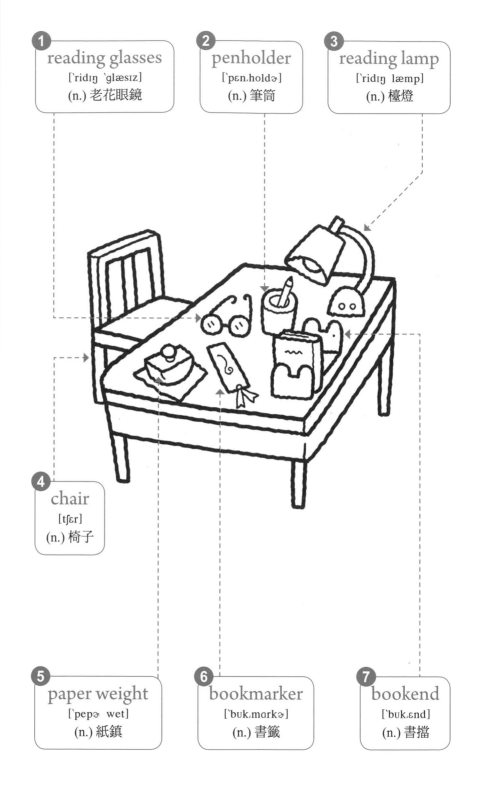

4 chair
[tʃɛr]
(n.) 椅子

5 paper weight
[ˈpepə wet]
(n.) 紙鎮

6 bookmarker
[ˈbʊk.mɑrkə]
(n.) 書籤

7 bookend
[ˈbʊk.ɛnd]
(n.) 書擋

❶ 老花眼鏡

Grandpa, I looked everywhere, but I can't find your reading glasses.

❷ 筆筒

Your pens and pencils are a mess. Get a penholder for them.

　　　　　　　　　　　　　　替它們找一個筆筒來

❸ 檯燈

Reading lamps will help save your eyes from straining in a dark room.

　　　　　　　　　　保護你的眼睛免於受損

❹ 椅子

The legs on this chair are getting weak so I'll need to get them fixed.

　　　　　　　　開始變得不穩

❺ 紙鎮

Harold has a gross paper weight with a scorpion inside it. Yuck!

❻ 書籤

What a beautiful bookmarker! Where did you get it?

❼ 書擋

Bookends help keep books from falling over.

學更多

❶ looked〈look（看）的過去式〉・everywhere〈到處〉・glasses〈眼鏡〉
❷ mess〈凌亂的狀態〉
❸ save...from〈保護…免於〉・straining〈strain（過勞而受損）的 ing 型態〉・dark〈暗的〉
❹ weak〈虛弱的〉・fixed〈fix（修理）的過去分詞〉
❺ gross〈令人噁心的〉・weight〈文鎮〉・scorpion〈蠍子〉
❻ beautiful〈漂亮的〉
❼ keep...from〈保持…免於〉・falling over〈fall over（倒下）的 ing 型態〉

中譯

❶ 祖父，我到處都找了，但我還是找不到你的老花眼鏡。
❷ 你的筆和鉛筆好亂。去找一個筆筒來裝。
❸ 檯燈有助於保護你的眼睛避免在太暗的房間閱讀而受損。
❹ 這張椅子的腳開始不穩了，所以我需要請人修理一下。
❺ Harold 有一個裡面有一隻蠍子的噁心紙鎮。嗯！
❻ 好漂亮的書籤！你在哪裡買的？
❼ 書擋會防止書本傾倒。

1 post-it note
[`postɪt not]
(n.) 便利貼

2 notebook
[`not.bʊk]
(n.) 記事本

3 pen
[pɛn]
(n.) 筆

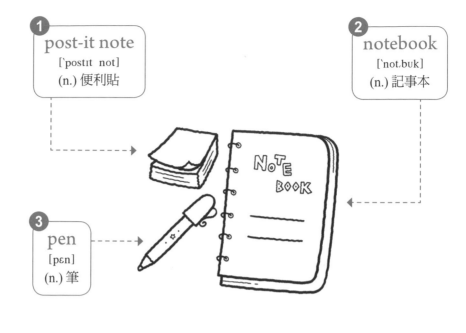

4 book
[bʊk]
(n.) 書籍

5 desk
[dɛsk]
(n.) 書桌

6 bookcase
[`bʊk.kes]
(n.) 書架

❶ 便利貼

Do you have any post-it notes I can use to <u>mark my textbook?</u>
在我的課本做標示

❷ 記事本

Mary, you left your notebook in the cafeteria.

❸ 筆

Don't write in that book with a pen!

❹ 書籍

What book are you currently reading? <u>Is it something you'd recommend?</u>
它是否值得你推薦

❺ 書桌

<u>Make sure you sweep</u> around the desk in the corner, honey.
你要記得清掃

❻ 書架

Bookcases are a necessary item in any home.

學更多

❶ post〈張貼〉‧note〈筆記〉‧mark〈標記、做記號〉‧textbook〈課本〉
❷ left〈leave（遺忘）的過去式〉‧cafeteria〈自助餐廳〉
❸ write〈書寫〉
❹ currently〈現在〉‧something〈值得重視的人事物〉‧recommend〈推薦〉
❺ make sure〈確定〉‧sweep〈打掃〉
❻ necessary〈必需的〉‧item〈物品〉

中譯

❶ 你有便利貼可以讓我在課本上做標示嗎？
❷ Mary，你把筆記本遺忘在餐廳了。
❸ 不要用筆在那本書裡寫字！
❹ 你最近在看哪一本書？那本書值得推薦嗎？
❺ 親愛的，要記得清掃角落書桌附近的地方。
❻ 書架是任何人家中的必需品。

046

客廳

MP3 046

1 ceiling
[ˋsilɪŋ]
(n.) 天花板

2 ceiling fan
[ˋsilɪŋ fæn]
(n.) 吊扇

3 painting
[ˋpentɪŋ]
(n.) 掛畫

4 sofa
[ˋsofə]
(n.) 沙發

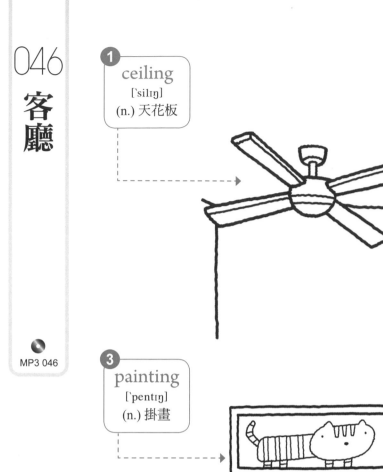
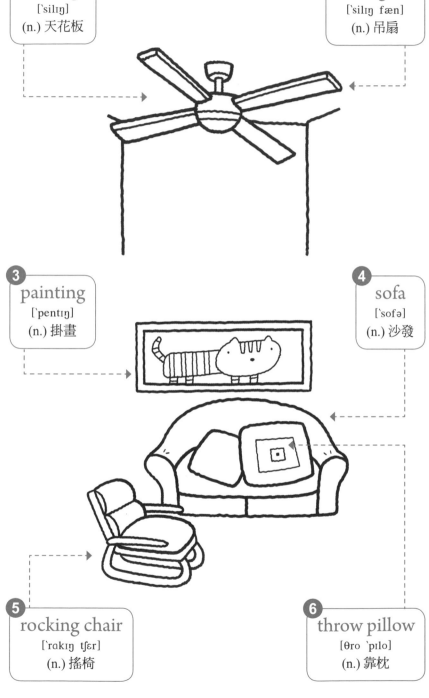

5 rocking chair
[ˋrɑkɪŋ tʃɛr]
(n.) 搖椅

6 throw pillow
[θro ˋpɪlo]
(n.) 靠枕

❶ 天花板

Can you help me dust the ceiling? It's too high for me to reach.

你可以幫我…

❷ 吊扇

My parents have ceiling fans in all the rooms in their home which keeps their air-conditioning bill low.

維持低廉的冷氣費用

❸ 掛畫

Tom collects paintings by new artists.

❹ 沙發

Dale is going shopping for a new brown sofa.

要去採購

❺ 搖椅

Mothers love rocking chairs which help rock their newborn babies to sleep.

❻ 靠枕

Those are lovely throw pillows on the sofa. Did you make them yourself?

你自己做這些

學更多

❶ dust〈除去…的灰塵〉・too...to...〈太…而無法…〉・reach〈達到〉
❷ fan〈風扇〉・air-conditioning〈空調〉・bill〈帳單〉・low〈低的〉
❸ collect〈收集〉・artist〈藝術家〉
❹ shopping〈shop（購物）的 ing 型態〉・brown〈咖啡色的〉
❺ chair〈椅子〉・rock〈搖〉・newborn〈新出生的〉・sleep〈睡覺〉
❻ lovely〈漂亮的〉・throw〈投擲〉・pillow〈枕頭〉・yourself〈你自己〉

中譯

❶ 你可以幫我去除天花板的灰塵嗎？那太高了我清理不到。
❷ 我父母家裡的每個房間都有吊扇，此舉讓他們的冷氣費用都維持得相當低。
❸ Tom 收集新畫家的畫作。
❹ Dale 要去買一張新的咖啡色沙發。
❺ 媽媽最喜歡搖椅可以幫助她們把新生兒搖到睡著。
❻ 那些沙發上的靠枕好漂亮。你自己做的嗎？

047

看電視

MP3 047

1 television
[ˈtɛləˌvɪʒən]
(n.) 電視

2 telephone
[ˈtɛləˌfon]
(n.) 電話

3 vase
[ves]
(n.) 花瓶

4 remote control
[rɪˈmot kənˈtrol]
(n.) 遙控器

5 coffee table
[ˈkɔfɪ ˈtebl̩]
(n.) 茶几

6 rug
[rʌg]
(n.) 地毯

❶ 電視

How do you like your new LCD television?

你覺得…如何

❷ 電話

The telephone is ringing. Someone answer it!

❸ 花瓶

Oh no! The dog just knocked the vase off the table and broke it.

把花瓶從桌上撞掉下來

❹ 遙控器

Hey, did you take the remote control somewhere? I want to watch TV.

❺ 茶几

Don't put your feet up on the coffee table!

把你的腳放在…之上

❻ 地毯

I need to vacuum the rug before the party starts.

❶ new〈新的〉・LCD〈液晶顯示〉

❷ ringing〈ring（響）的 ing 型態〉・someone〈某人〉・answer〈接電話〉

❸ knocked off〈knock off（撞倒）的過去式〉・broke〈break（打破）的過去式〉

❹ remote〈遙控的〉・control〈操縱裝置〉・somewhere〈某處〉

❺ feet〈foot（腳）的複數〉・coffee〈咖啡〉・table〈桌子〉

❻ vacuum〈用吸塵器清掃〉・party〈派對〉・start〈開始〉

中譯

❶ 你覺得你的新液晶電視如何？

❷ 電話在響，誰去接一下！

❸ 喔不！狗狗把花瓶從桌上撞掉下來，花瓶破了。

❹ 嘿，你有把遙控器拿去哪裡嗎？我想要看電視。

❺ 不要把你的腳放到茶几上！

❻ 派對開始前，我要用吸塵器清潔地毯。

048

玄關處

MP3 048

1 coat rack
[kot ræk]
(n.) 衣帽架

2 shoe cabinet
[ʃu ˋkæbənɪt]
(n.) 鞋櫃

3 hook
[hʊk]
(n.) 掛鉤

4 shoes
[ʃuz]
(n.) 鞋子

5 doormat
[ˋdor.mæt]
(n.) 腳踏墊

6 slippers
[ˋslɪpəz]
(n.) 室內拖鞋

7 shoehorn
[ˋʃu.hɔrn]
(n.) 鞋拔

❶ 衣帽架

Let me take your coat for you and put it here on the coat rack.

把它放到衣帽架上

❷ 鞋櫃

There is a shoe cabinet outside the door for guests.

門外

❸ 掛鉤

Just put your hat there on the hook.

❹ 鞋子

What a beautiful pair of shoes! Where did you buy them?

如此美麗的一雙…

❺ 腳踏墊

Make sure you wipe your dirty shoes on the doormat before you come in.

❻ 室內拖鞋

Would you like some slippers to wear inside the house?

你想要…　　　　　　　　　　　室內

❼ 鞋拔

My dad uses a shoehorn to put his shoes on.

學更多

❶ take〈拿〉．coat〈外套〉．put〈放〉．rack〈掛物架〉
❷ shoe〈鞋〉．cabinet〈櫃子〉． outside〈在外面〉．guest〈客人〉
❸ hat〈帽子〉
❹ a pair of...〈一雙、一對…〉．buy〈買〉
❺ make sure〈確認〉．wipe〈擦〉．dirty〈髒的〉．come in〈進來〉
❻ wear〈穿著〉．inside〈在裡面〉
❼ use〈使用〉．put on〈穿上〉

中譯

❶ 讓我替你拿你的外套，並把它掛在衣帽架上。
❷ 門外有一個鞋櫃給客人放置鞋子。
❸ 把你的帽子掛在掛鉤那兒就好了。
❹ 好漂亮的一雙鞋子！你在哪裡買的？
❺ 當你進來之前，要確認你已經在腳踏墊上將髒鞋子清潔乾淨。
❻ 在室內你需要穿室內拖鞋嗎？
❼ 我爸爸使用鞋拔穿鞋。

049

居家花園

MP3 049

1 sprinkler
[ˈsprɪŋklɚ]
(n.) 灑水器

2 lawn mower
[lɔn ˈmoɚ]
(n.) 除草機

3 watering can
[ˈwɔtərɪŋ kæn]
(n.) 澆花壺

4 gardener
[ˈgɑrdənɚ]
(n.) 園丁

5 flower
[ˈflauɚ]
(n.) 花卉

6 plant
[plænt]
(n.) 植物

❶ 灑水器

Please turn the sprinkler on and water the lawn.

開啟灑水器

❷ 除草機

Dad, I think the lawn mower needs oil in its engine.

引擎需要上油

❸ 澆花壺

Do you have a watering can I can use to water your plants for you?

❹ 園丁

Eric has a part-time summer job as a gardener.

當園丁

❺ 花卉

Mrs. Jones has a beautiful flower garden in her front yard.

❻ 植物

I love plants and have them all over my apartment and balcony.

學更多

❶ turn on〈打開、發動〉‧ water〈給…澆水〉‧ lawn〈草坪〉

❷ mower〈割草機〉‧ oil〈油〉‧ engine〈引擎〉

❸ watering〈澆水〉‧ can〈罐〉

❹ part-time〈兼職的〉‧ summer〈夏天〉‧ job〈工作〉‧ as〈作為、以…的身分〉

❺ garden〈花園〉‧ front〈前面的〉‧ yard〈庭院〉

❻ all over〈到處〉‧ apartment〈公寓〉‧ balcony〈陽台〉

中譯

❶ 請啟動灑水器,並給草皮澆水。

❷ 爸爸,我覺得除草機的引擎需要上油。

❸ 你有澆花壺可以讓我用來幫你的植物澆水嗎?

❹ Eric 夏天兼職當園丁。

❺ Jones 太太在她家前院有一個美麗的花園。

❻ 我愛植物,我的公寓和陽台到處都是植物。

050

居家庭園

MP3 050

1 bush
[bʊʃ]
(n.) 矮樹叢

2 fence
[fɛns]
(n.) 圍籬

3 garage
[gəˋrɑʒ]
(n.) 車庫

4 dog house
[dɔg haʊs]
(n.) 狗屋

5 swing
[swɪŋ]
(n.) 鞦韆

6 pond
[pɑnd]
(n.) 魚池

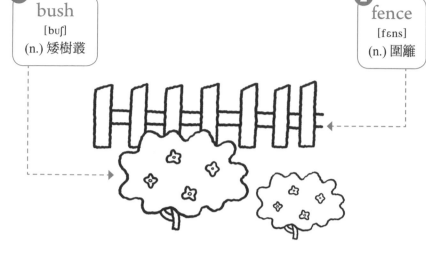

❶ 矮樹叢

Katie hid in the bushes while playing "hide and seek" with her friends.

躲在矮樹叢裡

❷ 圍籬

We have a tall fence that goes around our entire yard for privacy.

圍繞我們的整個庭院

❸ 車庫

You are so lucky to have a garage for your car!

❹ 狗屋

Is Skippy in his dog house outside or is he running around?

到處跑

❺ 鞦韆

Let's go and play on the swings in the backyard!

我們去玩盪鞦韆

❻ 魚池

Kevin has a pond in his backyard with goldfish swimming in it.

學更多

❶ hid〈hide（躲藏）的過去式〉・while〈當…的時候〉・hide and seek〈躲貓貓〉

❷ tall〈高大的〉・entire〈整個的〉・privacy〈隱私〉

❸ lucky〈幸運的〉

❹ house〈房子〉・outside〈在外面〉・running〈run（跑）的 ing 型態〉

❺ backyard〈後院〉

❻ goldfish〈金魚〉・swimming〈swim（游）的 ing 型態〉

中譯

❶ 跟朋友玩「躲貓貓」的時候，Katie 躲在矮樹叢裡。

❷ 為了隱私，我們整個庭院都用高高的圍籬圍繞。

❸ 你真幸運，有車庫可以停放自己的車子！

❹ Skippy 是在外面牠的狗屋裡？還是正到處亂跑？

❺ 我們去後院玩盪鞦韆吧！

❻ Kevin 的後院有一個魚池，裡面有金魚游來游去。

051

梳妝台上

MP3 051

1 cotton puff
[`kɑtn̩ pʌf]
(n.) 化妝棉

2 perfume
[`pɝfjum]
(n.) 香水

3 cosmetics
[kɑz`mɛtɪks]
(n.) 化妝品

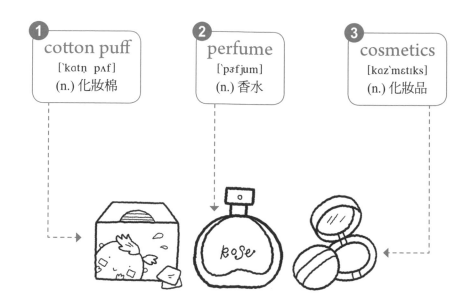

4 comb
[kom]
(n.) 梳子

5 mirror
[`mɪrɚ]
(n.) 鏡子

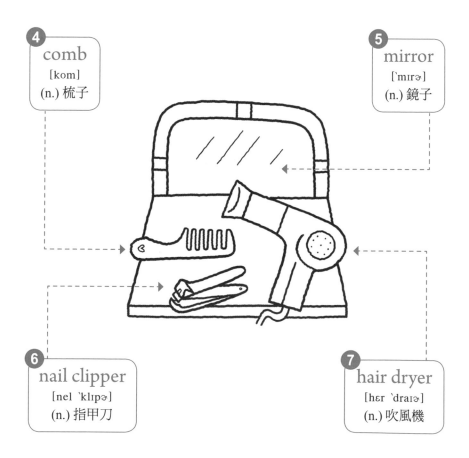

6 nail clipper
[nel `klɪpɚ]
(n.) 指甲刀

7 hair dryer
[hɛr `draɪɚ]
(n.) 吹風機

❶ 化妝棉

I use cotton puffs to remove my mascara.

❷ 香水

My mother likes very expensive perfume that has a musky scent.

❸ 化妝品

Jill spends most of her part-time job earnings on new cosmetics.

花費大部分的兼職收入

❹ 梳子

Wendy, did you take my comb? It used to be here in the bathroom.

拿走我的梳子　　　　　　　本來都在這裡

❺ 鏡子

I need a mirror to replace the one I broke this morning.

❻ 指甲刀

Sally, grab the nail clippers and give them to your dad.

把它給你爸爸

❼ 吹風機

Our neighbor, who is a model, uses her hair dryer at least twice a day.

至少一天兩次

學更多

❶ cotton〈棉花〉‧ puff〈粉撲〉‧ remove〈去掉〉‧ mascara〈睫毛膏〉
❷ expensive〈昂貴的〉‧ musky〈有麝香味的〉‧ scent〈氣味〉
❸ spend〈花費〉‧ most〈大部分的〉‧ earning〈收入〉‧ on〈有關〉
❹ used to〈過去一向〉‧ bathroom〈浴室〉
❺ replace〈取代〉‧ broke〈break（破裂）的過去式〉
❻ grab〈拿取〉‧ nail〈指甲〉‧ clipper〈指甲剪〉
❼ neighbor〈鄰居〉‧ model〈模特兒〉‧ dryer〈吹風機〉‧ at least〈至少〉‧ twice〈兩次〉

中譯

❶ 我用化妝棉卸掉我的睫毛膏。
❷ 我母親喜歡有麝香味的昂貴香水。
❸ Jill 兼職賺的錢，大部分都用來買新的化妝品。
❹ Wendy，你有拿我的梳子嗎？它本來在浴室裡。
❺ 我需要一個鏡子取代我早上打破的那面。
❻ Sally，拿指甲刀給你爸爸。
❼ 我們的鄰居是個模特兒，她每天至少使用吹風機兩次。

洗衣間

1 clothes dryer
[kloz `draɪɚ]
(n.) 烘衣機

2 washing machine
[`waʃɪŋ məʃɪn]
(n.) 洗衣機

3 laundry basket
[`lɔndrɪ `bæskɪt]
(n.) 洗衣籃

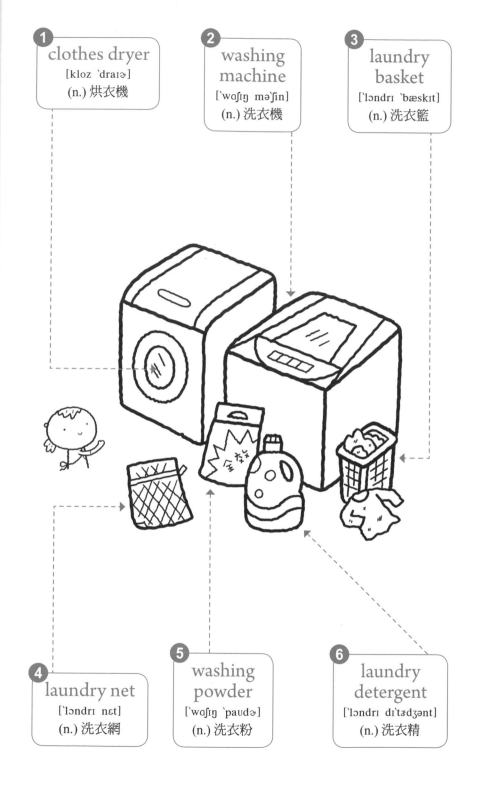

4 laundry net
[`lɔndrɪ nɛt]
(n.) 洗衣網

5 washing powder
[`waʃɪŋ `paʊdɚ]
(n.) 洗衣粉

6 laundry detergent
[`lɔndrɪ dɪ`tɝdʒənt]
(n.) 洗衣精

❶ 烘衣機

During the long, cold winter, it's nice to have a clothes dryer.
　　　　　　　　　　　　　　　　是很好的

❷ 洗衣機

Before I moved into my new apartment, my landlord bought a washing machine for me.

❸ 洗衣籃

Harry, can you bring the laundry basket over here?

❹ 洗衣網

Protect your delicate fabrics in the washing machine with a laundry net.
　　　　　敏感脆弱的布料

❺ 洗衣粉

Some folks like to use washing powder rather than a liquid.
　　有些人喜歡　　　　　　　　　　　　而不是液態洗衣精

❻ 洗衣精

What brand of laundry detergent do you prefer?
　哪一個品牌

學更多

❶ during〈在…的整個期間〉・winter〈冬天〉・dryer〈烘衣機〉

❷ moved into〈move into（搬進）的過去式〉・landlord〈房東〉・
　 bought〈buy（買）的過去式〉・machine〈機器〉

❸ bring〈拿來〉・laundry〈送洗、待洗的衣服〉・basket〈籃子〉・over here〈在這裡〉

❹ protect〈保護〉・delicate〈脆弱的〉・fabric〈布料〉・net〈網子〉

❺ folks〈人們〉・powder〈粉〉・rather than...〈而不是…〉・liquid〈液體〉

❻ brand〈品牌〉・detergent〈洗潔劑〉・prefer〈更喜歡〉

中譯

❶ 寒冷的長冬裡有烘衣機真好。

❷ 我搬進新公寓之前，我的房東為我買了一台洗衣機。

❸ Harry，你可以把洗衣籃拿過來這裡嗎？

❹ 使用洗衣網保護洗衣機裡脆弱的衣料。

❺ 有些人喜歡使用洗衣粉，而非液態洗衣精。

❻ 你比較喜歡哪一個品牌的洗衣精？

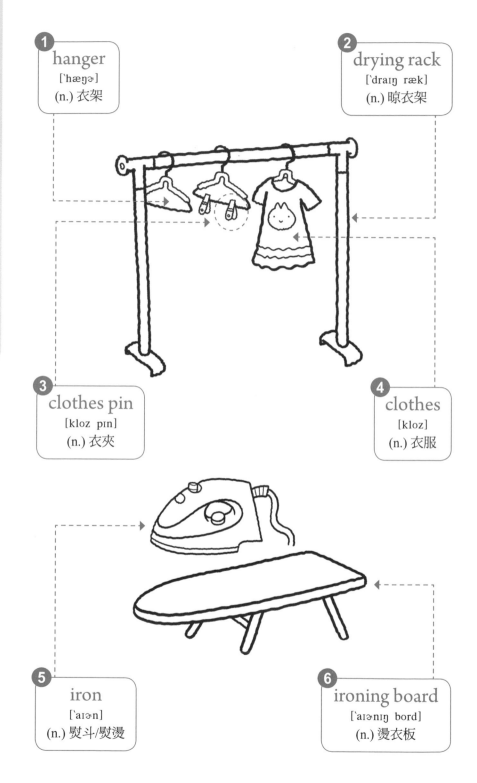

053

曬衣間

MP3 053

1 hanger [ˋhæŋɚ] (n.) 衣架

2 drying rack [ˋdraɪŋ ræk] (n.) 晾衣架

3 clothes pin [kloz pɪn] (n.) 衣夾

4 clothes [kloz] (n.) 衣服

5 iron [ˋaɪɚn] (n.) 熨斗/熨燙

6 ironing board [ˋaɪɚnɪŋ bord] (n.) 燙衣板

❶ 衣架

I've run out of hangers so I'm going to go and pick up some more at the store.
再買一些

❷ 晾衣架

Tina likes to use a drying rack inside her house during the wet winter months.

❸ 衣夾

Clothes pins help keep clothes from falling off the hangers.
避免衣服掉落

❹ 衣服

Don't bring in the clothes yet because they're still wet.
還不要把衣服拿進來

❺ 熨斗 / 熨燙

I hate to iron my clothes, so I pay my sister to do it for me.
我付錢給我妹妹

❻ 燙衣板

Becky bought an ironing board and dragged it home with her.
她拖著它回家

學更多

❶ run out of〈run out of（用完）的過去分詞〉・more〈更多的〉・store〈店〉
❷ drying〈使乾燥的〉・rack〈架子〉・wet〈濕的〉・month〈月份〉
❸ pin〈別針〉・keep...from...〈避免〉・falling off〈fall off（落下）的 ing 型態〉
❹ bring〈拿來〉・in〈進…、在裡面〉・yet〈還〉・still〈還是〉
❺ hate〈討厭〉・pay〈付款〉
❻ bought〈buy（買）的過去式〉・board〈板子〉・dragged〈drag（拖）的過去式〉

中譯

❶ 我的衣架用完了，所以我要去店裡再買一些。
❷ 在潮濕的冬季，Tina 喜歡在室內使用晾衣架。
❸ 衣夾有助於避免衣物從衣架滑落。
❹ 先不要把衣服收進來，因為它們還是濕的。
❺ 我討厭燙衣服，所以我都付錢給我妹妹請她幫我燙。
❻ Becky 買了一個燙衣板，並拖著它回家了。

054

動物園 (1)

MP3 054

1 ticket booth
['tɪkɪt buθ]
(n.) 售票口

2 exit
['ɛksɪt]
(n.) 出口

3 entrance
['ɛntrəns]
(n.) 入口

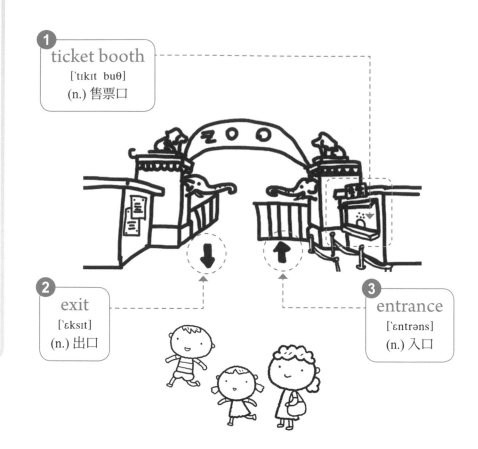

4 gift shop
[gɪft ʃɑp]
(n.) 紀念品商店

5 tourist information center
['tʊrɪst ˌɪnfəˈmeʃən ˈsɛntə]
(n.) 遊客中心

❶ 售票口
Let's get two adult tickets and two children's tickets at the ticket booth.
<u>兩張全票和兩張兒童票</u>

❷ 出口
The exits are clearly marked in case of an emergency.
<u>被標示得很清楚</u>

❸ 入口
Before the zoo opens, there's a crowd at the entrance waiting to be the first ones in.
<u>最先入園的人</u>

❹ 紀念品商店
Susie bought some postcards to send to her friends at the gift shop.
<u>寄給她的朋友們</u>

❺ 遊客中心
If you'd like some more information about the best places to see, just
如果你想要（= If you would like）　　　　　　必看景點
visit the tourist information center.

學更多

❶ adult〈成年人的〉‧children〈child（小孩）的複數〉‧booth〈售貨棚、售貨攤〉

❷ clearly〈清楚地〉‧marked〈mark（標明）的過去分詞〉‧in case of〈萬一、如果發生〉‧ emergency〈緊急情況〉

❸ open〈開門〉‧crowd〈人群〉‧waiting〈wait（等待）的 ing 型態〉‧crowd〈人群〉‧ first〈首先的〉

❹ bought〈buy（買）的過去式〉‧postcard〈明信片〉‧gift〈禮物〉

❺ information〈資訊〉‧place〈地點〉‧tourist〈遊客〉‧center〈中心、中心區〉

中譯

❶ 我們去售票口買兩張全票和兩張兒童票。

❷ 出口處都標示得很清楚，以防萬一有緊急狀況。

❸ 動物園開門之前，入口處會有一群人等著要成為最先入園的人。

❹ Susie 在紀念品商店買了一些明信片寄給她的朋友們。

❺ 如果你需要更多參觀景點的資訊，去問一下遊客中心就行了。

055

動物園(2)

MP3 055

1 guide book
[gaɪd bʊk]
(n.) 導覽手冊

2 park map
[pɑrk mæp]
(n.) 園區地圖

3 shuttle train
[`ʃʌtḷ tren]
(n.) 接駁車

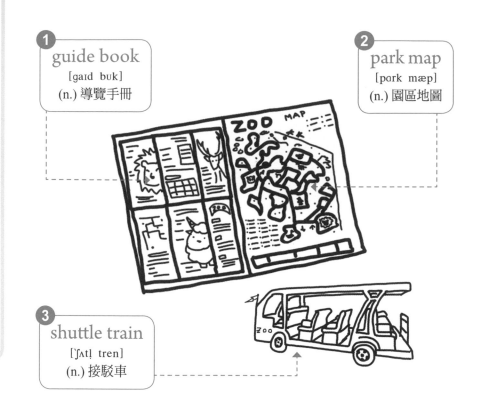

4 indoor display area
[`ɪn͵dor dɪ`sple `ɛrɪə]
(n.) 室內展示館

5 reptile
[`rɛptaɪl]
(n.) 爬蟲動物

❶ 導覽手冊

Pick up a guide book at the entrance. It's got great maps and information
inside.　　　　　　　　　　　　　　　　　那其中有很棒的地圖和資訊

❷ 園區地圖

Park maps are posted around the zoo to help visitors get around more easily.
　　　　　　　　　　　　　　　　　　　　　　　更方便到處走動

❸ 接駁車

There's a shuttle train in NYC between the east and west sides of town
that runs on 42nd street.　　　　　　在城市的西邊及東邊之間
　　　　　42 街

❹ 室內展示館

There's a beautiful indoor display area filled with different types of nocturnal
animals at the zoo.　　　　　　　　　　有各種不同的夜行性動物

❺ 爬蟲動物

I think the scariest reptile alive is the python which can squeeze people to
death.　　　現存最可怕的爬蟲類　　　　　　　　　　　將人纏捲至死

學更多

❶ pick up〈拿起〉．guide〈導覽〉．entrance〈入口〉．information〈資訊〉
❷ posted〈post（張貼）的過去分詞〉．visitor〈遊客〉．get around〈到處走動〉
❸ shuttle〈短程穿梭運行〉．train〈列車〉．NYC〈New York City（紐約市）的縮寫〉．
　east〈東方的〉．west〈西方的〉．side〈地區〉．town〈市區〉．run〈行駛〉
❹ indoor〈室內的〉．display〈展出〉．area〈區域〉．filled〈fill（充滿）的過去分詞〉．
　type〈種類〉．nocturnal〈夜行性的〉
❺ scariest〈最可怕的，scary（可怕的）的最高級〉．alive〈現存的〉．python〈蟒蛇〉．
　squeeze〈勒緊、擰〉

中譯

❶ 在入口處拿一本導覽手冊，裡面有很棒的地圖和資訊。
❷ 動物園內四處張貼著園區地圖，以便遊客能夠輕易地四處走動。
❸ 在紐約市的西邊和東邊之間，有一輛行駛於 42 街的接駁車。（註：此接駁車為地下
　鐵列車）
❹ 動物園內有一個美麗的室內展覽館，館內展示多種夜行性動物。
❺ 我覺得現存最可怕的爬蟲類是巨蟒，因為牠能將人纏捲至死。

056

動物園(3)

MP3 056

1 carnivore
[`kɑrnəˌvɔr]
(n.) 肉食動物

2 lion
[`laɪən]
(n.) 獅子

3 goat
[got]
(n.) 山羊

4 herbivore
[`hɝbəˌvɔr]
(n.) 草食動物

5 zoo keeper
[zu `kipɚ]
(n.) 動物園管理員

6 fence
[fɛns]
(n.) 圍欄

❶ 肉食動物
❷ 獅子

Tigers and lions are hunters by nature, and are carnivores of course.
　　　　　　　　　　　　　　　　天生是

❸ 山羊

The easiest way to tell the difference between a sheep and goat is to
look at their tails.　　　　　　辨別綿羊和山羊的差異

❹ 草食動物

A giraffe is a herbivore, so it only eats plants.

❺ 動物園管理員

If you want a job as a zoo keeper, it's important that you really love
animals.　　　從事動物管理員的工作

❻ 圍欄

You must stay behind the fence at all times for your protection.
　　　　　　退到圍欄之後

學更多

❶❷ tiger〈老虎〉‧ hunter〈獵食者〉‧ nature〈天性〉‧ of course〈當然〉

❸ easiest〈最簡單的，easy（簡單）的最高級〉‧ tell〈辨別〉‧ difference〈差異〉‧
between〈在…之間〉‧ look at〈看〉‧ tails〈尾巴〉

❹ giraffe〈長頸鹿〉‧ only〈只〉‧ plant〈植物〉

❺ keeper〈管理員〉‧ important〈重要的〉‧ animal〈動物〉

❻ stay〈停留〉‧ behind〈在…後面〉‧ at all times〈隨時〉‧ protection〈保護〉

中譯

❶❷ 老虎和獅子是天生的獵食者，所以當然是肉食性動物。

❸ 分辨綿羊和山羊差異最簡單的方法，就是看牠們的尾巴。

❹ 長頸鹿是草食性動物，所以牠只吃植物。

❺ 如果你想要當動物園管理員，很重要的一點是，你必須很愛動物。

❻ 為了你的安全著想，你必須隨時保持退到圍欄之後。

057

遊樂園設施(1)

🔘 MP3 057

1 merry-go-round
['mɛrɪgo,raʊnd]
(n.) 旋轉木馬

2 Ferris wheel
['fɛrɪs hwil]
(n.) 摩天輪

3 teacup ride
['ti,kʌp raɪd]
(n.) 咖啡杯

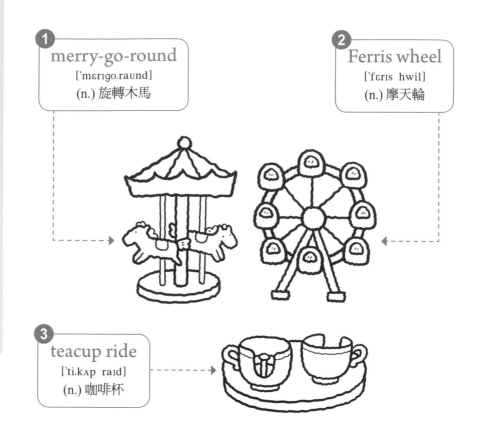

4 staff
[stæf]
(n.) 工作人員

5 ticket
['tɪkɪt]
(n.) 門票

6 park map
[pɑrk mæp]
(n.) 園區地圖

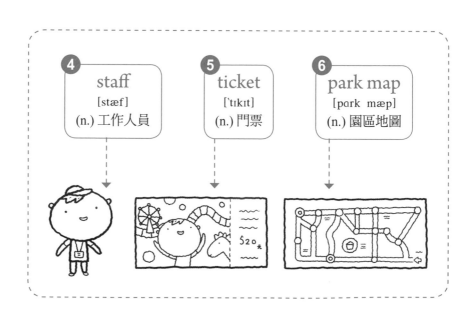

❶ 旋轉木馬

Beautifully painted horses on a merry-go-round go up and down on
poles. 被彩繪地極為漂亮的馬匹   上上下下

❷ 摩天輪

Neihu's Ferris wheel is a wonderful way to get a view of Taipei county.
                                                                    能夠飽覽新北市風景

❸ 咖啡杯

Doesn't the teacup ride make you dizzy?

❹ 工作人員

Staff at amusement parks must undergo frequent drug testing to ensure
visitors' safety.   經常接受毒品檢測

❺ 門票

Before you enter a ride, you must give your ticket to the worker.
    你搭乘一個遊樂設施之前

❻ 園區地圖

Amusement parks can be quite big. Remember to pick up a park map
when you go in.

學更多

❶ painted〈paint（繪圖）的過去分詞〉‧ merry〈歡樂的〉‧ round〈圓形〉‧ pole〈桿柱〉
❷ Ferris〈費里斯（最早的摩天輪的設計者）〉‧ wheel〈輪子〉‧ wonderful〈極好的〉
❸ teacup〈茶杯〉‧ ride〈搭乘〉‧ dizzy〈頭暈目眩的〉
❹ amusement park〈遊樂園〉‧ undergo〈接受〉‧ drug〈毒品〉‧ ensure〈確保〉
❺ enter〈進入〉‧ worker〈工作人員〉
❻ quite〈相當〉‧ remember〈記得〉‧ pick up〈拿起〉‧ go in〈進入〉

中譯

❶ 旋轉木馬上被彩繪地極為漂亮的馬匹，在桿柱上，上上下下地起伏。
❷ 內湖的摩天輪是讓你一覽新北市美景的好方法。
❸ 坐咖啡杯不會讓你頭暈嗎？
❹ 遊樂園的工作人員必須經常接受毒品檢測，以確保遊客的安全。
❺ 你搭乘一個遊樂設施之前，你必須把門票給工作人員。
❻ 遊樂園可能很大。記得進去後要拿一張園區地圖。

058

遊樂園設施(2)

MP3 058

1
roller coaster
['rolɚ `kostɚ]
(n.) 雲霄飛車

2
free fall ride
[fri fɔl raɪd]
(n.) 自由落體

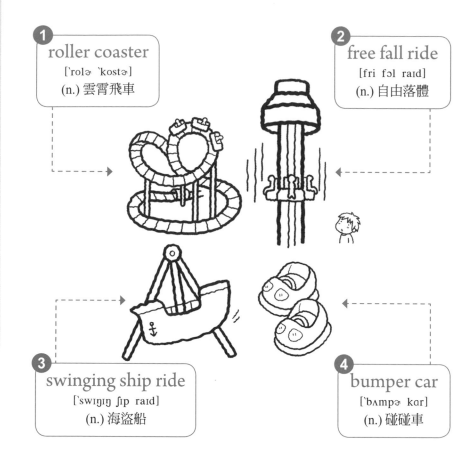

3
swinging ship ride
[`swɪŋɪŋ ʃɪp raɪd]
(n.) 海盜船

4
bumper car
[`bʌmpɚ kɑr]
(n.) 碰碰車

5
waterslide
[`wɔtɚ‚slaɪd]
(n.) 滑水道

6
haunted house
[`hɔntɪd haʊs]
(n.) 鬼屋

❶ 雲霄飛車

The first time Charlie rode a giant roller coaster, he threw up, but now he loves them!

❷ 自由落體

Disneyland's Tower of Terror is an example of a free fall ride.
迪士尼樂園的恐懼塔

❸ 海盜船

Small children are not allowed to ride the swinging ship ride. You must be at least 42cm tall. 不被允許

❹ 碰碰車

My dad loves bumper cars. He acts like a big kid in them.
舉止像個大孩子

❺ 滑水道

There's no better way to cool down and have some fun than on a waterslide.
沒有更好的方法　　　　　　　　　　　　除了玩滑水道

❻ 鬼屋

Mary loves to be scared, so she always heads straight to the haunted house at amusement parks. 直接前往

學更多

❶ rode〈ride（搭）的過去式〉‧ giant〈巨大的〉‧ threw up〈throw up（嘔吐）的過去式〉
❷ tower〈塔〉‧ terror〈驚駭〉‧ example〈例子〉‧ free〈自由的〉‧ fall〈降落〉
❸ allowed〈allow（允許）的過去分詞〉‧ swinging〈搖擺的〉‧ at least〈至少〉
❹ bumper〈車子保險桿〉‧ act〈表現〉‧ kid〈小孩〉
❺ better〈更好的〉‧ cool down〈變涼〉‧ than〈除了…之外〉
❻ scared〈scare（驚嚇）的過去分詞〉‧ head〈朝…出發〉‧ straight〈直接地〉‧
　 haunted〈鬧鬼的〉‧ amusement〈娛樂活動〉

中譯

❶ Charlie 第一次坐大型雲霄飛車時吐了，不過現在他非常愛玩！
❷ 迪士尼樂園的『恐懼塔』是自由落體遊樂設施的一種。
❸ 幼小的孩童不能搭乘海盜船，你至少要有 42 公分高。
❹ 我爸爸很愛玩碰碰車，在玩的時候，他好像一個大孩子。
❺ 能夠降溫又有趣味的最好方法，就是玩滑水道。
❻ Mary 最喜歡被嚇了，所以她到遊樂園都直接去鬼屋。

059

逛超市賣場

MP3 059

1 supermarket
[ˋsupɚˏmɑrkɪt]
(n.) 超市

2 customer
[ˋkʌstəmɚ]
(n.) 顧客

3 shopping cart
[ˋʃɑpɪŋ kɑrt]
(n.) 賣場推車

4 stall
[stɔl]
(n.) 攤位

5 free sample
[fri ˋsæmpl̩]
(n.) 試吃品

❶ 超市
Saturday is the busiest day of the week for supermarkets.

❷ 顧客
Remember to welcome your customers with a warm smile.
　　　　　　　　以熱情的笑容歡迎顧客

❸ 賣場推車
Honey, will you grab a shopping cart? I can't carry all these things.
　　　　　　　　　　　　　　拿不動全部的東西

❹ 攤位
After closing his stall for the night, the vendor threw his garbage away
into a nearby trash can.　　　　　　　　丟掉他的垃圾

❺ 試吃品
They offer free samples in the shop.

學更多

❶ Saturday〈週六〉‧ busiest〈最忙碌的，busy（忙碌的）的最高級〉‧ week〈一週〉
❷ welcome〈歡迎、款待〉‧ warm〈熱情的〉
❸ grab〈拿〉‧ cart〈推車〉‧ carry〈攜帶、搬運〉
❹ closing〈close（打烊）的 ing 型態〉‧ vendor〈攤販〉‧
　 threw...away〈throw...away（扔掉）的過去式〉‧ garbage〈垃圾〉‧
　 nearby〈附近的〉‧ trash can〈垃圾桶〉
❺ offer〈提供〉‧ free〈免費的〉‧ sample〈樣品、試用品〉

中譯

❶ 週六是超市一週內最忙碌的一天。
❷ 記得用熱情的笑容來接待你的顧客。
❸ 親愛的，你會去拿推車嗎？我沒辦法拿全部的東西。
❹ 晚上收攤之後，攤販把垃圾扔進附近的垃圾桶裡。
❺ 他們在店內提供試吃品。

060

超市賣場陳列區

MP3 060

1 household cleaners
[ˈhaʊsˌhold ˈklinəz]
(n.) 家庭清潔用品

2 beverage (section)
[ˈbɛvərɪdʒ (ˈsɛkʃən)]
(n.) 飲料(區)

3 dairy goods
[ˈdɛrɪ gʊdz]
(n.) 乳製品

清潔用品

飲料區

冷凍區

乳製品

蔬果

4 fruit and vegetable (section)
[frut ænd ˈvɛdʒətəbl̩ (ˈsɛkʃən)]
(n.) 蔬果(區)

5 frozen food
[ˈfrozn̩ fud]
(n.) 冷凍食品

❶ 家庭清潔用品

To prepare for Chinese New Year, folks stock up on all kinds of household cleaners.

各種的

❷ 飲料（區）

Linda slipped on the wet floor, and knocked some cans of soda off the shelf in the beverage section.

撞倒一些架上的罐裝汽水

❸ 乳製品

You'll find cheese and sour cream in the dairy goods.

❹ 蔬果（區）

I can't believe how big the fruit and vegetable section is here!

❺ 冷凍食品

Frank has a hectic job, so he buys a lot of frozen food to eat for dinner, rather than cook something fresh.

而不是烹調新鮮的食物

學更多

❶ prepare for...〈為…做準備〉‧ Chinese New Year〈農曆新年〉‧ folks〈人們〉‧ stock up〈囤積〉‧ kind〈種類〉‧ household〈家用的〉‧ cleaner〈清潔劑〉

❷ slipped〈slip（滑倒）的過去式〉‧ knocked off〈knock off（撞倒）的過去式〉‧ can〈罐裝〉‧ soda〈汽水〉‧ shelf〈架子〉‧ beverage〈飲料〉‧ section〈區域〉

❸ cheese〈起司〉‧ sour cream〈酸奶油〉‧ dairy〈乳製的〉‧ goods〈商品〉

❹ believe〈相信〉‧ fruit〈水果〉‧ vegetable〈蔬菜〉

❺ hectic〈忙碌的〉‧ frozen〈冷凍的〉‧ rather than〈而不是…〉‧ cook〈煮〉

中譯

❶ 為了準備過年，許多人會囤積各種家庭清潔用品。

❷ Linda 在潮濕的地板上滑倒了，並撞倒一些飲料區架子上的罐裝汽水。

❸ 你可以在乳製品區找到起司和酸奶。

❹ 我無法相信這裡的蔬果區竟然這麼大！

❺ Frank 的工作十分忙碌，所以他購買許多冷凍食品當晚餐，而不是烹調新鮮的食物。

061

結帳櫃檯

MP3 061

1 receipt
[rɪ`sit]
(n.) 發票

2 shopping bag
[`ʃɑpɪŋ bæg]
(n.) 購物袋

3 cash register
[kæʃ `rɛdʒɪstɚ]
(n.) 收銀機

4 cashier
[kæ`ʃɪr]
(n.) 收銀員

5 scanner
[`skænɚ]
(n.) 條碼掃描器

6 plastic bag
[`plæstɪk bæg]
(n.) 塑膠袋

❶ 發票

Did you check your receipts to see if you won any lottery money?
兌中獎金

❷ 購物袋

City Super sells their own cloth shopping bags at the check-out counter.

❸ 收銀機

Yvonne uses a cash register at her job at Family Mart.
在她的工作中

❹ 收銀員

Lori gave the cashier $1,000NT and got $550NT back in change.
找零回來 550 元台幣

❺ 條碼掃描器

I'm sorry, but this scanner is out of order. Please move to the next cashier.
移動到旁邊的收銀台

❻ 塑膠袋

Would you like a plastic bag or paper bag for your items, sir?
你想要…

學更多

❶ check〈檢查〉‧ see〈查看、發現〉‧ won〈win（贏得）的過去式〉‧ lottery〈彩券〉

❷ sell〈賣〉‧ cloth〈布料〉‧ bag〈袋子〉‧ check-out〈結帳〉‧ counter〈櫃檯〉

❸ cash〈現金〉‧ register〈登錄機、登記〉‧ job〈工作〉

❹ gave〈give（給）的過去式〉‧ got〈get（得到）的過去式〉‧ change〈找零、零錢〉

❺ out of order〈故障〉‧ move〈移動〉

❻ plastic〈塑膠〉‧ paper bag〈紙袋〉‧ item〈物品〉

中譯

❶ 你有檢查你的發票，看看有沒有中獎嗎？

❷ City Super 在結帳櫃檯有賣它們自家的布面購物袋。

❸ Yvonne 在全家便利商店的工作中，會使用收銀機。

❹ Lori 給收銀員 1000 元台幣，然後對方找回 550 元給她。

❺ 對不起，這個條碼掃瞄器壞了。請移至旁邊的收銀台結帳。

❻ 先生，請問你要塑膠袋還是紙袋裝你的東西？

062

結帳工具

MP3 062

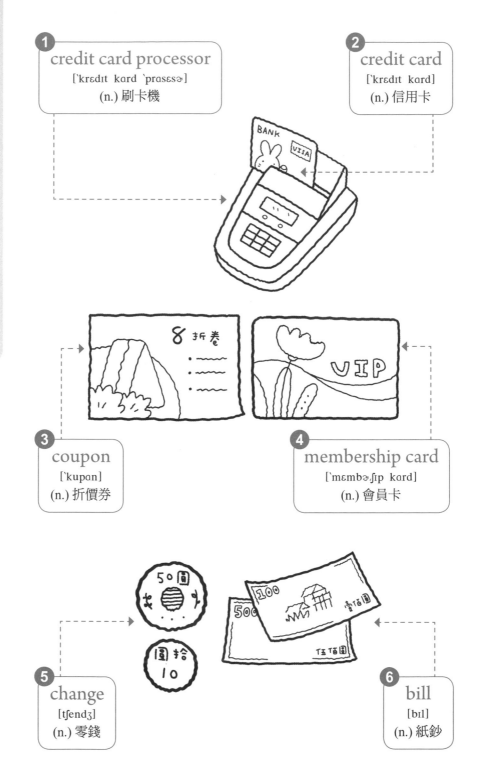

1 credit card processor
[ˈkrɛdɪt kɑrd ˈprɑsɛsɚ]
(n.) 刷卡機

2 credit card
[ˈkrɛdɪt kɑrd]
(n.) 信用卡

3 coupon
[ˈkupɑn]
(n.) 折價券

4 membership card
[ˈmɛmbɚʃɪp kɑrd]
(n.) 會員卡

5 change
[tʃendʒ]
(n.) 零錢

6 bill
[bɪl]
(n.) 紙鈔

❶ 刷卡機

Oh no! The credit card processor is broken. Can you pay with cash instead?

改用現金付款

❷ 信用卡

What is the expiration date on your credit card?

❸ 折價券

I collect coupons to save money on my purchases.

在消費時省錢

❹ 會員卡

Membership cards allow frequent shoppers to save money on the goods they buy.

經常消費的客人

❺ 零錢

Sir, can you please give me some change for this $100NT bill?

以這張 100 元鈔票交換

❻ 紙鈔

When Darren takes money out of his bank account, he always asks for small bills.

從他的銀行帳戶領錢

學更多

❶ processor〈數據處理機〉・broken〈損壞的〉・instead〈作為替代〉
❷ expiration date〈到期日〉
❸ collect〈蒐集〉・save〈節省〉・purchase〈購買、購買的東西〉
❹ membership〈會員〉・allow〈提供、容許〉・frequent〈頻繁的〉・goods〈商品〉
❺ can you please...〈能否麻煩你…〉・for〈以…交換〉
❻ bank〈銀行〉・account〈帳戶〉・ask〈要求〉・small bills〈小額紙鈔〉

中譯

❶ 喔不！刷卡機壞了，你能改用現金付款嗎？
❷ 你信用卡上的有效日期是什麼時候？
❸ 我蒐集折價券以便消費時折抵省錢。
❹ 會員卡讓經常消費的客人在購物時可以省錢。
❺ 先生，我可以用這 100 元鈔票跟你換些零錢嗎？
❻ Darren 從銀行帳戶領錢時，他都會要求要小額紙鈔。

063

海灘(1)

MP3 063

1 beach volleyball
[bitʃ ˋvɑlɪˌbɔl]
(n.) 沙灘排球

2 tourist
[ˋturɪst]
(n.) 遊客

3 bikini babe
[brˋkini beb]
(n.) 比基尼辣妹

4 crab
[kræb]
(n.) 螃蟹

5 sand sculpture
[sænd ˋskʌlptʃɚ]
(n.) 沙雕

6 sand
[sænd]
(n.) 沙子

7 shell
[ʃɛl]
(n.) 貝殼

① 沙灘排球

Let's get some exercise and play some beach volleyball here on the sand.

② 遊客

Kenting is crowded with beach lovers and tourists all year long.

擠滿沙灘愛好者

③ 比基尼辣妹

This beach is awesome! Take a look at all those gorgeous bikini babes over there!

看一下

④ 螃蟹

Fresh crabs are delicious if you cook them right.

⑤ 沙雕

I love your sand sculpture. It's a giant turtle, right?

⑥ 沙子

The sand on Florida beaches is incredibly soft – unlike the sand on California's beaches!

⑦ 貝殼

Jill is fascinated with shells, and collects as many of them as she can find.

她能找到多少就蒐集多少

學更多

① exercise〈運動〉・beach〈沙灘〉・volleyball〈排球〉
② be crowded with...〈擠滿…〉
③ awesome〈極好的〉・gorgeous〈美麗的〉・bikini〈比基尼泳裝〉・babe〈年輕女孩〉
④ delicious〈美味的〉・cook〈烹飪〉・right〈正確地〉
⑤ sculpture〈雕塑品〉・giant〈巨大的〉・turtle〈烏龜〉・right〈對的〉
⑥ incredibly〈難以置信地〉・unlike〈不像〉
⑦ be fascinated with...〈著迷於…〉

中譯

① 我們在這裡的沙灘上運動一下，打場沙灘排球吧。
② 墾丁一年到頭都擠滿了沙灘熱愛者和遊客。
③ 這裡的海灘好棒！你看看那邊那些美麗的比基尼女郎！
④ 新鮮的螃蟹如果烹飪得當，會非常美味。
⑤ 我喜歡你的沙雕作品，是一隻巨型烏龜對吧？
⑥ 佛羅里達海灘上的沙子非常柔軟，不像加州海灘的沙！
⑦ Jill 對貝殼著迷，而且她能找到多少就蒐集多少。

135

064

海灘(2)

MP3 064

1 beach umbrella
[bitʃ ʌmˋbrɛlə]
(n.) 大型遮陽傘

2 sunscreen
[ˋsʌn.skrin]
(n.) 防曬乳

3 flip-flops
[ˋflɪp.flɑps]
(n.) 夾腳拖鞋

4 lifeguard
[ˋlaɪf.gɑrd]
(n.) 救生員

5 life preserver
[laɪf prɪˋzɜvɚ]
(n.) 救生圈

① 大型遮陽傘

You have to protect your skin from the sun. Take the big beach umbrella with you! 保護你的皮膚避免陽光曬傷

② 防曬乳

Will you please help me apply this sunscreen on my back? 你可以幫我…

③ 夾腳拖鞋

Rather than walk barefoot on the beach, wear flip-flops to keep your 不要赤腳行走沙灘，而是… feet protected from glass and sharp objects.

④ 救生員

Paul wants to be a lifeguard when he grows up, so he's taking swimming lessons. 上游泳課

⑤ 救生圈

Don't forget to take some life preservers with you when you go out on a small boat. 搭乘小船出去

學更多

❶ protect A from B〈保護 A 免於 B〉．skin〈皮膚〉．beach〈海灘〉．umbrella〈傘〉
❷ apply〈塗…在表面〉．back〈背部〉
❸ rather than〈並非…而是…〉．barefoot〈赤腳地〉．protected〈protect（保護）的過去分詞〉．sharp〈尖銳的〉．object〈物體〉
❹ grow up〈長大〉．take lessons〈學習…〉
❺ forget〈忘記〉．preserver〈救生用具〉．boat〈船〉

中譯

❶ 你需要保護你的皮膚避免曬傷，帶著這把大型遮陽傘吧！
❷ 你可以幫我在背部塗上這防曬乳嗎？
❸ 不要赤腳在沙灘上行走，最好穿上夾腳拖鞋保護你的腳避免被玻璃或尖銳物割傷。
❹ Paul 長大後想要成為救生員，所以目前他正在上游泳課。
❺ 搭乘小船出去不要忘了攜帶救生圈。

065

露營區

MP3 065

1 firewood
[ˈfaɪrˌwʊd]
(n.) 木柴

2 tent
[tɛnt]
(n.) 帳棚

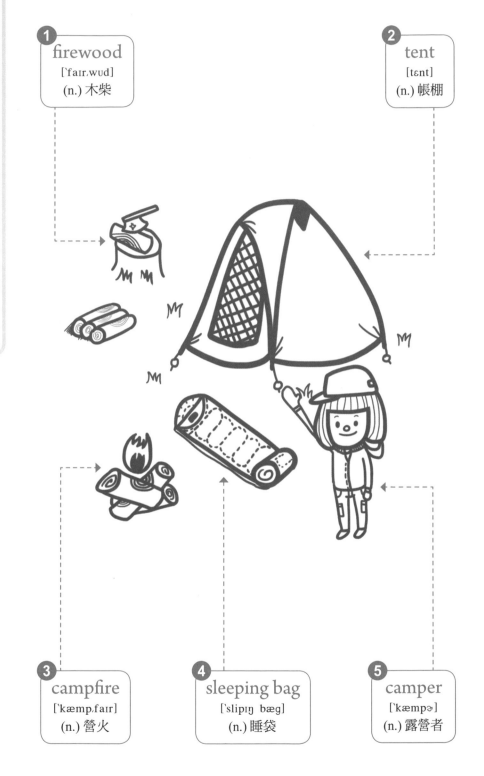

3 campfire
[ˈkæmpˌfaɪr]
(n.) 營火

4 sleeping bag
[ˈslipɪŋ bæg]
(n.) 睡袋

5 camper
[ˈkæmpə]
(n.) 露營者

❶ 木柴

It's cold this weekend, so I'll load up on firewood for our camping trip.
<u>裝載木柴</u>

❷ 帳棚

Dad bought a big tent to take camping this weekend!
露營

❸ 營火

Let's all sing songs around the campfire tonight!
<u>圍著營火</u>

❹ 睡袋

John's sleeping bag is huge and can hold two or three people inside.
裡面可以容納 2~3 人

❺ 露營者

This mountain has way too many campers. Let's go somewhere else.
去別的地方

學更多

❶ cold〈寒冷的〉・weekend〈週末〉・load〈裝載〉・camping〈露營〉・trip〈旅行〉
❷ bought〈buy（買）的過去式〉
❸ sing〈唱歌〉・song〈歌曲〉・around〈環繞、在…附近〉
❹ huge〈龐大的〉・hold〈容納〉・inside〈在裡面〉
❺ mountain〈山〉・way too many〈太多的〉・somewhere〈某處〉・else〈另外〉

中譯

❶ 這週末會冷，所以去露營我會多帶些木柴。
❷ 爸爸買了一個大帳棚，這週末要帶去露營！
❸ 我們今晚圍著營火唱歌吧！
❹ John 的睡袋超大，裡面可以容納 2~3 個人。
❺ 這座山有太多露營者了，我們去別的地方吧。

066

露營工具

MP3 066

1 flashlight
[ˈflæʃˌlaɪt]
(n.) 手電筒

2 compass
[ˈkʌmpəs]
(n.) 指南針

3 lighter
[ˈlaɪtə]
(n.) 打火機

4 bug spray
[bʌg spre]
(n.) 防蟲液

5 charcoal
[ˈtʃɑrˌkol]
(n.) 木炭

6 barbecue grill
[ˈbɑrbɪkju grɪl]
(n.) 烤肉架

7 folding chair
[ˈfoldɪŋ tʃɛr]
(n.) 折疊椅

❶ 手電筒

Hey, do you have a flashlight? My lantern went out.

❷ 指南針

I don't know where we are. It's a good thing you brought a compass.
<u>幸好</u>

❸ 打火機

Just use this lighter to get the campfire started.
<u>點燃營火</u>

❹ 防蟲液

Yikes! These mosquitoes are eating me alive. Where's the bug spray?
<u>正在咬我</u>

❺ 木炭

Where's the charcoal? I'll get the grill going so we can barbecue.
<u>生火、讓烤架運作</u>

❻ 烤肉架

What do you have cooking on the barbecue grill? It smells delicious.
<u>聞起來很香</u>

❼ 折疊椅

Get out the folding chairs, and let's sit around the campfire tonight and
tell ghost stories.
<u>圍坐在營火旁</u>

學更多

❶ lantern〈提燈〉・went out〈go out（熄滅）的過去式〉
❷ brought〈bring（帶來）的過去式〉
❸ campfire〈營火〉
❹ mosquito〈蚊子〉・alive〈有活力的〉・bug〈蟲子〉・spray〈噴液〉
❺ grill〈烤架〉・going〈go（運作）的 ing 型態〉・barbecue〈烤肉〉
❻ cooking〈cook（煮）的 ing 型態〉・smell〈聞〉・delicious〈香噴噴的〉
❼ get out〈拿出〉・folding〈折疊式的〉・ghost〈鬼〉

中譯

❶ 嘿，你有手電筒嗎？我的提燈熄滅了。
❷ 我不知道我們在哪裡，幸好你有帶指南針。
❸ 用這個打火機點燃營火。
❹ 天啊！這些蚊子正在咬我。防蟲液在哪？
❺ 木炭在哪？我要來生火，才能開始烤肉。
❻ 你在烤肉架上頭煮什麼？味道好香。
❼ 把折疊椅拿出來，我們今晚圍坐在營火旁講鬼故事吧。

馬戲團表演(1)

1 gorilla
[gəˋrɪlə]
(n.) 猩猩

2 big top
[bɪɡ tɑp]
(n.) 大帳棚

3 elephant
[ˋɛləfənt]
(n.) 大象

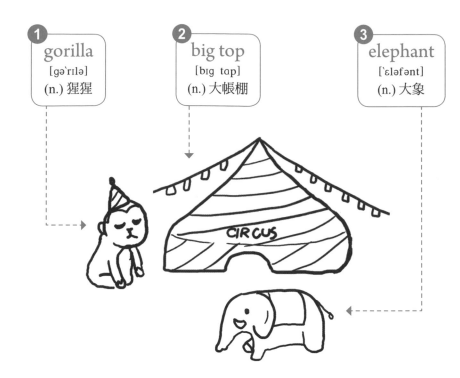

4 ring of fire
[rɪŋ ɑv faɪr]
(n.) 火圈

5 lion tamer
[ˋlaɪən ˋtemə]
(n.) 馴獸師

6 lion
[ˋlaɪən]
(n.) 獅子

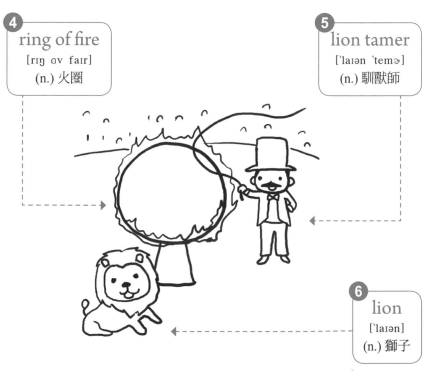

① 猩猩

That gorilla is huge! I bet he eats tons of food.
　　　　　　　　　　　　他吃很多食物

② 大帳棚

A circus performs under "the big top" as it travels from town to town.

③ 大象

Tina wants to work with elephants in a circus when she grows up.

④ 火圈

One circus trick that's cool is a ring of fire that is lit and hung up so that
a lion can jump through the middle of it.　　　　　　被點燃並吊起
　　　　　　　　　　從中間跳躍穿過

⑤ 馴獸師

Did you hear about the lion tamer that was attacked by his lion after 15
years? That's a very dangerous job!　　　　　被他的獅子攻擊

⑥ 獅子

Male lions are so beautiful with that thick mane of hair.
　　　　　　　　　　　　濃厚的鬃毛

學更多

① huge〈龐大的〉‧ bet〈斷言〉‧ tons of...〈極多的…〉

② circus〈馬戲團〉‧ perform〈表演〉‧ under〈在…裡面〉‧ top〈棚〉‧ town〈城鎮〉

③ grow up〈長大〉

④ trick〈特技〉‧ ring〈圈〉‧ lit〈light（點燃）的過去分詞〉‧
hung〈hang（吊掛）的過去分詞〉‧ jump〈跳〉‧ middle〈中間〉

⑤ hear about〈知道〉‧ tamer〈馴服師〉‧ attacked〈attack（攻擊）的過去分詞〉

⑥ male〈雄性的〉‧ thick〈濃厚的〉‧ mane〈鬃毛〉

中譯

① 那隻猩猩好龐大！我敢說他一定吃非常多食物。

② 馬戲團在城鎮與城鎮之間旅行時，都在大帳棚裡表演。

③ Tina 長大後想要在馬戲團和大象一起工作。

④ 一個很酷的馬戲團表演，是將火圈點燃並吊起，然後讓獅子從中間跳過去。

⑤ 你有聽說那個訓獸師 15 年之後被他的獅子攻擊的事嗎？那是非常危險的工作！

⑥ 公獅子的濃厚鬃毛好美。

馬戲團表演(2)

MP3 068

1 tightrope
[ˋtaɪt͵rop]
(n.) 鋼索

2 trapeze artist
[træˋpiz ˋɑrtɪst]
(n.) 空中飛人

3 unicycle
[ˋjunɪ͵saɪkḷ]
(n.) 單輪車

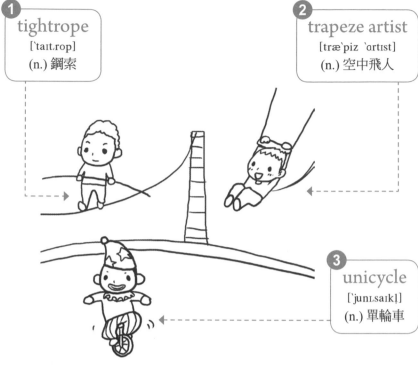

4 clown
[klaʊn]
(n.) 小丑

5 juggler
[ˋdʒʌglɚ]
(n.) 雜耍者

6 strongman
[ˋstrɔŋmæn]
(n.) 大力士

7 magician
[məˋdʒɪʃən]
(n.) 魔術師

❶ 鋼索

A tightrope is a long, thin wire placed high above the ground that circus performers attempt to walk across. 被安置在離地面很遠的高處

❷ 空中飛人

It's a good thing there's a net to catch the trapeze artists in case they fall.
有網子接住空中飛人

❸ 單輪車

I wonder how hard it is to ride a unicycle. You must need good balance.

❹ 小丑

Silly clowns dress up in costumes to perform in the circus.
穿上戲服

❺ 雜耍者

Jugglers can juggle at least three small objects at one time without dropping any of them.
不會掉任何一個

❻ 大力士

One famous strongman from history, could lift 168kg over his head with one hand!
舉起 168 公斤超過他的頭

❼ 魔術師

Tim can never figure out how magicians perform their magic tricks.

學更多

❶ wire〈金屬絲〉・placed〈place（安置）的過去分詞〉・attempt〈試圖〉・across〈穿過〉
❷ catch〈接住〉・trapeze〈高空鞦韆〉・artist〈技藝高超的人〉・in case〈以防萬一〉
❸ wonder〈想知道〉・hard〈困難的〉・balance〈平衡感〉
❹ silly〈糊塗的〉・dress up〈裝扮〉・costume〈服裝、戲服〉・circus〈馬戲團〉
❺ juggle〈玩雜耍〉・object〈物品〉・dropping〈drop（掉下）的 ing 型態〉
❻ famous〈著名的〉・history〈歷史〉・lift〈舉起〉
❼ figure out〈理解〉・perform〈表演〉・magic〈魔術的〉・trick〈把戲〉

中譯

❶ 鋼索是一條安置在距離地面很遠的高處的細長鋼絲，馬戲團的表演者會試圖走過它。
❷ 還好有網子可以接住空中飛人，以防萬一他們掉下來。
❸ 我不知道騎單輪車有多難，你應該需要很好的平衡感。
❹ 搞笑的小丑穿著戲服在馬戲團表演。
❺ 雜耍者可以一次至少耍三個小物品都不會掉。
❻ 一個歷史上有名的大力士，可以單手舉起 168 公斤超過他的頭。
❼ Tim 一直都搞不清楚魔術師是如何變出魔術戲碼的。

069

演場會 (1)

MP3 069

1
dancer
[ˋdænsɚ]
(n.) 舞者

2
singer
[ˋsɪŋɚ]
(n.) 歌手

3
special guest
[ˋspɛʃəl gɛst]
(n.) 特別嘉賓

4
stage
[stedʒ]
(n.) 舞台

5
fan
[fæn]
(n.) 歌迷

6
glow stick
[glo stɪk]
(n.) 螢光棒

7
microphone
[ˋmaɪkrəˌfon]
(n.) 麥克風

❶ 舞者
Tina is an amazing ballet dancer. She's been studying ballet for 12 years.
　　　　　　一位了不起的芭蕾舞者
❷ 歌手
I trained to be an opera singer, but I also sang musical theater in New
　我接受訓練成為
York City.
❸ 特別嘉賓
Tonight's special guest is YoYo Ma, who will be debuting two new pieces.
　　　　　　　　　　　　　　　　　　　　將首次發表兩首新曲
❹ 舞台
When Jay Chou walks onto the stage, the women in the audience
always scream.
❺ 歌迷
Fans can be really intense—some even stand in line for days to get
tickets to a concert.　　　　　　　　　排好幾天的隊
❻ 螢光棒
Linda bought some glow sticks to wave at the concert.
　　　　　　　　　　　　　　　在演唱會揮舞
❼ 麥克風
When the microphones stopped working, they had to stop the concert.

學更多

❶ amazing〈驚人的〉．ballet〈芭蕾舞〉．studying〈study（學習）的 ing 型態〉
❷ opera〈歌劇〉．sang〈song（唱歌）的過去式〉．musical〈音樂的〉．theater〈戲劇〉
❸ guest〈來賓〉．debuting〈debut（首度發表）的 ing 型態〉．piece〈作品、曲〉
❹ women〈woman（女人）的複數〉．audience〈觀眾席〉．scream〈尖叫〉
❺ intense〈熱情的〉．even〈甚至〉．stand in line〈排隊〉．concert〈音樂會、演唱會〉
❻ bought〈buy（買）的過去式〉．glow〈發光〉．stick〈棒子〉．wave〈搖擺〉
❼ stopped〈stop（停止）的過去式〉．working〈work（運作）的 ing 型態〉

中譯

❶ Tina 是個了不起的芭蕾舞者，她已經學芭蕾 12 年了。
❷ 我接受訓練成為歌劇演唱者，但我也曾在紐約唱過音樂劇。
❸ 今晚的特別嘉賓是馬友友，他將首度發表兩首新曲。
❹ 當周杰倫走到舞台上，觀眾席的女性觀眾都會尖叫。
❺ 歌迷有時候會很熱情，有些人甚至會排好幾天的隊，就為了買到演唱會門票。
❻ Linda 買了一些螢光棒，要拿去演唱會揮舞。
❼ 當麥克風停止運作，演唱會不得不暫停。

070
演場會(2)

MP3 070

1 band
[bænd]
(n.) 樂隊

2 choir
[kwaɪr]
(n.) 合音/合唱團

3 backstage
[`bæk`stedʒ]
(adv.)
在後台/往後台

4 bodyguard
[`badɪ͵gɑrd]
(n.) 貼身保鏢

5 staff
[stæf]
(n.) 工作人員

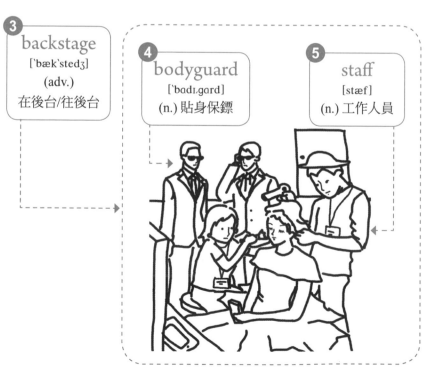

❶ 樂隊
Kelly is in her school's high school band.

❷ 合音 / 合唱團
Before joining the school choir as a soprano, Lisa accompanied the choir
for two years.
伴唱合音兩年

❸ 在後台 / 往後台
Fans can't go backstage after concerts. It's off-limits!
往後台去   那是禁止進入的

❹ 貼身保鑣
Lady Gaga travels with bodyguards when she is on tour.
在巡迴演出中

❺ 工作人員
Jolin Tsai has a handful of people on her staff.
有幾位她的工作人員

學更多

❶ high school〈高中〉
❷ soprano〈女高音〉・accompanied〈accompany（伴奏、伴唱）的過去式〉
❸ fan〈粉絲、…迷〉・concert〈演唱會〉・off-limits〈禁止進入的〉
❹ travel〈旅行、移動〉・tour〈旅遊、巡迴演出〉
❺ handful〈少數、少量〉・on〈屬於…、是…的成員〉

中譯

❶ Kelly 參加她學校的高中樂隊。
❷ 加入學校合唱團成為女高音之前，Lisa 擔任伴唱合音兩年。
❸ 演唱會之後歌迷不能往後台去，那是禁止進入的。
❹ 在巡迴演出時，女神卡卡活動時都會帶著她的貼身保鑣。
❺ 蔡依林有幾名工作人員。

MP3 071

1 curtain
[kɜtn̩]
(n.) 布幕

2 spotlight
[`spɑt͵laɪt]
(n.) 聚光燈

3 set
[sɛt]
(n.) 舞台布景

4 stage
[stedʒ]
(n.) 舞台

5 actress
[`æktrɪs]
(n.) 女演員

6 actor
[`æktə]
(n.) 演員/男演員

❶ 布幕

Quick! Sit down. The curtain's going up.
<u>布幕正在升起</u>

❷ 聚光燈

John's job at the theatre is to follow the lead actors with the spotlight.
<u>跟隨主要演員</u>

❸ 舞台布景

The sets for Phantom of the Opera are stunning—especially the chandelier.
<u>歌劇魅影的布景</u>

❹ 舞台

I can't see the stage clearly from here. Where are my glasses?

❺ 女演員

Patty is the lead actress in her high school play.
<u>女主角</u>

❻ 演員 / 男演員

The cast in this musical has very few actors.
<u>這齣音樂劇的演員陣容</u>

學更多

❶ quick〈快的〉‧ sit down〈坐下〉
❷ theatre〈劇院（英式說法）〉‧ follow〈跟隨〉‧ lead〈最重要的、領先的〉
❸ phantom〈幽靈、鬼魂〉‧ opera〈歌劇〉‧ stunning〈令人震驚的〉‧ chandelier〈吊燈〉
❹ clearly〈清楚地〉‧ glasses〈眼鏡〉
❺ high school〈高中〉‧ play〈戲劇〉
❻ cast〈演員陣容〉‧ musical〈音樂劇〉‧ few〈很少數的〉

中譯

❶ 快！坐下。布幕升起來了。
❷ John 在劇院的工作，是用聚光燈跟隨主要演員。
❸ 歌劇魅影的布景很震撼，尤其是那個吊燈。
❹ 從這邊我看不清楚舞台，我的眼鏡在哪？
❺ Patty 是她高中舞台劇的女主角（最重要的女演員）。
❻ 這齣音樂劇的演員很少。

072

舞台劇(2)

🔘 MP3 072

1
audience seating
[ˋɔdɪəns ˋsitɪŋ]
(n.) 觀眾席

2
box seat
[bɑks sit]
(n.) 包廂

3
binoculars
[bɪˋnɑkjələs]
(n.) 望遠鏡

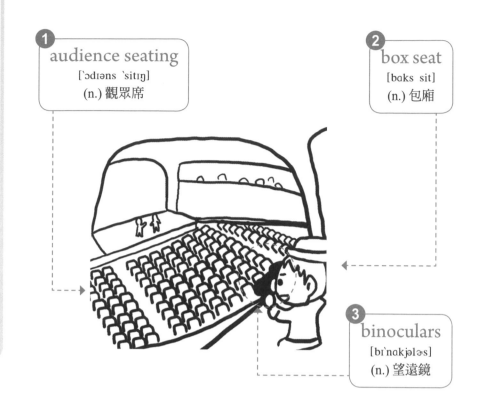

4
backstage
[ˋbækˋstedʒ]
(adv.)
在後台/往後台

5
costume
[ˋkɑstjum]
(n.) 戲服

❶ 觀眾席

The audience seating for the biggest theatre on Broadway in Manhattan
still only has 2,000 seats.

仍然只有 2000 個座位

❷ 包廂

You bought box seats for the play tonight? Those are expensive!

❸ 望遠鏡

We are up so high in the theatre that I need some binoculars to see the

我們在很高的位置

actors on stage.

❹ 在後台 / 往後台

Vivian has a quick costume change backstage because there's no time to

在後台進行快速更換戲服

reach her dressing room.

❺ 戲服

Their costumes are spectacular, but I bet they're really heavy.

我敢說它們一定很重

學更多

❶ audience〈觀眾〉‧ seating〈座位區〉‧ biggest〈最大的,big(大的)的最高級〉‧
theatre〈劇院(英式說法)〉‧ Broadway〈百老匯〉‧ still〈還是〉‧ seat〈座位〉
❷ play〈戲劇〉‧ expensive〈昂貴的〉
❸ up〈在上方〉‧ actor〈演員〉‧ stage〈舞台〉
❹ quick〈快的〉‧ change〈更換〉‧ reach〈到達〉‧ dressing room〈更衣間〉
❺ spectacular〈壯麗的〉‧ bet〈斷言〉‧ heavy〈重的〉

中譯

❶ 曼哈頓百老匯最大劇院的觀眾席,也只有兩千個座位。
❷ 今晚的舞台劇你買了包廂的票?那很貴的!
❸ 我們坐在劇院好高的地方,高到我需要用望遠鏡才看得到舞台上的演員。
❹ Vivian 在後台迅速更換戲服,因為沒有時間可以讓她去更衣間換。
❺ 這些戲服好華麗,不過我確定它們一定很重。

MP3 073

1 massage therapist
[məˋsɑʒ ˋθɛrəpɪst]
(n.) 按摩師

2 massage table
[məˋsɑʒ ˋtebḷ]
(n.) 按摩床

3 massage oil
[məˋsɑʒ ɔɪl]
(n.) 按摩油

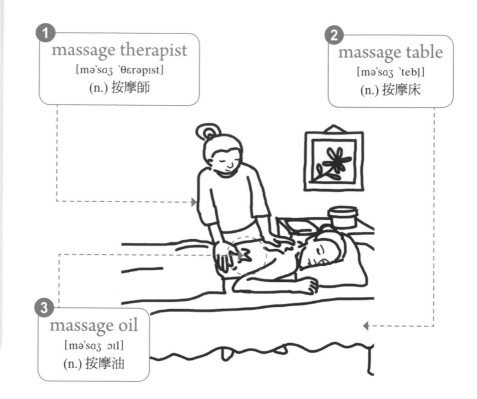

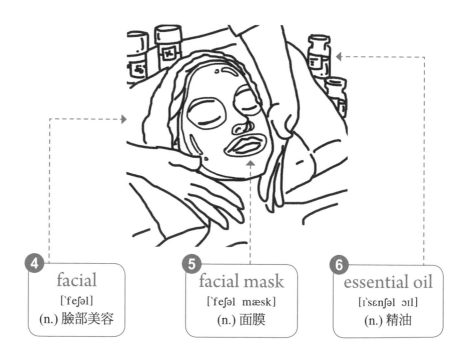

4 facial
[ˋfeʃəl]
(n.) 臉部美容

5 facial mask
[ˋfeʃəl mæsk]
(n.) 面膜

6 essential oil
[ɪˋsɛnʃəl ɔɪl]
(n.) 精油

❶ 按摩師

Bobby is training to be a professional massage therapist.
正接受訓練成為

❷ 按摩床

Sir, please lie on the massage table and we'll get started.
躺在⋯之上　　　　　　　　　　　　　我們將要開始

❸ 按摩油

I'll apply some massage oil to your back and legs.

❹ 臉部美容

There are different kinds of facials offered at beauty salons.
有各種不同的

❺ 面膜

Facial masks can help you moisturize your skin.
滋潤你的肌膚

❻ 精油

Essential oils are often used to scent a home.
經常使用於

學更多

❶ training〈train（訓練）的 ing 型態〉‧ professional〈專業的〉‧ massage〈按摩〉‧
therapist〈治療專家〉

❷ lie〈躺〉‧ table〈檯〉‧ started〈start（開始）的過去分詞〉

❸ apply〈將⋯塗在表面〉‧ back〈背部〉‧ leg〈腿〉

❹ different〈不同的〉‧ offered〈offer（提供）的過去分詞〉‧ beauty salon〈美容院〉

❺ facial〈臉的〉‧ mask〈面具〉‧ help〈幫助〉‧ moisturize〈濕潤〉‧ skin〈皮膚〉

❻ essential〈精華的〉‧ often〈常常〉‧ used〈use（使用）的過去分詞〉‧
scent〈使充滿氣味〉

中譯

❶ Bobby 正在受訓成為專業的按摩師。

❷ 先生，請躺在按摩床上，我們要開始了。

❸ 我要在你的背部和雙腿塗抹一些按摩油。

❹ 美容院提供各種不同的臉部美容療程。

❺ 面膜有助於滋潤你的肌膚。

❻ 精油常常用來讓家裡芳香。

三溫暖蒸氣室

MP3 074

1 thermometer
[θɚ`mɑmətə]
(n.) 溫度計

2 robe
[rob]
(n.) 浴袍

3 bath towel
[bæθ `tauəl]
(n.) 浴巾

4 sauna
[`saunə]
(n.) 三溫暖

5 steam
[stim]
(n.) 蒸氣

6 lounge chair
[laundʒ tʃɛr]
(n.) 躺椅

❶ 溫度計
The doctor used a thermometer to measure my body temperature.
量我的體溫

❷ 浴袍
After a relaxing swim, Janet grabbed a robe.

❸ 浴巾
Bath towels are provided free of charge.
不收費

❹ 三溫暖
Wrestlers often use saunas to lose a couple of pounds before matches.
減少一些磅數

❺ 蒸氣
Is there a steam room in the sauna?

❻ 躺椅
Save me a lounge chair by the pool, ok?

學更多

❶ doctor〈醫生〉・measure〈測量〉・body〈身體〉・temperature〈溫度〉
❷ relaxing〈令人輕鬆的〉・swim〈游泳〉・grabbed〈grab（抓取）的過去式〉
❸ bath〈洗澡〉・towel〈毛巾〉・provided〈provide（提供）的過去分詞〉・free〈免費的〉・charge〈費用〉
❹ wrestler〈摔角選手〉・lose〈失去〉・pound〈磅〉・match〈比賽〉
❺ Is there＋單數名詞〈有…嗎？〉・room〈房間〉
❻ save〈保留〉・lounge〈躺〉・by〈在…旁邊〉・pool〈游泳池〉

中譯

❶ 醫生用溫度計測量我的體溫。
❷ 輕鬆舒暢地游完泳之後，Janet 隨手抓了件浴袍。
❸ 我們免費提供浴巾。
❹ 摔角選手常常在比賽之前利用三溫暖減掉幾磅重量。
❺ 三溫暖內有蒸氣室嗎？
❻ 幫我留一個泳池邊的躺椅好嗎？

1 massage jet
[mə`saʒ dʒɛt]
(n.) 按摩水柱

2 hot tub
[hɑt tʌb]
(n.) 熱水池

3 cold plunge
[kold plʌndʒ]
(n.) 冷水池

4 hydrotherapy
[`haɪdrə`θɛrəpɪ]
(n.) 水療

5 hot spring
[hɑt sprɪŋ]
(n.) 溫泉

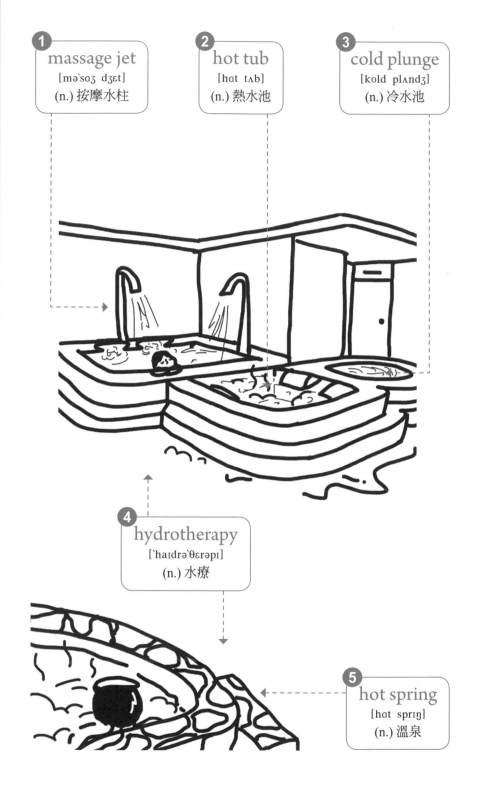

❶ 按摩水柱

The massage jets really give you a good massage.
給你一個舒服的按摩

❷ 熱水池

Sitting outside in a hot tub in the winter is so invigorating!
浸泡在戶外的熱水池

❸ 冷水池

After sitting in a hot tub or sauna, it's shocking to take a cold plunge.
泡入冷水池

❹ 水療

Hydrotherapy is used to help soothe sore muscles.
被使用於

❺ 溫泉

Do you have time to go to the hot springs with me this weekend?
你是否有空（做）…

學更多

❶ massage〈按摩〉‧ jet〈噴射器〉‧ really〈確實〉
❷ sitting〈sit（坐、棲身）的 ing 型態〉‧ outside〈在戶外〉‧ tub〈浴缸、桶〉‧
invigorating〈使精力充沛的〉
❸ shocking〈令人震驚的〉‧ plunge〈跳入〉
❹ used〈use（使用）的過去分詞〉‧ soothe〈緩和〉‧ sore〈痛的〉‧ muscle〈肌肉〉
❺ spring〈泉水〉‧ weekend〈週末〉

中譯

❶ 按摩水柱確實能把你按摩得很舒服。
❷ 冬天時，泡在戶外的熱水池裡讓人充滿活力！
❸ 棲身在熱水池或是三溫暖之後，再進入冷水池是很令人震撼的。
❹ 水療被使用於緩和痠痛的肌肉。
❺ 這個週末你有空跟我一起去泡溫泉嗎？

MP3 076

1 high ceiling
[haɪ `silɪŋ]
(n.) 挑高的天花板

2 chandelier
[ˌʃændl`ɪr]
(n.) 水晶吊燈

3 registration form
[ˌrɛdʒɪ`streʃən fɔrm]
(n.) 住宿登記表

4 front-desk clerk
[`frʌntˌdɛsk klɝk]
(n.) 服務台接待員

5 traveler
[`trævlɚ]
(n.) 旅客

6 reception desk
[rɪ`sɛpʃən dɛsk]
(n.) 接待櫃檯

7 flower arrangement
[`flauɚ ə`rendʒmənt]
(n.) 插花擺設

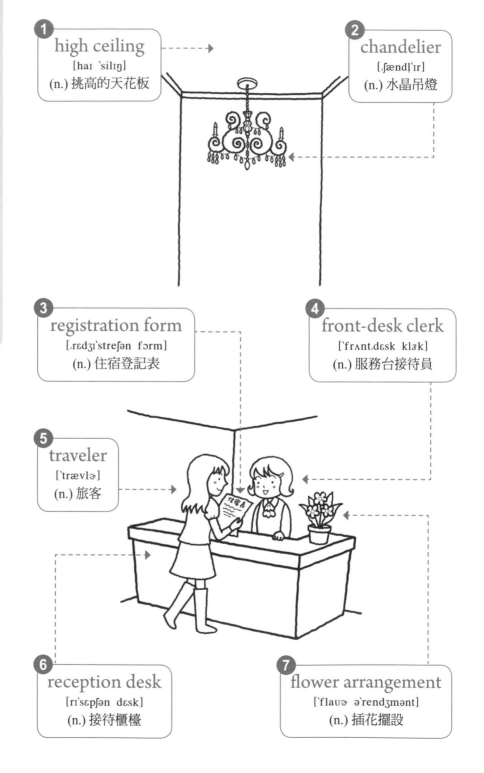

160

❶ 挑高的天花板
Look at those high ceilings! This place must have been built in the 1800's.
<u>被建造於 19 世紀</u>

❷ 水晶吊燈
Check out that chandelier! It must have cost a fortune.
<u>一定花了很多錢</u>

❸ 住宿登記表
Before checking in, you need to fill out a registration form.

❹ 服務台接待員
If you need to exchange some money, the front-desk clerk will help you.

❺ 旅客
This hotel has many travelers who frequently stay here.
<u>常來這裡住宿</u>

❻ 接待櫃檯
Please register here at the reception desk.

❼ 插花擺設
Most luxury hotels have fresh flower arrangements in the lobby.
大部分的高級飯店

學更多

❶ ceiling〈天花板〉‧place〈地點〉‧must〈一定是〉‧built〈build（建造）的過去分詞〉
❷ check out〈看看〉‧cost〈cost（花費）的過去分詞〉‧fortune〈巨款〉
❸ checking in〈check in（到達並登記）的 ing 型態〉‧fill out〈填寫〉‧registration〈登記〉
❹ exchange〈兌換〉‧front〈前面〉‧desk〈服務台〉‧clerk〈店員〉
❺ hotel〈飯店〉‧frequently〈頻繁地〉‧stay〈暫住〉
❻ register〈登記〉‧reception〈接待〉
❼ luxury〈奢華〉‧fresh〈新鮮的〉‧lobby〈大廳〉‧arrangement〈擺設〉

中譯

❶ 看看那些挑高的天花板！這個地方應該是 19 世紀建造的。
❷ 你看看那個水晶吊燈！那一定花了很多錢。
❸ 辦理入住之前，你需要先填寫住宿登記表。
❹ 如果你需要換鈔，服務台接待員可以幫你。
❺ 這間飯店有許多旅客常來這邊住宿。
❻ 請在這邊的接待櫃台登記。
❼ 大部分的高級飯店，在大廳都有新鮮的插花擺設。

旅館大廳(2)

1 revolving door
[rɪˋvɑlvɪŋ dor]
(n.) 旋轉門

2 doorman
[ˋdor͵mæn]
(n.) 門房

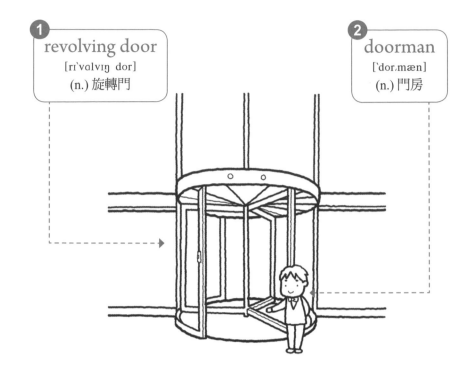

3 bellhop
[ˋbɛl͵hɑp]
(n.) 行李服務生

4 luggage cart
[ˋlʌgɪdʒ kɑrt]
(n.) 行李推車

5 luggage
[ˋlʌgɪdʒ]
(n.) 行李

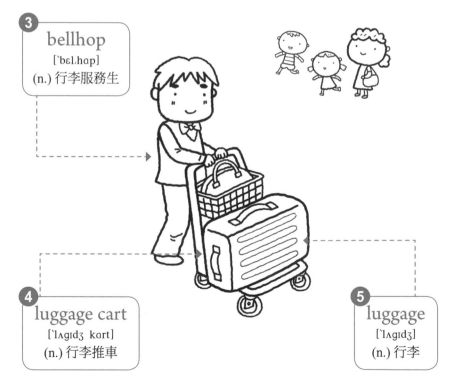

❶ 旋轉門

Please watch your children around the revolving door.

旋轉門周遭

❷ 門房

The doorman will hold the door open for you as you enter and exit.

替你把門開著

❸ 行李服務生

William, did you give that bellhop a nice tip?

❹ 行李推車

Sir, please put your luggage on the luggage cart, and I will take it all to your room.　把你的行李放到…之上　　全部帶到你的房間

❺ 行李

How many pieces of luggage did you bring with you?

幾件行李

學更多

❶ watch〈注意〉・children〈child（小孩）的複數〉・around〈在…四處〉・
　revolving〈旋轉的〉
❷ hold〈使保持著…〉・enter〈進入〉・exit〈出去〉
❸ nice〈好的〉・tip〈小費〉
❹ put A on B〈放 A 到 B 上面〉・luggage〈行李〉・cart〈推車〉
❺ piece〈一件、一片〉・bring〈帶來〉

中譯

❶ 在旋轉門周遭，請看好你的孩子。
❷ 當你進出時，門房會替你把門開著。
❸ William，你有給那位行李服務生合宜的小費嗎？
❹ 先生，請將你的行李放到行李推車上，我會幫全部帶到房間。
❺ 你隨身攜帶了幾件行李？

網咖設備

MP3 078

1 non-smoking area
[ˌnɑnˈsmokɪŋ ˈɛrɪə]
(n.) 禁煙區

2 smoking area
[ˈsmokɪŋ ˈɛrɪə]
(n.) 吸煙區

3 computer
[kəmˈpjutɚ]
(n.) 電腦

4 on-line game
[ˈɑnˌlaɪn gem]
(n.) 線上遊戲

5 mouse
[maʊs]
(n.) 滑鼠

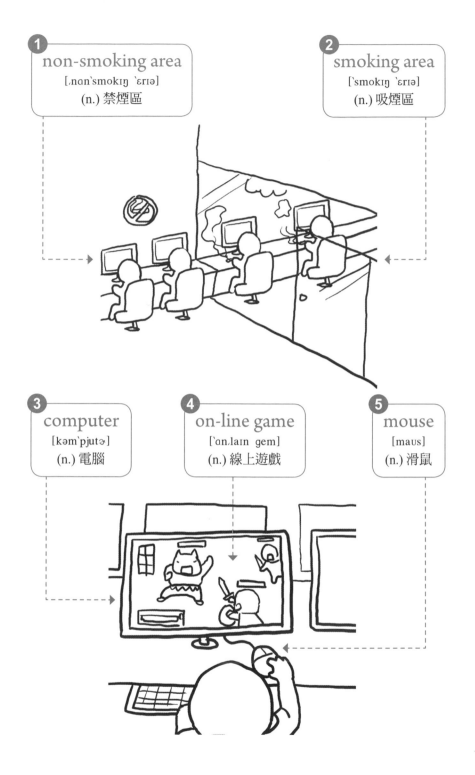

❶ 禁煙區

You may not smoke in non-smoking areas.
　　　　你不可以吸煙

❷ 吸煙區

Where's a smoking area in the airport?

❸ 電腦

Hey, my computer isn't working! Can I borrow yours to send a quick email?
　　　　　　　　　　　　　　　　　　　寄一封簡短的電子郵件

❹ 線上遊戲

You can't play on-line games until you finish your homework!

❺ 滑鼠

I don't use a mouse with my laptop.

学更多

❶ may〈可以〉‧ smoke〈吸煙〉‧ smoking〈吸煙〉‧ area〈區域〉
❷ airport〈機場〉
❸ working〈work（運作）的 ing 型態〉‧ borrow〈借用〉‧ send〈寄〉
❹ on-line〈線上的〉‧ until〈到…為止〉‧ finish〈完成〉‧ homework〈家庭作業〉
❺ laptop〈筆記型電腦〉

中譯

❶ 你不可以在禁煙區吸煙。
❷ 機場的吸煙區在哪裡？
❸ 嘿，我電腦不能用了！我可以借用你的電腦，寄封簡短的電子郵件嗎？
❹ 你還沒做完功課之前不准玩線上遊戲！
❺ 我操作筆記型電腦時，不使用滑鼠。

079

網咖臨檢

MP3 079

1 clerk
[klɝk]
(n.) 店員

2 counter
[ˈkaʊntɚ]
(n.) 櫃檯

3 raid
[red]
(v.) 臨檢

4 minor
[ˈmaɪnɚ]
(n.) 未成年者

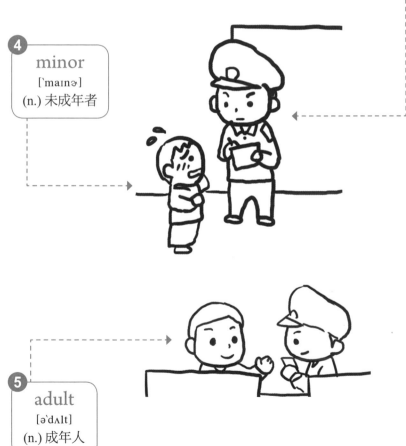

5 adult
[əˈdʌlt]
(n.) 成年人

❶ 店員

Larry works as a clerk in a cybercafé.

❷ 櫃檯

If you want some time on a computer here, then you'll need to pay a fee
at the counter. 　　使用一下這裡的電腦　　　　　　　　　　　　　　　付費

❸ 臨檢

That bar was raided last night because minors were being served alcohol.
　　　　　　　　　　　　　　　　　　　　　　　販賣酒精飲料給未成年人

❹ 未成年者

Minors are not allowed to drink alcoholic beverages.
　　　　　被禁止

❺ 成年人

If you want to see this movie, you will need to be with an adult.
　　　　　　　　　　　　　　　　　　　　　　需要有成年人陪同

學更多

❶ work〈工作〉・as〈作為〉・cybercafé〈網咖〉

❷ computer〈電腦〉・pay〈付款〉・fee〈費用〉

❸ bar〈酒吧〉・raided〈raid（臨檢）的過去分詞〉・served〈serve（供應）的過去分詞〉・
alcohol〈酒精〉

❹ allowed〈allow（允許）的過去分詞〉・drink〈喝〉・alcoholic〈酒精的〉・
beverage〈飲料〉

❺ movie〈電影〉・need〈需要〉

中譯

❶ Larry 的工作是在網咖當店員。

❷ 如果你想要使用一下這裡的電腦，你需要在櫃檯付費。

❸ 那間酒吧昨晚被臨檢了，因為它販賣酒精飲料給未成年人。

❹ 未成年者被禁止喝含酒精的飲料。

❺ 如果你想要看這部電影，你需要有成年人陪同。

080

網咖飲食

MP3 080

1 soda fountain
[ˈsodə ˈfaʊntɪn]
(n.) 飲料供應機

2 snack
[snæk]
(n.) 零食

3 instant noodles
[ˈɪnstənt ˈnudl̩z]
(n.) 泡麵

4 beverage
[ˈbɛvərɪdʒ]
(n.) 飲料

5 price list
[praɪs lɪst]
(n.) 價目表

❶ 飲料供應機

Subway has a soda fountain where customers can get their own drinks.

自己倒飲料

❷ 零食

I'm starving! Let's go get a snack.

吃點零食

❸ 泡麵

What are you having for lunch? I'm having some instant noodles.

❹ 飲料

Would you like a beverage with your cheeseburger?

你是否想要…

❺ 價目表

Can I see your price list, please?

我是否可以看…

學更多

❶ soda〈汽水〉‧ fountain〈水源、飲水器〉‧ customer〈顧客〉‧ own〈自己的〉‧ drink〈飲料〉

❷ starving〈飢餓的〉

❸ having〈have（吃、喝）的 ing 型態〉‧ lunch〈午餐〉‧ instant〈立即的〉‧ noodle〈麵條〉

❹ cheeseburger〈起司漢堡〉

❺ price〈價格〉‧ list〈列表〉‧ please〈請〉

中譯

❶ Subway 有飲料供應機讓顧客可以自己倒飲料。

❷ 我快餓死了！我們去吃點零食吧。

❸ 你中午打算吃什麼？我要吃泡麵。

❹ 你需要來杯飲料搭配你的起司漢堡嗎？

❺ 可以讓我看一下你們的價目表嗎？

081

賭桌上

MP3 081

1 gambling table
[ˋgæmblɪŋ ˋtebl]
(n.) 賭桌

2 dealer
[ˋdilə]
(n.) 發牌員

3 poker
[ˋpokə]
(n.) 撲克牌（遊戲）

4 dice
[daɪs]
(n.) 骰子

5 token
[ˋtokən]
(n.) 籌碼

6 gambler
[ˋgæmblə]
(n.) 賭客

❶ 賭桌
Seated around the gambling table were lots of good-looking men with beautiful dates.
身旁有漂亮女伴的英俊男士

❷ 發牌員
Sherry, ask the dealer to use a new deck of cards.
一副新的牌

❸ 撲克牌（遊戲）
How about a game of poker? Call your friends to come over tonight.
今晚過來

❹ 骰子
Roll the dice, ma'am. People are waiting.

❺ 籌碼
Tokens are worthless outside of casinos. Remember to cash them in before you leave.
在賭場外

❻ 賭客
Gamblers have to be careful or they might become addicted to gambling.
可能沉溺於賭博

學更多

❶ seated〈seat（使就座）的過去分詞〉‧ lots of〈許多〉‧ good-looking〈好看的〉‧ men〈man（男人）的複數〉‧ date〈約會對象〉
❷ ask〈要求〉‧ deck〈一副〉‧ card〈紙牌〉
❸ how about...?〈…如何〉‧ come over〈從遠方過來〉
❹ roll〈擲〉‧ ma'am〈女士〉‧ waiting〈wait（等待）的 ing 型態〉
❺ worthless〈無價值的〉‧ casino〈賭場〉‧ cash in〈兌成現金〉
❻ or〈否則〉‧ might〈可能〉‧ addicted〈入迷的、上癮的〉‧ gambling〈賭博〉

中譯

❶ 賭桌周圍坐著許多身旁有漂亮女伴的英俊男士。
❷ Sherry，請發牌員用一副新的牌。
❸ 要不要玩撲克牌？打電話叫你的朋友晚上過來。
❹ 女士，請擲骰子。大家都在等。
❺ 籌碼在賭場之外毫無價值。記得離開之前要去兌換成現金。
❻ 賭客要小心，不然可能沉溺於賭博。

082

宴會舞池

MP3 082

1 orchestra
[ˋɔrkɪstrə]
(n.) 管絃樂隊

2 balloon
[bəˋlun]
(n.) 氣球

3 formal gown
[ˋfɔrml̩ gaʊn]
(n.) 禮服

4 tuxedo
[tʌkˋsido]
(n.) 燕尾服

5 dance floor
[dæns flor]
(n.) 舞池

❶ 管絃樂隊

Hurry up! The orchestra is tuning, so they'll be starting any minute.

他們隨時都會開始

❷ 氣球

It really does look like a big celebration tonight, especially with all the

它看起來真的像是　　　盛大的慶祝晚會

colorful balloons.

❸ 禮服

Is a formal gown required at the ball tonight?

❹ 燕尾服

John, you look so handsome in your tuxedo.

你看起來很帥

❺ 舞池

Gary couldn't wait to hit the dance floor with his gorgeous date.

等不及要在舞池上跳舞

學更多

❶ hurry up〈趕緊〉‧ tuning〈tune（調音）的 ing 型態〉‧ starting〈start（開始）的 ing 型態〉‧
minute〈分〉

❷ celebration〈慶祝活動〉‧ especially〈尤其〉‧ colorful〈多彩的〉

❸ formal〈正式的〉‧ gown〈婦女穿的禮服〉‧ required〈必須的〉‧ ball〈舞會〉

❹ handsome〈帥氣的〉‧ in〈穿著、戴著〉

❺ hit〈到達〉‧ floor〈地板〉‧ gorgeous〈美麗的〉‧ date〈約會對象〉

中譯

❶ 快一點！管絃樂隊在調音了，所以他們隨時都會開始。

❷ 今晚看來真的是一個盛大的慶祝晚會，特別是還有繽紛多彩的氣球。

❸ 今晚的舞會需要穿正式禮服嗎？

❹ John，你穿著燕尾服看起來好帥氣。

❺ Gary 等不及要跟他美麗的女伴在舞池上跳舞。

083

賓主同歡

MP3 083

1 goblet
[ˋgablɪt]
(n.) 高腳杯

2 waiter
[ˋwetɚ]
(n.) 服務生

3 hostess
[ˋhostɪs]
(n.) 女主人

4 host
[host]
(n.) 男主人/東道主/主持人

5 guest
[gɛst]
(n.) 賓客

❶ 高腳杯

These are such beautiful goblets, dear, aren't they?

你說它們是不是這樣？

❷ 服務生

Waiter, may I have another glass of white wine?

是否可以給我

❸ 女主人

The hostess will introduce you to any guests you have not met yet.

你還未認識

❹ 男主人 / 東道主 / 主持人

Mr. Samuel Smith will be your host tonight.

將是你們的主持人

❺ 賓客

I heard there were over 300 guests invited tonight.

我聽說有…

學更多

❶ such〈如此的〉‧ beautiful〈美麗的〉‧ dear〈親愛的〉
❷ another〈再一〉‧ glass〈杯〉‧ white wine〈白葡萄酒〉
❸ introduce〈介紹〉‧ any〈任一〉‧ met〈meet（認識）的過去分詞〉‧ yet〈尚未〉
❹ Mr.〈Mister（先生）的簡稱〉‧ tonight〈今晚〉
❺ heard〈hear（聽說）的過去式〉‧ over〈超過〉‧ invited〈invite（邀請）的過去分詞〉

中譯

❶ 親愛的，這些高腳杯好美喔！對不對？
❷ 服務生，可以再給我一杯白酒嗎？
❸ 女主人會介紹你認識那些你還不認識的客人。
❹ Samuel Smith 先生將是你們今晚的主持人。
❺ 我聽說今晚邀請了超過 300 位賓客。

084

宴會餐飲

MP3 084

1 fizzy drink
[ˈfɪzɪ drɪŋk]
(n.) 氣泡飲料

2 cocktail
[ˈkɑk.tel]
(n.) 雞尾酒

3 champagne
[ʃæmˈpen]
(n.) 香檳

4 food
[fud]
(n.) 餐點

5 punchbowl
[ˈpʌntʃbol]
(n.) 調酒壺

❶ 氣泡飲料

Oh good, they are serving some fizzy drinks along with the alcoholic
beverages.

酒精飲料

❷ 雞尾酒

Can I get you another cocktail, Jenny?

是否可以幫你取得⋯

❸ 香檳

I would like to order a sandwich and a bottle of champagne.

我想要⋯   一瓶

❹ 餐點

Don't you think the food here tonight is superb?

❺ 調酒壺

Do you think the punch in the punchbowl was spiked or is it non-alcoholic?

不含酒精的

學更多

❶ serving〈serve（供應）的 ing 型態〉・fizzy〈起泡沫的〉・along with〈和⋯一起〉・
alcoholic〈酒精的〉・beverage〈飲料〉

❷ get〈為⋯取得〉・another〈再一個〉

❸ order〈點餐〉・sandwich〈三明治〉・bottle〈瓶〉

❹ think〈認為〉・tonight〈今晚〉・superb〈極好的〉

❺ punch〈一種果汁調酒〉・spiked〈spike（把烈酒加入⋯）的過去分詞〉

中譯

❶ 太好了，除了酒精飲料之外，他們還提供氣泡飲料。

❷ Jenny，我再幫你拿一杯雞尾酒好嗎？

❸ 我想點一份三明治及一瓶香檳。

❹ 你不覺得今晚這裡的餐點非常好吃嗎？

❺ 你覺得調酒壺裡的果汁調酒，有加入烈酒？還是不含酒精的？

085

服飾賣場

MP3 085

1 women's department
[ˈwɪmɪnz dɪˈpɑrtmənt]
(n.) 女裝部

2 men's department
[mɛnz dɪˈpɑrtmənt]
(n.) 男裝部

3 mannequin
[ˈmænəkɪn]
(n.) 服裝人體模特兒

4 children's department
[ˈtʃɪldrənz dɪˈpɑrtmənt]
(n.) 童裝部

5 discount
[ˈdɪskaunt]
(n.) 折扣

❶ 女裝部

The women's department has lots of different sizes, from XS to XL.
　　　　　　　　　　　　　很多不同尺寸

❷ 男裝部

Trisha works in the men's department at SOGO.

❸ 服裝人體模特兒

Clothing being displayed on a mannequin is sold faster.
　　　　　衣服穿在人體模特兒身上展示

❹ 童裝部

Judy is so tiny that she still shops for clothes in the children's department,
even though she's 13.　　　　　買衣服

❺ 折扣

If I buy more, can I get a discount?
　　　　　　　　　獲得折扣

學更多

❶ women〈woman（女士）的複數〉・women's〈女士們的〉・department〈部門〉・
different〈不同的〉・size〈尺寸〉

❷ work〈工作〉・men〈man（男人）的複數〉・men's〈男士們的〉

❸ clothing〈衣服〉・displayed〈display（陳列）的過去分詞〉・sold〈sell（賣）的過去分詞〉・
faster〈較快的，fast（快的）的比較級〉

❹ tiny〈極小的〉・shop〈購物〉・clothes〈衣服〉・children〈child（孩童）的複數〉・
even though〈即使〉

❺ buy〈購買〉・more〈更多〉・get〈獲得〉

中譯

❶ 女裝部有很多不同尺寸的衣服，從 XS 到 XL。

❷ Trisha 在 SOGO 百貨的男裝部上班。

❸ 衣服穿在人體模特兒上展示，會比較快售出。

❹ Judy 的身型太小了，所以她仍然要到童裝部買衣服，即使她已經 13 歲了。

❺ 如果我多買幾個，可以打折嗎？

086

百貨陳列

MP3 086

1 toy department
[tɔɪ dɪˋpɑrtmənt]
(n.) 玩具部

2 home furnishings department
[hom ˋfɝnɪʃɪŋz dɪˋpɑrtmənt]
(n.) 家具區

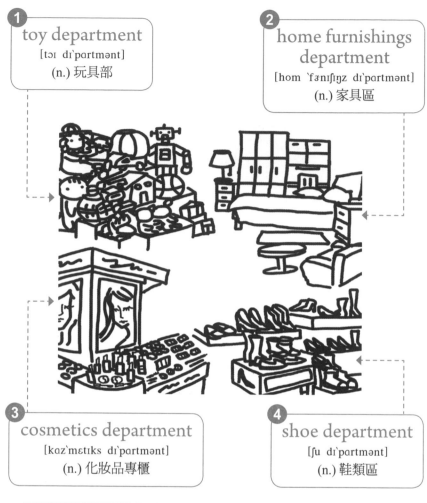

3 cosmetics department
[kɑzˋmɛtɪks dɪˋpɑrtmənt]
(n.) 化妝品專櫃

4 shoe department
[ʃu dɪˋpɑrtmənt]
(n.) 鞋類區

5 emergency exit
[ɪˋmɝdʒənsɪ ˋɛksɪt]
(n.) 逃生門

6 food court
[fud kort]
(n.) 美食廣場

❶ 玩具部

Right before Christmas, the toy department is always crowded with
shoppers.
　　　　　　　　　　　　　　　　　　　　　總是擠滿

❷ 家具區

I hope we can find a nice sofa in the home furnishings department.

❸ 化妝品專櫃

They are offering free makeovers in the cosmetics department today.

❹ 鞋類區

Jennifer's mom refuses to go to the shoe department with her daughter
because Jennifer takes too long to decide which shoes to buy.
　　　　　　　　花太多時間做決定

❺ 逃生門

In case of fire, please use the emergency exits as quickly as possible.
　　　　　　　　　　　　　　　　　　　　　　愈快愈好

❻ 美食廣場

I'm starving! Let's head down to the food court in the basement.
　　　　　　往樓下走

學更多

❶ right〈正好〉・Christmas〈聖誕節〉・be crowded with...〈擠滿…〉・shopper〈顧客〉
❷ hope〈希望〉・sofa〈沙發〉・furnishings〈家具〉
❸ offering〈offer（提供）的 ing 型態〉・makeover〈美容〉・cosmetics〈化妝品〉
❹ refuse〈拒絕〉・shoe〈鞋〉・daughter〈女兒〉・decide〈決定〉
❺ in case of〈假如碰上〉・exit〈出口〉・as...as possible〈愈…愈好〉
❻ starving〈飢餓的〉・head〈朝向…出發〉・court〈場地〉・basement〈地下室〉

中譯

❶ 聖誕節之前，玩具部總是擠滿了顧客。
❷ 我希望我們能在家具區找到一張好沙發。
❸ 今天在化妝品專櫃有提供免費的化妝服務。
❹ Jennifer 的媽媽拒絕跟她女兒一起去鞋類區，因為 Jennifer 總是花太多時間決定要買
　哪雙鞋子。
❺ 萬一發生火災，請盡快從逃生門離開。
❻ 我好餓！我們下樓到地下室的美食廣場吧。

087

協尋服務&停車

MP3 087

1 locker
[ˈlɑkə]
(n.) 置物櫃

2 customer service center
[ˈkʌstəmə ˈsɝvɪs ˈsɛntə]
(n.) 服務台

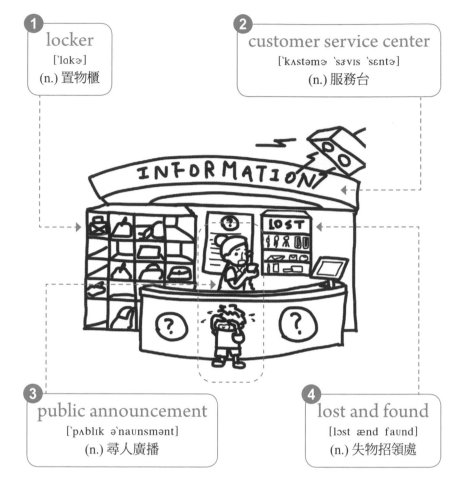

3 public announcement
[ˈpʌblɪk əˈnaʊnsmənt]
(n.) 尋人廣播

4 lost and found
[lɔst ænd faʊnd]
(n.) 失物招領處

5 parking lot
[ˈpɑrkɪŋ lɑt]
(n.) 停車場

6 shopping cart
[ˈʃɑpɪŋ kɑrt]
(n.) 購物推車

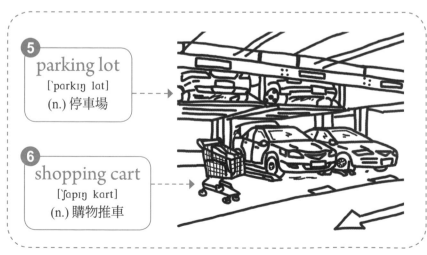

❶ 置物櫃

Yvonne uses a locker at the mall to keep her valuables safe while she's
working.
安全存放她的貴重物品

❷ 服務台

Ellen likes working in the customer service center and helping customers.

❸ 尋人廣播

Public announcements are used to let everyone know when a child is missing
被用來　　　　　　　　　　　　　　　　　　　　　有孩童走失
or a lost child is found.
發現走失的孩童

❹ 失物招領處

See if your wallet has been turned in to lost and found.

❺ 停車場

Did you find a parking space in the parking lot? It looked full to me.
找到停車位

❻ 購物推車

We need a shopping cart for all of our items.
我們所有的物品

學更多

❶ mall〈購物中心〉・keep〈存放〉・valuables〈貴重物品〉・safe〈安全的〉
❷ customer〈顧客〉・service〈服務〉・center〈中心〉
❸ public〈公眾的〉・announcement〈佈告〉・missing〈失蹤的〉・lost〈迷途的〉
❹ wallet〈皮夾〉・turned in〈turn in（交出）的過去分詞〉
❺ parking space〈停車位〉・lot〈一塊地〉・looked〈look（看起來）的過去式〉・full〈滿的〉
❻ cart〈推車〉・all〈全部的〉・our〈我們的〉・item〈物品〉

中譯

❶ Yvonne 上班時使用購物中心的置物櫃，安全存放她的貴重物品。
❷ Ellen 喜歡在服務台工作，幫助顧客。
❸ 尋人廣播是用來讓大家知道有孩童走失，或是發現走失的孩童。
❹ 看看你的皮夾是不是已經被撿到失物招領處。
❺ 你在停車場有找到停車位嗎？我看到都好像停滿了。
❻ 我們需要購物推車，來裝我們的物品。

088

酒吧內(1)

MP3 088

1 bartender
[ˋbɑr,tɛndɚ]
(n.) 調酒師

2 beer
[bɪr]
(n.) 啤酒

3 bar
[bɑr]
(n.) 吧檯/酒吧

4 alcoholic beverage
[ˌælkəˋhɔlɪk ˋbɛvərɪdʒ]
(n.) 酒精飲料

5 bar stool
[bɑr stul]
(n.) 高腳椅

6 drunk
[ˋdrʌŋk]
(n.) 醉漢/酒鬼

❶ 調酒師

Nathan works as a bartender on the weekends for extra cash.
賺外快

❷ 啤酒

How about some beer and chips while we play?

❸ 吧檯／酒吧

Let's sit at the bar and eat some burgers, ok?

❹ 酒精飲料

Bars serve all kinds of alcoholic beverages, but they also serve soda for
non-drinkers.　　　　各種酒精飲料

❺ 高腳椅

Charlie was really drunk and actually fell off his bar stool.
竟然從高腳椅上跌下來

❻ 醉漢／酒鬼

Yuck! I think that drunk is coming over here to flirt with us.
就要過來這邊

學更多

❶ weekend〈週末〉・extra〈額外的〉・cash〈錢〉
❷ how about...〈…如何〉・chip〈洋芋片〉・while〈當…的時候〉
❸ sit〈坐〉・burger〈漢堡〉
❹ serve〈提供〉・all kinds of...〈各式各樣的…〉・alcoholic〈酒精的〉・beverage〈飲料〉・
　 soda〈汽水〉・non-drinker〈不喝酒的人〉
❺ drunk〈喝醉的〉・actually〈竟然〉・fell off〈fall off（落下）的過去式〉・bar〈吧檯〉・
　 stool〈凳子〉
❻ coming〈come（來）的 ing 型態〉・flirt with...〈和…調情〉

中譯

❶ Nathan 週末當調酒師賺外快。
❷ 我們在玩的時候，來一點啤酒和洋芋片如何？
❸ 我們坐在吧檯吃漢堡好嗎？
❹ 酒吧提供各種酒精飲料，不過他們也提供汽水給不喝酒的客人。
❺ Charlie 喝得太醉，而且竟然從高腳椅上跌下來。
❻ 噁！那個醉漢好像要過來這邊和我們搭訕。

089

酒吧內(2)

MP3 089

1
slot machine
[slɑt məˈʃɪn]
(n.) 吃角子老虎機

2
video game
[ˈvɪdɪo gem]
(n.) 電動遊戲機

3
dartboard
[ˈdɑrtˌbɔrd]
(n.) 飛鏢靶

4
dart
[dɑrt]
(n.) 飛鏢

5
pool table
[pul ˈtebl̩]
(n.) 撞球檯

6
disk jockey
[dɪsk ˈdʒɑkɪ]
(n.) DJ

「disk jockey」可縮
寫為「DJ」。

❶ 吃角子老虎機

Do you have any change? I feel lucky. I want to try that slot machine.
<u>我覺得好運降臨</u>

❷ 電動遊戲機

Frank played video games at the bar all night.

❸ 飛鏢靶

The goal is to hit the center of the dartboard with the darts.
<u>射中飛標靶中心點</u>

❹ 飛鏢

Be careful with those darts. You might hurt someone if you don't aim correctly.
<u>如果你沒有精準瞄準</u>

❺ 撞球檯

Hey, this place has a pool table! Let's play!

❻ DJ

Mike's my favorite disk jockey（DJ）. He mixes songs so well.
<u>他很會混音</u>

學更多

❶ change〈零錢〉・feel〈覺得〉・lucky〈好運的〉・try〈嘗試〉・slot〈吃角子老虎〉

❷ played〈play（玩）的過去式〉・video〈影像的〉・bar〈酒吧〉

❸ goal〈目標〉・hit〈擊中〉・center〈中心點〉

❹ careful〈小心的〉・might〈可能〉・hurt〈傷害〉・aim〈瞄準〉・correctly〈正確地〉

❺ place〈地方〉・pool〈撞球〉・table〈檯〉

❻ favorite〈最喜歡的〉・disk〈唱片〉・jockey〈操作者〉・mix〈混合〉・song〈歌曲〉

中譯

❶ 你有沒有零錢？我覺得好運降臨，我要去那台吃角子老虎機試試運氣。

❷ Frank 整晚都在酒吧玩電動遊戲機。

❸ 目標是要用飛鏢射中飛鏢靶的中心點。

❹ 玩飛鏢要小心，如果沒有瞄準好，你可能會傷到人。

❺ 嘿，這邊有一個撞球檯！我們來玩吧！

❻ Mike 是我最喜歡的 DJ，他很會混音。

博物館入口處

MP3 090

1 ticket counter
[ˈtɪkɪt ˈkaʊntɚ]
(n.) 購票處

2 information desk
[ˌɪnfɚˈmeʃən dɛsk]
(n.) 詢問處

3 floor directory
[flor dəˈrɛktərɪ]
(n.) 樓層簡介

4 coat check
[kot tʃɛk]
(n.) 物品寄放處

5 locker
[ˈlɑkɚ]
(n.) 置物櫃

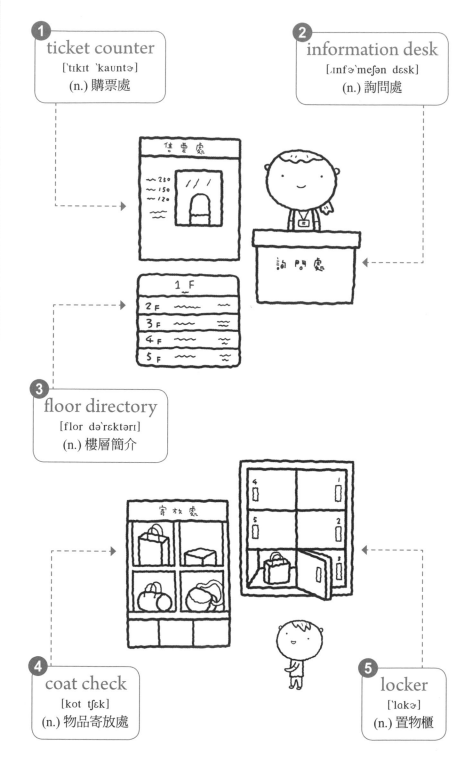

❶ 購票處
There's a long line at the ticket counter.
有一列很長的隊伍

❷ 詢問處
Katie works at the information desk at the National Palace Museum.
工作於

❸ 樓層簡介
Check the floor directory to see what floor the sculptures are on.
雕塑作品在哪一層樓

❹ 物品寄放處
You can leave your jacket and bags for safekeeping at the coat check.
留下你的外套和包包

❺ 置物櫃
Do you have any lockers we can rent for the day?
我們可以租用一天

學更多

❶ long〈長的〉‧ line〈行列〉‧ ticket〈票〉‧ counter〈櫃檯〉
❷ information〈資訊〉‧ desk〈服務檯〉‧ national〈國立的〉‧ palace〈宮殿〉‧
museum〈博物館〉
❸ check〈檢查〉‧ floor〈樓層〉‧ directory〈指南〉‧ see〈查看、知道〉‧
sculpture〈雕塑品〉
❹ leave〈留下〉‧ jacket〈外套〉‧ bag〈包包〉‧ safekeeping〈安全保護〉
❺ rent〈租用〉

中譯

❶ 購票處排了很長的隊伍。
❷ Katie 在國立故宮博物院的詢問處工作。
❸ 看一下樓層簡介，看看雕塑作品在哪一層樓。
❹ 你可以將你的外套和包包寄放在物品寄放處保管。
❺ 你們有置物櫃可以給我們租用一天嗎？

1 security camera
[sɪˋkjʊrətɪ ˋkæmərə]
(n.) 錄影監視器

2 painting
[ˋpentɪŋ]
(n.) 繪畫作品

3 sculpture
[ˋskʌlptʃɚ]
(n.) 雕塑作品

4 exhibition area
[ɛksəˋbɪʃən ˋɛrɪə]
(n.) 展覽區

5 tour guide
[tʊr gaɪd]
(n.) 導覽員

❶ 錄影監視器

Security cameras are everywhere, protecting the valuables inside.
保護貴重物品

❷ 繪畫作品

Do you think my paintings will be in a museum like this someday?
將會擺在博物館裡

❸ 雕塑作品

My favorite sculptures are by a sculptor named Rodin.

❹ 展覽區

There is a toy exhibition downtown where the exhibition area is quite
spacious.　　　玩具展　　　　　　　　　　　　　　　　　相當寬敞

❺ 導覽員

Wendy Chen is a tour guide for Chinese tourists who visit New York City.
遊覽紐約的中國遊客

學更多

❶ security〈防護〉・camera〈攝影機〉・everywhere〈到處〉・
protecting〈protect（保護）的 ing 型態〉・valuables〈貴重物品〉・inside〈在屋內的〉
❷ museum〈博物館〉・like〈宛如〉・someday〈有朝一日〉
❸ favorite〈最喜歡的〉・sculptor〈雕塑家〉・named〈name（取名）的過去分詞〉
❹ exhibition〈展覽〉・downtown〈市中心〉・spacious〈寬敞的〉
❺ tour〈旅遊〉・guide〈導遊〉・tourist〈遊客〉・visit〈參觀〉

中譯

❶ 到處都設置錄影監視器保護裡面的貴重物品。
❷ 你覺得我的繪畫作品有一天也會像這樣擺在博物館裡嗎？
❸ 我最喜歡的雕塑作品出自名叫 Rodin 的雕塑家。
❹ 市中心有個玩具展，那兒的展覽區相當大。
❺ Wendy Chen 是一位替遊覽紐約的中國遊客進行導覽的導覽員。

092

教室內

MP3 092

1 student
['stjudn̩t]
(n.) 學生

2 textbook
['tɛkst.bʊk]
(n.) 教科書

3 chair
[tʃɛr]
(n.) 椅子

4 desk
[dɛsk]
(n.) 桌子

5 trash can
[træʃ kæn]
(n.) 垃圾桶

6 broom
[brum]
(n.) 掃把

7 dustpan
['dʌst.pæn]
(n.) 畚箕

❶ 學生
Ms. Chen teaches 25 students in her 3rd grade classroom.
三年級教室

❷ 教科書
Jerry carries a backpack to school filled with his textbooks.
裝滿

❸ 椅子
Oh no! The leg on this chair is broken.

❹ 桌子
The desks are quite small because the students are only 6 years old.

❺ 垃圾桶
Frank, will you please put that candy wrapper in the trash can?
把糖果包裝紙放入垃圾桶

❻ 掃把
Brooms are useful for sweeping the classroom floor.
清掃教室地板

❼ 畚箕
We need to buy a new dustpan. This one is broken.

學更多

❶ teach〈教〉・grade〈年級〉・classroom〈教室〉
❷ carry〈攜帶〉・backpack〈背包〉・filled with〈fill with（充滿）的過去分詞〉
❸ leg〈腳〉・broken〈損壞的〉
❹ quite〈相當〉・only〈只有〉
❺ candy〈糖果〉・wrapper〈包裝紙〉・trash〈垃圾〉・can〈容器〉
❻ useful〈有幫助的〉・sweeping〈sweep（打掃）的 ing 型態〉・floor〈地板〉
❼ buy〈買〉・new〈新的〉

中譯

❶ 陳小姐所教的這一班三年級學生，有 25 人。
❷ Jerry 帶著裝滿教科書的背包到學校。
❸ 喔不！這椅子的椅腳壞了。
❹ 桌子都相當小，因為使用的學生才六歲大。
❺ Frank，可以請你把糖果包裝紙丟到垃圾桶嗎？
❻ 掃把用來清掃教室地板很方便。
❼ 我們需要買一個新的畚箕。這個壞了。

1 blackboard
[`blæk.bord]
(n.) 黑板

2 teacher
[`titʃə]
(n.) 老師

3 eraser
[ɪ`resə]
(n.) 板擦/橡皮擦

4 chalk
[tʃɔk]
(n.) 粉筆

5 platform
[`plæt.fɔrm]
(n.) 講台

❶ 黑板

The blackboard is cleaned every day after school by the students.
　　　黑板被清潔

❷ 老師

What's your teacher like? Is she nice or really strict?
　　　你的老師像什麼樣子

❸ 板擦 / 橡皮擦

Can I borrow your eraser? I can't find mine.
　　我可以借用你的…嗎

❹ 粉筆

We're out of chalk. Tommy, will you go get some more in the storage closet?　缺少粉筆　　　　　　　　　　　　再拿一些

❺ 講台

Ms. Lee, who is quite short, uses the platform in her class to teach her students.　　他的個子矮小

學更多

❶ cleaned〈clean（清潔）的過去分詞〉‧ after school〈放學後〉
❷ like〈類似的〉‧ nice〈友好的〉‧ strict〈嚴格的〉
❸ borrow〈借〉‧ find〈找到〉‧ mine〈我的〉
❹ out of...〈缺少…〉‧ storage〈儲藏〉‧ closet〈櫃子〉
❺ short〈矮的〉‧ class〈班級〉‧ teach〈教〉

中譯

❶ 每天放學之後，學生都會清潔黑板。
❷ 你的老師是怎麼樣的人？她人很好？還是很嚴格？
❸ 我可以借用你的橡皮擦嗎？我找不到我的。
❹ 我們沒有粉筆了。Tommy，你可以去儲藏櫃再拿一些來嗎？
❺ 個子矮小的李老師，在課堂上教學生時，會使用講台。

1 flag-raising ceremony
[ˋflæɡˋrezɪŋ ˋsɛrə.monɪ]
(n.) 升旗典禮

2 stage
[stedʒ]
(n.) 司令台/舞台

3 flagpole
[ˋflæɡ.pol]
(n.) 旗杆

4 student
[ˋstjudn̩t]
(n.) 學生

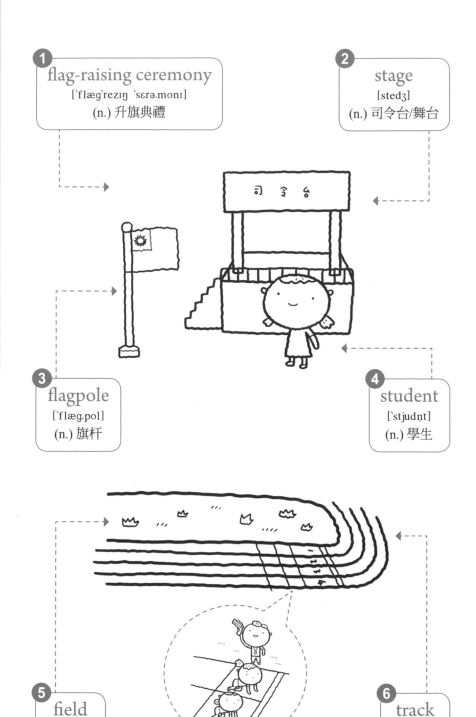

5 field
[fild]
(n.) 操場

6 track
[træk]
(n.) 跑道

❶ 升旗典禮

Every morning, Johnny's school has a flag-raising ceremony before beginning class.

❷ 司令台 / 舞台

Sometimes, students stand on the stage outside to sing together for special events.
站上室外舞台合唱

❸ 旗杆

The country's flag is raised on the flagpole every morning.
被升上旗桿

❹ 學生

All the students run out on the playground as soon as they hear the recess bell.
跑到操場

❺ 操場

There is a big field behind the school where the kids can play baseball.

❻ 跑道

Let's go run on the track this weekend.
在跑道上跑步

學更多

❶ flag〈旗〉・raising〈raise（升起）的 ing 型態〉・ceremony〈典禮〉・beginning〈begin（開始）的 ing 型態〉

❷ stand〈站〉・special〈特殊的〉・event〈事件〉

❸ country〈國家〉・raised〈raise（升起）的過去分詞〉

❹ playground〈操場〉・as soon as...〈一…就…〉・recess〈休息〉・bell〈鐘聲〉

❺ behind〈在…的後面〉・baseball〈棒球〉

❻ run〈跑步〉・weekend〈週末〉

中譯

❶ 每天早上開始上課前，Johnny 的學校都會舉行升旗典禮。

❷ 有時候，為了特別的活動，學生們會站上室外的舞台合唱歌曲。

❸ 每天早上國旗都會被升上旗桿。

❹ 只要聽到下課鐘聲，所有的學生就會跑到操場。

❺ 學校後方有一個大操場可以讓小朋友打棒球。

❻ 我們這週末到（操場）跑道上跑步吧。

操場上的遊樂設施

MP3 095

1 soccer pitch
[`sɑkə pɪtʃ]
(n.) 足球場

2 basketball court
[`bæskɪt͵bɔl kort]
(n.) 籃球場

3 jungle gym
[`dʒʌŋɡl dʒɪm]
(n.) 攀登架（爬格子）

4 sand box
[sænd bɑks]
(n.) 沙坑

5 chin-up bar
[`tʃɪn͵ʌp bɑr]
(n.) 單槓

6 swing
[swɪŋ]
(n.) 鞦韆

❶ 足球場

The soccer pitch is the name of the field where soccer is played.
場地的名稱

❷ 籃球場

Hey, do you want to play some hoops tonight on the basketball court?
打籃球

❸ 攀登架（爬格子）

Sam fell off the jungle gym and broke his arm.
摔斷了他的手臂

❹ 沙坑

Most kids love to play in the sand box—especially if they can add some
water to the sand.
加水到沙子裡

❺ 單槓

My daddy is always doing chin-ups on the chin-up bar to keep his
muscles big and strong.
在單槓上拉單槓

❻ 鞦韆

Jill loves to have her mom push her on the swings.
讓她媽媽推她

學更多

❶ soccer〈足球〉‧ pitch〈運動場地〉‧ field〈場地〉‧ played〈play（踢球）的過去分詞〉
❷ hoops〈籃球〉‧ basketball〈籃球〉‧ court〈運動場地〉
❸ fell off〈fall off（掉下）的過去式〉‧ jungle〈叢林〉‧ gym〈體育〉‧
broke〈break（折斷）的過去式〉
❹ most〈大部分的〉‧ sand〈沙子〉‧ especially〈尤其〉‧ add〈添加〉
❺ chin-up〈拉單槓使身體上升，下顎與單槓平〉‧ bar〈條狀物〉‧ muscle〈肌肉〉
❻ have＋某人〈讓某人、使某人〉‧ push〈推〉

中譯

❶ 足球場是踢足球的場地的名稱。
❷ 嘿，你今晚要在籃球場打籃球嗎？
❸ Sam 從攀登架上掉下來，摔斷了手臂。
❹ 大部分的孩子喜歡在沙坑玩，尤其是如果他們能夠加水到沙子裡。
❺ 我爸爸總是利用拉單槓，讓他的肌肉保持強壯。
❻ Jill 最愛在鞦韆上讓媽媽推她。

096

書店

🔊 MP3 096

1 best-seller
[ˌbɛstˋsɛlə]
(n.) 暢銷品/暢銷書

2 best-seller list
[ˌbɛstˋsɛlə list]
(n.) 暢銷排行榜

3 book
[bʊk]
(n.) 書籍

4 new arrival
[nju əˋraɪvl̩]
(n.) 新書

5 bookshelf
[ˋbʊkˌʃɛlf]
(n.) 書架

6 clerk
[klɝk]
(n.) 店員

7 consumer
[kənˋsjumə]
(n.) 消費者

❶ 暢銷品 / 暢銷書

Let's check the list of best-sellers this month.
　　　　　　　　暢銷排行榜

❷ 暢銷排行榜

Have you seen The New York Times best-seller list this week?

❸ 書籍

Can you reach that book by James Chen for me? I'm too short.
　　　　　　　那本 James Chen 寫的書

❹ 新書

Typically, bookstores display the new arrivals in the shop windows.
　　　　　　　　　　　　　　　展示新書

❺ 書架

There is a great selection here. They have rows and rows of bookshelves.
　　　　　　　有很多選擇　　　　　　　　　　　　　　一排一排的書架

❻ 店員

What a cute clerk they have working here! We should come here more often.

❼ 消費者

"Brick and mortar" bookstores have been struggling lately as more
　　　　　　　　　　　　　　　　　最近陷入營運困難

consumers go online to purchase books.
　　　　　　上網買書

學更多

❶ check〈檢查〉・list〈表〉・seller〈銷售物〉・month〈月〉
❷ seen〈see（看）的過去分詞〉・week〈週〉
❸ reach〈伸手去拿〉・short〈矮的〉
❹ typically〈典型地〉・display〈展示〉・arrival〈到達的物品〉・shop window〈陳列窗〉
❺ great〈數量大的〉・selection〈選擇、精選品〉・row〈排〉
❻ cute〈可愛的〉・working〈work（工作）的 ing 型態〉・more often〈更常〉
❼ struggling〈struggle（掙扎）的 ing 型態〉・lately〈最近〉・as〈因為〉・purchase〈購買〉

中譯

❶ 我們來看看這個月的暢銷品排行榜。
❷ 你有看到 The New York Times 這週的暢銷排行榜嗎？
❸ 你可以幫我拿一下那本 James Chen 寫的書嗎？我太矮了（拿不到）。
❹ 通常，書店都會將新書展示在櫥窗內。
❺ 在這兒可以有很多選擇，他們有一排又一排的書架。
❻ 在這邊工作的店員好可愛啊！我們應該要常來光顧。
❼ Brick and mortar 書店最近陷入營運困難，因為越來越多消費者上網買書。

097

書店陳列區

MP3 097

1 stationery
[ˈsteʃənˌɛrɪ]
(n.) 文具

2 children's book
[ˈtʃɪldrənz bʊk]
(n.) 童書

3 bookworm
[ˈbʊkˌwɝm]
(n.) 喜歡看書的人

4 magazine
[ˌmægəˈzin]
(n.) 雜誌

5 comic book
[ˈkɑmɪk bʊk]
(n.) 漫畫書

❶ 文具

I need some stationery to write some personal letters this weekend.
寫些私人信件

❷ 童書

David is only seven, so his parents buy him children's books to read.
買童書給他

❸ 喜歡看書的人

He's a bookworm and loves just hanging around bookshelves stacked with
放滿書的書架
books.

❹ 雜誌

Allie spends lots of time looking at the fashion magazines at the
花很多時間
bookstore.

❺ 漫畫書

You'll find the comic books if you just follow the kids.
只要你跟隨著小孩

學更多

❶ write〈寫〉・personal〈個人的〉・letter〈信件〉
❷ only〈只〉・parents〈雙親〉・read〈閱讀〉
❸ hanging around〈hang around（徘徊）的 ing 型態〉・stacked〈stack（堆放）的過去分詞〉
❹ spend〈花費〉・looking at〈look at（看）的 ing 型態〉・fashion〈時尚〉
❺ find〈找到〉・comic〈連環漫畫〉・follow〈跟隨〉・kid〈小孩〉

中譯

❶ 我需要一些文具，讓我在這個週末寫些私人信件。
❷ David 才七歲，所以他的父母親買童書給他閱讀。
❸ 他是個書蟲，最愛在堆滿書的書架間徘徊。
❹ Allie 花很多時間在書店翻閱時尚雜誌。
❺ 只要你跟隨小孩的腳步，就會找到漫畫書。

098

書籍櫃位

MP3 098

1 literature
[ˈlɪtərətʃə]
(n.) 文學作品

2 non-fiction
[ˌnɑnˈfɪkʃən]
(n.) 非虛構文學/非小說類文學

3 financial book
[faɪˈnænʃəl bʊk]
(n.) 財經書

4 language learning
[ˈlæŋgwɪdʒ ˈlɜnɪŋ]
(n.) 語言學習

5 foreign language book
[ˈfɔrɪn ˈlæŋgwɪdʒ bʊk]
(n.) 外文書

❶ 文學作品

Where is the literature section? I want to buy a classic novel today.
經典小說

❷ 非虛構文學 / 非小說類文學

He doesn't have a favorite genre; he likes fiction, as well as non-fiction.
最愛的文藝作品類型

❸ 財經書

Tony is a business student, and loves to browse through the financial books
in the bookstore.
翻閱財經書

❹ 語言學習

I'm learning Russian at school. Can you tell me where the language learning
books are located?
語言學習書放在哪裡

❺ 外文書

Are the foreign language books on the first or second floor?
在一樓或二樓

學更多

❶ section〈區域〉‧classic〈經典的〉‧novel〈小說〉
❷ genre〈文藝作品的類型〉‧fiction〈小說〉‧as well as...〈也…〉
❸ business〈商業〉‧browse〈瀏覽〉‧financial〈金融的〉‧bookstore〈書店〉
❹ Russian〈俄文〉‧language〈語言〉‧located〈locate（設置於…）的過去分詞〉
❺ foreign〈外國的〉‧first〈第一的〉‧second〈第二的〉‧floor〈樓層〉

中譯

❶ 文學作品區在哪裡？我今天想要買一本經典小說。
❷ 他沒有最愛的文藝作品類型；他喜歡小說類，也喜歡非虛構文學。
❸ Tony 是商學院的學生，而且很愛在書店翻閱財經書。
❹ 我現在在學校學俄文。你能告訴我語言學習書放在哪裡嗎？
❺ 外文書是在一樓，還是二樓？

099

醫療中心(1)

1
doctor
[ˋdɑktɚ]
(n.) 醫生

2
nurse
[nɝs]
(n.) 護士

3
patient
[ˋpeʃənt]
(n.) 病人

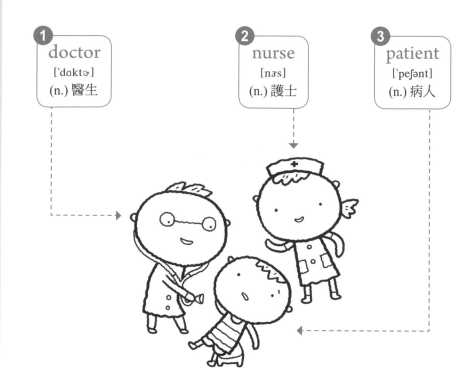

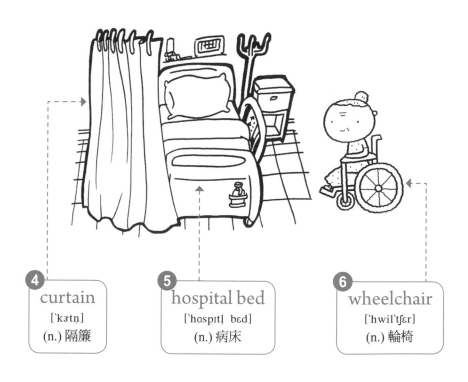

4
curtain
[ˋkɝtn̩]
(n.) 隔簾

5
hospital bed
[ˋhɑspɪtl̩ bɛd]
(n.) 病床

6
wheelchair
[ˋhwilˋtʃɛr]
(n.) 輪椅

❶ 醫生

James is in medical school, studying to be a doctor.
　　　　　　　 醫學院

❷ 護士

Currently, there is a shortage of nurses around the world.
　　　　　　　　　　 護士短缺

❸ 病人

Once a patient is admitted to the hospital, they will receive good care.
　　　　　　病人被送進醫院

❹ 隔簾

For more privacy, you can ask the nurse to close the curtain around your
bed.　　　　　　　　　　　　　　　　　　　 拉上環繞你床邊的隔簾

❺ 病床

There aren't enough hospital beds for all the patients who need them.
　　　　　　　　　　　　　　　　　　　 所有需要病床的病人

❻ 輪椅

Eric's grandfather needs a wheelchair to leave the hospital because he's
still quite weak.

學更多

❶ medical〈醫學的〉・studying〈study（學習）的 ing 型態〉
❷ currently〈現在〉・shortage〈缺少〉・around〈在…四處〉・world〈世界〉
❸ once〈一旦〉・admitted〈admit（准許進入）的過去分詞〉・receive〈接受〉・
　 care〈照顧〉
❹ more〈更多的〉・privacy〈隱私〉・ask〈要求〉・close〈關閉〉・around〈環繞〉
❺ enough〈足夠的〉・hospital〈醫院〉
❻ grandfather〈祖父〉・leave〈離開〉・still〈還是〉・quite〈很〉・weak〈虛弱的〉

中譯

❶ James 正在讀醫學院，學習如何成為醫生。
❷ 目前在世界各處，都有護士短缺的情形。
❸ 病人一旦被送進醫院，就會受到良好的照顧。
❹ 為了更能保護隱私，你可以要求護士將環繞床邊的隔簾拉起來。
❺ 醫院沒有足夠的病床提供給所有需要的病人。
❻ Eric 的祖父需要坐輪椅離開醫院，因為他身體還是很虛弱。

100

醫療中心(2)

MP3 100

1 bandage
[ˋbændɪdʒ]
(n.) 繃帶

2 patient
[ˋpeʃənt]
(n.) 病人

3 crutch
[krʌtʃ]
(n.) 柺杖

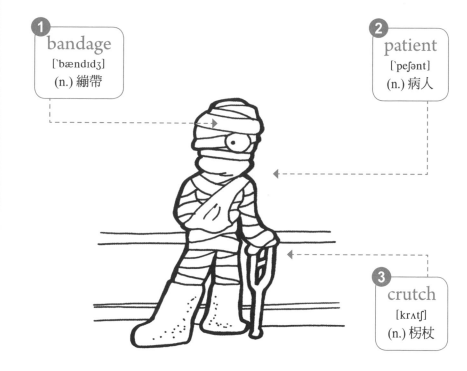

4 first aid kit
[fɝst ed kɪt]
(n.) 急救箱

5 iodine
[ˋaɪəˌdaɪn]
(n.) 碘酒

6 cotton ball
[ˋkɑtn̩ bɔl]
(n.) 棉球

7 gauze
[gɔz]
(n.) 紗布

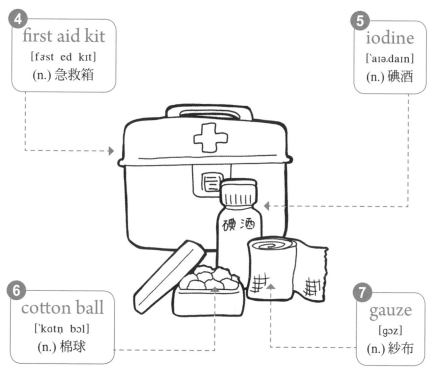

❶ 繃帶

Patty needs some bandages for the blisters on her feet from new shoes.
　　　　　　　　　　　　　　　　她腳上的水泡

❷ 病人

Some hospitals refuse to treat uninsured patients.
　　　　　　　　　　　　　　　沒有投保的病人

❸ 枴杖

Andy needs two crutches to walk with his broken leg.
　　　　　　　　　　　　　和他摔斷的腿一起走路

❹ 急救箱

All homes, schools, and businesses should have a first aid kit.

❺ 碘酒

After Harry cut his foot, he applied iodine to clean the wound before
　　　　　　　　　　　　　　　　　　　　　　　　　清理傷口
putting a bandage on it.
　　用繃帶包紮傷口

❻ 棉球

Cotton balls are useful in applying antiseptic liquids like iodine.
　　　　　　　　　　　　　塗抹抗菌液體

❼ 紗布

Gauze is a thin, cotton fabric used to bandage wounds.
　　　　　　　　　　　　　　用來包紮傷口

學更多

❶ blister〈水泡〉．feet〈foot（腳）的複數〉．shoe〈鞋子〉
❷ hospital〈醫院〉．refuse〈拒絕〉．treat〈治療〉．uninsured〈沒有投保的〉
❸ walk〈走路〉．with〈和⋯一起〉．broken〈損壞的〉．leg〈腿〉
❹ business〈公司〉．first〈最先的〉．aid〈救助〉．kit〈工具箱〉
❺ cut〈cut（割）的過去式〉．applied〈apply（將⋯塗在表面）的過去式〉．wound〈傷口〉
❻ cotton〈棉〉．ball〈球〉．useful〈有用的〉．antiseptic〈抗菌的〉．liquid〈液體〉
❼ thin〈薄的〉．fabric〈布料〉．used〈use（使用）的過去分詞〉．bandage〈包紮〉

中譯

❶ Patty 需要一些繃帶包裹她腳上因為穿新鞋而長出的水泡。
❷ 有些醫院會拒絕治療沒有投保的病人。
❸ Andy 需要兩支拐杖輔助他摔斷的腿一起走路。
❹ 所有的家庭、學校和公司,都該有個急救箱。
❺ Harry 割傷腳後,在用繃帶包紮之前,他先塗抹碘酒清理傷口。
❻ 棉球拿來塗抹碘酒之類的抗菌液體,是很好用的。
❼ 紗布是用來包紮傷口的薄棉布。

學校宿舍(1)

MP3 101

1 resident assistant
[ˈrɛzədənt əˈsɪstənt]
(n.) 舍監

2 curfew
[ˈkɝfju]
(n.) 宵禁時間

「resident assistant」可縮寫為「RA」。

3 girl's dormitory
[gɝlz ˈdɔrməˌtorɪ]
(n.) 女宿

4 boy's dormitory
[bɔɪz ˈdɔrməˌtorɪ]
(n.) 男宿

5 bunk bed
[bʌŋk bɛd]
(n.) 雙層床

6 roommate
[ˈrumˌmet]
(n.) 室友

7 dormitory room
[ˈdɔrməˌtorɪ rum]
(n.) 寢室

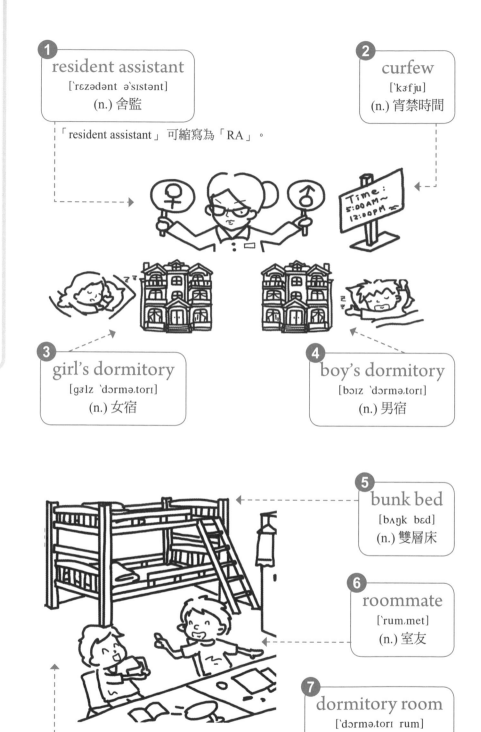

❶ 舍監

Stacy is working as a resident assistant this year in a college dorm.
擔任舍監

❷ 宵禁時間

There's a curfew in dorms because schools don't want the students to stay out too late.
在外逗留太晚

❸ 女宿

Linda decided to live in the girl's dormitory as a college freshman.

❹ 男宿

The boy's dormitory is located on the south side of campus.
位於　　　　　　校區的南邊

❺ 雙層床

How about getting a bunk bed to save space in our room?
買雙層床

❻ 室友

Who is your roommate, Ken? Do you like him?

❼ 寢室

Most dormitory rooms are quite small, with just beds and desks.
只能容納床跟書桌

學更多

❶ resident〈居民〉‧ assistant〈助手〉‧ college〈大學〉‧ dorm〈宿舍〉
❷ stay〈逗留〉‧ out〈在外〉‧ late〈晚的〉
❸ live〈住〉‧ dormitory〈宿舍〉‧ freshman〈一年級生、新生〉
❹ located〈locate（坐落於…）的過去分詞〉‧ south〈南方的〉‧ side〈邊〉‧ campus〈校區〉
❺ bunk〈上下床鋪〉‧ save〈節省〉‧ space〈空間〉‧ our〈我們的〉‧ room〈房間〉
❻ your〈你的〉‧ like〈喜歡〉
❼ quite〈相當〉‧ small〈小的〉‧ just〈只有〉‧ desk〈書桌〉

中譯

❶ Stacy 今年在大學的宿舍擔任舍監。
❷ 宿舍有宵禁時間，因為學校不希望學生在外面逗留到太晚。
❸ 成為了大學新鮮人，Linda 決定住在學校的女生宿舍。
❹ 男生宿舍位於校區的南邊。
❺ 要不要買張雙層床，來節省我們房間的空間？
❻ Ken，你的室友是誰？你喜歡他嗎？
❼ 大多數宿舍的寢室都挺小的，只能容納床和書桌。

1 laundry room
[ˈlɔndrɪ rum]
(n.) 洗衣間

2 bathroom / restroom
[ˈbæθˌrum] / [ˈrɛstˌrum]
(n.) 廁所

兩個單字都是「廁所」。

3 shower
[ˈʃaʊɚ]
(n.) 淋浴間

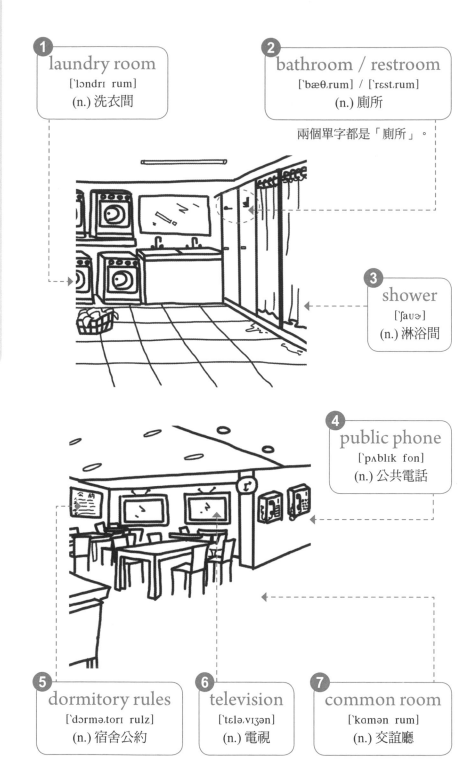

4 public phone
[ˈpʌblɪk fon]
(n.) 公共電話

5 dormitory rules
[ˈdɔrməˌtorɪ rulz]
(n.) 宿舍公約

6 television
[ˈtɛləˌvɪʒən]
(n.) 電視

7 common room
[ˈkɑmən rum]
(n.) 交誼廳

❶ 洗衣間
Jenny's in the laundry room in the dorm basement.
　　　　　　　　　　　　　　在宿舍的地下室

❷ 廁所
Cleaning the bathrooms in a dormitory is no fun.
　　　　　　　　　　　　　　一點都不好玩

❸ 淋浴間
There are several showers on each floor of the dormitory.
　　　　　　　　　　　每一層樓

❹ 公共電話
My cell isn't working, so I'll just use the public phone.
　　　沒有在運作

❺ 宿舍公約
If you don't follow the dormitory rules, you will be kicked out!
　　　　　　　　　　　　　　　　　被趕出去

❻ 電視
Now that Ron is in college, he doesn't have much time to watch television.

❼ 交誼廳
Let's meet tonight in the common room to watch our favorite TV show!
　　　　　　　　今晚在交誼廳碰面

學更多

❶ laundry〈洗衣店〉‧dorm〈宿舍〉‧basement〈地下室〉
❷ cleaning〈clean（清潔）的 ing 型態〉‧dormitory〈學生宿舍〉‧fun〈樂趣〉
❸ several〈幾個的〉‧each〈每一個〉‧floor〈樓層〉
❹ cell〈手機〉‧working〈work（運作）的 ing 型態〉‧use〈使用〉‧public〈公共的〉
❺ follow〈遵守〉‧rule〈規定〉‧kicked out〈kick out（驅趕出去）的過去分詞〉
❻ now that〈既然、因為〉‧college〈大學〉‧much〈許多的〉
❼ meet〈碰面〉‧common〈公眾的〉‧favorite〈最喜歡的〉‧show〈節目〉

中譯

❶ Jenny 在宿舍地下室的洗衣間。
❷ 清潔宿舍的廁所，一點都不好玩。
❸ 在宿舍的每一層樓，都有好幾間淋浴間。
❹ 我的手機不能使用，所以我要去打一下公共電話。
❺ 如果你不遵守宿舍公約，你會被趕出去。
❻ 既然 Ron 是大學生了，他就沒有很多時間看電視了。
❼ 我們今晚在交誼廳碰面，一起看最喜歡的電視節目吧！

1 examination sheet
[ɪgˌzæməˈneʃən ʃit]
(n.) 考卷/試題卷

2 answer sheet
[ˈænsɚ ʃit]
(n.) 答案卡

3 2B pencil
[ˈtuˋbi ˈpɛnsḷ]
(n.) 2B 鉛筆

4 examination supervisor
[ɪgˌzæməˈneʃən ˌsupɚˈvaɪzɚ]
(n.) 監考人員

5 exam attendee
[ɪgˈzæm əˈtɛndi]
(n.) 考生

❶ 考卷 / 試題卷

I don't have an examination sheet, sir, can you give me one?
<u>給我一份</u>

❷ 答案卡

Make sure you mark your answers very clearly on the answer sheet.
<u>很清楚地畫記你的答案</u>

❸ 2B鉛筆

You must use a 2B pencil when taking exams.
<u>當考試的時候</u>

❹ 監考人員

Mr. Brink is the examination supervisor and he's really strict!
<u>他很嚴格</u>

❺ 考生

There are over 200 exam attendees waiting to take the exam.
<u>正等著接受考試</u>

學更多

❶ examination〈考試〉．sheet〈一張紙〉．sir〈先生、老師、長官〉．give〈給〉
❷ make sure〈確定〉．mark〈做標記〉．answer〈答案〉．clearly〈清楚地〉
❸ must〈必須〉．use〈使用〉．pencil〈鉛筆〉．exam〈考試〉
❹ supervisor〈監督者〉．really〈很〉．strict〈嚴格的〉
❺ over〈超過〉．attendee〈出席的人〉．waiting〈wait（等待）的 ing 型態〉

中譯

❶ 先生，我沒有考卷，你可以給我一份嗎？
❷ 要確定你有把答案清楚地畫在答案卡上。
❸ 考試的時候，你必須使用 2B 鉛筆。
❹ Brink 先生是監考人員，而且他很嚴格。
❺ 有超過 200 位考生正等著接受考試。

考試用具

MP3 104

1 admission ticket
[əd`mɪʃən `tɪkɪt]
(n.) 准考證

2 identification / ID
[aɪ.dɛntəfə`keʃən] / [`aɪ`di]
(n.) 身份證

縮寫為「ID」。

3 eraser
[ɪ`resɚ]
(n.) 橡皮擦

4 pen
[pɛn]
(n.) 原子筆

5 white-out
[`hwaɪt.aʊt]
(n.) 立可白

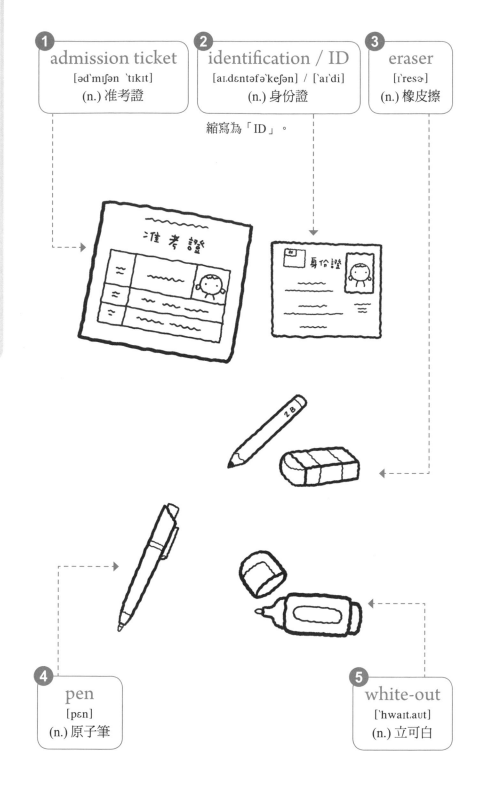

216

❶ 准考證

You need an admission ticket to gain entrance.
<u>有權利進入</u>

❷ 身份證

Don't forget to bring your ID on examination day.
<u>攜帶你的身份證</u>

❸ 橡皮擦

You'd better bring a good eraser to the exam. You'll need it.
<u>你最好…</u>

❹ 原子筆

Pens are not allowed to be used on exams at all.
<u>不被允許使用</u>

❺ 立可白

I prefer to use white-out, rather than an eraser with a pencil.
<u>橡皮擦和鉛筆</u>

學更多

❶ need〈需要〉‧ admission〈進入許可〉‧ ticket〈許可證〉‧ gain〈得到〉‧
entrance〈進入的權利〉

❷ forget〈忘記〉‧ bring〈帶來〉‧ examination〈考試〉

❸ good〈好的〉‧ exam〈考試〉

❹ allowed〈allow（准許）的過去分詞〉‧ used〈use（使用）的過去分詞〉‧ at all〈完全〉

❺ prefer〈更喜歡〉‧ white〈白色〉‧ rather than〈而不是…〉‧ pencil〈鉛筆〉

中譯

❶ 你需要有准考證才可以進入。

❷ 考試當天，不要忘記攜帶你的身份證。

❸ 你最好帶一個好用的橡皮擦去考試，你會需要它的。

❹ 考試時，完全禁止使用原子筆。

❺ 比起橡皮擦和鉛筆，我更喜歡使用立可白。

105

幼稚園(1)

MP3 105

1 school bus
[skul bʌs]
(n.) 娃娃車

2 school gate
[skul get]
(n.) 校門

3 teacher
[ˈtitʃɚ]
(n.) 老師

4 principal
[ˈprɪnsəpl̩]
(n.) 園長/校長

5 children
[ˈtʃɪldrən]
(n.) 小朋友

6 parents
[ˈpɛrənts]
(n.) 家長

❶ 娃娃車

Timmy, hurry up! You're going to miss the school bus!

<u>你快要錯過娃娃車了</u>

❷ 校門

Once the school gate is closed, you need permission to either enter or leave.

<u>進入或出去</u>

❸ 老師

Yvonne's favorite teacher, Ms. Lee, is very kind.

❹ 園長 / 校長

Roger was so naughty today that his teacher sent him to the principal's office.

<u>把他帶到校長室</u>

❺ 小朋友

Mrs. Chang teaches twenty-five children in her kindergarten class.

<u>在她的幼稚園班級</u>

❻ 家長

Every morning I can see lots of parents taking their kids to school.

<u>帶他們的小孩去學校</u>

學更多

❶ hurry up〈趕緊〉・miss〈錯過〉・school〈學校〉・bus〈公車〉

❷ once〈一旦〉・gate〈大門〉・closed〈關閉的〉・permission〈許可〉・
either...or...〈不是…就是…〉・enter〈進入〉・leave〈離開〉

❸ favorite〈最喜歡的〉・kind〈親切的〉

❹ naughty〈調皮的〉・sent〈send（送）的過去式〉・office〈辦公室〉

❺ teach〈教〉・kindergarten〈幼稚園〉・class〈班級〉

❻ lots of〈許多〉・taking〈take（帶去）的 ing 型態〉・kid〈小孩〉

中譯

❶ Timmy，動作快！你快要錯過娃娃車了！

❷ 一旦校門關閉，你需要獲得許可才能進入或離開。

❸ Yvonne 最喜歡的老師——李老師，為人非常和藹可親。

❹ Roger 今天太調皮了，所以他的老師把他帶到校長辦公室。

❺ 張太太在她的幼稚園班級裡，教導 25 個小朋友。

❻ 每天早上，我都會看到許多家長帶他們的孩子去上學。

106

幼稚園(2)

MP3 106

1 bulletin board
[ˈbʊlətɪn bord]
(n.) 布告欄

2 artworks
[ˈɑrt.wɝks]
(n.) 美勞作品

3 classroom
[ˈklæs.rum]
(n.) 教室

4 nurse's office
[ˈnɝsɪz ˈɔfɪs]
(n.) 保健室

5 office
[ˈɔfɪs]
(n.) 辦公室

6 playground
[ˈple.graʊnd]
(n.) 遊戲場

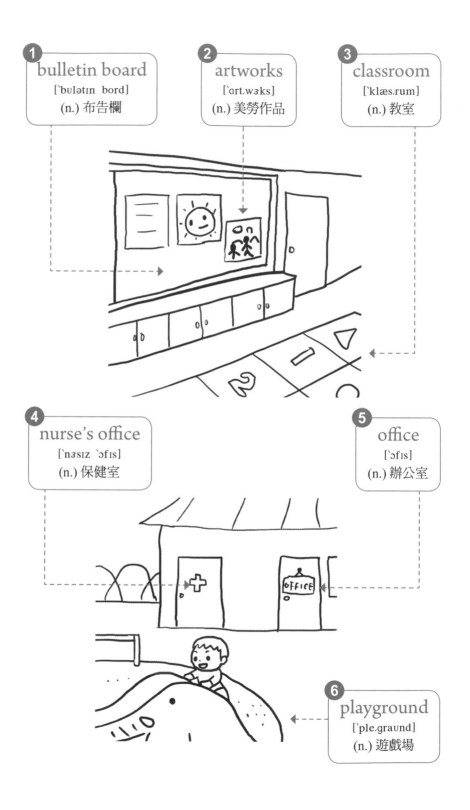

❶ 布告欄
Did you check the bulletin board for any announcements?

❷ 美勞作品
The students' artworks will be featured in their classrooms for parents
to see.
將成為教室的特色

❸ 教室
Classrooms can be quite warm in the summer heat.
夏季的高溫

❹ 保健室
Holly had a tummy ache, so she went to the nurse's office.
肚子痛

❺ 辦公室
If you're late, you'd better go to the office first to check in.
先去辦公室報到

❻ 遊戲場
It's recess time! Let's go outside to the playground.
下課時間

學更多

❶ check〈檢查〉‧bulletin〈公布〉‧board〈布告牌〉‧announcement〈公告〉
❷ featured〈feature（作為主要角色）的過去分詞〉‧parents〈家長〉
❸ warm〈溫暖的〉‧summer〈夏天〉‧heat〈高溫〉
❹ tummy〈肚子〉‧ache〈疼痛〉‧went〈go（去）的過去式〉‧nurse〈護士〉
❺ late〈遲到的〉‧first〈首先〉‧check in〈報到〉
❻ recess〈休息〉‧time〈時間〉‧outside〈外面〉

中譯

❶ 你有檢查布告欄，看看有沒有任何公告嗎？
❷ 學生們的美勞作品將成為教室內的一大特色，供家長們觀賞。
❸ 在夏季的高溫之下，教室會變得很溫暖。
❹ Holly 肚子痛，所以她去了一趟保健室。
❺ 如果你遲到了，最好先去辦公室報到。
❻ 現在是下課時間，我們到外面的遊戲場玩！

107

野生動物保護區

MP3 107

1 wildlife
[ˈwaɪldˌlaɪf]
(n.) 野生動物

2 plant
[plænt]
(n.) 植物

3 protected area
[prəˈtɛktɪd ˈɛrɪə]
(n.) 保護區

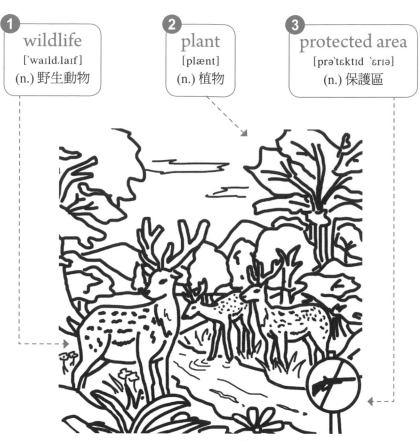

進入「野生動物保護區」需事先辦理申請，並禁止任何騷擾、虐待、獵捕、宰殺野生動物，或破壞野生動植物棲地之行為。

梅花鹿：因背上白色的梅花斑而得名。因早期遭到任意獵捕，幾乎瀕臨絕種，目前所見皆為透過復育計劃由人工飼養的鹿隻。

4 endangered species
[ɪnˈdendʒəd ˈspiʃiz]
(n.) 瀕臨絕種的動物

5 ranger
[ˈrendʒə]
(n.) 管理員

❶ 野生動物

Let's go to a national park today! I love to see the wildlife living there.
<u>生活在那裡的野生動物</u>

❷ 植物

The plants here are flourishing. Plants love the rain and humidity.

❸ 保護區

The area you are now entering is a protected area, and is off-limits to
<u>你現在正要進入的區域</u>
any non-park personnel.
<u>任何非園方人員</u>

❹ 瀕臨絕種的動物

It is illegal to go hunting for any endangered species.
<u>獵捕任何瀕臨絕種的動物</u>

❺ 管理員

Daddy, the ranger is coming over. Are we in trouble for building a campfire?
<u>正走過來</u>　　　　　　　　　<u>因為升營火而惹上麻煩</u>

學更多

❶ national〈國家的〉・park〈公園〉・living〈live（生活）的 ing 型態〉
❷ flourishing〈茂盛的〉・rain〈雨水〉・humidity〈濕氣〉
❸ area〈區域〉・entering〈enter（進入）的 ing 型態〉・protected〈受保護的〉・
off-limits〈禁止進入的〉・personnel〈人員〉
❹ illegal〈違法的〉・hunting〈狩獵〉・endangered〈瀕臨絕種的〉・species〈物種〉
❺ coming over〈come over（從遠方過來）的 ing 型態〉・in trouble〈在危險的處境中〉・
building〈build（生火）的 ing 型態〉・campfire〈營火〉

中譯

❶ 今天我們去國家公園吧！我喜歡看生活在那裡的野生動物。
❷ 這邊的植物長得很茂盛。植物喜愛雨水及潮濕。
❸ 你現在正要進入的區域是保護區，是禁止任何非園方人員進入的。
❹ 獵捕任何瀕臨絕種的動物都是違法的。
❺ 爸爸，管理員走過來了，是因為我們升營火所以惹上麻煩嗎？

大自然生態

MP3 108

1 valley
[`vælɪ]
(n.) 峽谷

2 mountain
[`mauntn̩]
(n.) 山

3 cliff
[klɪf]
(n.) 懸崖

4 forest
[`fɔrɪst]
(n.) 森林

5 stream
[strim]
(n.) 溪流

❶ 峽谷

If you look down from the mountaintop, you'll see a lovely little valley
<u>從山頂俯瞰</u>
below.

❷ 山

After Zoe hiked up the mountain with her friends, she took out her lunch
<u>健行上山</u>   <u>拿出她的午餐來吃</u>
to eat.

❸ 懸崖

Watch out! You're way too close to the edge of the cliff!
<u>你的位置太靠近…</u>

❹ 森林

It's easy to get lost in a forest if you don't have a trail to follow.
<u>沿著小徑走</u>

❺ 溪流

Is that stream water clean enough to drink? I'm so thirsty!
<u>乾淨到可以喝</u>

學更多

❶ look〈看〉・down〈向下〉・mountaintop〈山頂〉・lovely〈美麗的〉・little〈小的〉・
below〈在下方〉

❷ hiked〈hike（健行）的過去式〉・up〈向上〉・took out〈take out（拿出）的過去式〉・
lunch〈午餐〉

❸ watch out〈當心〉・be way too〈太過…〉・close〈接近的〉・edge〈邊緣〉

❹ easy〈容易的〉・get lost〈迷路〉・trail〈小徑〉・follow〈沿著…行進〉

❺ clean〈乾淨的〉・enough〈足夠的〉・drink〈喝〉・thirsty〈口渴的〉

中譯

❶ 如果你從山頂俯瞰，你會看到下方有一個美麗的小峽谷。

❷ Zoe 與她的朋友健行上山之後，她就把午餐拿出來吃了。

❸ 小心！你的位置太靠近懸崖邊了！

❹ 如果沒有沿著小徑走，很容易在森林裡迷路。

❺ 那條溪流的水是否乾淨到可以直接喝？我的口好渴！

109 夏令營

MP3 109

1 camping
[ˈkæmpɪŋ]
(n.) 露營

2 summer camping
[ˈsʌmɚ ˈkæmpɪŋ]
(n.) 夏令營

3 guidebook
[ˈgaɪd.bʊk]
(n.) 導覽手冊

4 cottage
[ˈkɑtɪdʒ]
(n.) 小木屋

5 volunteer
[ˌvɑlənˈtɪr]
(n.) 義工

6 park interpreter
[pɑrk ɪnˈtɜprɪtɚ]
(n.) 園區解說員

NATIONAL PARK

❶ 露營

It's cold this weekend, so I'll load up on firewood for our camping trip.
                          装載木柴

❷ 夏令營

Please be advised that no summer camping will be allowed in this
            謹此告知   禁止舉辦夏令營

national park.

❸ 導覽手冊

Make sure you pick up a guidebook, Charles, so we'll know where we're going.
                                                    我們會到哪裡

❹ 小木屋

The cottage in the forest looks really nice.

❺ 義工

What are you doing this summer, Mike? I'm going to spend the time working
as a volunteer in a national park.   花時間當義工

❻ 園區解說員

In order to accommodate the foreign visitors, there is a park interpreter
                        照顧外國觀光客

provided to help translate.

學更多

❶ cold〈寒冷的〉・weekend〈週末〉・load〈裝載〉・firewood〈木柴〉・trip〈旅行〉
❷ advised〈advise（告知）的過去分詞〉・allowed〈allow（准許）的過去分詞〉
❸ make sure〈確定〉・pick up〈拿起〉・know〈知道〉
❹ forest〈森林〉・look〈看起來〉・nice〈好的〉
❺ spend〈花費〉・working〈work（工作）的 ing 型態〉・as〈作為、以⋯的身分〉
❻ in order to〈為了〉・accommodate〈照顧到〉・foreign〈外國的〉・
interpreter〈解釋者〉・provided〈provide（準備）的過去分詞〉・translate〈翻譯〉

中譯

❶ 這週末會冷，所以去露營我會多帶些木柴。
❷ 謹此告知：在此國家公園內，禁止舉辦夏令營。
❸ Charles，要確定你拿了一份導覽手冊，這樣我們才知道會走去哪裡。
❹ 森林裡的小木屋看起來很不錯。
❺ Mike，你這個暑假打算做什麼？我打算利用這段時間在國家公園當義工。
❻ 為了照顧外國觀光客，有準備一位解說員幫忙翻譯。

110

畫室裡(1)

MP3 110

1 acrylic paint
[æ`krɪlɪk pent]
(n.) 壓克力顏料

2 painter
[`pentɚ]
(n.) 畫家

3 mixing tray
[`mɪksɪŋ tre]
(n.) 調色盤

4 brush
[brʌʃ]
(n.) 畫筆

5 draft
[dræft]
(n.) 草稿 (v.) 打草稿

❶ 壓克力顏料

We have all kinds of acrylic paint in the shop.

各式各樣

❷ 畫家

It is important for a painter to be creative.

富有創造力

❸ 調色盤

You should have all the colors you need on the mixing tray before you start painting.

讓你需要的所有顏色都在調色盤上

❹ 畫筆

You should always clean your brush with water after using it.

用水清洗畫筆

❺ 草稿 / 打草稿

It's always better to get a handle on your topic before you start drafting it.

掌握你的主題

學更多

❶ all〈所有的〉‧ kind〈種類〉‧ acrylic〈丙烯酸的、壓克力的〉‧ paint〈顏料〉‧ shop〈店〉

❷ important〈重要的〉‧ creative〈有創造力的〉

❸ color〈顏色〉‧ mixing〈混合〉‧ tray〈托盤〉‧ before〈在…之前〉‧ start〈開始〉‧ painting〈paint（繪畫）的 ing 型態〉

❹ clean〈清潔〉‧ after〈在…之後〉‧ using〈use（使用）的 ing 型態〉

❺ better〈更好的〉‧ get a handle on...〈理解、掌握…〉‧ topic〈主題〉‧ drafting〈draft（打草稿）的 ing 型態〉

中譯

❶ 我們店裡有各式各樣的壓克力顏料。

❷ 對一名畫家來說，富有創造力是很重要的。

❸ 開始作畫前，你應該讓調色盤上都有你需要的所有顏色。

❹ 每次使用之後，你都應該用水清洗畫筆。

❺ 開始打草稿之前，先掌握你的主題總是比較好。

111

畫室裡(2)

MP3 111

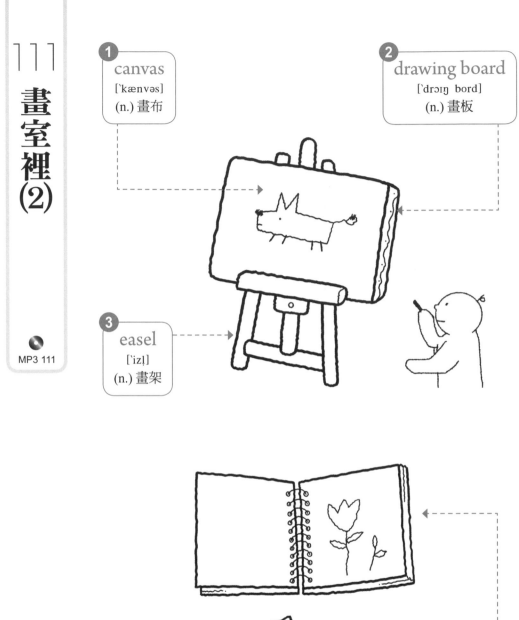

1 canvas
[ˋkænvəs]
(n.) 畫布

2 drawing board
[ˋdrɔɪŋ bord]
(n.) 畫板

3 easel
[ˋizl̩]
(n.) 畫架

4 charcoal
[ˋtʃɑr͵kol]
(n.) 炭筆

5 sketchbook
[ˋskɛtʃ͵bʊk]
(n.) 素描本

❶ 畫布

I bought a lot of canvases for my new art studio.
我的新畫室

❷ 畫板

This looks like a good drawing board. How much is it?
看起來是一個不錯的畫板

❸ 畫架

A multifunctional easel can usually be folded for easy storage.
方便收納

❹ 炭筆

I use charcoal for shading in my art work.
在畫作中畫出明暗對比

❺ 素描本

I always keep my sketchbook handy so that I can draw whenever I feel inspired.
隨身攜帶我的素描本　　　　　　　　　　　　每當我有靈感時

學更多

❶ bought〈buy（購買）的過去式〉‧ a lot of〈許多〉‧ art〈藝術〉‧ studio〈畫室〉

❷ look like〈看起來像…〉‧ drawing〈描繪〉‧ board〈板子〉

❸ multifunctional〈多功能的〉‧ usually〈通常〉‧ folded〈fold（摺疊）的過去分詞〉‧ easy〈容易的〉‧ storage〈收納〉

❹ use〈使用〉‧ shading〈shade（畫陰影）的 ing 型態〉‧ work〈作品〉

❺ keep〈保持〉‧ handy〈手邊的〉‧ so that〈以便〉‧ draw〈畫〉‧ whenever〈每當〉‧ feel〈感覺〉‧ inspired〈有靈感的〉

中譯

❶ 我為我的新畫室添購了許多畫布。

❷ 這個畫板看起來很不錯，它的售價是多少？

❸ 為了方便收納，多功能畫架通常都可以摺疊起來。

❹ 在畫作中，我使用炭筆畫出明暗對比。

❺ 我總是隨身攜帶素描本，以便靈感湧現時，都能隨時創作。

1 stationary bike
[ˋsteʃənˏɛrɪ baɪk]
(n.) 健身腳踏車

2 treadmill
[ˋtrɛdˏmɪl]
(n.) 跑步機

3 dumbbell
[ˋdʌmˏbɛl]
(n.) 啞鈴

4 power rack
[ˋpauə ræk]
(n.) 舉重架

5 yoga
[ˋjogə]
(n.) 瑜珈

6 personal trainer
[ˋpɝsn̩l ˋtrenə]
(n.) 私人教練

❶ 健身腳踏車
I prefer to use the stationary bike for my warm up.
作為我的暖身運動

❷ 跑步機
I usually spend the first 15 minutes on the treadmill when I work out.
先花費 15 分鐘

❸ 啞鈴
Dumbbell exercises are highly effective for building shoulders muscles.
強化肩膀的肌肉

❹ 舉重架
Power racks help weightlifters work out safely and efficiently.
安全且有效率地健身

❺ 瑜珈
Some people believe that yoga can help both your body and mind.
對你的身心都有幫助

❻ 私人教練
A personal trainer will teach you how to train appropriately.
如何正確地鍛鍊

學更多

❶ prefer〈較喜歡〉・stationary〈不動的〉・bike〈腳踏車〉・warm up〈暖身運動〉
❷ usually〈通常〉・spend〈花費〉・first〈最先的〉・work out〈健身〉
❸ effective〈有效的〉・building〈build（增長）的 ing 型態〉・shoulder〈肩膀〉・muscle〈肌肉〉
❹ rack〈架子〉・weightlifter〈舉重者〉・safely〈安全地〉・efficiently〈有效率地〉
❺ believe〈相信〉・both〈兩者都〉・body〈身體〉・mind〈心〉
❻ personal〈個人的、私人的〉・trainer〈教練〉・train〈訓練〉・appropriately〈適當地〉

中譯

❶ 我比較喜歡踩健身腳踏車作為暖身運動。
❷ 我健身時，通常會先在跑步機上跑 15 分鐘。
❸ 啞鈴運動對於強化肩膀肌肉是非常有效的。
❹ 舉重架可以幫助舉重的人安全又有效率地健身。
❺ 有些人相信瑜珈對於身心都有幫助。
❻ 私人教練會教導你如何正確地鍛鍊身體。

113

健身中心設施

MP3 113

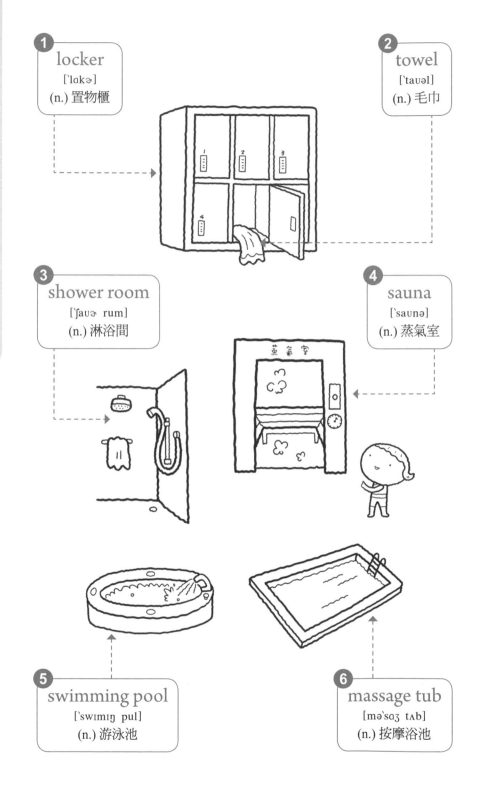

1 locker
['lɑkɚ]
(n.) 置物櫃

2 towel
['tauəl]
(n.) 毛巾

3 shower room
['ʃauɚ rum]
(n.) 淋浴間

4 sauna
['saunə]
(n.) 蒸氣室

蒸氣室

5 swimming pool
['swɪmɪŋ pul]
(n.) 游泳池

6 massage tub
[mə'sɑʒ tʌb]
(n.) 按摩浴池

❶ 置物櫃

It is safer and more convenient to lock up your personal belongings in the locker when you work out. 把你的私人物品鎖在置物櫃

❷ 毛巾

You should bring a towel with you to the sauna.
攜帶一條毛巾

❸ 淋浴間

I always take a quick shower in the shower room after a workout.
快速沖澡

❹ 蒸氣室

Before you go into the sauna, you should take a shower first.
進入蒸氣室

❺ 游泳池

The swimming pool is usually crowded during the summer.

❻ 按摩浴池

I like to soak in the massage tub after a long day at work to relax.
工作一整天

學更多

❶ convenient〈方便的〉‧ lock up〈上鎖〉‧ belongings〈攜帶物品〉‧ work out〈健身〉
❷ should〈應該〉‧ bring〈帶來〉
❸ always〈總是〉‧ quick〈快速的〉‧ shower〈淋浴〉‧ workout〈健身〉
❹ before〈在…之前〉‧ go into〈進入〉‧ first〈首先〉
❺ swimming〈游泳〉‧ pool〈游泳池〉‧ crowded〈擁擠的〉‧ during〈在…的整個期間〉
❻ soak〈浸泡〉‧ massage〈按摩〉‧ tub〈浴缸〉‧ relax〈放鬆〉

中譯

❶ 當你健身時,將私人物品鎖在置物櫃會更安全、更方便。
❷ 去蒸氣室時,你應該攜帶一條毛巾。
❸ 健身之後,我都會在淋浴間快速地沖個澡。
❹ 進入蒸氣室之前,你應該要先沖個澡。
❺ 夏季時,游泳池通常很擁擠。
❻ 辛苦工作一整天之後,我喜歡在按摩浴池裡泡澡來放鬆自己。

114

田徑場競技

MP3 114

1 hurdle
[`hɝdḷ]
(n.) 跨欄

2 pole vault
[pol vɔlt]
(n.) 撐竿跳

3 vaulting box
[`vɔltɪŋ bɑks]
(n.) 跳箱

4 long jump
[lɔŋ dʒʌmp]
(n.) 跳遠

5 mattress
[`mætrɪs]
(n.) 安全墊

6 high jump
[haɪ dʒʌmp]
(n.) 跳高

❶ 跨欄

The horse jumped over the hurdles with ease.
越過跨欄

❷ 撐竿跳

Running ability is the key to doing well in the pole vault.
是做得好的關鍵

❸ 跳箱

It is much harder than it seems to straddle over a vaulting box.
兩腿叉開跨越跳箱

❹ 跳遠

When you do long jump, you should try to jump as far as possible.
跳得越遠越好

❺ 安全墊

There is a very thick mattress so it's perfectly safe to jump down.
絕對安全的

❻ 跳高

If you want to do high jump well, you need strong and flexible back muscles.
強壯而柔軟的背部肌肉

學更多

❶ horse〈馬〉・jumped〈jump（跳躍）的過去式〉・over〈越過〉・with ease〈從容地〉

❷ ability〈能力〉・key〈關鍵〉・well〈很好地〉・pole〈竿〉・vault〈撐物跳躍〉

❸ seem〈看起來〉・straddle〈兩腿叉開〉・vaulting〈跳越〉・box〈箱子〉

❹ long〈遠的〉・try〈試圖〉・far〈遠的〉・as...as possible〈盡可能、愈…愈好〉

❺ thick〈厚的〉・perfectly〈絕對地〉・down〈向下〉

❻ high〈高的〉・strong〈強壯的〉・flexible〈柔軟的〉・back〈背部〉・muscle〈肌肉〉

中譯

❶ 這匹馬輕而易舉地躍過了跨欄。

❷ 跑步能力，是撐竿跳跳得好的關鍵。

❸ 實際跳跳箱比看起來困難多了！

❹ 跳遠時，你應該試著跳得越遠越好。

❺ 下方有一塊很厚的安全墊，所以往下跳是絕對安全的。

❻ 如果你希望跳高跳得好，你必須擁有強壯而柔軟的背部肌肉。

115

賽跑

MP3 115

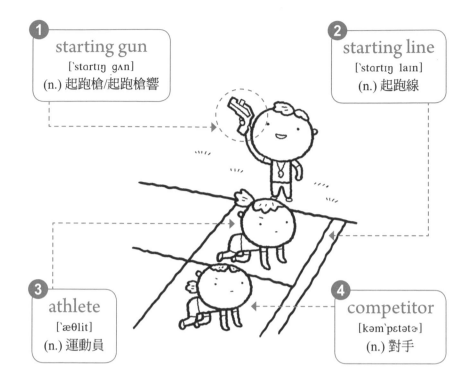

1 starting gun
[ˋstɑrtɪŋ gʌn]
(n.) 起跑槍/起跑槍響

2 starting line
[ˋstɑrtɪŋ laɪn]
(n.) 起跑線

3 athlete
[ˋæθlɪt]
(n.) 運動員

4 competitor
[kəmˋpɛtətɚ]
(n.) 對手

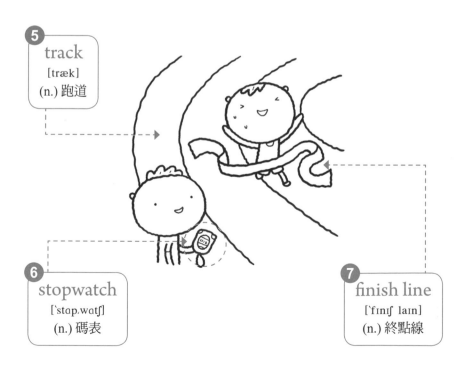

5 track
[træk]
(n.) 跑道

6 stopwatch
[ˋstɑp͵wɑtʃ]
(n.) 碼表

7 finish line
[ˋfɪnɪʃ laɪn]
(n.) 終點線

❶ 起跑槍 / 起跑槍響
You should only start running when you hear the starting gun.

❷ 起跑線
All the runners should standby at the starting line in 5 minutes.
在起跑線預備

❸ 運動員
The athlete won two gold medals in the Olympics.
贏得兩面金牌

❹ 對手
It's not always bad to have competitors because you might learn something
並不總是壞事
from them.

❺ 跑道
He runs around the track every morning to stay in shape.
保持良好的健康狀況

❻ 碼表
A stopwatch will accurately record your time.

❼ 終點線
Even though he sprained his ankle, he still made it to the finish line.
成功抵達終點線

學更多

❶ only〈只〉・running〈run（跑）的 ing 型態〉・starting〈開始〉・gun〈槍〉
❷ runner〈賽跑者〉・standby〈準備行動〉・line〈線條〉・minute〈分鐘〉
❸ gold〈金的〉・medal〈獎章〉・Olympics〈奧林匹克運動會、奧運〉
❹ always〈總是〉・bad〈壞的〉・learn〈學習〉・something〈某事〉
❺ around〈環繞〉・morning〈早晨〉・stay〈保持〉・in shape〈處於良好的健康狀況〉
❻ accurately〈準確地〉・record〈記錄〉
❼ even though〈即使〉・sprained〈sprain（扭傷）的過去式〉・ankle〈腳踝〉

中譯

❶ 只有聽到起跑槍響時，你才能起跑。
❷ 所有的跑者都必須在五分鐘內，到起跑線準備就緒。
❸ 這名運動員在奧運中勇奪兩面金牌。
❹ 有對手不見得是壞事，因為你也許能從他們身上學到東西。
❺ 他每天早上都會繞著跑道跑步，藉以保持身體健康。
❻ 碼表可以準確地記錄你所花費的時間。
❼ 即使扭傷腳踝，他仍然成功抵達終點線。

116

游泳池(1)

MP3 116

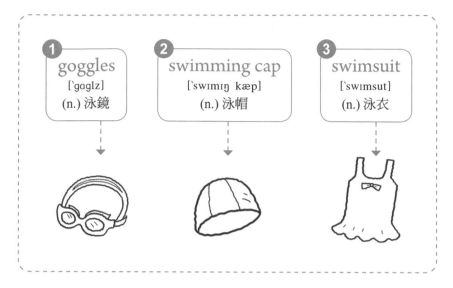

1 goggles
['gɑglz]
(n.) 泳鏡

2 swimming cap
['swɪmɪŋ kæp]
(n.) 泳帽

3 swimsuit
['swɪmsut]
(n.) 泳衣

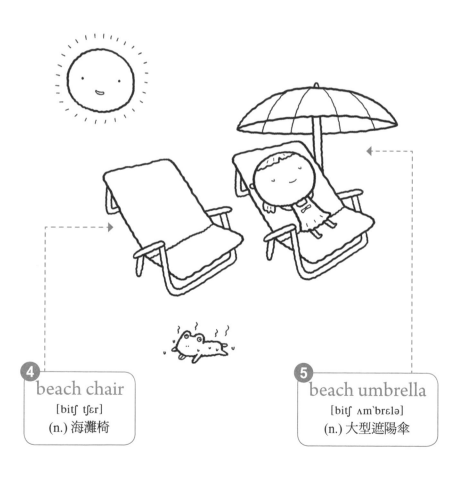

4 beach chair
[bitʃ tʃɛr]
(n.) 海灘椅

5 beach umbrella
[bitʃ ʌm`brɛlə]
(n.) 大型遮陽傘

240

❶ 泳鏡

You should protect your eyes by wearing goggles.
戴泳鏡

❷ 泳帽

You have to wear a swimming cap when you go to the public swimming pool.
必須戴泳帽

❸ 泳衣

Please put on your swimsuit before you go into the swimming pool.
穿上你的泳衣　　　　　　　　　　　進入游泳池

❹ 海灘椅

Beach chairs are perfect for people who enjoy sunbathing on the beach.
喜愛在海灘做日光浴的人

❺ 大型遮陽傘

Beach umbrellas block the sunlight and help prevent sunburn.
阻擋陽光　　　　　　　幫助防止曬傷

學更多

❶ should〈應該〉‧ protect〈保護〉‧ wearing〈wear（配戴）的 ing 型態〉

❷ swimming〈游泳〉‧ cap〈帽子〉‧ public〈公眾的〉‧ pool〈游泳池〉

❸ put on〈穿上〉‧ before〈在…之前〉‧ go into〈進入〉

❹ beach〈海灘〉‧ chair〈椅子〉‧ perfect〈最適當的〉‧ enjoy〈喜愛〉‧
sunbathing〈sunbathe（做日光浴）的 ing 型態〉

❺ umbrella〈傘〉‧ block〈阻擋〉‧ sunlight〈陽光〉‧ help〈幫助〉‧ prevent〈防止〉‧
sunburn〈曬傷〉

中譯

❶ 你應該要戴泳鏡保護你的眼睛。

❷ 當你到公共泳池游泳時，必須戴上泳帽。

❸ 進入泳池之前，請先換上你的泳衣。

❹ 海灘椅非常適合那些喜愛在海灘做日光浴的人。

❺ 大型遮陽傘可以阻擋陽光，並有助於防止曬傷。

1 kickboard
[ˈkɪkˌbord]
(n.) 浮板

2 children's pool
[ˈtʃɪldrənz pul]
(n.) 兒童池

3 diving board
[ˈdaɪvɪŋ bord]
(n.) 跳板

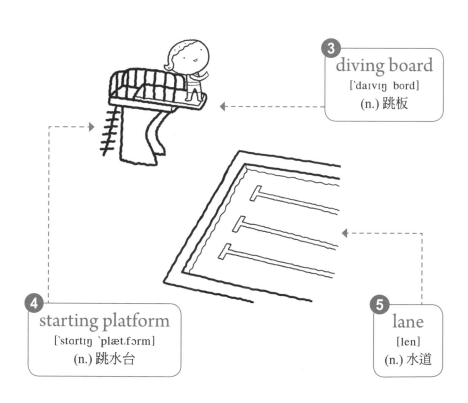

4 starting platform
[ˈstɑrtɪŋ ˈplætˌfɔrm]
(n.) 跳水台

5 lane
[len]
(n.) 水道

❶ 浮板

If you just started learning to swim, you should use a kickboard in the pool.
剛開始學游泳

❷ 兒童池

Please make sure the kids stay in the children's pool only.
只待在兒童池裡

❸ 跳板

There should not be a diving board if the water is not deep enough.
不應該有　　　　　　　　　　　　水不夠深

❹ 跳水台

The starting platform should be used by trained swimmers only.
只有受過訓練的游泳選手能夠使用

❺ 水道

Typically, a pool is divided into three or more lanes.
被劃分成三個或更多的水道

學更多

❶ just〈剛要〉‧ started〈start（開始）的過去式〉‧ learning〈learn（學習）的 ing 型態〉‧ swim〈游泳〉‧ pool〈游泳池〉

❷ make sure〈確定〉‧ kid〈小孩〉‧ stay〈停留〉‧ children〈child（孩童）的複數〉‧ only〈只〉

❸ should〈應該〉‧ diving〈跳水〉‧ board〈板子〉‧ deep〈深的〉‧ enough〈足夠的〉

❹ starting〈開始〉‧ platform〈平台〉‧ trained〈受過訓練的〉‧ swimmer〈游泳者〉

❺ typically〈典型地〉‧ divided into〈divide into（劃分成⋯）的過去分詞〉

中譯

❶ 如果你剛開始學游泳，在泳池裡你就應該使用浮板。

❷ 請確定小孩子都只待在兒童池。

❸ 如果水不夠深，那個地方就不該設置跳板。

❹ 只有受過訓練的游泳選手，才能使用跳水台。

❺ 通常，游泳池會被劃分出 3 個以上的水道。

1 locker
[ˈlɑkɚ]
(n.) 置物櫃

2 clothes for changing
[kloz fɔr ˈtʃendʒɪŋ]
(n.) 換洗衣物

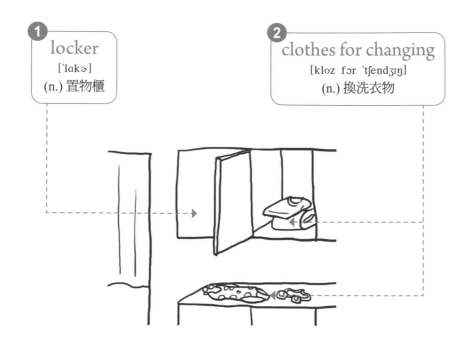

3 mirror
[ˈmɪrɚ]
(n.) 鏡子

4 hair dryer
[hɛr ˈdraɪɚ]
(n.) 吹風機

5 hook
[hʊk]
(n.) 掛鉤

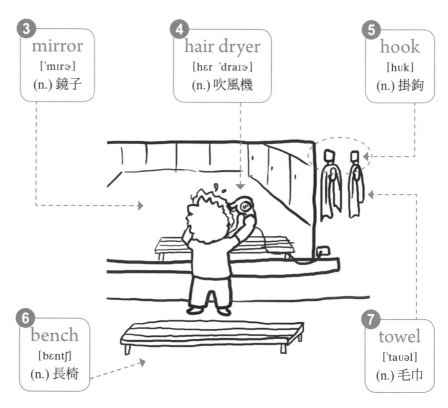

6 bench
[bɛntʃ]
(n.) 長椅

7 towel
[ˈtaʊəl]
(n.) 毛巾

❶ 置物櫃

You can leave your stuff in the locker when you go swim.
把你的東西留在置物櫃裡

❷ 換洗衣物

Did you remember to bring clothes for changing?

❸ 鏡子

I need to use the mirror when I blow dry my hair.
用吹風機吹乾我的頭髮

❹ 吹風機

There are hair dryers in the changing room if you want to use them.

❺ 掛鉤

You can hang your towel on the hook in the shower room.
把你的毛巾掛在掛鉤上

❻ 長椅

You can sit on the bench when you put your shoes on.
穿上你的鞋子

❼ 毛巾

I always bring my own towel when I go swimming.

學更多

❶ leave〈留下〉‧ stuff〈物品〉‧ swim〈游泳〉
❷ remember〈記得〉‧ bring〈帶來〉‧ clothes〈衣服〉‧ changing〈change（更換）的 ing 型態〉
❸ use〈使用〉‧ blow dry〈用吹風機吹乾〉‧ hair〈頭髮〉
❹ dryer〈吹風機〉‧ changing room〈更衣室〉
❺ hang〈把⋯掛起〉‧ towel〈毛巾〉‧ shower room〈淋浴間〉
❻ sit〈坐〉‧ put on〈穿上〉‧ shoes〈shoe（鞋子）的複數〉
❼ bring〈帶來〉‧ own〈自己的〉‧ swimming〈swim（游泳）的 ing 型態〉

中譯

❶ 當你去游泳時，可以把東西放在置物櫃裡。
❷ 你有記得帶來換洗衣物嗎？
❸ 使用吹風機吹乾頭髮的時候，我需要照鏡子。
❹ 如果你需要使用吹風機，更衣室裡面有。
❺ 你可以把你的毛巾掛在淋浴間的掛鉤上。
❻ 當你要穿鞋子的時候，可以坐在長椅上。
❼ 我每次去游泳時，都會攜帶自己的毛巾。

119

泳池更衣室(2)

MP3 119

1 faucet
[ˋfɔsɪt]
(n.) 水龍頭

2 shower head
[ˋʃaʊɚ hɛd]
(n.) 蓮蓬頭

3 shower room
[ˋʃaʊɚ rum]
(n.) 淋浴間

4 basin
[ˋbesn̩]
(n.) 洗手台

5 slip-proof mat
[ˋslɪpˏpruf mæt]
(n.) 防滑墊

6 slippers
[ˋslɪpɚz]
(n.) 拖鞋

7 drain
[dren]
(n.) 排水口

❶ 水龍頭

Please remember to turn off the faucet after every use.
在每一次使用後

❷ 蓮蓬頭

You can adjust the height of the shower head as you would like.
依照你的需要

❸ 淋浴間

There are usually a lot of shower rooms in the changing room.

❹ 洗手台

Please place your swimsuit in the basin and let it soak for 10 minutes.
讓它浸泡 10 分鐘

❺ 防滑墊

There is a slip-proof mat to prevent you from slipping.
防止你滑倒

❻ 拖鞋

Would you like some slippers to wear inside the house?
室內

❼ 排水口

The drain in the shower room needs repairing.

學更多

❶ remember〈記得〉・turn off〈關掉〉・every〈每一〉・use〈使用〉
❷ adjust〈調整〉・height〈高度〉・shower〈淋浴器〉・head〈物品的頭部〉
❸ usually〈通常〉・a lot of〈許多〉・shower〈淋浴〉・changing room〈更衣室〉
❹ place〈放置〉・swimsuit〈泳衣〉・soak〈浸泡〉・minute〈分鐘〉
❺ proof〈防…的〉・mat〈墊子〉・prevent A from B〈防止 A 避免 B〉・
  slipping〈slip（滑倒）的 ing 型態〉
❻ wear〈穿著〉・inside〈在裡面〉
❼ need〈需要〉・repairing〈repair（修理）的 ing 型態〉

中譯

❶ 請記得每一次使用水龍頭後,都要把它關好。
❷ 你可以依照自己的需要,調整蓮蓬頭的高度。
❸ 更衣室裡,通常有很多淋浴間。
❹ 請將你的泳衣放入洗手台,讓它在水裡浸泡 10 分鐘。
❺ 那裡有一個防滑墊,用來防止你滑倒。
❻ 在室內你需要穿拖鞋嗎?
❼ 淋浴間的排水口需要修理。

1 boxer
[ˋbɑksə]
(n.) 拳擊手

2 headgear
[ˋhɛd͵gɪr]
(n.) 頭部護具

3 boxing gloves
[ˋbɑksɪŋ glʌvz]
(n.) 拳擊手套

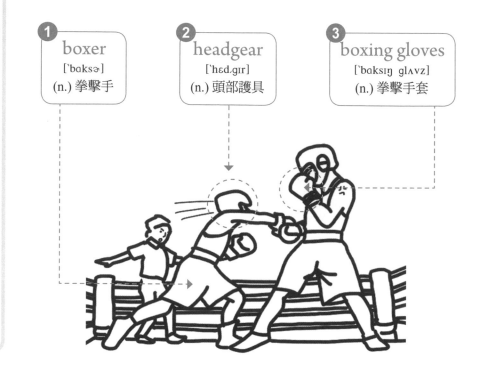

4 paramedic
[͵pærəˋmɛdɪk]
(n.) 場邊救護人員

5 stretcher
[ˋstrɛtʃə]
(n.) 擔架

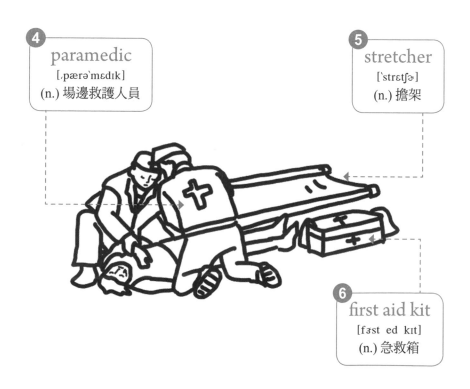

6 first aid kit
[fɝst ed kɪt]
(n.) 急救箱

❶ 拳擊手
All professional boxers follow a special diet and nutrition program.
特殊的飲食營養計劃

❷ 頭部護具
Headgear will protect your head from getting hurt.
受到傷害

❸ 拳擊手套
Boxers need to wear boxing gloves during boxing matches.
在進行拳擊比賽時

❹ 場邊救護人員
Paramedics can be found at boxing matches in case of emergency medical
可以找到場邊救護人員　　　　　　　　　　萬一、如果發生
situations.

❺ 擔架
The sick old woman was carried away on a stretcher.
被搬走

❻ 急救箱
Everyone should keep a first aid kit at home in case of emergency.
有急救箱

學更多

❶ professional〈職業的〉・diet〈飲食〉・nutrition〈營養〉・program〈計劃〉
❷ prevent A from B〈保護 A 避免 B〉・head〈頭部〉・getting〈get（得到）的 ing 型態〉
❸ boxing〈拳擊〉・glove〈手套〉・during〈在…的整個期間〉・match〈比賽〉
❹ found〈find（發現）的過去分詞〉・emergency〈緊急狀況〉・medical〈醫療的〉・
　situation〈情況〉
❺ sick〈生病的〉・old〈老的〉・carried away〈carry away（搬走）的過去式〉
❻ keep〈持有〉・first〈最先的〉・aid〈救助〉・kit〈工具箱〉

中譯

❶ 所有的職業拳擊手，都遵循特殊的飲食營養計劃。
❷ 頭部護具可以保護你的頭部，避免受到傷害。
❸ 拳擊手在比賽時，必須戴上拳擊手套。
❹ 萬一發生緊急醫療狀況，拳擊比賽現場都能找到場邊救護人員。
❺ 生病的老太太躺在擔架上被抬走了。
❻ 每個人家裡都該有急救箱，以防萬一發生緊急狀況。

拳擊賽(2)

MP3 121

1 winner
[ˋwɪnɚ]
(n.) 贏家

2 referee
[ˌrɛfəˋri]
(n.) 裁判

3 lose
[luz]
(v.) 輸/戰敗

4 boxing ring
[ˋbɑksɪŋ rɪŋ]
(n.) 拳擊台

5 rope
[rop]
(n.) 圍繩

❶ 贏家

The winner for this match will be awarded one million dollars!
將被授予

❷ 裁判

Who is the referee for the boxing match?
拳擊賽

❸ 輸 / 戰敗

Our team lost by five points.
以五分之差

❹ 拳擊台

The boxers must stay in the boxing ring throughout a boxing match.
整場拳擊比賽

❺ 圍繩

There are ropes around the ring to prevent the competitors from falling.
擂台四周環繞圍繩

學更多

❶ match〈比賽〉‧awarded〈award（授予）的過去分詞〉‧million〈百萬〉

❷ boxing〈拳擊〉

❸ our〈我們的〉‧team〈隊伍〉‧lost〈lose（輸）的過去式〉‧point〈分數〉

❹ boxer〈拳擊手〉‧stay〈停留〉‧ring〈擂台〉‧throughout〈從頭到尾〉

❺ there are...〈有…〉‧around〈圍繞〉‧prevent A from B〈防止 A 避免 B〉‧
competitor〈選手〉‧falling〈fall（墜落）的 ing 型態〉

中譯

❶ 這場比賽的贏家，將獲得一百萬元的獎金。

❷ 這場拳擊賽的裁判是誰？

❸ 我們這隊以五分之差輸了。

❹ 在整場拳賽中，拳擊手都必須留在拳擊台上。

❺ 擂台四周環繞圍繩，以免選手摔下擂台。

122

拳擊賽(3)

MP3 122

1 straight punch
[stret pʌntʃ]
(n.) 直拳

2 uppercut
[ˈʌpɚˌkʌt]
(n.) 上鉤拳

3 left hook
[lɛft hʊk]
(n.) 左鉤拳

4 punch
[pʌntʃ]
(n.) 拳頭/出拳

5 right hook
[raɪt hʊk]
(n.) 右鉤拳

❶ 直拳

The straight punch is an effective blow to deal a fighting opponent.
有效的一擊　　　　　　戰鬥的對手

❷ 上鉤拳

The uppercut is a punch used in boxing that usually aims at the opponent's chin.
一種用於拳擊的拳法　　　　瞄準對手的下巴

❸ 左鉤拳

The opponent countered the attack with a left hook to the temple and won the game.
一記擊中太陽穴的左鉤拳

❹ 拳頭 / 出拳

John was so angry at his boxing partner that he threw a punch at his face.
對他的拳擊搭檔很生氣　　　　朝他的臉部揮拳

❺ 右鉤拳

The boxer swayed to the right and ducked under a right hook.
偏向右側且蹲低

學更多

❶ straight〈直的〉・effective〈有效的〉・blow〈一擊〉・deal〈予以攻擊〉・
fighting〈戰鬥的〉・opponent〈對手〉

❷ used〈use（使用）的過去分詞〉・boxing〈拳擊〉・aim〈瞄準〉・chin〈下巴〉

❸ countered〈counter（還擊）的過去式〉・attack〈攻擊〉・left〈左邊〉・hook〈鉤拳〉・
temple〈太陽穴〉・won〈win（獲勝）的過去式〉

❹ angry〈生氣的〉・partner〈搭檔〉・threw〈throw（揮拳）的過去式〉・face〈臉〉

❺ swayed〈sway（傾斜、轉向）的過去式〉・right〈右邊〉・
ducked〈duck（躲避）的過去式〉・under〈在…下方〉

中譯

❶ 直拳是用來攻擊對戰對手的有效一擊。

❷ 上鉤拳是一種拳擊中使用的拳法，通常會瞄準對手的下巴出拳。

❸ 對手回擊一記擊中太陽穴的左鉤拳，贏得了比賽。

❹ 約翰對他的拳擊搭檔很生氣，朝他臉部揍了一拳。

❺ 這名拳擊手將身體偏向右側且蹲低，躲過了一記在他上方的右鉤拳。

123

農牧場(1)

MP3 123

1 tree
[tri]
(n.) 樹木

2 mower
[ˈmoɚ]
(n.) 除草機

3 lawn
[lɔn]
(n.) 草地/草坪

4 fruit farm
[frut fɑrm]
(n.) 果園

5 vegetable garden
[ˈvɛdʒətəbḷ ˈgɑrdṇ]
(n.) 菜園

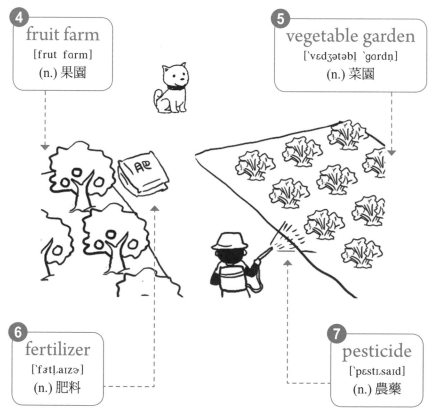

6 fertilizer
[ˈfɝtḷˌaɪzɚ]
(n.) 肥料

7 pesticide
[ˈpɛstɪˌsaɪd]
(n.) 農藥

❶ 樹木

I have never met anyone who doesn't love trees.

我從未遇見

❷ 除草機

My gardener taught me how to work the mower properly.

❸ 草地 / 草坪

You need to mow the lawn properly to keep it nice and healthy.

適當地替草坪除草

❹ 果園

My grandfather has a big fruit farm at his house in the country.

在他鄉下的房子

❺ 菜園

We grow organic vegetables in our vegetable garden.

我們種植有機蔬菜

❻ 肥料

You should use organic fertilizer to grow healthy plants.

種植健康的農作物

❼ 農藥

You should think twice about using pesticide, because it kills both the bad and the good bugs.

重新考慮　　　　　　　　　　　　　　　同時殺死害蟲和益蟲

學更多

❶ never〈從未〉‧ met〈meet（遇見）的過去分詞〉‧ love〈喜愛〉
❷ gardener〈園丁〉‧ taught〈teach（教導）的過去式〉‧ work〈操作〉‧ properly〈正確地〉
❸ mow〈除草〉‧ properly〈恰當地〉‧ keep〈維持〉‧ healthy〈健康的〉
❹ fruit〈水果〉‧ farm〈農場〉‧ country〈鄉下〉
❺ grow〈種植、栽培〉‧ organic〈有機的〉‧ vegetable〈蔬菜〉‧ garden〈菜園〉
❻ use〈使用〉‧ plant〈農作物〉
❼ twice〈兩次〉‧ about〈關於〉‧ kill〈殺害〉‧ both〈兩者都〉‧ bug〈蟲子〉

中譯

❶ 我從未遇見不喜愛樹木的人。
❷ 我的園丁教我如何正確地操作除草機。
❸ 你必須適當地替草坪除草，才能維持它的美觀與健康。
❹ 我爺爺在鄉下的房子，有一個大果園。
❺ 我們在自己的菜園種植有機蔬菜。
❻ 你應該使用有機肥料來栽培健康的農作物。
❼ 你應該重新考慮是否使用農藥，因為它會同時殺死害蟲和益蟲。

124

農牧場(2)

MP3 124

1 livestock
['laɪv.stɑk]
(n.) 家畜

2 milking machine
['mɪlkɪŋ məˈʃin]
(n.) 擠奶器

3 feed
[fid]
(n.) 飼料

4 poultry
['poltrɪ]
(n.) 家禽

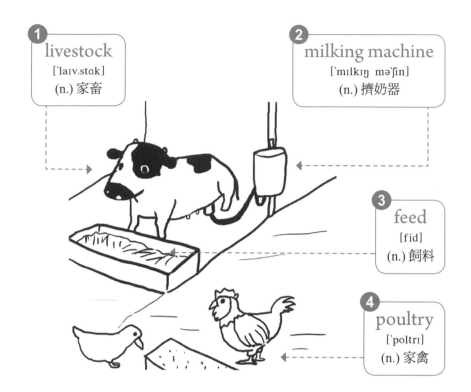

5 pickup truck
['pɪkˌʌp trʌk]
(n.) 小貨車

6 fence
[fɛns]
(n.) 籬笆

7 owner
['onɚ]
(n.) 主人

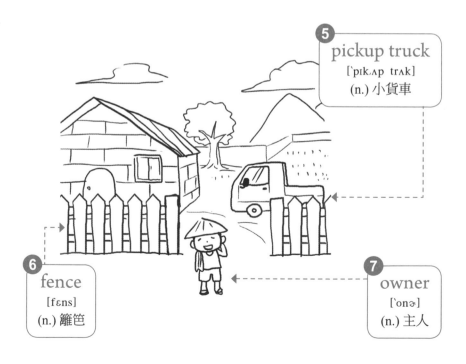

❶ 家畜

The livestock on the farm are grazing in the meadow.

❷ 擠奶器

There are several milking machines on the farm for cows, goats and sheep.

❸ 飼料

Corn is used as animal feed on the farm.
<u>被當作…使用</u>

❹ 家禽

The farm breeds a wide range of poultry.
<u>種類廣泛的…</u>

❺ 小貨車

The farmers use pickup trucks to deliver fresh farm products to the market every day.
<u>運送新鮮的農產品</u>

❻ 籬笆

He built a fence around his rose garden.
<u>在他的玫瑰園四周</u>

❼ 主人

The owner of the farm is a retired millionaire.
<u>退休的百萬富翁</u>

學更多

❶ farm〈農場〉‧ grazing〈graze（吃草）的 ing 型態〉‧ meadow〈牧草地〉
❷ milking〈擠奶〉‧ machine〈機器〉‧ cow〈乳牛〉‧ goat〈山羊〉‧ sheep〈綿羊〉
❸ corn〈玉米〉‧ used〈use（使用）的過去分詞〉‧ as〈當作〉‧ animal〈牲口〉
❹ breed〈飼養〉‧ wide〈廣泛的〉‧ range〈類別〉
❺ pickup〈小卡車〉‧ truck〈卡車〉‧ deliver〈運送〉‧ product〈產品〉‧ market〈市場〉
❻ built〈build（建築）的過去式〉‧ around〈圍繞〉‧ rose〈玫瑰〉‧ garden〈花園〉
❼ retired〈退休的〉‧ millionaire〈百萬富翁〉

中譯

❶ 農場裡的家畜正在草地上吃草。
❷ 農場裡有好幾種擠奶器，用來幫乳牛、山羊、及綿羊擠奶。
❸ 農場裡，玉米被用來作為牲口的飼料。
❹ 這間農場飼養了種類多樣的家禽。
❺ 農夫每天駕駛小貨車，將新鮮的農產品運送到市場。
❻ 他在他的玫瑰園四周築起了一道籬笆。
❼ 這間農場的主人，是一位退休的百萬富翁。

125 宇宙中 (1)

1 galaxy
['gæləksɪ]
(n.) 星系

宇宙的基本單位。

2 black hole
[blæk hol]
(n.) 黑洞

恆星於核心燃料耗盡後，所產生的重力塌縮現象。

包含太陽、以及以太陽為中心，受太陽引力影響環繞運行的天體。

3 Solar System
['solɚ 'sɪstəm]
(n.) 太陽系

4 natural satellite
['nætʃərəl 'sætḷ.aɪt]
(n.)（天然）衛星

環繞行星周圍運行的天體。

5 star
[stɑr]
(n.) 恆星/星星

本身能散發光和熱的天體。太陽就是距離地球最近的恆星。

在宇宙中依一定軌道，環繞恆星周圍運行的天體。如金星、木星等。

6 comet
['kɑmɪt]
(n.) 彗星

太陽系形成之初遺留的小天體，俗稱為「掃把星」或「掃帚星」。

7 planet
['plænɪt]
(n.) 行星

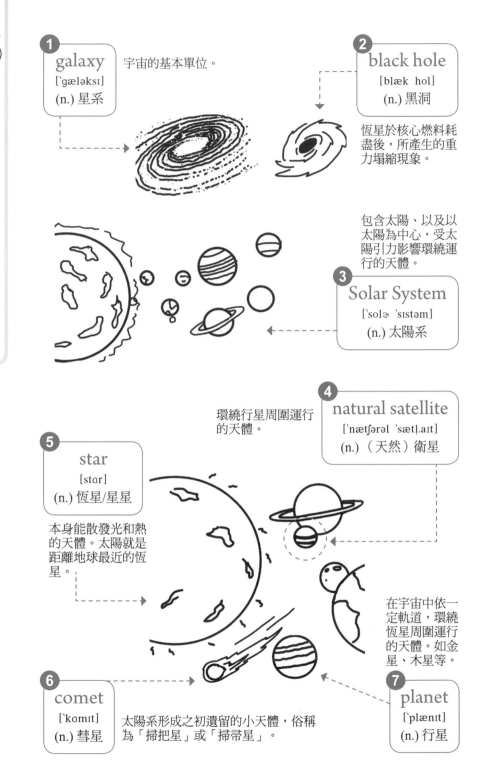

❶ 星系

These galaxy images are so beautiful!

❷ 黑洞

A black hole is a place in space where the pull of gravity is so strong that anything going near it will be sucked in.
　　　　　　任何靠近它的事物

❸ 太陽系

Did you know the Solar System was formed over four billion years ago?
　　　　　　　　　　　　　　　　超過四十億年以前

❹（天然）衛星

The Moon is one of many natural satellites in outer space.

❺ 恆星／星星

The stars in the sky are shining so brightly tonight.
　　　　　　　　　　　閃閃發亮

❻ 彗星

We can see comets only when they come close to the Earth.
　　　　　　　　　　　　　　　接近地球

❼ 行星

The planets move around the Sun.
　　　　　繞著太陽運轉

學更多

❶ image〈影像〉・beautiful〈美麗的〉
❷ space〈太空〉・pull〈引力〉・gravity〈重力〉・sucked〈suck（吞沒）的過去分詞〉
❸ solar〈太陽的〉・system〈體系〉・formed〈form（形成）的過去分詞〉・billion〈十億〉
❹ Moon〈月球〉・natural〈天然的〉・satellite〈衛星〉・outer space〈外太空〉
❺ sky〈天空〉・shining〈shine（發亮）的 ing 型態〉・brightly〈閃亮地〉
❻ see〈看〉・only〈只〉・come〈來〉・close〈接近的〉・Earth〈地球〉
❼ move〈移動〉・around〈環繞〉

中譯

❶ 這些星系的影像真美！
❷ 黑洞是太空中一個重力強大的地方，它的重力強到任何靠近它的東西都會被捲入。
❸ 你知道太陽系是在四十億年前形成的嗎？
❹ 月球是外太空中眾多衛星的其中之一。
❺ 今晚夜空中的星星閃閃發光。
❻ 只有當彗星接近地球時，我們才能看見它們。
❼ 行星繞著太陽運轉。

宇宙中(2)

MP3 126

1 UFO (unidentified flying object)
[ˌʌnaɪˈdɛtɪˌfaɪd ˈflaɪɪŋ ˈɑbdʒɪkt]
(n.) 飛碟

2 artificial satellite
[ˌɑrtəˈfɪʃəl ˈsætḷˌaɪt]
(n.) 人造衛星

3 alien
[ˈelɪən]
(n.) 外星人

4 astronaut
[ˈæstrəˌnɔt]
(n.) 太空人

5 space station
[spes ˈsteʃən]
(n.) 太空站

6 spacecraft
[ˈspesˌkræft]
(n.) 太空船

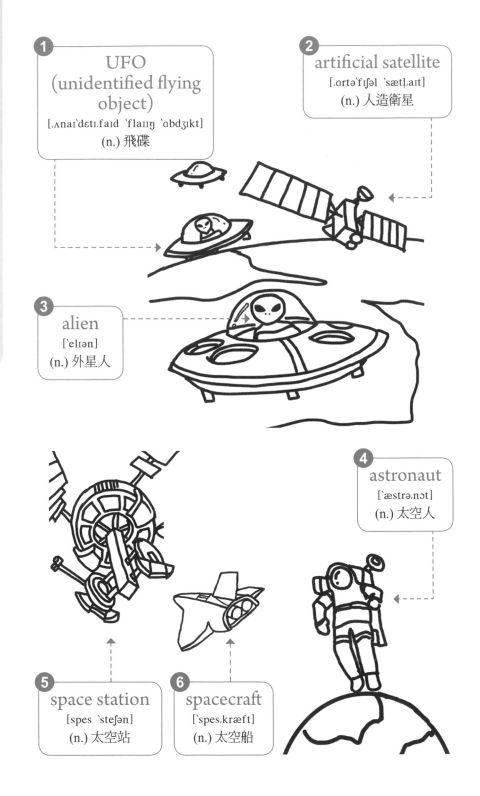

❶ 飛碟
Have you ever seen a UFO before?!

❷ 人造衛星
The Soviet Union launched the first artificial satellite back in 1957.
發射第一枚人造衛星

❸ 外星人
Do you believe that aliens exist?
你相信…嗎？

❹ 太空人
Neil Armstrong is the first astronaut to ever walk on the Moon.
曾經在月球上漫步

❺ 太空站
I would love to go to the space station one day.
我想要做…

❻ 太空船
Spacecraft are vehicles used to fly in outer space.
用來飛行

學更多

❶ ever〈至今〉‧ seen〈see（看）的過去分詞〉‧ unidentified〈未辨別出的〉‧ flying〈飛行的〉‧ object〈物體〉

❷ The Soviet Union〈蘇聯〉‧ launched〈launch（發射）的過去式〉‧ artificial〈人造的〉‧ satellite〈衛星〉‧ back in〈追溯到過去的某個時間點〉

❸ believe〈相信〉‧ exist〈存在〉

❹ first〈第一的〉‧ ever〈曾經、從來〉‧ walk〈走〉‧ Moon〈月球〉

❺ would〈想〉‧ space〈太空〉‧ station〈站〉‧ one day〈有一天〉

❻ vehicle〈飛行器〉‧ fly〈飛行〉‧ outer space〈外太空〉

中譯

❶ 你之前曾經看過飛碟嗎？
❷ 蘇聯在 1957 年發射了第一枚人造衛星。
❸ 你相信外星人存在嗎？
❹ 尼爾阿姆斯壯是第一位漫步在月球的太空人。
❺ 我希望有朝一日能去太空站看看。
❻ 太空船是飛行於外太空的交通工具。

127

天空中 (1)

MP3 127

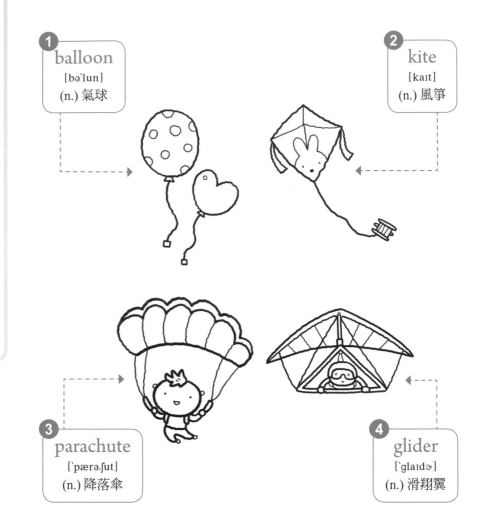

1 balloon
[bə`lun]
(n.) 氣球

2 kite
[kaɪt]
(n.) 風箏

3 parachute
[`pærə,ʃut]
(n.) 降落傘

4 glider
[`glaɪdə]
(n.) 滑翔翼

5 star
[stɑr]
(n.) 星星

6 moon
[mun]
(n.) 月亮

❶ 氣球

The girl was startled when the balloon exploded.

這個女孩嚇了一跳

❷ 風箏

She had never learned to fly a kite.

從未學過　　　　　放風箏

❸ 降落傘

Parachute jumping is fun and exciting!

跳降落傘

❹ 滑翔翼

I would like to ride a glider one day.

搭乘滑翔翼

❺ 星星

I'm a Gemini. What star sign are you?

❻ 月亮

The full moon lit up the whole area.

滿月

學更多

❶ startled〈受驚嚇的〉‧exploded〈explode（爆炸）的過去式〉

❷ learned〈learn（學習）的過去分詞〉‧fly〈使…飛〉

❸ jumping〈跳躍〉‧fun〈有趣的〉‧exciting〈刺激的〉

❹ would like〈想要〉‧ride〈搭乘〉‧one day〈總有一天〉

❺ Gemini〈雙子座〉‧star sign〈星座〉

❻ full〈滿的〉‧lit up〈light up（照亮）的過去式〉‧whole〈整個的〉‧area〈區域〉

中譯

❶ 這女孩在氣球爆破時嚇了一跳。

❷ 她從未學過放風箏。

❸ 玩降落傘既有趣又刺激！

❹ 我希望有朝一日可以駕駛滑翔翼。

❺ 我是雙子座，你是什麼星座的？

❻ 滿月照亮了整個區域。

天空中(2)

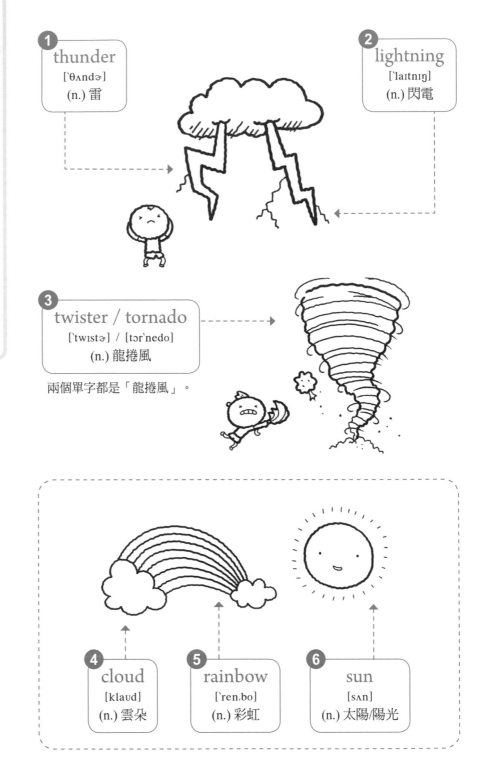

1 thunder
[ˈθʌndɚ]
(n.) 雷

2 lightning
[ˈlaɪtnɪŋ]
(n.) 閃電

3 twister / tornado
[ˈtwɪstɚ] / [tɔrˈnedo]
(n.) 龍捲風

兩個單字都是「龍捲風」。

4 cloud
[klaʊd]
(n.) 雲朵

5 rainbow
[ˈren.bo]
(n.) 彩虹

6 sun
[sʌn]
(n.) 太陽/陽光

❶ 雷

The sound of the thunder scared the baby to tears.
<u>把小嬰兒嚇哭</u>

❷ 閃電

After the lightning came the thunder.
<u>雷聲到來</u>

❸ 龍捲風

The fierce tornado destroyed the village.
<u>摧毀村落</u>

❹ 雲朵

The sky was suddenly covered with dark clouds.
<u>烏雲密布</u>

❺ 彩虹

The beautiful rainbow formed a perfect arc in the sky.
<u>形成完美的弧形</u>

❻ 太陽／陽光

The sun is pretty strong today, so remember to wear your sunglasses.
<u>戴上你的太陽眼鏡</u>

學更多

❶ sound〈聲音〉・scared〈scare（驚嚇）的過去式〉・baby〈嬰兒〉・tear〈眼淚〉
❷ after〈在…之後〉・came〈come（到來）的過去式〉
❸ fierce〈猛烈的〉・destroyed〈destroy（毀壞）的過去式〉・village〈村落〉
❹ suddenly〈突然〉・covered〈cover（覆蓋）的過去分詞〉・dark〈顏色深的〉
❺ formed〈form（形成）的過去式〉・perfect〈完美的〉・arc〈弧形〉
❻ pretty〈相當〉・strong〈強烈的〉・remember〈記得〉・sunglasses〈太陽眼鏡〉

中譯

❶ 雷聲把小嬰兒嚇哭了。
❷ 閃電之後，接著雷聲到來。
❸ 猛烈的龍捲風摧毀了村落。
❹ 天空忽然變得烏雲密布。
❺ 美麗的彩虹在空中畫出一道完美的圓弧。
❻ 今天的陽光非常強烈，所以要記得戴上你的太陽眼鏡。

山區
(1)

MP3 129

1 cable car
[ˈkebḷ kɑr]
(n.) 纜車

2 power tower
[ˈpaʊɚ ˈtaʊɚ]
(n.) 電塔

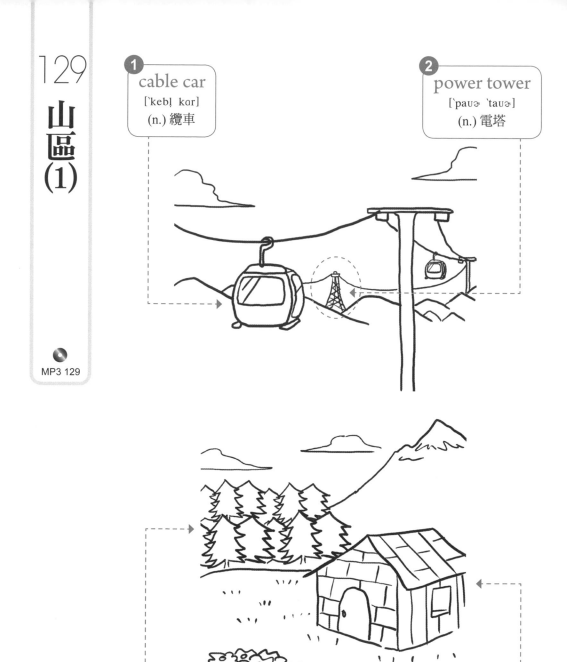

3 forest
[ˈfɔrɪst]
(n.) 森林

4 mountain plant
[ˈmaʊntṇ plænt]
(n.) 高山植物

5 cottage
[ˈkɑtɪdʒ]
(n.) 小木屋

❶ 纜車

The view from the cable car is breathtaking.

從纜車內看出去的風景

❷ 電塔

It can be dangerous to be near the power tower.

❸ 森林

Most of the ancient forests in the world have been destroyed.

古老的森林　　　　　　　　　　已經被破壞

❹ 高山植物

I don't know any of these mountain plants.

任何一種高山植物

❺ 小木屋

The cottage in the forest looks really nice.

學更多

❶ view〈風景〉‧ cable〈纜線〉‧ car〈纜車的吊艙〉‧ breathtaking〈驚人的〉

❷ dangerous〈危險的〉‧ near〈近的〉‧ power〈電力〉‧ tower〈塔〉

❸ ancient〈古老的〉‧ world〈世界〉‧ destroyed〈desroy（破壞）的過去分詞〉

❹ know〈認識、知道〉‧ any〈任何一個〉‧ mountain〈山〉‧ plant〈植物〉

❺ look〈看起來〉‧ really〈很〉‧ nice〈好的〉

中譯

❶ 從纜車內向外眺望的風景，美得令人屏息。

❷ 太靠近電塔可能會發生危險。

❸ 世界上大多數歷史悠久的森林，都已經遭受破壞。

❹ 這些高山植物我全都不認識。

❺ 森林裡的小木屋看起來很不錯。

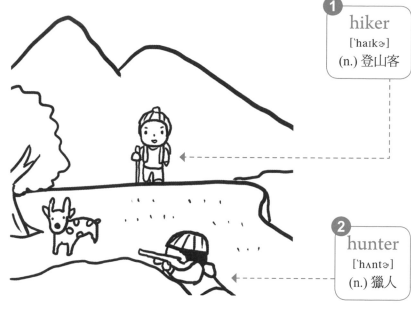

1 hiker
[ˈhaɪkɚ]
(n.) 登山客

2 hunter
[ˈhʌntɚ]
(n.) 獵人

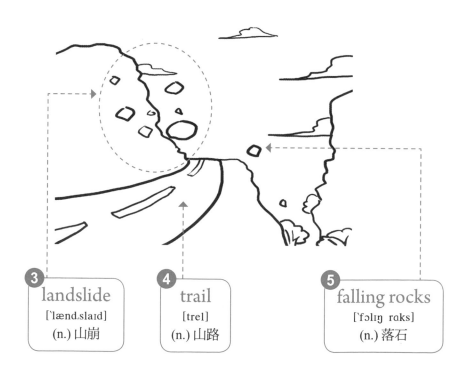

3 landslide
[ˈlænd,slaɪd]
(n.) 山崩

4 trail
[trel]
(n.) 山路

5 falling rocks
[ˈfɔlɪŋ rɑks]
(n.) 落石

❶ 登山客
Hikers are usually nature lovers.
　　　　　　　　　大自然愛好者

❷ 獵人
David was a very brave, young hunter.

❸ 山崩
The landslide destroyed the little village.

❹ 山路
Let's take a different trail this time.
　　　　　　走不同的山路

❺ 落石
Watch out for falling rocks when you drive on an unstable gravel road.
　　小心⋯　　　　　　　　　　　　　一條不穩固的礫石子路

學更多

❶ usually〈通常〉‧ nature〈自然〉‧ lover〈愛好者〉
❷ brave〈勇敢的〉‧ young〈年輕的〉
❸ destroyed〈destroy（破壞）的過去式〉‧ little〈小的〉‧ village〈村落〉
❹ take〈採取〉‧ different〈不同的〉‧ time〈次〉
❺ watch out〈小心〉‧ falling〈墜落的〉‧ rock〈岩石〉‧ unstable〈不穩固的〉‧
gravel〈礫石〉

中譯

❶ 登山客通常都是大自然的愛好者。
❷ 大衛是個非常勇敢的年輕獵人。
❸ 山崩摧毀了小村落。
❹ 我們這次走不同的山路吧。
❺ 開車行經顛簸的礫石子路時，要小心落石。

131

山區
(3)

MP3 131

1 fog
[fɑɡ]
(n.) 霧

2 waterfall
[`wɔtɚˌfɔl]
(n.) 瀑布

3 spring
[sprɪŋ]
(n.) 山泉

4 hot spring
[hɑt sprɪŋ]
(n.) 溫泉

5 stream
[strim]
(n.) 小溪

❶ 霧

Driving in heavy fog is way too dangerous.

在濃霧中開車

❷ 瀑布

The river came pouring down in a waterfall off the hill.

傾瀉而下

❸ 山泉

Does spring water really taste different?

❹ 溫泉

Hot springs in the winter are the best!

❺ 小溪

This stream is so clear that you can see the pebbles below.

你可以看見下面的小卵石

學更多

❶ driving〈drive（開車）的 ing 型態〉・heavy〈濃烈的〉・dangerous〈危險的〉
❷ river〈河〉・came〈come（來）的過去式〉・pouring〈pour（傾瀉）的 ing 型態〉・
off〈從…掉下〉・hill〈小山〉
❸ water〈水〉・really〈真地〉・taste〈喝起來〉・different〈不同的〉
❹ hot〈熱的〉・winter〈冬天〉・best〈最好的〉
❺ so...that...〈如此…以致於…〉・clear〈清澈的〉・pebble〈小卵石〉・below〈在下面〉

中譯

❶ 在濃霧中開車是非常危險的。
❷ 河流從山上傾瀉而下，形成一道瀑布。
❸ 山泉水喝起來真的不一樣嗎？
❹ 冬天時泡溫泉最棒了！
❺ 這條小溪很清澈，所以你能清楚看見溪底的小卵石。

132

餐車(1)

MP3 132

1 price list
[praɪs lɪst]
(n.) 價目表

2 awning
[`ɔnɪŋ]
(n.) 遮雨棚

3 trademark
[`trɛd,mɑrk]
(n.) 商標

4 customer
[`kʌstəmɚ]
(n.) 顧客

5 owner
[`onɚ]
(n.) 老闆

6 show case
[ʃo kes]
(n.) 陳列櫃

7 freezer
[`frizɚ]
(n.) 冷藏櫃

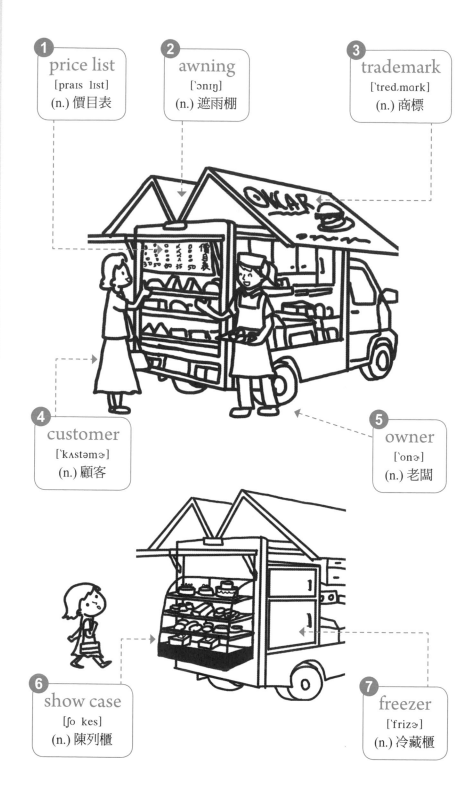

❶ 價目表
All the items for sell are listed clearly on the price list.
　　　　　　　　　　　　　清楚地被列出

❷ 遮雨棚
The place where they sat was shaded from the sun by green awnings.
　　　　　　　　　　　　　被遮蔽以避開陽光

❸ 商標
The new trademark looks very fancy.

❹ 顧客
He has been a regular customer for the past 10 years.
　　　　　　　　　　常客

❺ 老闆
My uncle knows the owner so I always get a discount.
　　　　　　　　　　　　　　享有折扣

❻ 陳列櫃
The new spring collection is displayed in the show case.
　　　　　　　　　　　被展示

❼ 冷藏櫃
Mom bought a new freezer today.

學更多

❶ item〈物品〉‧ listed〈list（編成列表）的過去分詞〉‧ clearly〈清楚地〉‧ list〈清單〉
❷ sat〈sit（坐）的過去式〉‧ shaded〈shade（遮陰）的過去分詞〉‧ green〈綠色的〉
❸ new〈新的〉‧ look〈看起來〉‧ fancy〈別緻的、花俏的〉
❹ regular〈固定的〉‧ past〈過去的〉
❺ uncle〈舅舅〉‧ know〈認識〉‧ always〈總是〉‧ get〈得到〉‧ discount〈折扣〉
❻ spring〈春季〉‧ collection〈系列新品〉‧ displayed〈display（展示）的過去分詞〉
❼ bought〈buy（買）的過去式〉‧ today〈今天〉

中譯

❶ 所有的販售物都清楚地列在價目表上。
❷ 他們坐的地方有綠色的遮雨棚遮陰，以避開陽光。
❸ 新的商標看起來相當花俏。
❹ 過去十年來，他一直是店裡的常客。
❺ 我舅舅認識老闆，所以我總是享有優惠價。
❻ 春季系列新品被放在陳列櫃裡展示。
❼ 媽媽今天買了一個新的冷藏櫃。

133
餐車(2)

MP3 133

1 straw
[strɔ]
(n.) 吸管

2 pepper
[ˋpɛpɚ]
(n.) 胡椒

3 ketchup
[ˋkɛtʃəp]
(n.) 蕃茄醬

4 chopping board
[ˋtʃɑpɪŋ bord]
(n.) 砧板

5 paper cup
[ˋpepɚ kʌp]
(n.) 紙杯

6 paper napkin
[ˋpepɚ ˋnæpkɪn]
(n.) 紙巾

7 paper bag
[ˋpepɚ bæg]
(n.) 紙袋

❶ 吸管

The straps in the store come in all different colors.
<u>可以買到各種顏色</u>

❷ 胡椒

I would like some pepper in my soup.
我想要⋯

❸ 蕃茄醬

I always eat my fries with a lot of ketchup.
<u>配很多番茄醬</u>

❹ 砧板

I prefer to use wooden chopping boards.
<u>木製砧板</u>

❺ 紙杯

There are plenty of paper cups in the kitchen cupboard.

❻ 紙巾

Please pass me a paper napkin.

❼ 紙袋

I need a paper bag for the groceries.

學更多

❶ store〈店〉・come in〈有貨、可以買到〉・different〈各種的〉・color〈顏色〉
❷ would like〈想要〉・some〈一些〉・soup〈湯〉
❸ prefer〈較喜歡〉・wooden〈木製的〉・chopping〈切〉・board〈板子〉
❹ always〈總是〉・fries〈炸薯條〉・a lot of〈許多〉
❺ plenty of〈很多的〉・paper〈紙的〉・cup〈杯子〉・kitchen〈廚房〉・cupboard〈櫥櫃〉
❻ pass〈傳遞〉・napkin〈餐巾〉
❼ need〈需要〉・bag〈袋子〉・groceries〈食品雜貨〉

中譯

❶ 在這間店可以買到各種顏色的吸管。
❷ 我想要在我的湯裡灑些胡椒。
❸ 吃薯條時，我總是沾很多蕃茄醬。
❹ 我比較喜歡使用木製的砧板。
❺ 廚房的櫥櫃裡有很多紙杯。
❻ 請遞給我一張紙巾。
❼ 我需要一個紙袋來裝這些食品雜貨。

速食店點餐

MP3 134

1 clerk
[klɝk]
(n.) 店員

2 menu
[`mɛnju]
(n.) 菜單

3 order
[`ɔrdə]
(v.) 點餐

4 line
[laɪn]
(v.) 排隊
(n.) 隊伍

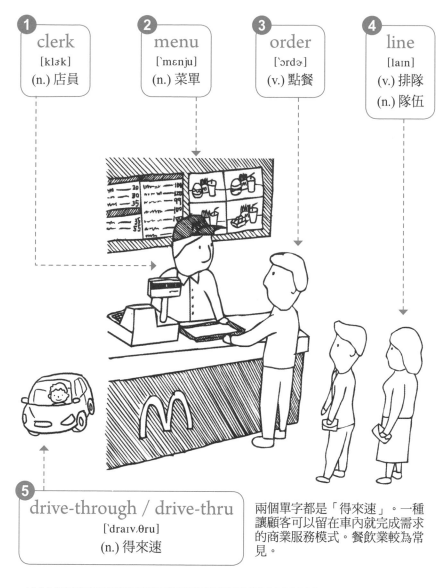

5 drive-through / drive-thru
[`draɪv.θru]
(n.) 得來速

兩個單字都是「得來速」。一種讓顧客可以留在車內就完成需求的商業服務模式。餐飲業較為常見。

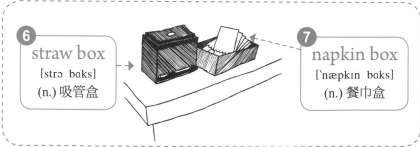

6 straw box
[strɔ bɑks]
(n.) 吸管盒

7 napkin box
[`næpkɪn bɑks]
(n.) 餐巾盒

❶ 店員

Her first job was as a store clerk.
<u>作為一位商店店員</u>

❷ 菜單

You can take a look at the menu.

❸ 點餐

Let me know when you are ready to order.
<u>當你準備好要點餐的時候</u>

❹ 排隊 / 隊伍

Please wait in line for your order.
<u>在隊伍中等候</u>

❺ 得來速

Thanks to the drive-thru, I can order food from my car.
<u>從我的車內點餐</u>

❻ 吸管盒

There are no more straws in the straw box.
<u>沒有更多的吸管</u>

❼ 餐巾盒

We need more napkin boxes.

學更多

❶ first〈第一的〉‧job〈工作〉‧store〈店〉
❷ take a look at...〈看一看…〉
❸ let〈讓〉‧know〈知道〉‧ready〈準備好的〉
❹ please〈請〉‧wait〈等待〉
❺ thanks to...〈幸虧…〉‧drive〈開車〉‧through〈通過〉‧food〈食物〉
❻ more〈更多的〉‧straw〈吸管〉‧box〈盒子〉
❼ need〈需要〉‧napkin〈餐巾〉‧boxes〈box（盒子）的複數〉

中譯

❶ 她的第一份工作，是商店的店員。
❷ 你可以看一下菜單。
❸ 當你準備好要點餐時，請跟我說。
❹ 請排成隊伍等候點餐。
❺ 多虧有得來速，我可以坐在車內點餐。
❻ 吸管盒裡面沒有吸管了。
❼ 我們需要更多的餐巾盒。

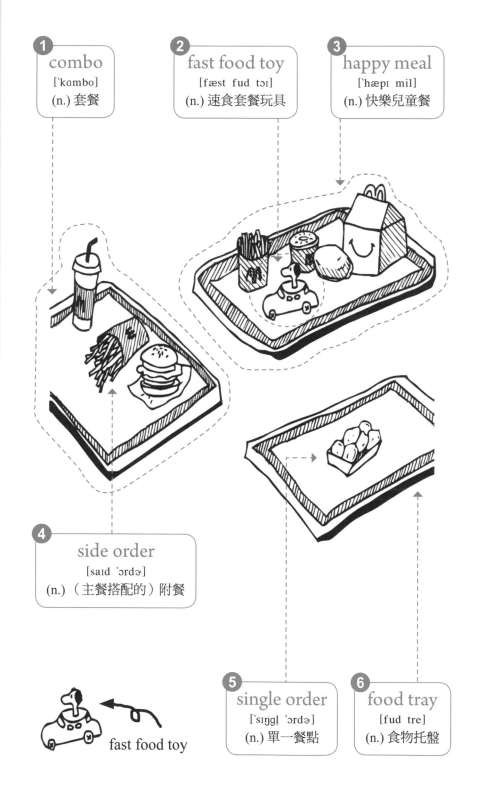

1 combo
[ˋkɑmbo]
(n.) 套餐

2 fast food toy
[fæst fud tɔɪ]
(n.) 速食套餐玩具

3 happy meal
[ˋhæpɪ mil]
(n.) 快樂兒童餐

4 side order
[saɪd ˋɔrdɚ]
(n.)（主餐搭配的）附餐

5 single order
[ˋsɪŋgḷ ˋɔrdɚ]
(n.) 單一餐點

6 food tray
[fud tre]
(n.) 食物托盤

fast food toy

❶ 套餐
Would you like to try our combo?
　　　　你想要…嗎

❷ 速食套餐玩具
There are five fast food toys to choose from.
　　　　　　　　　　　　　　從中選擇

❸ 快樂兒童餐
Do you also provide happy meals?

❹（主餐搭配的）附餐
What side orders would you like?

❺ 單一餐點
I'm not really hungry so a single order will be fine.
　　　　　　　　　　　　　　一個單一餐點就夠了

❻ 食物托盤
We can share a food tray.
　　　共用一個食物托盤

學更多

❶ try〈嘗試〉・our〈我們的〉
❷ fast food〈速食〉・toy〈玩具〉・choose〈選擇〉
❸ also〈也〉・provide〈提供〉・happy〈高興的〉・meal〈餐〉
❹ side〈附帶的〉・order〈點餐〉
❺ really〈很〉・hungry〈飢餓的〉・single〈單一的〉・fine〈好的〉
❻ can〈可以〉・share〈分享〉・food〈食物〉・tray〈托盤〉

中譯

❶ 你要試試看我們的套餐嗎？
❷ 有五種速食套餐玩具可供選擇。
❸ 你們也有供應快樂兒童餐嗎？
❹ 附餐你想要點什麼呢？
❺ 我沒有很餓，所以點一個單點就夠了。
❻ 我們可以共用一個食物托盤。

麵包店陳列

1 basket
[`bæskɪt]
(n.) 麵包籃

2 bread
[brɛd]
(n.) 麵包

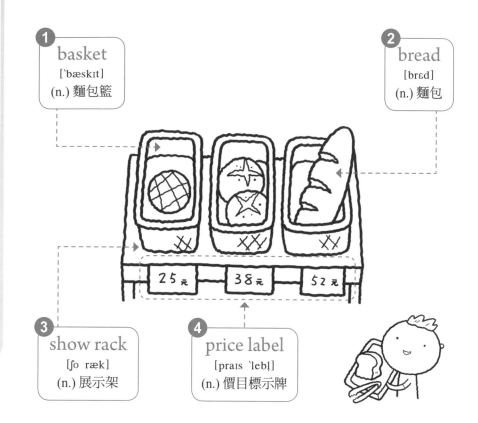

3 show rack
[ʃo ræk]
(n.) 展示架

4 price label
[praɪs `lebḷ]
(n.) 價目標示牌

5 birthday cake
[`bɝθˌde kek]
(n.) 生日蛋糕

6 display refrigerator
[dɪ`sple rɪ`frɪdʒəˌretɚ]
(n.) 冷藏展示櫃

❶ 麵包籃

Help me choose a bread basket.

❷ 麵包

I love the smell of freshly baked bread.

剛烘烤出爐的麵包

❸ 展示架

There is a variety of bread on the show rack.

各式各樣的

❹ 價目標示牌

I don't see the price label, so please tell me the price.

❺ 生日蛋糕

The surprise birthday cake made her cry with happy tears.

讓她開心地哭了

❻ 冷藏展示櫃

All the cakes in the store are placed in the display refrigerator.

被放在

學更多

❶ help〈幫助〉‧choose〈選擇〉

❷ smell〈氣味〉‧freshly〈剛剛〉‧baked〈烘烤的〉

❸ variety〈多種類型〉‧show〈展示〉‧rack〈架子〉

❹ see〈看到〉‧price〈價錢〉‧label〈標籤〉‧tell〈告訴〉

❺ surprise〈驚喜〉‧birthday〈生日〉‧cake〈蛋糕〉‧cry〈哭〉‧tear〈眼淚〉

❻ placed〈place（放置）的過去分詞〉‧display〈展示〉‧refrigerator〈冰箱〉

中譯

❶ 幫我選一個麵包籃。

❷ 我喜愛剛烘烤出爐的麵包香味。

❸ 展示架上放著各式各樣的麵包。

❹ 我沒有看到價目標示牌，所以請告訴我價錢。

❺ 這個驚喜的生日蛋糕，讓她開心地哭了。

❻ 店內所有的蛋糕，都放在冷藏展示櫃裡。

137

麵包店櫃檯

MP3 137

1 cash register
[kæʃ `rɛdʒɪstə]
(n.) 收銀機

2 clerk
[klɜk]
(n.) 店員

3 customer
[`kʌstəmə]
(n.) 顧客

4 toast
[tost]
(n.) 烤吐司

5 tongs
[tɔŋz]
(n.) 夾子

6 tray
[tre]
(n.) 托盤

❶ 收銀機
Please pay at the cash register.

❷ 店員
The clerk has a friendly smile.

❸ 顧客
Remember to <u>welcome your customers</u> with a warm smile.
　　　　　　歡迎你的顧客

❹ 烤吐司
I always eat <u>toast with butter</u>.
　　　　　　搭配奶油

❺ 夾子
<u>Could you please</u> bring more tongs?
　可以請你⋯

❻ 托盤
You can <u>put the bread on the tray</u>.
　　把麵包放在⋯上面

學更多

❶ pay〈付款〉‧cash〈現金〉‧register〈收銀機〉
❷ friendly〈友善的〉‧smile〈笑容〉
❸ remember〈記得〉‧welcome〈接待〉‧warm〈熱情的〉
❹ always〈總是〉‧butter〈奶油〉
❺ could〈可以〉‧bring〈拿來〉‧more〈更多的〉
❻ can〈可以〉‧put〈放〉‧bread〈麵包〉

中譯

❶ 請至收銀機結帳。
❷ 這名店員的笑容很友善。
❸ 記得用熱情的笑容接待你的顧客。
❹ 吃烤吐司時，我都會塗上奶油。
❺ 可以請你再拿一些夾子過來嗎？
❻ 你可以把麵包放在托盤上。

138

露天咖啡廳

MP3 138

1 outdoor coffee shop
[ˈaʊtˌdor ˈkɔfɪ ʃɑp]
(n.) 露天咖啡廳

2 live band show
[laɪv bænd ʃo]
(n.) 現場演奏

3 musician
[mjuˈzɪʃən]
(n.) 樂手

4 tables and chairs
[ˈtebḷz ɛnd tʃɛrz]
(n.) 桌椅

5 sun umbrella
[sʌn ʌmˈbrɛlə]
(n.) 遮陽傘

6 waiter
[ˈwetɚ]
(n.) 侍者

7 menu
[ˈmɛnju]
(n.) 菜單

① 露天咖啡廳
⑤ 遮陽傘

I like sitting under the sun umbrella at an outdoor coffee shop.

② 現場演奏

They have live band shows every Wednesday night.

③ 樂手

Musicians read a score to tell them what to play.

　　　　　　　　　　　讓樂手們知道要演奏什麼

④ 桌椅

There are plenty of tables and chairs here at this café.

⑥ 侍者

Remind me to tip the waiter.

　　　　　　　給侍者小費

⑦ 菜單

Did you change your menu?

學更多

①⑤ sitting〈sit（坐）的 ing 型態〉・under〈在…下面〉・umbrella〈傘〉・
outdoor〈戶外的〉・coffee shop〈咖啡廳〉
② live〈現場的〉・band〈樂隊〉・show〈表演〉・every〈每個〉・Wednesday〈星期三〉
③ read〈讀〉・score〈樂譜〉・tell〈顯示某訊息〉・play〈演奏〉
④ plenty of...〈很多的…〉・table〈桌子〉・chair〈椅子〉・café〈咖啡廳〉
⑥ remind〈提醒〉・tip〈給…小費〉
⑦ change〈改變〉・your〈你們的〉

中譯

①⑤ 在露天咖啡廳時，我喜歡坐在遮陽傘下。
② 每週三晚上，他們都有現場演奏。
③ 樂手們看樂譜來演奏。
④ 這間咖啡廳有很多張桌椅。
⑥ 提醒我要給侍者小費。
⑦ 你們已經換新菜單了嗎？

139

下午茶點心

MP3 139

1 waffle
[`wafl̩]
(n.) 鬆餅

2 sugar jar
[`ʃʊgɚ dʒɑr]
(n.) 糖罐

3 cake
[kek]
(n.) 蛋糕

4 coffee
[`kɔfɪ]
(n.) 咖啡

5 tea
[ti]
(n.) 茶

6 coffee cup
[`kɔfɪ kʌp]
(n.) 咖啡杯

7 cream
[krim]
(n.) 奶油球

❶ 鬆餅

That coffee shop has the best <u>waffles</u> in town.

有最好吃的鬆餅

❷ 糖罐

Please pass me the sugar jar.

❸ 蛋糕

I would like a cheesecake please. （起司蛋糕的「cheese」和「cake」通常會連在一起）

我想要…

❹ 咖啡

I always drink black <u>coffee</u>.

黑咖啡

❺ 茶

I like my <u>tea</u> with lots of milk.

加很多牛奶

❻ 咖啡杯

These coffee cups look expensive.

❼ 奶油球

Would you like more cream?

你想要…

學更多

❶ coffee shop〈咖啡廳〉・best〈最好的〉・town〈城市〉
❷ pass〈傳遞〉・sugar〈糖〉・jar〈罐〉
❸ cheese〈起司〉・please〈請〉
❹ always〈總是〉・drink〈喝〉・black〈不加牛奶的〉
❺ like〈喜歡〉・lots of〈很多〉・milk〈牛奶〉
❻ these〈這些〉・cup〈杯子〉・expensive〈昂貴的〉
❼ more〈更多的〉

中譯

❶ 那間咖啡廳有城裡最好吃的鬆餅。
❷ 請將糖罐遞給我。
❸ 請給我一塊起司蛋糕。
❹ 我都喝黑咖啡。
❺ 我喜歡在茶裡加很多牛奶。
❻ 這些咖啡杯看起來很昂貴。
❼ 你想要更多奶油球嗎？

1 notebook computer
[ˋnot͵bʊk kəmˋpjutɚ]
(n.) 筆記型電腦

2 computer monitor
[kəmˋpjutɚ ˋmɑnətɚ]
(n.) 電腦螢幕

3 keyboard
[ˋki͵bord]
(n.) 鍵盤

4 mouse pad
[maʊs pæd]
(n.) 滑鼠墊

5 mouse
[maʊs]
(n.) 滑鼠

❶ 筆記型電腦
I always carry my notebook computer with me.

❷ 電腦螢幕
I prefer a big computer monitor because it helps me see more clearly.
幫助我看得更清楚

❸ 鍵盤
My keyboard is damaged. I need to buy a new one.
買一副新的

❹ 滑鼠墊
The mouse functions better if you use a mouse pad.
更好操作

❺ 滑鼠
A mouse makes using the computer so much easier.
更加容易

學更多

❶ always〈總是〉‧ carry〈攜帶〉‧ notebook〈筆記本、筆記型電腦〉‧ computer〈電腦〉
❷ prefer〈較喜歡〉‧ monitor〈電腦螢幕〉‧ because〈因為〉‧ help〈幫助〉‧ see〈看〉‧
more〈更加〉‧ clearly〈清楚地〉
❸ damaged〈毀損的〉‧ need〈需要〉‧ new〈新的〉
❹ function〈運作〉‧ better〈更好地〉‧ use〈使用〉‧ pad〈墊〉
❺ make〈使得〉‧ using〈use（使用）的 ing 型態〉‧ easier〈更容易的，easy（容易的）的
比較級〉

中譯

❶ 我總是隨身攜帶我的筆記型電腦。
❷ 我比較喜歡大一點的電腦螢幕，因為它幫助我看得更清楚。
❸ 我的鍵盤壞掉了，我需要買一副新的。
❹ 如果你使用滑鼠墊，滑鼠會更好操作。
❺ 滑鼠使得電腦更容易操作。

141

辦公桌上 (2)

MP3 141

1 telephone
[ˈtɛləˌfon]
(n.) 電話

2 tape dispenser
[tep dɪˈspɛnsɚ]
(n.) 膠帶台

3 reading lamp
[ˈridɪŋ læmp]
(n.) 檯燈

4 post-it
[ˈpostɪt]
(n.) 便利貼

5 calculator
[ˈkælkjəˌletɚ]
(n.) 計算機

6 folder
[ˈfoldɚ]
(n.) 檔案夾

7 penholder / pen holder
[ˈpɛnˌholdɚ] / [pɛn ˈholdɚ]
(n.) 筆筒

❶ 電話

Please leave your telephone number; we will contact you soon.

❷ 膠帶台

I prefer a small tape dispenser so it doesn't take up too much space.

占用太多的空間

❸ 檯燈

Remember to always turn on the reading lamp during work.

在工作期間

❹ 便利貼

I marked the contents that need revisions with the post-it.

在需要修正的內容上做記號

❺ 計算機

Does anyone have a calculator here?

❻ 檔案夾

I keep all the relevant information in the same folder.

相關資料

❼ 筆筒

I use a penholder for all my pens so my desk looks neat.

用一個筆筒裝我所有的筆

學更多

❶ leave〈留下〉・number〈號碼〉・contact〈聯絡〉・soon〈很快地〉
❷ prefer〈較喜歡〉・tape〈膠帶〉・dispenser〈分配器〉・take up〈佔用〉・space〈空間〉
❸ remember〈記得〉・turn on〈打開〉・reading〈閱讀的〉・lamp〈燈〉
❹ marked〈mark（標記）的過去式〉・content〈內容〉・revision〈修正〉・post〈張貼〉
❺ anyone〈任何人〉・here〈這裡〉
❻ keep〈存放〉・relevant〈有關的〉・information〈資料〉・same〈同一個的〉
❼ use〈使用〉・holder〈支撐物〉・desk〈書桌〉・look〈看起來〉・neat〈整潔的〉

中譯

❶ 請留下你的電話號碼，我們會盡快跟你聯絡。
❷ 我比較喜歡小型膠帶台，因為它不會占用太多空間。
❸ 每次工作時，都要記得打開檯燈。
❹ 需修正的內容，我貼上便利貼做記號。
❺ 現場有人有計算機嗎？
❻ 我會把所有相關資料存放在同一個檔案夾。
❼ 我所有的筆都裝在筆筒裡，所以我的桌面看起來很整齊。

142

辦公室(1)

MP3 142

1 partition screen
[par`tɪʃən skrin]
(n.) 隔板屏風

2 cubicle
[`kjubɪk!]
(n.) 辦公座位

3 file cabinet
[faɪl `kæbənɪt]
(n.) 檔案櫃

4 reception room
[rɪ`sɛpʃən rum]
(n.) 會客室

5 pantry
[`pæntrɪ]
(n.) 茶水間

❶ 隔板屏風

Let's use this partition screen to divide the room into two areas.

把房間劃分成兩個區域

❷ 辦公座位

I like to decorate my cubicle so it looks unique.

裝飾我的辦公座位

❸ 檔案櫃

All the files you need can be found in the file cabinet.

可以被找到

❹ 會客室

Please wait in the reception room.

❺ 茶水間

There is a steam heating box for your lunch in the pantry.

給你的午餐使用

學更多

❶ partition〈隔板〉‧ screen〈屏風〉‧ divide〈劃分〉‧ room〈房間〉‧ area〈區域〉

❷ decorate〈裝飾〉‧ look〈看起來〉‧ unique〈獨特的〉

❸ file〈檔案〉‧ found〈find（找到）的過去分詞〉‧ cabinet〈櫃子〉

❹ wait〈等待〉‧ reception〈接待〉

❺ steam〈蒸汽〉‧ heating〈加熱的〉‧ box〈箱子〉‧ lunch〈午餐〉

中譯

❶ 我們用隔板屏風把房間分成兩個區域吧。

❷ 我喜歡裝飾我的辦公座位，所以它看起來與眾不同。

❸ 你需要的文件全都在檔案櫃裡。

❹ 請在會客室稍候片刻。

❺ 茶水間裡的蒸汽加熱箱，可以用來加熱你的午餐。

143

辦公室(2)

MP3 143

1 air conditioning system
[ɛr kənˈdɪʃənɪŋ ˈsɪstəm]
(n.) 空調系統

2 time clock
[taɪm klɑk]
(n.) 打卡鐘

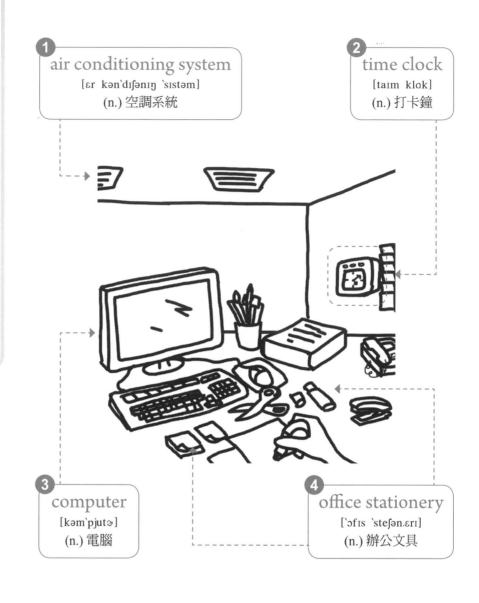

3 computer
[kəmˈpjutə]
(n.) 電腦

4 office stationery
[ˈɔfɪs ˈsteʃənˌɛrɪ]
(n.) 辦公文具

5 photocopier
[ˈfotəˌkɑpɪə]
(n.) 影印機

❶ 空調系統

Which type of air conditioning system do you prefer?
哪一種類型的空調系統

❷ 打卡鐘

The time clock records our working hours.
工作時數

❸ 電腦

Remember to keep a backup file on your computer.
存放一個備份檔案

❹ 辦公文具

The office stationery is free.

❺ 影印機

Can you please fix the broken photocopier before noon?
修理故障的印表機

學更多

❶ type〈類型〉‧ air〈空氣〉‧ conditioning〈調節〉‧ system〈系統〉‧ prefer〈較喜歡〉
❷ time〈時間〉‧ clock〈時鐘〉‧ record〈記錄〉‧ our〈我們的〉‧ working〈工作的〉‧
hour〈時間〉
❸ remember〈記得〉‧ keep〈存放〉‧ backup〈備用的〉‧ file〈檔案〉
❹ office〈辦公室〉‧ stationery〈文具〉‧ free〈免費的〉
❺ fix〈修理〉‧ broken〈損壞的、故障的〉‧ before〈在…之前〉‧ noon〈中午〉

中譯

❶ 你比較喜歡哪一種類型的空調系統？
❷ 打卡鐘記錄我們的工作時數。
❸ 記得在你電腦裡存一個備份檔案。
❹ 辦公文具可以免費取用。
❺ 可以請你在中午之前修好故障的影印機嗎？

辦公室(3)

MP3 144

1 printer
[`prɪntɚ]
(n.) 印表機

2 fax machine
[fæks məˋʃin]
(n.) 傳真機

3 employer
[ɪmˋplɔɪɚ]
(n.) 老闆

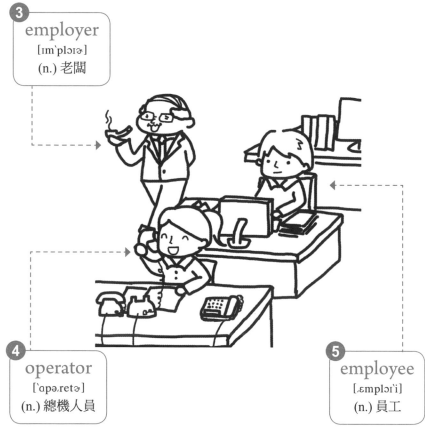

4 operator
[`ɑpə,retɚ]
(n.) 總機人員

5 employee
[,ɛmplɔɪˋi]
(n.) 員工

❶ 印表機

The color printer is not working.
　　　　　　　　　　　沒有在運作

❷ 傳真機

Please teach me how to use the fax machine.

❸ 老闆

You are lucky to have such a nice employer!
　　　　　　　　　　　一個這麼好的老闆

❹ 總機人員

This is the operator, how may I direct your call?
　　　　　　　　　　　　　　　轉接你的電話

❺ 員工

How many employees do you have?

學更多

❶ color〈彩色〉‧working〈work（運作）的 ing 型態〉
❷ teach〈教〉‧use〈使用〉‧fax〈傳真〉‧machine〈機器〉
❸ lucky〈幸運的〉‧such〈這樣的〉‧nice〈好的〉
❹ direct〈將…轉向、指向〉‧call〈電話〉
❺ how many〈多少〉‧have〈有〉

中譯

❶ 彩色印表機沒有在運作。
❷ 請教我如何使用傳真機。
❸ 你真是幸運能有一個這麼好的老闆！
❹ 這裡是總機，請問要我幫您轉接給誰？
❺ 你有幾位員工呢？

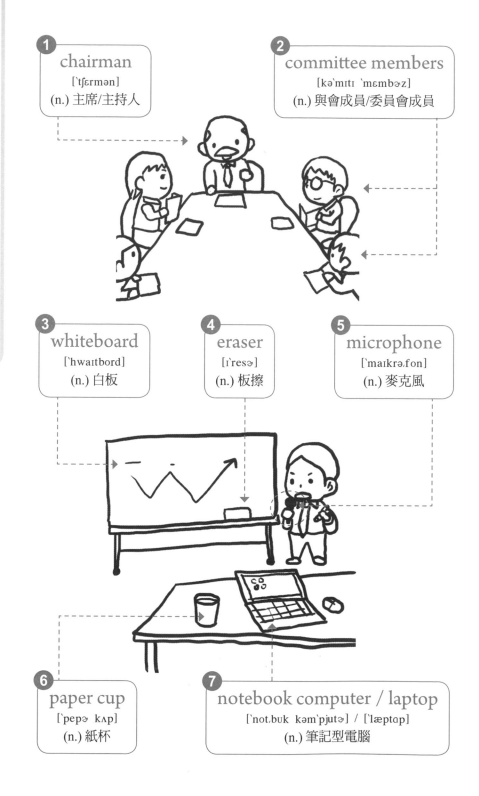

1 chairman
[`tʃɛrmən]
(n.) 主席/主持人

2 committee members
[kə`mɪtɪ `mɛmbəz]
(n.) 與會成員/委員會成員

3 whiteboard
[`hwaɪtbord]
(n.) 白板

4 eraser
[ɪ`resə]
(n.) 板擦

5 microphone
[`maɪkrə.fon]
(n.) 麥克風

6 paper cup
[`pepə kʌp]
(n.) 紙杯

7 notebook computer / laptop
[`not.bʊk kəm`pjutə] / [`læptɑp]
(n.) 筆記型電腦

❶ 主席 / 主持人

Allow me to introduce our chairman for tonight's event.
容我介紹

❷ 與會成員 / 委員會成員

Please let me introduce my committee members to you.

❸ 白板

Please put your name on the whiteboard.
寫上你的名字

❹ 板擦

After school, one student cleans the blackboard, erasers and replenishes the chalk.
補充粉筆

❺ 麥克風

Let's do a microphone test first.
測試麥克風

❻ 紙杯

The paper cups are in the drawer.

❼ 筆記型電腦

I always carry my notebook computer with me when I travel.

學更多

❶ allow〈允許〉‧ introduce〈介紹〉‧ tonight〈今晚〉‧ event〈活動〉
❷ committee〈委員會〉‧ member〈成員〉
❸ please〈請〉‧ put〈寫上〉‧ name〈名字〉
❹ clean〈打掃〉‧ blackboard〈黑板〉‧ replenish〈把…再補足〉‧ chalk〈粉筆〉
❺ test〈測試〉‧ first〈首先〉
❻ paper〈紙的〉‧ cup〈杯子〉‧ drawer〈抽屜〉
❼ carry〈攜帶〉‧ notebook〈筆記本、筆記型電腦〉‧ computer〈電腦〉‧ travel〈旅行〉

中譯

❶ 請容我介紹今晚活動的主席。
❷ 請讓我向你介紹我們的與會成員。
❸ 請將你的名字寫在白板上。
❹ 放學後,一名學生要負責清理黑板、板擦和補充粉筆。
❺ 我們先來測試麥克風吧。
❻ 紙杯放在抽屜裡。
❼ 旅行時,我總是隨身攜帶筆記型電腦。

146

會議室(2)

MP3 146

1 screen
[skrin]
(n.) 放映布幕

2 video conference
[ˈvɪdɪo ˈkɑnfərəns]
(n.) 視訊會議

3 folding chair
[ˈfoldɪŋ tʃɛr]
(n.) 折疊椅

4 projector
[prəˈdʒɛktə]
(n.) 投影機

5 conference table
[ˈkɑnfərəns ˈtebl]
(n.) 會議桌

兩個單字都是「會議記錄」。

6 PowerPoint presentation
[ˈpauəˌpɔɪnt ˌprizɛnˈteʃən]
(n.) 電子檔簡報

7 meeting notes
[ˈmitɪŋ nots]
meeting minutes
[ˈmitɪŋ ˈmɪnɪts]
(n.) 會議記錄

❶ 放映布幕
Please put down the screen for us.
降下放映布幕

❷ 視訊會議
The video conference is in 10 minutes.
在十分鐘後

❸ 折疊椅
There are more folding chairs in the room next door.
隔壁房間裡

❹ 投影機
Charles, I'd like you to set up the projector for me.
我想要（＝I would like）　　架設投影機

❺ 會議桌
Please take a seat at the conference table.
坐下

❻ 電子檔簡報
The PowerPoint presentation was well done.
做得好

❼ 會議記錄
Who is taking the meeting notes this time?
做會議記錄

學更多

❶ put down〈放下〉・us〈我們〉
❷ video〈影像的〉・conference〈會議〉・in〈在…以後〉・minute〈分鐘〉
❸ more〈更多的〉・folding〈折疊式的〉・chair〈椅子〉・next〈緊鄰的〉
❹ would like〈想要〉・set up〈設置〉
❺ please〈請〉・seat〈座位〉・table〈桌子〉
❻ PowerPoint〈微軟公司的簡報軟體〉・presentation〈報告〉・well done〈做得好的〉
❼ meeting〈會議〉・note〈筆記〉・minutes〈會議記錄〉・time〈次、回〉

中譯

❶ 請幫我們降下放映布幕。
❷ 視訊會議將在十分鐘後舉行。
❸ 隔壁房間裡還有更多的折疊椅。
❹ Charles，我想請你幫我把投影機準備好。
❺ 請在會議桌就座。
❻ 這個電子檔簡報做得很棒。
❼ 這次由誰做會議記錄呢？

147

公園(1)

MP3 147

1 seesaw
[ˋsiˌsɔ]
(n.) 蹺蹺板

2 lawn
[lɔn]
(n.) 草坪

3 slide
[slaɪd]
(n.) 溜滑梯

4 chin-up bar
[ˋtʃɪnˌʌp bɑr]
(n.) 單槓

5 swing
[swɪŋ]
(n.) 鞦韆

6 kite
[kaɪt]
(n.) 風箏

此字為複數，單數
是「child」。

7 children
[ˋtʃɪldrən]
(n.) 小孩（們）

❶ 蹺蹺板

I have never played on a seesaw before.
我從未玩過

❷ 草坪

It's time to mow the lawn.
替草坪除草

❸ 溜滑梯

Can I play on the slide after school?
放學後

❹ 單槓

The chin-up bar seems like a difficult activity.
看起來像是

❺ 鞦韆

It's fun to play on the swings with friends.
在鞦韆上玩

❻ 風箏

Do you know how to fly a kite?
放風箏

❼ 小孩（們）

I love playing with children; they are so cute.

學更多

❶ never〈從未〉‧ played〈play（玩）的過去分詞〉‧ before〈以前〉
❷ time〈時機〉‧ mow〈除草〉
❸ after〈在…之後〉‧ school〈上學〉
❹ chin-up〈拉單槓使身體上升，下顎與單槓平〉‧ difficult〈困難的〉‧ activity〈活動〉
❺ fun〈有趣的〉‧ friend〈朋友〉
❻ know〈知道〉‧ fly〈放（風箏）〉
❼ love〈喜愛〉‧ playing〈play（玩）的 ing 型態〉‧ cute〈可愛〉

中譯

❶ 之前我從來沒玩過蹺蹺板。
❷ 是該替草坪除草的時候了。
❸ 放學後我可以玩溜滑梯嗎？
❹ 單槓看起來似乎是一項很困難的活動。
❺ 跟朋友們一起盪鞦韆很好玩。
❻ 你知道要怎麼放風箏嗎？
❼ 我喜愛和小孩一同嬉戲，他們真是可愛。

148

公園(2)

MP3 148

1 Frisbee
[ˈfrɪzbi]
(n.) 飛盤

2 fountain
[ˈfaʊntɪn]
(n.) 噴泉

3 sculpture
[ˈskʌlptʃɚ]
(n.) 雕塑品

4 gazebo
[gəˈzibo]
pavilion
[pəˈvɪljən]
(n.) 涼亭

兩個單字都是
「涼亭」。

兩個單字都是
「健康步道」。
5 fitness trail
[ˈfɪtnɪs trel]
fitness path
[ˈfɪtnɪs pæθ]
(n.) 健康步道

兩個單字都是「垃圾桶」。
6 trash can / garbage can
[træʃ kæn] / [ˈgɑrbɪdʒ kæn]
(n.) 垃圾桶

❶ 飛盤
Frisbee is such a fun game.
　　　　　如此好玩的遊戲
❷ 噴泉
There are many coins in the fountain.

❸ 雕塑品
It is anticipated that the sculpture will sell for as much as a million dollars.
　　　　　　　　　　　　　　　　　　　　　　　　多達
❹ 涼亭
What a beautiful gazebo they have over there in the park.
　　　　　　　　　　　　他們擁有
❺ 健康步道
Let's take a walk on the fitness trail.
　我們去散步、走走
❻ 垃圾桶
Please throw the trash in the trash can.
　　　　　　　丟垃圾

學更多

❶ fun〈有趣的〉‧game〈遊戲〉
❷ many〈許多的〉‧coin〈硬幣〉
❸ anticipated〈anticipate（預期）的過去分詞〉‧sell〈出售〉‧million〈百萬〉‧dollar〈美元〉
❹ beautiful〈漂亮的〉‧over there〈在那裡〉‧park〈公園〉
❺ take a walk〈散步〉‧fitness〈健康〉‧trail〈小徑〉‧path〈小徑〉
❻ throw〈扔〉‧trash〈垃圾〉‧can〈容器〉‧garbage〈垃圾〉

中譯

❶ 飛盤真是好玩的遊戲。
❷ 噴泉裡有很多硬幣。
❸ 這件雕塑品的售價，預期將高達一百萬美金。
❹ 公園那邊的涼亭真是漂亮呀！
❺ 我們去走一走健康步道吧。
❻ 請將垃圾扔進垃圾桶內。

149

騎樓(1)

MP3 149

1 house number
[haʊs ˋnʌmbə]
(n.) 門牌號碼

2 residence
[ˋrɛzədəns]
(n.) 住家/居住

3 store sign
[stor saɪn]
(n.) 商店招牌

（門牌號碼放大圖）

4 vending machine
[ˋvɛndɪŋ məˋʃin]
(n.) 自動販賣機

5 street vendor
[strit ˋvɛndə]
(n.) 騎樓攤販/路邊攤販

6 shop
[ʃɑp]
(n.) 商店

❶ 門牌號碼

What is your house number?

❷ 住家 / 居住

I learned Spanish during my residence in Mexico.
我居住在墨西哥的時候

❸ 商店招牌

They don't have a store sign outside for the shop.

❹ 自動販賣機

I'll get a coke from the vending machine.
從自動販賣機

❺ 騎樓攤販 / 路邊攤販

Why are there so many street vendors?

❻ 商店

Let's go to the shop to buy some juice.
我們去商店吧

學更多

❶ your〈你的〉‧house〈住宅〉‧number〈號碼〉
❷ learned〈learn（學習）的過去式〉‧Spanish〈西班牙語〉‧during〈在…的期間〉‧
Mexico〈墨西哥〉
❸ store〈商店〉‧sign〈招牌〉‧outside〈在外面〉
❹ get〈買到〉‧coke〈可樂〉‧vending〈販賣的〉‧machine〈機器〉
❺ many〈許多的〉‧street〈街道〉‧vendor〈攤販〉
❻ buy〈買〉‧some〈一些〉‧juice〈果汁〉

中譯

❶ 你家的門牌號碼是幾號？
❷ 我居住在墨西哥時，學了西班牙語。
❸ 他們的店外面沒有商店招牌。
❹ 我要去自動販賣機買一瓶可樂。
❺ 為什麼有這麼多騎樓攤販呢？
❻ 我們去商店買一些果汁吧。

150

騎樓(2)

MP3 150

1
motorcycle
[ˈmotɚˌsaɪkl̩]
(n.) 摩托車

引導視障者行進的磚塊。磚面上有直線、圓點等紋路，指引視障者前進方向、危險或暫停。

2
curbs for the blind
[kɝbz fɔr ðə blaɪnd]
(n.) 導盲磚

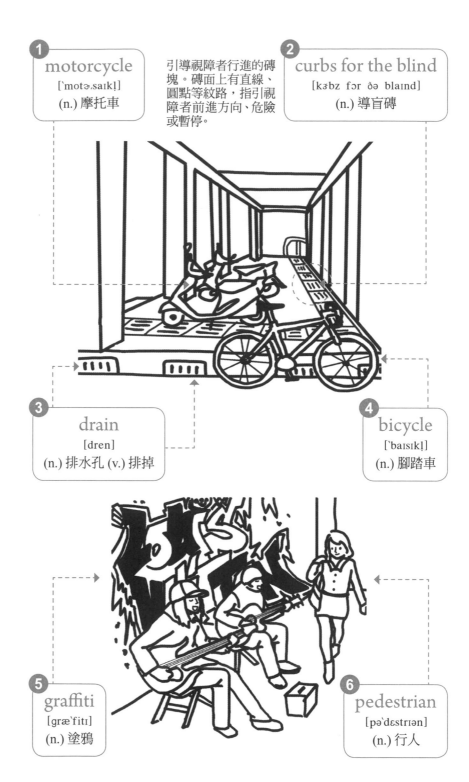

3
drain
[dren]
(n.) 排水孔 (v.) 排掉

4
bicycle
[ˈbaɪsɪkl̩]
(n.) 腳踏車

5
graffiti
[græˈfitɪ]
(n.) 塗鴉

6
pedestrian
[pəˈdɛstrɪən]
(n.) 行人

❶ 摩托車
My brother bought a motorcycle for me.

❷ 導盲磚
What you see here are the curbs for the blind.
你在這裡看到的

❸ 排水孔 / 排掉
Ditches were dug to drain water from the swamp.
從沼澤地排水

❹ 腳踏車
Please teach me how to ride a bicycle.
騎腳踏車

❺ 塗鴉
How long did you spend doing this graffiti?
你花多久時間

❻ 行人
Watch out for pedestrians when driving.
注意行人

學更多

❶ brother〈兄弟〉‧ bought〈buy（買）的過去式〉
❷ see〈看到〉‧ curb〈人行道旁邊的鑲邊石〉‧ the blind〈盲人〉
❸ ditch〈渠道〉‧ dug〈dig（挖掘）的過去分詞〉‧ swamp〈沼澤〉
❹ please〈請〉‧ teach〈教〉‧ ride〈騎〉
❺ how long〈有多久〉‧ spend〈花費〉‧ doing〈do（做、畫）的 ing 型態〉
❻ watch out〈注意〉‧ driving〈drive（開車）的 ing 型態〉

中譯

❶ 我哥哥幫我買了一部摩托車。
❷ 你眼前所見的就是導盲磚。
❸ 渠道是為了從沼澤地排掉水而挖掘的。
❹ 請教我騎腳踏車。
❺ 你花了多久時間完成這幅塗鴉？
❻ 開車時，要注意路上的行人。

151

地下道 (1)

MP3 151

1 road sign
[rod saɪn]
(n.) 路標

2 directional sign
[dəˋrɛkʃənḷ saɪn]
(n.) 方向指示牌

3 poster
[ˋpostɚ]
(n.) 海報

4 rail
[rel]
(n.) 扶手/欄杆

5 stair
[stɛr]
(n.) 階梯

6 curbs for the blind
[kɝbz fɔr ðə blaɪnd]
(n.) 導盲磚

❶ 路標

You should pay attention to the road signs when you drive.
注意路標

❷ 方向指示牌

The directional sign says to turn left.
顯示要左轉

❸ 海報

Some of the posters on the wall are from many years ago.
從好幾年前

❹ 扶手 / 欄杆

He kept his hand on the rail as he climbed the steps.
把他的手放在扶手上

❺ 階梯

We climbed the stairs to the tower.
爬階梯

❻ 導盲磚

The city passed a new law saying all major roads must have curbs for the blind built.
通過一項新法令

學更多

❶ should〈應該〉・pay attention to...〈注意⋯〉・sign〈標誌〉・drive〈開車〉

❷ directional〈方向的〉・say〈顯示〉・turn〈轉彎〉・left〈左邊〉

❸ wall〈牆壁〉・many〈許多的〉・ago〈在⋯以前〉

❹ kept〈keep（保持）的過去式〉・as〈當⋯時〉・climbed〈climb（攀登、爬）的過去式〉

❺ tower〈塔樓、高樓〉

❻ passed〈pass（通過）的過去式〉・saying〈say（說明、宣稱）的 ing 型態〉・
   major〈主要的〉・curb〈人行道旁邊的鑲邊石〉・built〈build（建造）的過去分詞〉

中譯

❶ 當你開車時，要注意路標。

❷ 方向指示牌上寫著要左轉。

❸ 牆上有些海報貼了好幾年。

❹ 當他上樓梯時，把手放在樓梯的扶手上。

❺ 我們爬階梯上了塔樓。

❻ 這個城市通過一項新法令：所有要道皆須設置導盲磚。

152

地下道(2)

MP3 152

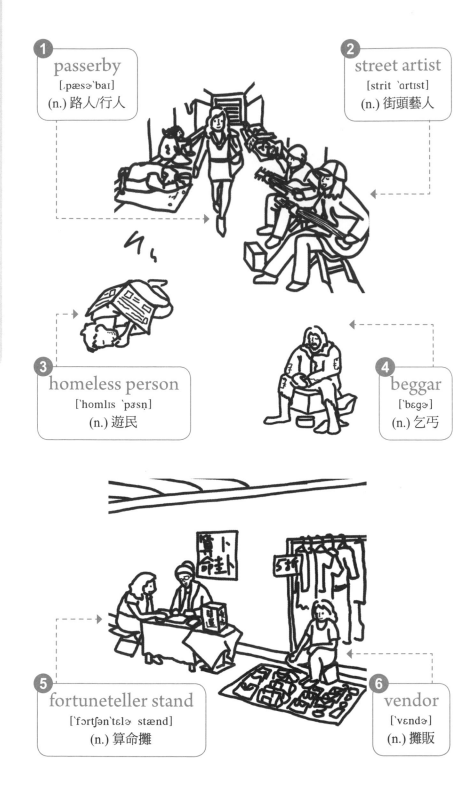

1 passerby
[ˌpæsəˋbaɪ]
(n.) 路人/行人

2 street artist
[strit ˋɑrtɪst]
(n.) 街頭藝人

3 homeless person
[ˋhomlɪs ˋpɜsn̩]
(n.) 遊民

4 beggar
[ˋbɛɡə]
(n.) 乞丐

5 fortuneteller stand
[ˋfɔrtʃənˏtɛlə stænd]
(n.) 算命攤

6 vendor
[ˋvɛndə]
(n.) 攤販

❶ 路人 / 行人

Beware of passersby when you drive.

小心注意…

❷ 街頭藝人

Many of the street artists you see are students at music schools.

你看到的街頭藝人

❸ 遊民

He is a homeless person so he sleeps on a bench in the park.

❹ 乞丐

There are so many beggars in the underpass.

❺ 算命攤

There is a fortuneteller stand right at the corner.

就在轉角處

❻ 攤販

This vendor only comes once a week.

一週一次

學更多

❶ beware of...〈小心…〉‧ passersby〈passerby（路人、行人）的複數〉‧ drive〈開車〉
❷ street〈街道〉‧ artist〈藝人〉‧ student〈學生〉‧ music〈音樂〉
❸ homeless〈無家可歸的〉‧ person〈人〉‧ sleep〈睡〉‧ bench〈長椅〉‧ park〈公園〉
❹ many〈許多的〉‧ underpass〈地下道〉
❺ fortuneteller〈算命師〉‧ stand〈攤子〉‧ right〈正好〉‧ corner〈轉角〉
❻ only〈只〉‧ once〈一次〉

中譯

❶ 當你開車時，要留意路人。
❷ 你看到的街頭藝人，很多都是音樂學院的學生。
❸ 他是個無家可歸的遊民，所以睡在公園的長椅上。
❹ 地下道裡有非常多乞丐。
❺ 轉角處就有一個算命攤。
❻ 這個攤販每週只來擺攤一次。

便利商店櫃位(1)

1 cigarette rack
[͵sɪgəˋrɛt ræk]
(n.) 香菸櫃位

2 check-out counter
[ˋtʃɛk͵aʊt ˋkaʊntə]
(n.) 結帳櫃檯

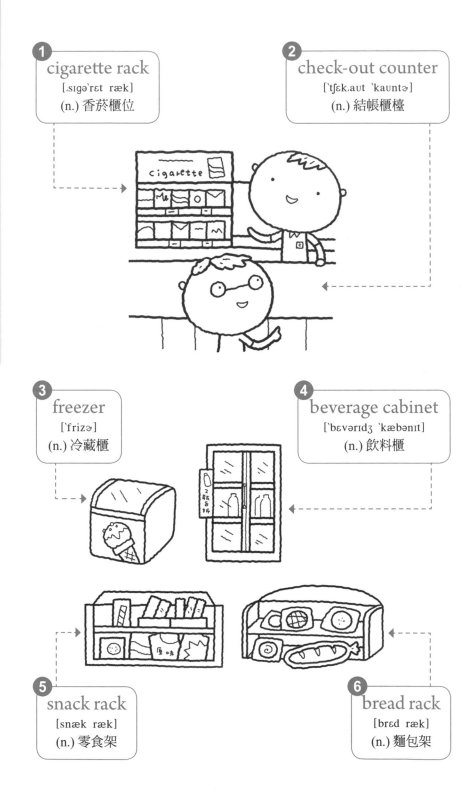

3 freezer
[ˋfrizə]
(n.) 冷藏櫃

4 beverage cabinet
[ˋbɛvərɪdʒ ˋkæbənɪt]
(n.) 飲料櫃

5 snack rack
[snæk ræk]
(n.) 零食架

6 bread rack
[brɛd ræk]
(n.) 麵包架

❶ 香菸櫃位
The cigarette rack is right behind the check-out counter.

❷ 結帳櫃檯
Please settle your payment at the check-out counter.
結算款項

❸ 冷藏櫃
The ice cream is in the freezer.

❹ 飲料櫃
Please bring more green tea from the beverage cabinet.
拿來更多的綠茶

❺ 零食架
There are no more chocolate bars on the snack rack.
沒有任何巧克力棒

❻ 麵包架
The freshly baked bread on the bread rack smells so good!
剛出爐的麵包

學更多

❶ cigarette〈香菸〉‧ rack〈架子〉‧ right〈正好〉‧ behind〈在⋯的後面〉
❷ settle〈結算〉‧ payment〈款項〉‧ check-out〈結帳離開〉‧ counter〈櫃檯〉
❸ ice cream〈冰淇淋〉
❹ bring〈拿來〉‧ green tea〈綠茶〉‧ beverage〈飲料〉‧ cabinet〈櫥櫃〉
❺ more〈另外的〉‧ chocolate〈巧克力〉‧ bar〈棒〉‧ snack〈零食〉
❻ freshly〈剛剛〉‧ baked〈烘烤的〉‧ bread〈麵包〉‧ smell〈有⋯氣味〉

中譯

❶ 香菸櫃位就在結帳櫃檯的後方。
❷ 請至結帳櫃檯完成結帳。
❸ 冰淇淋放在冷藏櫃裡。
❹ 請從飲料櫃裡多拿一些綠茶出來。
❺ 零食架上沒有任何巧克力棒。
❻ 麵包架上剛出爐的麵包聞起來真香！

154 便利商店櫃位(2)

MP3 154

1 newspaper rack
[`njuz,pepɚ ræk]
(n.) 報紙架

2 book shelf
[bʊk ʃɛlf]
(n.) 書籍櫃位

3 magazine shelf
[,mægəˋzin ʃɛlf]
(n.) 雜誌架

4 ATM
[`e`ti`ɛm]
(n.) 自動櫃員機

5 fax machine
[fæks məˋʃin]
(n.) 傳真機

6 photocopier
[ˋfotə,kɑpɪɚ]
(n.) 影印機

❶ 報紙架

All the newspapers can be found on the newspaper rack.
<u>可以被找到</u>

❷ 書籍櫃位

I can't find the book I want on the book shelf.
<u>我想要的書</u>

❸ 雜誌架

Can you tell me where I can find the magazine shelf?
<u>我可以在哪裡找到雜誌架</u>

❹ 自動櫃員機

Do you have an ATM in your store?

❺ 傳真機

Please load the paper in the fax machine.
<u>裝入紙張</u>

❻ 影印機

This photocopier is not working.
<u>沒有在運作</u>

學更多

❶ newspaper〈報紙〉・found〈find（找到）的過去分詞〉・rack〈架子〉
❷ find〈找到〉・want〈想要〉・shelf〈書櫥架子〉
❸ tell〈告訴〉・magazine〈雜誌〉
❹ have〈有〉・store〈店〉
❺ load〈裝載〉・paper〈紙〉・fax〈傳真〉・machine〈機器〉
❻ working〈work（運作）的 ing 型態〉

中譯

❶ 報紙架上，可以看到各家的報紙。
❷ 在書籍櫃位上，我找不到我想要的書。
❸ 可以告訴我雜誌架在哪裡嗎？
❹ 你們店裡有自動櫃員機嗎？
❺ 請裝入傳真機內的紙張。
❻ 這台影印機不能用了。

155

郵局(1)

MP3 155

1 mail drop
[mel drɑp]
(n.) 郵筒

2 letter
[ˈlɛtɚ]
(n.) 信件

3 mailman
[ˈmelˌmæn]
(n.) 郵差

4 sea mail
[si mel]
(n.) 海運郵件

5 air mail
[ɛr mel]
(n.) 航空郵件

以航空或路運方式優先
處理，並於最短時間內
送達收件人的郵件寄送
方式。

6 express mail
[ɪkˈsprɛs mel]
(n.) 快捷郵件

❶ 郵筒
What is the mail drop used for?
　　　　　　　　　　　　用於

❷ 信件
He wrote me a letter last month.

❸ 郵差
The mailman delivers letters and parcels every morning.
　　　　　　　　遞送信件和包裹

❹ 海運郵件
I sent the letters to the US via sea mail.
　　　　　　　　　　　　藉由海運郵件

❺ 航空郵件
How long does air mail usually take?

❻ 快捷郵件
Would you like to send it by express mail?
　　你想要…嗎

學更多

❶ mail〈郵件〉．drop〈投信口〉．used〈use（使用）的過去分詞〉
❷ wrote〈write（寫）的過去式〉．last〈上一個〉．month〈月〉
❸ deliver〈運送〉．parcel〈包裹〉．morning〈早晨〉
❹ sent〈send（寄）的過去式〉．via〈藉由〉．sea〈海洋〉
❺ air〈天空〉．usually〈通常地〉．take〈花費〉
❻ send〈寄〉．express〈快遞〉

中譯

❶ 郵筒的用途是什麼？
❷ 他上個月寫了一封信件給我。
❸ 每天早上郵差都會遞送信件和包裹。
❹ 我用海運郵件寄信到美國。
❺ 航空郵件通常要花多久時間寄達？
❻ 你想要使用快捷郵件寄送嗎？

156

郵局(2)

MP3 156

1 registered mail
[ˈrɛdʒɪstəd mel]
(n.) 掛號信

2 stamp
[stæmp]
(n.) 郵票

3 postmark
[ˈpostˌmɑrk]
(n.) 郵戳

4 envelope
[ˈɛnvəˌlop]
(n.) 信封

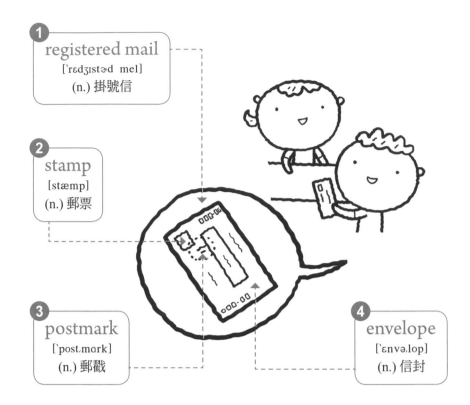

5 package
[ˈpækɪdʒ]
(n.) 包裹

6 postcard
[ˈpostˌkɑrd]
(n.) 明信片

320

❶ 掛號信
The registered mail arrived this morning.

❷ 郵票
I would like to buy a $10NT stamp.

❸ 郵戳
The letter bore a postmark of March 8, 1983.
　　　　　　　　蓋有一個郵戳

❹ 信封
I will put your allowance in the envelope.
　　　　　　　把你的零用錢放進…

❺ 包裹
The package arrived yesterday afternoon.

❻ 明信片
Please send me a postcard when you arrive in Hawaii.
　　　　　　寄明信片給我

學更多

❶ registered〈已掛號的〉・mail〈郵件〉・arrived〈arrive（到達）的過去式〉
❷ would like〈想要〉・buy〈購買〉
❸ letter〈信件〉・bore〈bear（印有）的過去式〉・March〈三月〉
❹ put in〈把…放進〉・allowance〈零用錢〉
❺ yesterday〈昨天〉・afternoon〈下午〉
❻ send〈寄〉・arrive〈到達〉・Hawaii〈夏威夷〉

中譯

❶ 掛號信已於今天早上送達。
❷ 我想要買一張 10 元的郵票。
❸ 這封信上蓋著 1983 年 3 月 8 日的郵戳。
❹ 我會把你的零用錢裝進信封裡。
❺ 包裹已於昨天下午寄達。
❻ 當你抵達夏威夷時，請寄明信片給我。

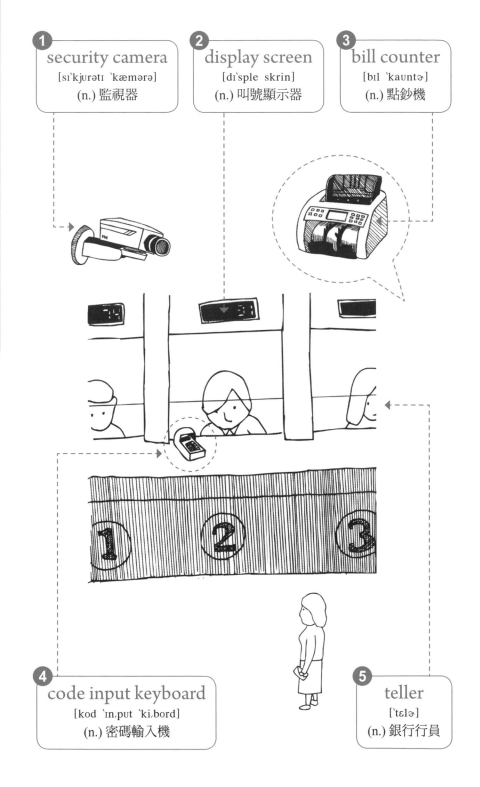

157 銀行櫃檯(1)

MP3 157

1 security camera
[sɪˋkjʊrətɪ ˋkæmərə]
(n.) 監視器

2 display screen
[dɪˋsple skrin]
(n.) 叫號顯示器

3 bill counter
[bɪl ˋkaʊntɚ]
(n.) 點鈔機

4 code input keyboard
[kod ˋɪnˌpʊt ˋkiˌbord]
(n.) 密碼輸入機

5 teller
[ˋtɛlɚ]
(n.) 銀行行員

1 監視器

There are security cameras everywhere in the bank.

2 叫號顯示器

Your number will be shown on the display screen when it's your turn.

輪到你

3 點鈔機

A bill counter makes counting the bills so much easier.

數鈔票

4 密碼輸入機

Please enter your code with the code input keyboard.

輸入你的密碼

5 銀行行員

She works as a teller in a bank.

以銀行行員的身分工作

---

1 security〈防備〉‧camera〈攝影機〉‧everywhere〈到處〉‧bank〈銀行〉

2 shown〈show（顯示）的過去分詞〉‧display〈顯示〉‧screen〈螢幕〉‧
turn〈輪到的一次機會〉

3 bill〈鈔票〉‧counter〈計數器〉‧counting〈count（數）的 ing 型態〉‧
easier〈更簡單的，easy（簡單的）的比較級〉

4 enter〈輸入〉‧code〈密碼〉‧input〈輸入〉‧keyboard〈鍵盤〉

5 work〈工作〉‧as〈作為、以…的身分〉

中譯

1 銀行裡到處都有監視器。

2 當輪到你的時候，你的號碼會顯示在叫號顯示器上。

3 點鈔機使得數鈔票變得容易許多。

4 請在密碼輸入機輸入你的密碼。

5 她的工作是銀行行員。

MP3 158

1 deposit slip
[dɪˋpɑzɪt slɪp]
deposit form
[dɪˋpɑzɪt fɔrm]
(n.) 存款單

兩個單字都是「存款單」。

2 withdrawal slip
[wɪðˋdrɔəl slɪp]
withdrawal form
[wɪðˋdrɔəl fɔrm]
(n.) 提款單

兩個單字都是「提款單」。

3 passbook
[ˋpæsˌbʊk]
(n.) 存摺

4 foreign currency
[ˋfɔrɪn ˋkɝənsɪ]
(n.) 外幣

5 bill
[bɪl]
(n.) 鈔票

6 check
[tʃɛk]
(n.) 支票

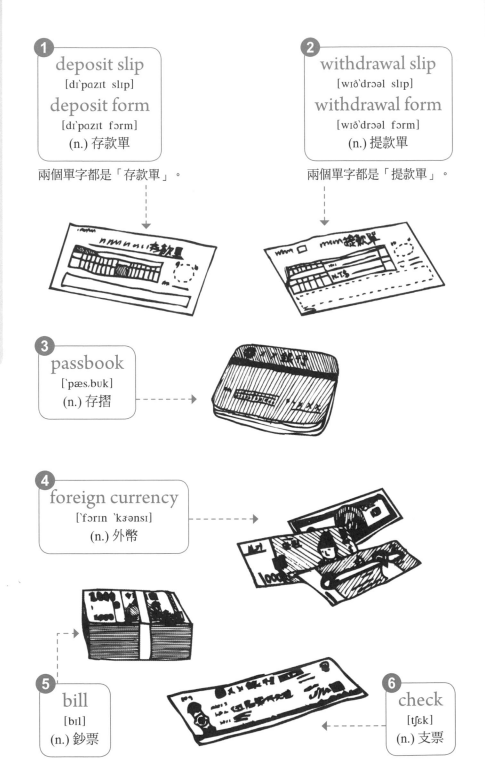

❶ 存款單

I need the deposit form please.

❷ 提款單

Do I have to fill in the <u>withdrawal form</u> first?

先填好提款單

❸ 存摺

I can't believe I lost my passbook!

❹ 外幣

Where is the foreign currency <u>exchange counter</u>?

兌換櫃檯

❺ 鈔票

I only have a $10 dollar <u>bill left</u>.

剩下一張 10 美元的鈔票

❻ 支票

Would you like to <u>pay by check</u>?

用支票的方式

學更多

❶ need〈需要〉・deposit〈存款〉・slip〈紙條〉・form〈表格〉
❷ fill in〈填寫〉・withdrawal〈提款〉・first〈首先〉
❸ believe〈相信〉・lost〈lose（遺失）的過去式〉
❹ foreign〈外國的〉・currency〈貨幣〉・exchange〈兌換〉・counter〈櫃檯〉
❺ only〈只〉・dollar〈美元〉・left〈leave（剩下）的過去分詞〉
❻ pay〈付款〉

中譯

❶ 請給我存款單。
❷ 我需要先填好提款單嗎？
❸ 我不敢相信我竟然把存摺弄丟了！
❹ 外幣兌換櫃檯在哪裡？
❺ 我只剩下一張 10 美元的鈔票。
❻ 你想要用支票付款嗎？

1 tablet
[`tæblɪt]
(n.) 藥片/藥丸

2 capsule
[`kæps!]
(n.) 膠囊

3 pharmacist
[`fɑrməsɪst]
(n.) 藥師

4 cough syrup
[kɔf `sɪrəp]
(n.) 咳嗽糖漿

5 vitamin
[`vaɪtəmɪn]
(n.) 維他命

6 ointment
[`ɔɪntmənt]
(n.) 藥膏

❶ 藥片 / 藥丸

Can you please pass me the blue tablets?
　　　　　　拿給我

❷ 膠囊

I prefer capsules to powdered medicine.
　　　　　　　　　　　　藥粉

❸ 藥師

I want to become a pharmacist when I grow up.

❹ 咳嗽糖漿

The cough syrup relieves my throat pain.
　　　　　　　　減輕我的喉嚨痛

❺ 維他命

Our bodies need vitamins to function properly.
　　　　　　　　　　　　　　正常地運作

❻ 藥膏

The ointment will cure your wound.
　　　　　　　　治療你的傷口

學更多

❶ please〈請〉・pass〈傳遞〉・blue〈藍色的〉
❷ prefer〈較喜歡〉・powdered〈粉末狀的〉・medicine〈藥〉
❸ want〈想要〉・become〈成為〉・grow up〈長大〉
❹ cough〈咳嗽〉・syrup〈糖漿〉・relieve〈緩和〉・throat〈喉嚨〉・pain〈疼痛〉
❺ our〈我們的〉・bodies〈body（身體）的複數〉・function〈運作〉・properly〈正確地〉
❻ cure〈治療〉・wound〈傷口〉

中譯

❶ 可以請你把藍色的藥片拿給我嗎？
❷ 我喜歡膠囊勝過於藥粉。
❸ 長大後，我希望成為一名藥師。
❹ 咳嗽糖漿舒緩了我喉嚨痛的症狀。
❺ 我們的身體需要維他命維持正常運作。
❻ 藥膏能夠治療你的傷口。

藥局(2)

MP3 160

1 first aid kit
[fɝst ed kɪt]
(n.) 急救箱

2 bandage
[`bændɪdʒ]
(n.) 繃帶

3 band-aid
[`bænd͵ed]
(n.) OK 繃

4 sanitary napkin
[`sænə͵tɛrɪ `næpkɪn]
(n.) 衛生棉

5 condom
[`kɑndəm]
(n.) 保險套

6 diaper
[`daɪəpə]
(n.) 尿布

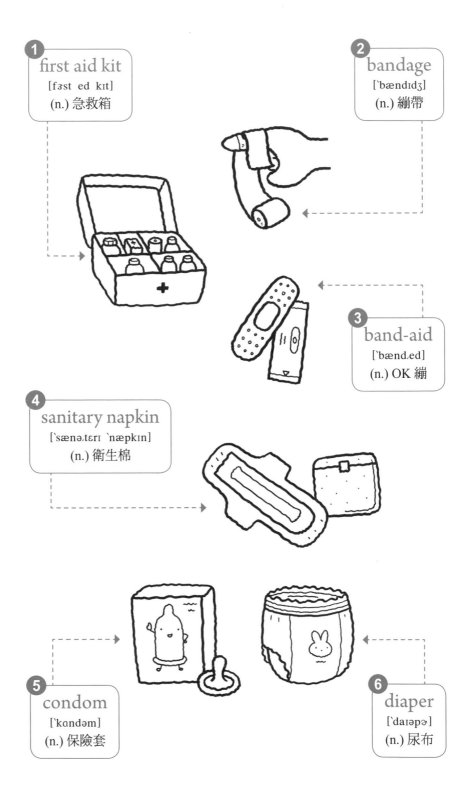

❶ 急救箱

Everyone should keep a first aid kit at home in case of emergency.
　　　　　　　　　　　　　　　　　　　　　　　　　　　萬一、如果發生

❷ 繃帶

He wrapped a bandage around his injured arm.
　　　　　　　　　　　　　　環繞他受傷的手臂

❸ OK 繃

Do you have a band-aid that I can use?

❹ 衛生棉

Please do not flush sanitary napkins.

❺ 保險套

Condoms should be used for protection.
　　　　　　　　　被使用於

❻ 尿布

I need someone to help me change the baby's diaper.
　　　　我需要有人幫忙我

學更多

❶ keep〈持有〉‧ first〈最先的〉‧ aid〈救助〉‧ kit〈工具箱〉‧ emergency〈緊急狀況〉
❷ wrapped〈wrap（纏繞）的過去式〉‧ around〈環繞〉‧ injured〈受傷的〉
❸ band〈鬆緊帶〉‧ use〈使用〉
❹ flush〈沖水〉‧ sanitary〈衛生的〉‧ napkin〈衛生棉〉
❺ used〈use（使用）的過去分詞〉‧ protection〈保護〉
❻ someone〈有人〉‧ help〈幫助〉‧ change〈更換〉‧ baby〈嬰兒〉

中譯

❶ 每個人家裡都應該要有急救箱，以防萬一發生緊急狀況。
❷ 他用繃帶纏繞他受傷的手臂。
❸ 你有 OK 繃可以給我使用嗎？
❹ 請不要（用馬桶）沖掉衛生棉。
❺ 應該使用保險套作為防護措施。
❻ 我需要有人幫我替嬰兒換尿布。

161

傳統市場(1)

MP3 161

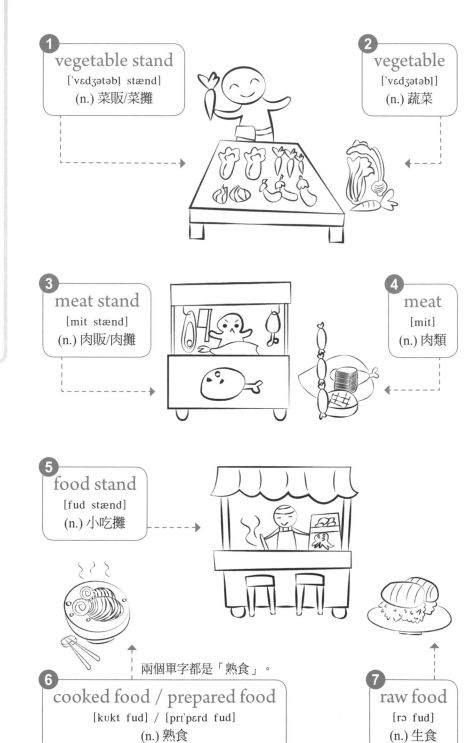

1 vegetable stand
[ˈvɛdʒətəbl̩ stænd]
(n.) 菜販/菜攤

2 vegetable
[ˈvɛdʒətəbl̩]
(n.) 蔬菜

3 meat stand
[mit stænd]
(n.) 肉販/肉攤

4 meat
[mit]
(n.) 肉類

5 food stand
[fud stænd]
(n.) 小吃攤

兩個單字都是「熟食」。

6 cooked food / prepared food
[kʊkt fud] / [prɪˈpɛrd fud]
(n.) 熟食

7 raw food
[rɔ fud]
(n.) 生食

❶ 菜販 / 菜攤

I also want to buy some cabbage from the vegetable stand.

❷ 蔬菜

We have a small vegetable garden in our backyard.
　　　　　　一小塊的蔬菜園

❸ 肉販 / 肉攤

You can find the meat you want at the meat stand.
　　　　你想要的肉類

❹ 肉類

A traditional market sells all kinds of different meats: pork, beef,chicken and lamb.
　　　　　　　　　各種不同的肉類

❺ 小吃攤

You can find a variety of food stands in the night markets.
　　　　各式各樣的

❻ 熟食

I prefer cooked food to raw food.

❼ 生食

Some people are afraid of eating raw food.
　　　　　害怕

學更多

❶ also〈也〉・buy〈購買〉・cabbage〈高麗菜〉・stand〈攤子〉
❷ small〈小的〉・garden〈菜園〉・our〈我們的〉・backyard〈後院〉
❸ find〈找到〉・want〈想要〉
❹ traditional〈傳統的〉・pork〈豬肉〉・beef〈牛肉〉・chicken〈雞肉〉・lamb〈羊肉〉
❺ food〈食物〉・night market〈夜市〉
❻ prefer〈更喜歡〉・cooked〈煮熟的〉・prepared〈經過調製的〉・raw〈生的〉
❼ afraid〈害怕的〉・eating〈eat（吃）的 ing 型態〉

中譯

❶ 我也想要去菜攤買一些高麗菜。
❷ 我們的後院裡，有一小塊蔬菜園。
❸ 你可以在肉攤找到你想要的肉類。
❹ 傳統市場販賣各種肉類：豬肉、牛肉、雞肉和羊肉。
❺ 在夜市裡，你可以看到各式各樣的小吃攤。
❻ 比起生食，我更喜歡吃熟食。
❼ 有些人害怕吃生食。

❶ 家庭主婦

Mary became a full-time housewife after she got married last year.

全職的家庭主婦　　　　　　　　　　　去年結婚了

❷ 菜籃車

Put everything you want in the shopping cart.

❸ 水果

These organic fruits taste really good!

有機水果

❹ 乾貨

It is important to store dry food properly.

❺ 醃漬物

She can make jams and pickles.

❻ 海鮮

My father is allergic to seafood so he never eats it.

對…過敏

❼ 磅秤

Please use the scale to weigh the meat.

秤肉的重量

學更多

❶ became〈become（變成）的過去式〉‧ full-time〈全日制的、專職的〉
❷ put〈放〉‧ everything〈每件東西〉‧ shopping〈購物〉‧ cart〈手推車〉
❸ organic〈有機的〉‧ taste〈吃起來〉‧ really〈很〉
❹ important〈重要的〉‧ store〈貯存〉‧ dry〈乾燥的〉‧ properly〈正確地〉
❺ can〈會〉‧ make〈製作〉‧ jam〈果醬〉
❻ father〈父親〉‧ allergic〈過敏的〉‧ never〈從未〉
❼ use〈用〉‧ weigh〈秤…的重量〉‧ meat〈肉〉

中譯

❶ 瑪莉去年結婚後，就變成了全職的家庭主婦。
❷ 把所有你想要的東西，都放進菜籃車裡。
❸ 這些有機水果真的很好吃！
❹ 正確地貯存乾貨是很重要的。
❺ 她會做果醬和醃漬物。
❻ 我爸爸對海鮮過敏，所以他從來不吃。
❼ 請使用磅秤秤肉的重量。

電梯(1)

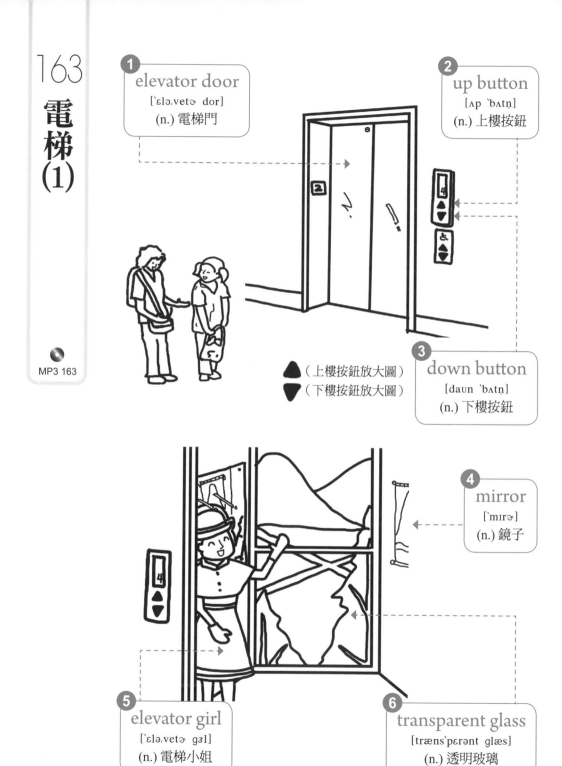

① elevator door
[ˈɛləˌvetɚ dor]
(n.) 電梯門

② up button
[ʌp ˈbʌtn̩]
(n.) 上樓按鈕

③ down button
[daʊn ˈbʌtn̩]
(n.) 下樓按鈕

▲（上樓按鈕放大圖）
▼（下樓按鈕放大圖）

④ mirror
[ˈmɪrɚ]
(n.) 鏡子

⑤ elevator girl
[ˈɛləˌvetɚ gɝl]
(n.) 電梯小姐

⑥ transparent glass
[trænsˈpɛrənt glæs]
(n.) 透明玻璃

❶ 電梯門
When the elevator doors opened on the first floor, everyone got out.
　　　　　　　　　在一樓開門

❷ 上樓按鈕
Press the up button if you want to go to the top floor.
　　　　　　　　　　　　　　　　到頂樓

❸ 下樓按鈕
I'm going down to the first floor. Please press the down button.
　　下去到一樓

❹ 鏡子
Sandy checked her hair in the mirror.
　　　　看一看她的頭髮

❺ 電梯小姐
The elevator girl asked me which floor I wanted.
　　　　　　　　　　　　　　我要到哪一層樓

❻ 透明玻璃
I can see my friend through the transparent glass.

學更多

❶ elevator〈電梯〉‧ opened〈open（開）的過去式〉‧ got out〈get out（離去）的過去式〉
❷ press〈按〉‧ up〈向上的〉‧ button〈按鈕〉‧ top〈頂的〉‧ floor〈樓層〉
❸ going down〈go down（下去）的 ing 型態〉‧ first〈第一個〉‧ down〈向下的〉
❹ checked〈check（檢查）的過去式〉‧ hair〈頭髮〉
❺ asked〈ask（問）的過去式〉‧ wanted〈want（想要）的過去式〉
❻ friend〈朋友〉‧ through〈透過〉‧ transparent〈透明的〉‧ glass〈玻璃〉

中譯

❶ 當抵達一樓，電梯門打開後，所有人都走出了電梯。
❷ 如果你要到頂樓，就按上樓按鈕。
❸ 我要下去一樓，請按下樓按鈕。
❹ Sandy 照鏡子看一看她的頭髮。
❺ 電梯小姐詢問我要到哪一層樓。
❻ 我可以從透明玻璃看到我的朋友。

電梯(2)

MP3 164

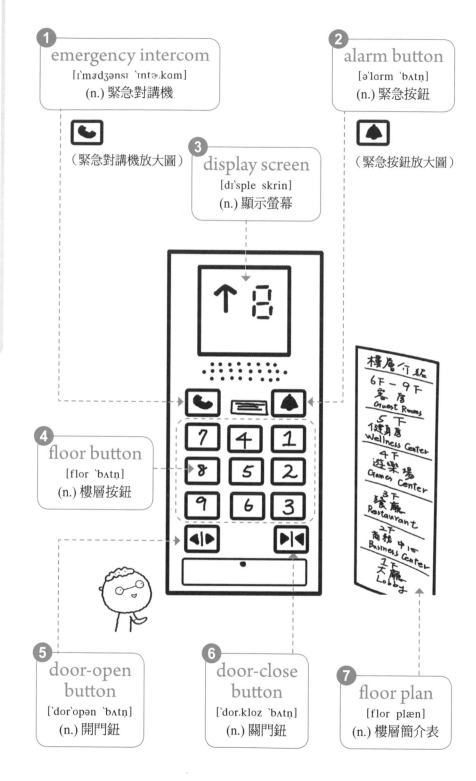

1 emergency intercom
[ɪˋmɝdʒənsɪ ˋɪntɚˌkɑm]
(n.) 緊急對講機

（緊急對講機放大圖）

2 alarm button
[əˋlɑrm ˋbʌtn̩]
(n.) 緊急按鈕

（緊急按鈕放大圖）

3 display screen
[dɪˋsple skrin]
(n.) 顯示螢幕

4 floor button
[flor ˋbʌtn̩]
(n.) 樓層按鈕

5 door-open button
[ˋdorˋopən ˋbʌtn̩]
(n.) 開門鈕

6 door-close button
[ˋdorˌkloz ˋbʌtn̩]
(n.) 關門鈕

7 floor plan
[flor plæn]
(n.) 樓層簡介表

樓層介紹
6F - 9F
客房
Guest Rooms
5 F
健身房
Wellness Center
4 F
遊樂場
Games Center
3 F
餐廳
Restaurant
2 F
商務中心
Business Center
1 F
大廳
Lobby

❶ 緊急對講機

If the elevator stops, talk to the security guard on the emergency intercom.
聯絡警衛

❷ 緊急按鈕

You should only press the alarm button in emergencies.
在緊急狀況時

❸ 顯示螢幕

The display screen in the elevator shows what floor we're on.
我們目前在哪一層樓

❹ 樓層按鈕

Tell me which floor you want, and I'll press the right floor button.

❺ 開門鈕

Pressing the door-open button will keep the doors open longer.
讓門開得比較久

❻ 關門鈕

Nobody else is waiting. Press the door-close button.
沒有其他人

❼ 樓層簡介表

The shoppers looked at the floor plan to see where the restrooms were.
廁所在哪裡

學更多

❶ elevator〈電梯〉‧ security guard〈警衛〉‧ emergency〈緊急情況〉‧ intercom〈對講機〉
❷ press〈按〉‧ alarm〈警報〉‧ button〈按鈕〉
❸ display〈顯示〉‧ screen〈螢幕〉‧ show〈顯示〉‧ floor〈樓層〉
❹ tell〈告訴〉‧ want〈想要〉‧ right〈正確的〉
❺ keep〈使…保持在某一狀態〉‧ longer〈較長久地，long（長久地）的比較級〉
❻ nobody〈沒有人〉‧ else〈其他〉‧ waiting〈wait（等待）的 ing 型態〉‧ close〈關閉〉
❼ shopper〈顧客〉‧ looked at...〈look at...（看…）的過去式〉‧ see〈查看〉‧ restroom〈廁所〉

中譯

❶ 如果電梯停擺，請使用緊急對講機聯絡警衛。
❷ 只有在緊急狀況時，你才能按下緊急按鈕。
❸ 電梯裡的顯示螢幕，會顯示出我們目前所在的樓層。
❹ 告訴我你要到哪一層樓，我會幫你按正確的樓層按鈕。
❺ 按住開門鈕會讓電梯門開得比較久。
❻ 沒有人（等著）要進電梯了，可以按下關門鈕。
❼ 顧客看了樓層簡介表，就知道廁所在哪裡。

165

花店(1)

MP3 165

1 wrapping paper
[ˈræpɪŋ ˈpepɚ]
(n.) 包裝紙

2 wrapped bouquet
[ræpt buˋke]
(n.) 花束

3 card
[kɑrd]
(n.) 卡片

4 ribbon
[ˈrɪbən]
(n.) 緞帶

5 flower basket
[ˈflaʊɚ ˈbæskɪt]
(n.) 花籃

338

❶ 包裝紙

The gift was covered in wrapping paper.
　　　　　　　　　被包裝紙包住

❷ 花束

If you want your flowers to look more special, get them in a wrapped
bouquet.
　　　　　　　　　　　　　　　　　　　讓它們變成一個花束

❸ 卡片

The card that came with the flowers said, "I love you."
　　　　　　　　隨花到來

❹ 緞帶

To make the flower pot look nicer, Mary tied some ribbon round it.
　　　　　　　　　　　　　　　　　　　　繞著花盆

❺ 花籃

Penny collected flowers in a flower basket.

學更多

❶ gift〈禮物〉・covered〈cover（覆蓋）的過去分詞〉・wrapping〈包裝材料〉
❷ look〈看起來〉・special〈特別的〉・wrapped〈有包裝的〉・bouquet〈花束〉
❸ came〈come（來）的過去式〉・said〈say（表達）的過去式〉
❹ pot〈花盆〉・tied〈tie（繫上）的過去式〉・round〈環繞〉
❺ collected〈collect（採集）的過去式〉・basket〈籃子〉

中譯

❶ 禮物用包裝紙包好。
❷ 如果要讓你的花看起來更特別，就把它們綁成一個花束。
❸ 隨花所附的卡片上面寫著「我愛你」。
❹ 為了讓花盆更加美觀，Mary 為花盆繫上了緞帶。
❺ Penny 摘了一些花，並裝在花籃裡。

166

花店(2)

MP3 166

1 rubber glove
[ˈrʌbɚ glʌv]
(n.) 橡膠手套

2 apron
[ˈeprən]
(n.) 圍裙

3 flower pot
[ˈflauɚ pɑt]
(n.) 花盆

4 fertilizer
[ˈfɝtḷˌaɪzɚ]
(n.) 肥料

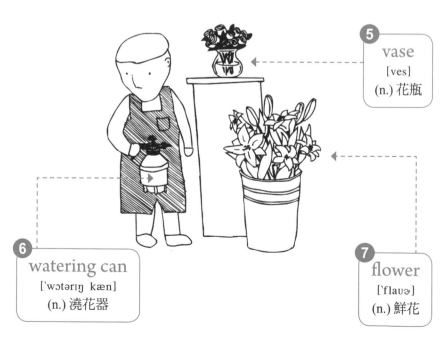

5 vase
[ves]
(n.) 花瓶

6 watering can
[ˈwɔtərɪŋ kæn]
(n.) 澆花器

7 flower
[ˈflauɚ]
(n.) 鮮花

❶ 橡膠手套

Rubber gloves keep your hands clean when you're holding dirty things.
保持你的手部乾淨

❷ 圍裙

Daphne puts an apron over her clothes when she cooks.
覆蓋在她的衣服上

❸ 花盆

Wendy has a few flowers in flower pots next to her window.
在她的窗戶邊

❹ 肥料

Fertilizer helps plants grow.

❺ 花瓶

Polly put her flowers in a vase with some water.
加入一些水

❻ 澆花器

Rachel used a watering can to put water on her plants.
澆她的植物

❼ 鮮花

The old woman loved to smell the flowers in her garden.
喜歡聞花香

學更多

❶ rubber〈橡膠〉．glove〈手套〉．holding〈hold（握、抓）的 ing 型態〉．dirty〈髒的〉
❷ put〈穿衣〉．over〈在…上面〉．cook〈烹飪〉
❸ a few〈一些〉．pot〈盆〉．next〈緊鄰的〉．window〈窗戶〉
❹ help〈幫助〉．plant〈植物〉．grow〈成長〉
❺ put〈放〉．water〈水〉
❻ watering〈灑水〉．can〈容器〉
❼ old〈老的〉．woman〈女人〉．smell〈聞〉．garden〈花園〉

中譯

❶ 當你要拿髒東西時，戴上橡膠手套可以讓你的手保持乾淨。
❷ Daphne 做菜時，都會在衣服外面套上圍裙。
❸ Wendy 在窗戶旁用花盆種了一些花。
❹ 肥料有助於植物生長。
❺ Polly 把花放進花瓶裡，並加了一些水。
❻ Rachel 使用澆花器幫她的植物澆水。
❼ 那位老太太喜歡聞她花園裡的花香。

美容院(1)

MP3 167

1 salon hair dryer
[sə`lɑn hɛr `draɪɚ]
(n.) 燙髮機

2 hairdresser
[`hɛr,drɛsɚ]
(n.) 髮型設計師

3 barber's cape
[`bɑrbɚz kep]
(n.) 剪髮袍

4 basin
[`besn̩]
(n.) 沖水台

5 foam
[fom]
(n.) 泡沫

❶ 燙髮機

The woman sat under the salon hair dryer for 30 minutes, and then the hairdresser styled her hair for her.
為她設計她的髮型

❷ 髮型設計師

The hairdresser loves cutting hair every day.
剪頭髮

❸ 剪髮袍

A barber's cape is used to keep cut hair off the customer and his clothes.
使剪下的頭髮遠離…

❹ 沖水台

Put your head over the basin so I can wash your hair.
把你的頭枕在…上

❺ 泡沫

Foam or shaving cream is used to help someone shave more comfortably.

學更多

❶ woman〈女人〉‧ sat〈sit（坐）的過去式〉‧ under〈在…下面〉‧ minute〈分鐘〉‧ styled〈style（設計）的過去式〉

❷ cutting〈cut（剪）的 ing 型態〉‧ hair〈頭髮〉

❸ barber〈理髮師〉‧ cape〈斗篷〉‧ used〈use（使用）的過去分詞〉‧ keep〈使…保持在某一狀態〉‧ cut〈切下的〉‧ off〈偏離〉‧ customer〈顧客〉

❹ over〈在…上面〉‧ wash〈洗〉

❺ shaving〈刮鬍子〉‧ cream〈膏狀物〉‧ help〈幫助〉‧ someone〈某人〉‧ shave〈刮毛髮〉‧ comfortably〈舒適地〉

中譯

❶ 那名女子坐在燙髮機底下整燙了 30 分鐘，接著美髮師便為她設計髮型。

❷ 髮型設計師樂於每天剪髮。

❸ 剪髮袍用來避免剪下的頭髮沾到顧客身上和衣服上。

❹ 把你的頭枕在沖水台上，好讓我幫你洗頭。

❺ 泡沫或刮鬍膏是用來讓人更舒適地刮鬍子。

MP3 168

1 comb
[kom]
(n.) 梳子

2 hair dryer
[hɛr `draɪə]
(n.) 吹風機

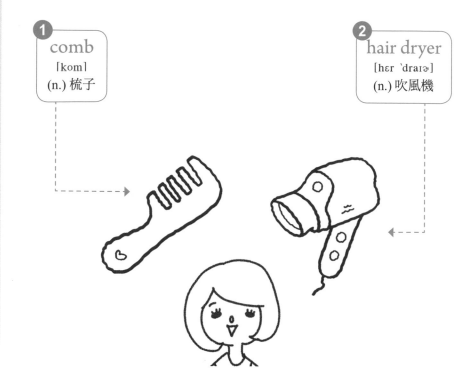

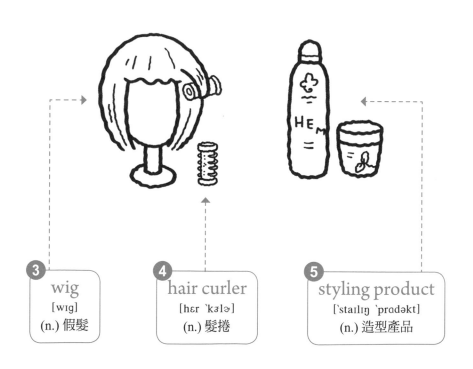

3 wig
[wɪg]
(n.) 假髮

4 hair curler
[hɛr `kɝlə]
(n.) 髮捲

5 styling product
[`staɪlɪŋ `prɑdəkt]
(n.) 造型產品

❶ 梳子

David used a comb to put his hair in place.

把他的頭髮梳好

❷ 吹風機

After getting out of the shower, Rebecca used a hair dryer to dry her hair.

走出淋浴間

❸ 假髮

He doesn't have any hair. He wears a wig.

戴假髮

❹ 髮捲

Put the hair curlers in your hair to make it curly.

在你的頭髮上上髮捲

❺ 造型產品

Styling products like mousse help you style your hair.

有助於你造型頭髮

學更多

❶ used〈use（使用）的過去式〉‧hair〈頭髮〉‧in place〈在適當的地方、適當的〉

❷ getting out of〈get out of（從⋯離開）的 ing 型態〉‧shower〈淋浴間〉‧dryer〈吹風機〉‧dry〈弄乾〉

❸ have〈有〉‧any〈絲毫〉‧wear〈戴著〉

❹ curler〈捲髮夾〉‧make〈使得〉‧curly〈捲的〉

❺ styling〈造型〉‧product〈產品〉‧mousse〈慕斯〉‧help〈幫助〉‧style〈設計〉

中譯

❶ David 用梳子將他的頭髮梳理好。

❷ 走出淋浴間之後，Rebecca 用吹風機吹乾頭髮。

❸ 他完全沒有頭髮。他戴假髮。

❹ 在你的頭髮上上髮捲，讓頭髮變捲。

❺ 類似慕斯之類的造型產品，有助於你造型頭髮。

169
戶外廣場(1)

MP3 169

1
tourist
[ˈturɪst]
(n.) 遊客

2
vendor
[ˈvɛndɚ]
(n.) 攤販

3
street performer
[strit pɚˈfɔrmɚ]
(n.) 街頭藝人

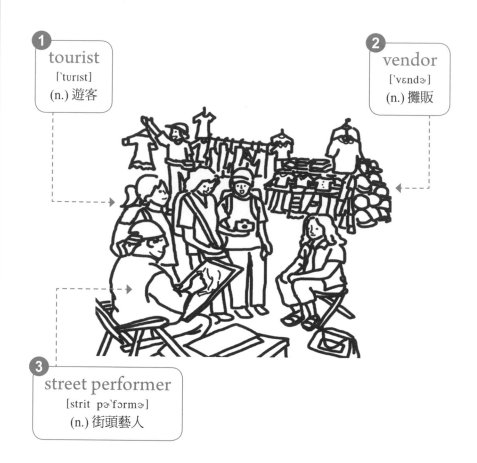

4
flea market
[fli ˈmɑrkɪt]
(n.) 跳蚤市場

5
market
[ˈmɑrkɪt]
(n.) 市集

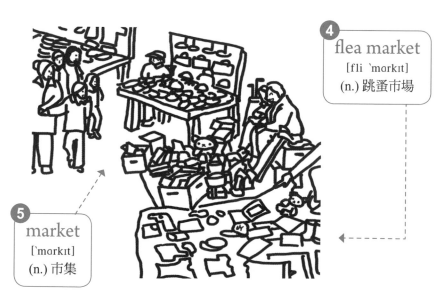

❶ 遊客

The tourists took pictures of the famous buildings.
　　　　　　　拍…的相片

❷ 攤販

After closing his stall for the night, the vendor threw his garbage away
　　　收起他的攤位　　　　　　　　　　　　　　　　把他的垃圾扔掉

into a nearby trash can.

❸ 街頭藝人

The street performer is entertaining crowds on the street.
　　　　　　　　　　　娛樂群眾

❹ 跳蚤市場

People sell lots of old things at flea markets.
　　販賣許多舊物

❺ 市集

You can usually buy things more cheaply in the market.
　　　　　　　　　　　更便宜地

學更多

❶ took pictures〈take pictures（照相）的過去式〉‧famous〈有名的〉‧building〈建築物〉

❷ closing〈close（打烊）的 ing 型態〉‧stall〈攤位〉‧
threw...away〈throw...away（扔掉）的過去式〉‧nearby〈附近的〉

❸ street〈街道〉‧performer〈表演者〉‧entertaining〈entertain（使娛樂）的 ing 型態〉‧
crowd〈人群〉

❹ sell〈販賣〉‧lots of〈很多〉‧old〈舊的〉‧flea〈跳蚤〉‧market〈市場〉

❺ usually〈通常〉‧more〈更加〉‧cheaply〈便宜地〉

中譯

❶ 遊客拍了一些著名建築物的照片。

❷ 晚上收攤之後，攤販把垃圾扔進附近的垃圾桶裡。

❸ 街頭藝人正在街上娛樂群眾。

❹ 人們在跳蚤市場販賣許多舊物。

❺ 通常你可以在市集裡買到比較便宜的東西。

MP3 170

1 fountain
[ˈfaʊntɪn]
(n.) 噴泉

2 statue
[ˈstætʃʊ]
(n.) 雕像

3 flower bed
[ˈflaʊɚ ˈbɛd]
(n.) 花壇

4 pigeon
[ˈpɪdʒɪn]
(n.) 鴿子

5 music concert
[ˈmjuzɪk ˈkɑnsɚt]
(n.) 音樂會

❶ 噴泉
The water in the fountain looks so nice in the summer.

❷ 雕像
The government wants to put a statue of the great president on the street.
　　　　　　　　　　　　　　　　豎立偉大總統的雕像

❸ 花壇
The flower beds in the park look very pretty in the summer.
　　　　　　　　　　　　　　　看起來非常漂亮

❹ 鴿子
Lots of people hate pigeons, and some are even scared when the birds fly past them.
　　　　　　　　　　　　　　有些人甚至會被嚇到　　　　　這些鳥飛過

❺ 音樂會
Lots of singers performed at the music concert.

學更多

❶ look〈看起來、好像〉・nice〈美好的〉・summer〈夏天〉
❷ government〈政府〉・great〈偉大的〉・president〈總統〉・street〈街道〉
❸ bed〈花壇〉・park〈公園〉・pretty〈漂亮的〉
❹ hate〈討厭〉・even〈甚至〉・scared〈scare（驚嚇）的過去分詞〉・fly〈飛〉・
　 past〈經過〉
❺ singer〈歌手〉・performed〈perform（表演）的過去式〉・concert〈音樂會〉

中譯

❶ 夏季時，噴泉的水看起來覺得很舒服（讓人覺得很涼快）。
❷ 政府想要在街道上豎立一座偉大總統的雕像。
❸ 夏季時，公園的花壇看起來賞心悅目。
❹ 許多人討厭鴿子，當鴿子飛過身邊時，有些人甚至會受到驚嚇。
❺ 許多歌手在音樂會上做了表演。

1 firework
[ˈfaɪr.wɝk]
(n.) 煙火

2 flag
[flæg]
(n.) 旗幟

3 clock tower
[klɑk ˈtaʊɚ]
(n.) 鐘塔

4 wishing pond
[ˈwɪʃɪŋ pɑnd]
(n.) 許願池

5 monument
[ˈmɑnjəmənt]
(n.) 紀念碑

❶ 煙火

People love watching the fireworks at 101 on New Year's Eve.
<u>新年前夕</u>

❷ 旗幟

There's a Taiwanese flag flying outside the presidential building.
<u>在總統府外飄揚</u>

❸ 鐘塔

The clock tower in the center of the town has stopped working.
<u>已經停止運作了</u>

❹ 許願池

Kim threw a coin in the wishing pond and made a wish.
<u>許下了願望</u>

❺ 紀念碑

The monument was built to honor soldiers who died in the war.
<u>在戰爭中逝去的人</u>

學更多

❶ watching〈watch（觀看）的 ing 型態〉‧New Year〈新年〉‧Eve〈前夕〉
❷ flying〈fly（飄揚）的 ing 型態〉‧presidential〈總統的〉‧building〈建築物〉
❸ clock〈時鐘〉‧tower〈塔〉‧center〈中心〉‧town〈城鎮〉‧
stopped〈stop（停止）的過去分詞〉‧working〈work（運作）的 ing 型態〉
❹ threw〈throw（扔）的過去式〉‧coin〈硬幣〉‧pond〈池塘〉‧wish〈願望〉
❺ built〈build（建造）的過去分詞〉‧honor〈給…榮譽〉‧soldier〈兵〉‧
died〈die（死）的過去式〉‧war〈戰爭〉

中譯

❶ 即將跨年時，人們喜歡在台北 101 觀賞煙火。
❷ 有一面台灣的國旗在總統府外飄揚。
❸ 位在城鎮中心的鐘塔，已經停止運作了。
❹ Kim 將一枚硬幣丟入許願池，並許了一個願望。
❺ 這座紀念碑是為了紀念那些在戰爭中逝去的士兵而建的。

172

行李箱內(1)

MP3 172

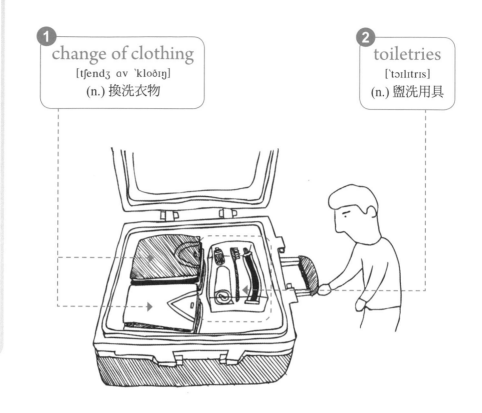

1 change of clothing
[tʃendʒ ɑv `kloðɪŋ]
(n.) 換洗衣物

2 toiletries
[`tɔɪlɪtrɪs]
(n.) 盥洗用具

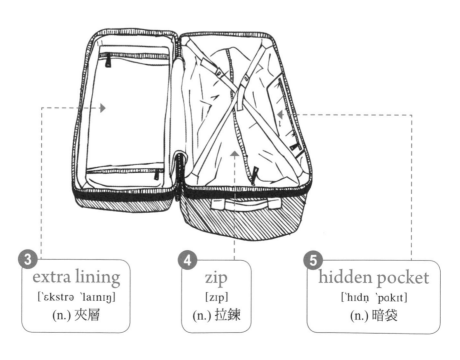

3 extra lining
[`ɛkstrə `laɪnɪŋ]
(n.) 夾層

4 zip
[zɪp]
(n.) 拉鍊

5 hidden pocket
[`hɪdn̩ `pɑkɪt]
(n.) 暗袋

❶ 換洗衣物

We'll be there for two days, so bring a change of clothing.
在那裡待上兩天

❷ 盥洗用具

Do you have your toiletries—you know, your toothbrush and soap and stuff?
你的牙刷、肥皂等等

❸ 夾層

Extra lining in luggage helps keep clothes better organized.
把衣服收得更整齊

❹ 拉鍊

The zip on Jean's coat is broken, so she can't zip it up.
她無法拉上拉鍊

❺ 暗袋

There's a hidden pocket inside the jacket. You can put valuable things in
there.
在外套裡面

學更多

❶ bring〈帶來〉・change〈更換〉・clothing〈衣服〉
❷ know〈知道〉・toothbrush〈牙刷〉・soap〈肥皂〉・and stuff〈等等、…之類的〉
❸ extra〈額外的〉・lining〈內層〉・luggage〈行李〉・keep〈保持在某一狀態〉・
clothes〈衣服〉・better〈更好地〉・organized〈有條理的〉
❹ coat〈外套〉・broken〈損壞的〉・zip up〈拉上…的拉鍊〉
❺ hidden〈隱藏的〉・pocket〈口袋〉・inside〈內側〉・jacket〈外套〉・put〈放〉・
valuable〈貴重的〉

中譯

❶ 我們會在那裡待上兩天，所以要帶換洗衣物。
❷ 你有帶你的盥洗用具——就是，你的牙刷、肥皂等等嗎？
❸ 行李中的夾層有助於將衣服收納得更整齊。
❹ Jean 外套的拉鍊壞了，所以她沒辦法拉上拉鍊。
❺ 外套內側有一個暗袋，你可以將貴重物品放在裡面。

173

行李箱內(2)

MP3 173

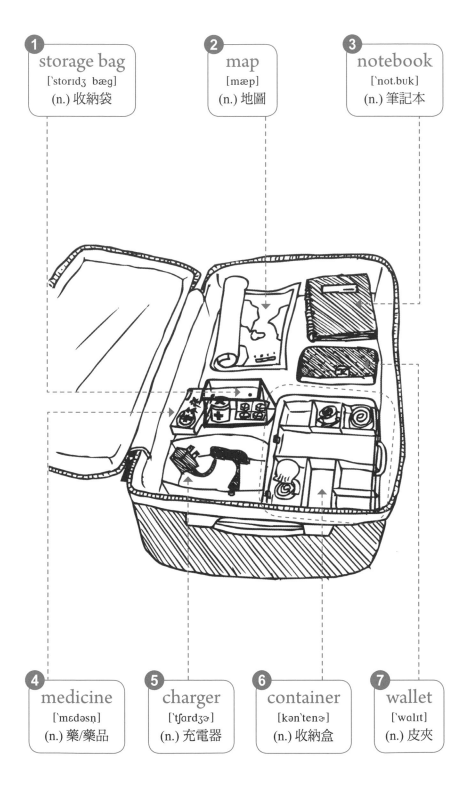

1 storage bag
[ˈstorɪdʒ bæg]
(n.) 收納袋

2 map
[mæp]
(n.) 地圖

3 notebook
[ˈnot.bʊk]
(n.) 筆記本

4 medicine
[ˈmɛdəsn̩]
(n.) 藥/藥品

5 charger
[ˈtʃɑrdʒɚ]
(n.) 充電器

6 container
[kənˈtenɚ]
(n.) 收納盒

7 wallet
[ˈwɑlɪt]
(n.) 皮夾

❶ 收納袋

Lily put her coat in a storage bag during the summer.
<u>把她的外套放入收納袋</u>

❷ 地圖

Zach didn't know where to go, so he looked at his map.
<u>要往哪裡</u>

❸ 筆記本

The writer often writes down ideas for stories in his notebook.
<u>寫下故事的點子</u>

❹ 藥 / 藥品

Andy's got some medicine for his sore throat.
<u>Andy 已經拿了一些藥</u>

❺ 充電器

My cellphone battery is low. I need a charger.
<u>電量低</u>

❻ 收納盒

Lindsey couldn't finish her food, so she put it in a container and put
<u>吃不完她的食物</u>　　　　　　　<u>把它放進收納盒</u>

that in the fridge.

❼ 皮夾

Do you keep your money in a wallet?

學更多

❶ put〈put（放）的過去式〉‧ coat〈外套〉‧ storage〈貯藏〉‧ during〈在…期間〉
❷ know〈知道〉‧ looked at...〈look at（看…）的過去式〉
❸ writer〈作者〉‧ often〈常常〉‧ write down...〈把…寫下〉‧ idea〈點子〉
❹ got〈get（得到）的過去式〉‧ sore throat〈喉嚨痛〉
❺ cellphone〈手機〉‧ battery〈電池〉‧ low〈低的〉
❻ finish〈吃完〉‧ fridge〈冰箱〉
❼ keep〈存放〉‧ money〈錢〉

中譯

❶ 在夏季期間，Lily 會將她的外套放入收納袋。
❷ Zach 不知道要往哪走，所以看了一下他的地圖。
❸ 作者常常會將故事的點子寫在自己的筆記本裡。
❹ Andy 有拿一些藥來治療他的喉嚨痛。
❺ 我的手機快沒電了，我需要充電器。
❻ Lindsey 吃不完她的餐點，所以她把餐點放入收納盒，並冰在冰箱裡。
❼ 你都把錢放在皮夾裡嗎？

174

車禍現場(1)

MP3 174

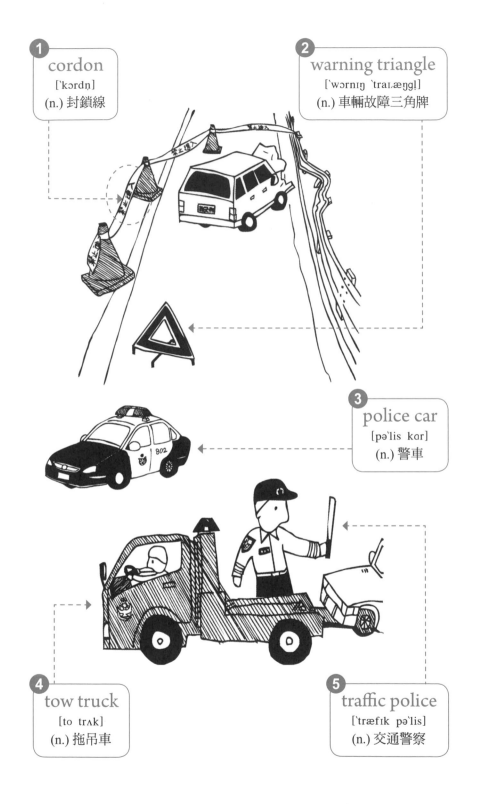

1 cordon
[ˈkɔrdn̩]
(n.) 封鎖線

2 warning triangle
[ˈwɔrnɪŋ ˈtraɪæŋgl̩]
(n.) 車輛故障三角牌

3 police car
[pəˈlis kɑr]
(n.) 警車

4 tow truck
[to trʌk]
(n.) 拖吊車

5 traffic police
[ˈtræfɪk pəˈlis]
(n.) 交通警察

❶ 封鎖線

The police set up a cordon around the crashed cars.
　　　　　　　　　設置封鎖線

❷ 車輛故障三角牌

Watch out ahead! There's a warning triangle you need to go around.
　　　　　　　　　　　　　　　　　　　　你必須繞過去

❸ 警車

The bad man was taken away in a police car.
　　　　　　　　被帶走

❹ 拖吊車

A tow truck was called in to take away the damaged cars.

❺ 交通警察

The traffic police arrived to look at the car crash scene.
　　　　　　　　　　　　　　　　勘查車禍現場

學更多

❶ police〈警察〉．set up〈擺放〉．crashed〈被碰撞的〉
❷ watch out〈小心〉．ahead〈在前面〉．warning〈警告〉．triangle〈三角形的物品〉．around〈繞過〉
❸ bad〈壞的〉．taken away〈take away（帶走）的過去分詞〉
❹ tow〈拖〉．truck〈卡車〉．called in〈call in（請…來）的過去分詞〉．damaged〈受損壞的〉
❺ traffic〈交通〉．arrived〈arrive（抵達）的過去式〉．look at〈檢查、研究〉．car crash〈車禍〉．scene〈現場〉

中譯

❶ 警察在遭撞毀車輛的四周，架起了封鎖線。
❷ 小心前面！那裡有一個車輛故障三角牌，你必須繞過去。
❸ 壞人被警車載走了。
❹ 叫來一輛拖吊車，拖走受損的車輛。
❺ 交通警察抵達現場，並進行車禍現場勘查工作。

175

車禍現場(2)

MP3 175

1 stretcher
[ˈstrɛtʃɚ]
(n.) 擔架

2 ambulance
[ˈæmbjələns]
(n.) 救護車

3 injured person
[ˈɪndʒəd ˈpɝsn]
(n.) 傷患

4 paramedic
[ˌpærəˈmɛdɪk]
(n.) 醫護人員

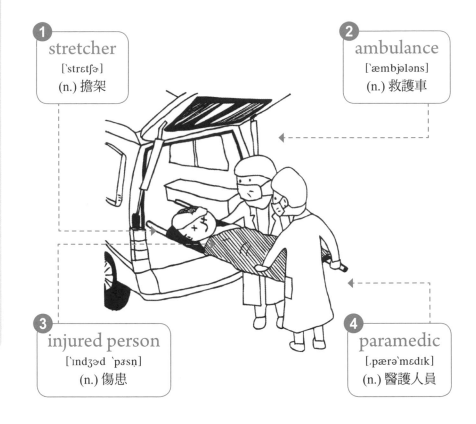

5 reporter
[rɪˈportɚ]
(n.) 記者

6 photographer
[fəˈtɑgrəfɚ]
(n.) 攝影師

7 SNG car
[ˈɛsˈɛnˈdʒi kɑr]
(n.) 衛星連線車

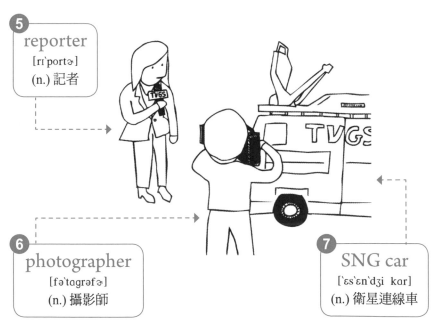

❶ 擔架

The boy with a broken leg <u>was carried to an ambulance on a</u> stretcher.
被抬到救護車上

❷ 救護車

The injured woman <u>was taken to the hospital in an</u> ambulance.
被載往醫院

❸ 傷患

Call an ambulance. There's an injured person here.

❹ 醫護人員

The paramedics arrived to help the people <u>who were injured in the car crash</u>.
在車禍中受傷的人

❺ 記者

A reporter went to the scene to interview people about <u>what had happened</u>.
發生了什麼事

❻ 攝影師

The photographer took pictures of the <u>famous star</u>.
知名影星

❼ 衛星連線車

The SNG car was driven to the site of the <u>car crash</u>.
車禍地點

學更多

❶ broken〈折斷的〉・leg〈腿〉・carried〈carry（抬）的過去分詞〉・on〈以…方式〉
❷ injured〈受傷的〉・taken〈take（帶去）的過去分詞〉・hospital〈醫院〉
❸ call〈呼叫〉・person〈人〉
❹ arrived〈arrive（抵達）的過去式〉・car crash〈車禍〉
❺ went〈go（去）的過去式〉・scene〈現場〉・interview〈訪問〉
❻ took pictures〈take pictures（照相）的過去式〉・famous〈有名的〉・star〈明星〉
❼ SNG〈Satellite News Gathering（衛星連線）的簡稱〉・driven〈drive（開車）的過去分詞〉

中譯

❶ 斷了腿的小男孩被用擔架抬到救護車上。
❷ 受傷的女人被救護車載往醫院。
❸ 叫救護車！這裡有一名傷患。
❹ 醫護人員前來幫助那些在車禍中受傷的傷者。
❺ 記者到現場訪問人們發生了什麼事。
❻ 攝影師拍了一些知名影星的照片。
❼ 衛星連線車開到了車禍現場。

176

火災現場 (1)

MP3 176

1 fire
[faɪr]
(n.) 大火

2 water hose
[ˋwɔtɚ hoz]
(n.) 消防水柱

3 smoke
[smok]
(n.) 黑煙

4 firefighter
[ˋfaɪrˏfaɪtɚ]
(n.) 消防員

5 rescue air cushion
[ˋrɛskju ɛr ˋkuʃən]
(n.) 救生氣墊

6 fire extinguisher
[faɪr ɪkˋstɪŋgwɪʃɚ]
(n.) 滅火器

7 bystander
[ˋbaɪˏstændɚ]
(n.) 旁觀民眾

1 大火

The fire burnt down the building.

2 消防水柱

The firefighters used water hoses to put out the fire.

把火撲滅

3 黑煙

The thick smoke made it hard for people to breathe.

讓…變得困難

4 消防員

The firefighters rescued people from the burning building.

從著火的建築物裡

5 救生氣墊

The man jumped from the roof down onto the rescue air cushion.

從屋頂往下跳到…

6 滅火器

Neil used a small fire extinguisher to put out a fire in his hotel room.

7 旁觀民眾

A bystander witnessed the accident and told police what had happened.

目擊了意外　　　　發生了什麼事

學更多

1 burnt down〈burn down（燒毀）的過去式〉・building〈建築物〉
2 water〈水〉・hose〈軟管、水龍帶〉・put out〈撲滅〉・fire〈火〉
3 thick〈濃厚的〉・hard〈困難的〉・breathe〈呼吸〉
4 rescued〈rescue（援救）的過去式〉・burning〈著火的〉
5 jumped〈jump（跳）的過去式〉・roof〈屋頂〉・air〈空氣〉・cushion〈墊狀物〉
6 small〈小的〉・extinguisher〈滅火器〉・hotel〈飯店〉
7 witnessed〈witness（目擊）的過去式〉・accident〈意外〉・police〈警察〉

中譯

1 大火燒毀了建築物。
2 消防員利用消防水柱滅火。
3 濃煙讓人們呼吸困難。
4 消防員從起火的建築物，將人們搶救出來。
5 那個男人從屋頂往下跳到救生氣墊上。
6 Neil 使用小型滅火器，將他飯店房間裡的火給撲滅了。
7 一位旁觀民眾目擊了意外，並將案發過程告訴警方。

177

火災現場(2)

MP3 177

1 fire engine
[faɪr `ɛndʒən]
(n.) 消防車

2 ladder truck
[`lædə trʌk]
(n.) 雲梯車

3 ambulance
[`æmbjələns]
(n.) 救護車

4 stretcher
[`strɛtʃə]
(n.) 擔架

5 injured person
[`ɪndʒəd `pɝsn̩]
(n.) 傷患

6 oxygen mask
[`ɑksədʒən mæsk]
(n.) 氧氣罩

❶ 消防車

A fire engine is racing down the street. There must be a fire somewhere.
　　　　　　　　正沿著街道疾駛

❷ 雲梯車

The firefighters used the ladder truck to get up to the eighth floor of the
building.　　　　　　　　　　　　　　　　　抵達八樓

❸ 救護車

When people were brought out of the burning building, they were
　　　　　　　　從起火的大樓被帶出

taken to an ambulance for medical care.

❹ 擔架

The sick old woman was carried away on a stretcher.
　　　　　　　　　　　　被搬走

❺ 傷患

After the car crash, an injured person was left lying on the road.
　　　　　　　　　　　　　　處於倒臥在路上的狀態

❻ 氧氣罩

Before the firefighter went into the building, he put on an oxygen mask
to help him breathe.　　　　　　　　　　　　戴上氧氣罩

學更多

❶ racing〈race（全速行進）的 ing 型態〉・down〈沿著〉・street〈街道〉
❷ firefighter〈消防員〉・ladder〈梯子〉・truck〈卡車〉・floor〈樓層〉・building〈建築物〉
❸ brought out〈bring out（把…帶到戶外）的過去分詞〉・burning〈著火的〉・medical〈醫療的〉
❹ sick〈生病的〉・old〈老的〉・carried away〈carry away（搬走）的過去式〉
❺ car cash〈車禍〉・left〈leave（使處於某種狀態）的過去式〉・lying〈lie（躺）的 ing 型態〉
❻ put on〈put on（戴上）的過去式〉・oxygen〈氧氣〉・mask〈口罩〉・breathe〈呼吸〉

中譯

❶ 消防車正沿著街道疾駛而過，一定是某處發生了火災。
❷ 消防員利用雲梯車，抵達建築物的八樓。
❸ 當人們從起火的大樓被救出時，他們會被帶到救護車上接受醫療照顧。
❹ 生病的老太太躺在擔架上被抬走了。
❺ 車禍發生之後，一名傷患倒臥在馬路上。
❻ 消防員進入大樓之前，先戴上氧氣罩幫助自己呼吸。

178

警察局(1)

MP3 178

1 badge
[bædʒ]
(n.) 警徽

2 police hat
[pə`lis hæt]
(n.) 警帽

3 patrol car
[pə`trol kɑr]
(n.) 警用巡邏車

4 patch
[pætʃ]
(n.) 臂章

5 handgun
[`hænd͵gʌn]
(n.) 配槍

6 nightstick
[`naɪt͵stɪk]
(n.) 警棍

❶ 警徽

Police officers carry badges as forms of ID.

<u>作為身分證明的形式</u>

❷ 警帽

The police officer put her police hat on her head and left the café.

<u>將警帽戴在她的頭上</u>

❸ 警用巡邏車

A police officer got out of his patrol car to ask the man what he was doing.

<u>從他的警車裡出來</u>

❹ 臂章

The mother sewed the patch onto her son's shirt.

❺ 配槍

The police officer took out his handgun because the criminal was shooting people.

<u>拿出他的槍</u>

❻ 警棍

Police officers sometimes use nightsticks to help them control dangerous criminals.

<u>控制危險的罪犯</u>

學更多

❶ carry〈配戴〉．as〈作為〉．form〈類型、形式〉．ID〈身分證明〉

❷ put on〈戴上〉．police〈警察〉．hat〈帽子〉．left〈leave（離開）的過去式〉

❸ got out〈get out（下車）的過去式〉．patrol〈巡邏〉．ask〈問〉

❹ sewed〈sew（縫上）的過去式〉．son〈兒子〉．shirt〈襯衫〉

❺ took out〈take out（拿出）的過去式〉．criminal〈罪犯〉．
shooting〈shoot（開槍）的 ing 型態〉

❻ sometimes〈有時〉．control〈控制〉．dangerous〈危險的〉

中譯

❶ 警察會配戴警徽作為身分證明的形式。

❷ 那位警官戴上她的警帽，離開了咖啡廳。

❸ 當時一名警察從警用巡邏車上走了出來，詢問該男子在做什麼。

❹ 這名母親將臂章縫在兒子的襯衫上。

❺ 警察掏出了他的配槍，因為當時罪犯正朝著人們開槍。

❻ 警察有時候會利用警棍來幫助自己控制危險的罪犯。

1 police car
[pəˋlis kɑr]
(n.) 警車

2 criminal
[ˋkrɪmənl]
(n.) 犯人

3 police
[pəˋlis]
(n.) 警察

4 handcuff
[ˋhænd͵kʌf]
(n.) 手銬

5 gun
[gʌn]
(n.) 槍枝

❶ 警車

Oh no! That police car wants us to pull over.
<u>要我們把車開到路邊</u>

❷ 犯人

The criminal was caught trying to get into someone's house.
<u>企圖侵入某一戶人家</u>

❸ 警察

The police are looking for the bad man now.
<u>正在找尋</u>

❹ 手銬

The criminal has handcuffs on his wrists.

❺ 槍枝

He put his hand into his pocket and pulled a gun.
<u>掏出一把槍</u>

學更多

❶ pull over〈靠邊停車〉

❷ caught〈catch（逮捕）的過去分詞〉・get into〈進入〉・house〈房子〉

❸ looking for〈look for（尋找）的 ing 型態〉・bad〈壞的〉

❹ wrist〈手腕〉

❺ put...into〈把…放進〉・pocket〈口袋〉・pulled〈pull（拔）的過去式〉

中譯

❶ 喔不！那台警車要我們靠邊停車。

❷ 該名罪犯因為企圖侵入民宅而被捕了。

❸ 目前警察正在找尋那名壞人。

❹ 罪犯的手腕上銬著手銬。

❺ 他把手伸進口袋裡，然後掏出一把槍。

1 doctor in charge
[ˈdɑktə ɪn tʃɑrdʒ]
(n.) 主治醫師

2 nurse on duty
[nɝs ɑn djutɪ]
(n.) 值班護士

3 critical patient
[ˈkrɪtɪkḷ ˈpeʃənt]
(n.) 重症患者

4 facemask
[ˈfesˌmæsk]
(n.) 口罩

5 hospital bed
[ˈhɑspɪtḷ bɛd]
(n.) 病床

6 scrubs
[skrʌbz]
(n.) 隔離衣/罩袍

7 curtain
[ˈkɝtṇ]
(n.) 隔簾

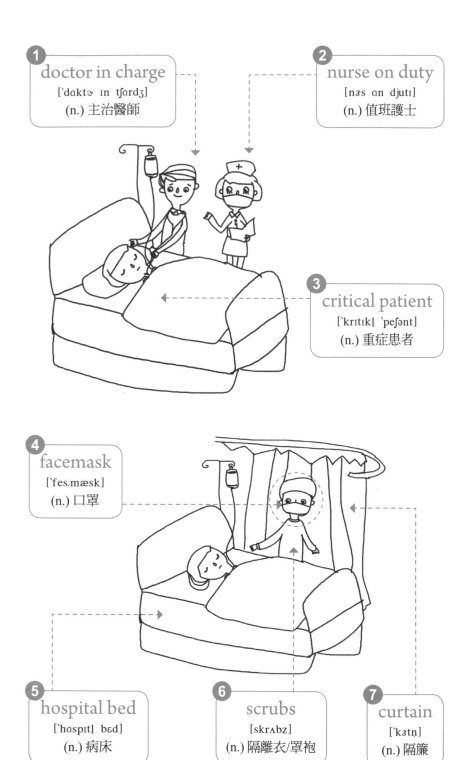

❶ 主治醫師

The doctor in charge told the other doctors what they should do.
　　　　　　　　　　　　　其餘的醫生們

❷ 值班護士

The nurse on duty checked on all the patients in the room.

❸ 重症患者

The nurses closely watched the critical patient. He could need a doctor
　　　　　　密切地注意

at any time.　　密切地注意
隨時

❹ 口罩

If you have a cold, put on a facemask so that you won't pass on your illness.
　　得了感冒　　　　　　　　　　　　　　　　把疾病傳染出去

❺ 病床

After spending three weeks in the hospital, Mark was happy to leave his

hospital bed behind.　　　　　　　　　　　　　離開他的病床

❻ 隔離衣 / 罩袍

Scrubs are the clothes surgeons wear when they do operations.
　　　　　　外科醫生穿的衣物

❼ 隔簾

Pulling the curtain around the bed will give the patient some privacy.
　　　　　　圍繞病床的隔簾

學更多

❶ in charge〈負責〉・other〈其他的〉・should〈應該〉
❷ on duty〈值班〉・checked on〈check on（檢查）的過去式〉・room〈房間〉
❸ nurse〈護士〉・closely〈密切地〉・critical〈危急的〉・patient〈病人〉
❹ cold〈感冒〉・put on〈戴上〉・pass on〈傳染〉・illness〈疾病〉
❺ spending〈spend（度過）的 ing 型態〉・leave...behind〈留下…離開〉・hospital〈醫院〉
❻ clothes〈衣服〉・surgeon〈外科醫生〉・wear〈穿著〉・operation〈手術〉
❼ pulling〈pull（拉）的 ing 型態〉・around〈圍繞〉・privacy〈隱私〉

中譯

❶ 主治醫師告知其他醫師他們該做的事。
❷ 值班護士檢視了房間裡所有的病患。
❸ 護士密切注意這名重症患者，他隨時都可能需要醫生。
❹ 如果你感冒了，請戴上口罩，這樣才不會把疾病傳染出去。
❺ 在醫院待了三週之後，Mark 很開心終於能離開他的病床。
❻ 隔離衣是外科醫生進行手術時所穿的衣物。
❼ 拉起環繞病床的隔簾，可以給病患一些隱私。

加護病房(2)

1 emergency call button
[ɪˈmɛdʒənsɪ kɔl ˈbʌtn̩]
(n.) 緊急呼叫鈴

2 electrocardiogram
[ɪˌlɛktroˈkɑrdɪəˌgræm]
(n.) 心電圖

「electrocardiogram」可縮寫為「EKG」。

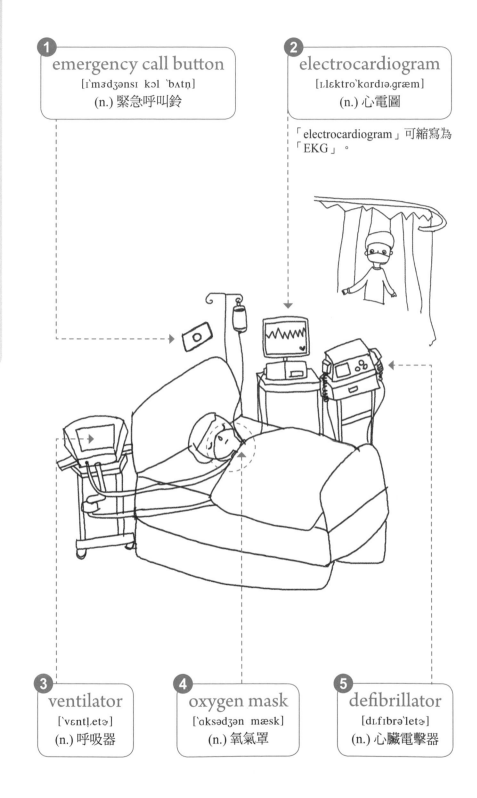

3 ventilator
[ˈvɛntl̩ˌetɚ]
(n.) 呼吸器

4 oxygen mask
[ˈɑksədʒən mæsk]
(n.) 氧氣罩

5 defibrillator
[dɪˌfɪbrəˈletɚ]
(n.) 心臟電擊器

❶ 緊急呼叫鈴

The patient was in pain, so he pressed the emergency call button.
病患覺得不舒服

❷ 心電圖

Andy had been having problems with his heart, so the doctor gave him an EKG.
他的心臟有些問題　　　　　　　　　　　替他做心電圖

❸ 呼吸器

The ventilator will help you breathe.

❹ 氧氣罩

The patient's having trouble breathing, so he was given an oxygen mask.
呼吸困難

❺ 心臟電擊器

The defibrillator was used to put an electrical current through the man's heart.
施加電流通過⋯

學更多

❶ patient〈病人〉‧ in pain〈在痛苦中〉‧ pressed〈press（按）的過去式〉‧
　emergency〈緊急情況〉‧ call〈呼叫〉‧ button〈按鈕〉
❷ problem〈問題〉‧ heart〈心臟〉‧ gave〈give（給予）的過去式〉
❸ help〈幫助〉‧ breathe〈呼吸〉
❹ trouble〈困難〉‧ given〈give（給予）的過去分詞〉‧ oxygen〈氧氣〉‧ mask〈口罩〉
❺ put〈施加〉‧ electrical〈電的〉‧ current〈電流〉‧ through〈通過〉

中譯

❶ 病患覺得不舒服，所以按下了緊急呼叫鈴。
❷ Andy 的心臟有些問題，所以醫生替他做心電圖。
❸ 呼吸器會幫助你呼吸。
❹ 病患呼吸困難，所以給他戴上氧氣罩。
❺ 利用心臟電擊器施加電流通過該名男子的心臟。

182

電視節目現場 (1)

🔊 MP3 182

①
clerk
[klɜk]
(n.) 場記

記錄拍攝現場
狀況、負責拿
拍板的人。

場記拍板：記錄節目名稱、場次、鏡次等。拍攝時讓攝影機錄下拍板上的資料，有助於縮短後製剪輯的時間。

②
producer
[prəˋdjusɚ]
(n.) 製作人

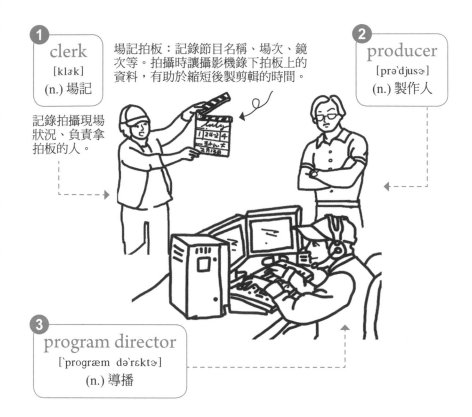

③
program director
[ˋprogræm dəˋrɛktɚ]
(n.) 導播

④
cameraman
[ˋkæmərəˏmæn]
(n.) 攝影師

⑤
gaffer
[ˋgæfɚ]
(n.) 燈光師

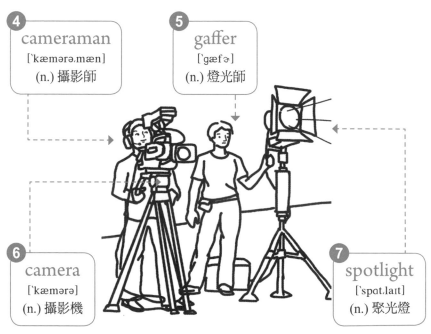

⑥
camera
[ˋkæmərə]
(n.) 攝影機

⑦
spotlight
[ˋspɑtˏlaɪt]
(n.) 聚光燈

❶ 場記

The clerk took notes about what happened in the day's filming.

　　　　記錄發生了什麼事情

❷ 製作人

The producer prepared everything the presenter needed for the show.

　　　　　　主持人需要的所有東西

❸ 導播

The program director is in charge of the show.

　　　　　負責節目

❹ 攝影師

The cameraman pointed the camera at the presenter.

　　　　把攝影機對著

❺ 燈光師

The gaffer controls all the technical equipment.

❻ 攝影機

The newsreader looked into the camera when he read the news.

　　　　看著攝影機

❼ 聚光燈

The bright spotlight shone on the singer.

　　　　照向歌手

學更多

❶ took notes〈take note（做筆記）的過去式〉‧ filming〈拍攝〉
❷ prepared〈prepare（準備）的過去式〉‧ presenter〈節目主持人〉
❸ program〈節目〉‧ director〈導演〉‧ in charge〈負責〉
❹ pointed...at〈point...at（把…對準）的過去式〉‧ camera〈攝影機、照相機〉
❺ control〈控制〉‧ technical〈科技的〉‧ equipment〈設備〉
❻ newsreader〈新聞播報員〉‧ read〈read（讀出）的過去式〉‧ news〈新聞〉
❼ bright〈亮的〉‧ shone〈shine（照向）的過去式〉‧ singer〈歌手〉

中譯

❶ 場記記錄了當天拍攝時所發生的事。
❷ 製作人為主持人準備了節目裡需要的所有東西。
❸ 導播要負責整個節目。
❹ 攝影師將攝影機對準主持人。
❺ 燈光師要控制所有的儀器。
❻ 新聞主播看著攝影機播報新聞。
❼ 明亮的聚光燈投射在歌手身上。

183

電視節目現場(2)

MP3 183

1 background
[ˋbæk͵graʊnd]
(n.) 背景

2 prop
[prɑp]
(n.) 道具

3 mini mic
[ˋmɪnɪ maɪk]
(n.) 迷你麥克風

4 artist
[ˋɑrtɪst]
(n.) 藝人

5 master of ceremony
[ˋmæstɚ ɑv ˋsɛrə͵monɪ]
(n.) 主持人

「master of ceremony」
可縮寫為「MC」。

6 artist's assistant
[ɑrˋtɪstɪz əˋsɪstənt]
(n.) 藝人助理

7 makeup artist
[ˋmek͵ʌp ˋɑrtɪst]
(n.) 化妝師

❶ 背景

He isn't an important actor. He just stands in the <u>background</u> of the shot.
站在背景裡

❷ 道具

<u>Props</u> are the objects used in TV shows and movies.
被用於電視節目和電影之中

❸ 迷你麥克風

The presenter had a <u>mini mic</u> clipped onto her jacket.
將迷你麥克風夾在她的外套上

❹ 藝人

The <u>artist</u>'s performance entertained the crowds.

❺ 主持人

The <u>MC</u> introduced each performer.

❻ 藝人助理

Wendy is an <u>artist's assistant</u>. She makes sure that the singer is OK.

❼ 化妝師

The <u>makeup artist</u> applied makeup to the actress's face.
將化妝品塗在…

學更多

❶ important〈重要的〉‧ actor〈演員〉‧ stand〈站著〉‧ shot〈拍攝〉
❷ object〈物品〉‧ show〈節目〉‧ movie〈電影〉
❸ presenter〈節目主持人〉‧ clipped〈clip（夾住）的過去分詞〉‧ jacket〈外套〉
❹ performance〈表演〉‧ entertained〈entertain（娛樂）的過去式〉‧ crowd〈大眾〉
❺ master〈有控制權的人〉‧ ceremony〈儀式、典禮〉‧ performer〈表演者〉
❻ assistant〈助理〉‧ make sure〈確保〉‧ singer〈歌手〉
❼ artist〈大師〉‧ applied〈apply（將…塗在表面）的過去式〉‧ actress〈女演員〉

中譯

❶ 他並非要角，拍攝時他只需要站在背景裡。
❷ 道具是電視節目和電影裡所使用的物品。
❸ 主持人在她的外套上夾了一個迷你麥克風。
❹ 藝人的表演娛樂了大眾。
❺ 主持人介紹了每一位表演者。
❻ Wendy 是藝人助理，她要確保歌手的一切都沒問題。
❼ 化妝師在女演員的臉部上妝。

184

動物醫院 (1)

🔊 MP3 184

1 registration desk
[ˌrɛdʒɪˈstreʃən dɛsk]
(n.) 掛號處

2 waiting room
[ˈwetɪŋ rum]
(n.) 候診室

3 operating room
[ˈɑpəretɪŋ rum]
(n.) 手術室

4 examination room
[ɪgˌzæmənˈneʃən rum]
(n.) 診療室

5 veterinarian
[ˌvɛtərəˈnɛrɪən]
(n.) 獸醫

6 nurse
[nɝs]
(n.) 護士

7 animal
[ˈænəm!]
(n.) 動物

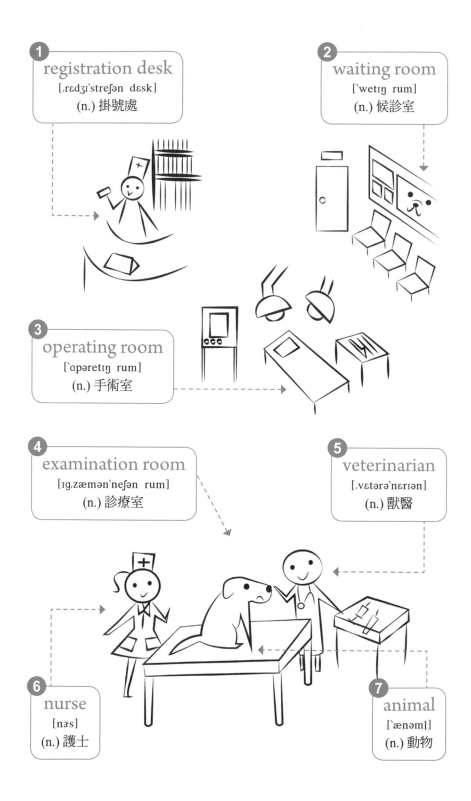

376

❶ 掛號處

When you arrive at a hospital, you need to go to the registration desk to make an appointment.
預約

❷ 候診室

The patient sat in the waiting room, waiting for the doctor.

❸ 手術室

The patient was taken into the operating room for the operation.
被帶進手術室

❹ 診療室

The doctor looked at the patient in the examination room.
檢視病患

❺ 獸醫

Veterinarians care for sick animals.

❻ 護士

The nurse went to check on a patient.

❼ 動物

Sam loves animals. He has three cats and a rabbit.

學更多

❶ arrive〈抵達〉‧ registration〈掛號〉‧ desk〈櫃檯〉‧ appointment〈約定〉
❷ sat〈sit（坐）的過去式〉‧ waiting〈等候〉‧ waiting for〈wait for（等待…）的 ing 型態〉
❸ taken〈take（帶去）的過去分詞〉‧ operating〈外科手術的〉‧ operation〈手術〉
❹ looked at〈look at（看）的過去式〉‧ examination〈檢查〉‧ room〈房間〉
❺ care〈照顧〉‧ sick〈病的〉
❻ went〈go（去）的過去式〉‧ check on〈檢查〉
❼ love〈喜愛〉‧ cat〈貓〉‧ rabbit〈兔子〉

中譯

❶ 到達醫院後，你必須去掛號處辦理預約。
❷ 病患坐在候診室等候醫生看診。
❸ 病患被送往手術室進行手術。
❹ 醫生在診療室替病患看診。
❺ 獸醫照顧生病的動物。
❻ 護士去檢視病患的狀況。
❼ Sam 喜愛動物。他養了三隻貓和一隻兔子。

動物醫院(2)

MP3 185

1
cage
[kedʒ]
(n.) 籠子

2
scale
[skel]
(n.) 磅秤

3
thermometer
[θəˋmɑmətə]
(n.) 體溫計

4
anesthesia
[͵ænəsˋθiʒə]
(n.) 麻醉/麻醉劑

5
injection
[ɪnˋdʒɛkʃən]
(n.) 注射

6
syringe
[ˋsɪrɪndʒ]
(n.) 針筒

❶ 籠子

My neighbor keeps her dog locked up in a cage.
<u>被鎖在籠子裡</u>

❷ 磅秤

A scale was used to weigh the animal.
<u>秤動物的體重</u>

❸ 體溫計

The nurse used a thermometer to take my temperature.
<u>量我的體溫</u>

❹ 麻醉 / 麻醉劑

When you're under anesthesia, you won't be able to feel any pain.
<u>處於麻醉的狀況</u>　　　　　　　<u>可以感覺到</u>

❺ 注射

The dog was given an injection of medicine.
<u>被注射</u>

❻ 針筒

Syringes are used to give injections.
<u>打針</u>

學更多

❶ neighbor〈鄰居〉・keep〈使保持在某一狀態〉・locked up〈lock up（鎖起來）的過去分詞〉

❷ used〈use（使用）的過去分詞〉・weigh〈秤重〉・animal〈動物〉

❸ used〈use（使用）的過去式〉・take〈量取〉・temperature〈體溫〉

❹ under〈處於…情況之下〉・able〈會〉・feel〈感覺〉・pain〈疼痛〉

❺ given〈give（給予）的過去分詞〉・medicine〈藥物〉

❻ used〈use（使用）的過去分詞〉

中譯

❶ 我的鄰居把她的狗鎖在籠子裡。

❷ 磅秤被用來測量動物的體重。

❸ 護士用體溫計幫我量體溫。

❹ 當你處於麻醉狀態時，你不會感覺到任何疼痛。

❺ 那隻狗被打了一針（那隻狗被注射藥品）。

❻ 針筒是用來打針的。

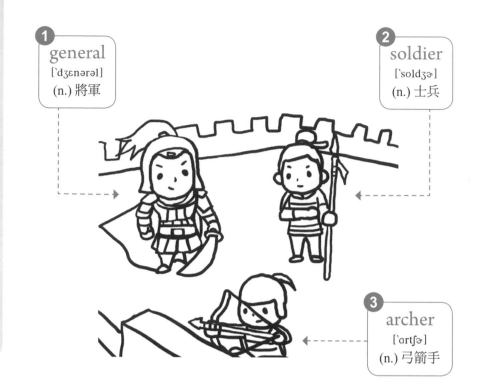

1 general
[ˈdʒɛnərəl]
(n.) 將軍

2 soldier
[ˈsoldʒɚ]
(n.) 士兵

3 archer
[ˈɑrtʃɚ]
(n.) 弓箭手

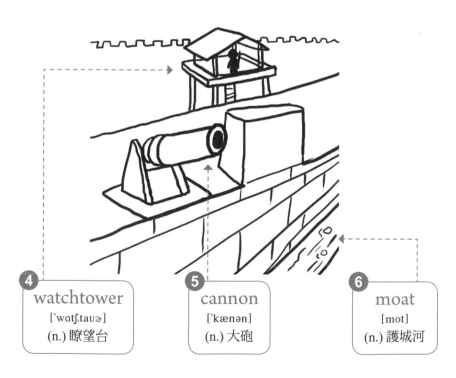

4 watchtower
[ˈwɑtʃˌtauɚ]
(n.) 瞭望台

5 cannon
[ˈkænən]
(n.) 大砲

6 moat
[mot]
(n.) 護城河

❶ 將軍

The general ordered his soldiers into battle.

❷ 士兵

The soldiers fought each other on the battlefield.
<u>互相廝殺</u>

❸ 弓箭手

Archers fire arrows from their bows.
<u>射箭</u>

❹ 瞭望台

A soldier stood in the watchtower to look out for enemy soldiers.
<u>注意敵方士兵</u>

❺ 大砲

The huge cannon was fired at the enemy soldiers.
<u>被射向敵軍</u>

❻ 護城河

The moat around the castle is filled with water.
<u>被注滿了水</u>

學更多

❶ ordered〈order（命令）的過去式〉・battle〈戰役〉
❷ fought〈fight（戰鬥）的過去式〉・each other〈互相〉・battlefield〈戰場〉
❸ fire〈射擊〉・arrow〈箭〉・bow〈弓〉
❹ stood〈stand（站）的過去式〉・look out〈注意〉・enemy〈敵方的〉
❺ huge〈巨大的〉・fired〈fire（射擊）的過去分詞〉
❻ around〈圍繞〉・castle〈城堡〉・filled with...〈fill with（充滿）的過去分詞〉

中譯

❶ 將軍命令他的士兵上戰場。
❷ 士兵在戰場上互相廝殺。
❸ 弓箭手拉弓射箭。
❹ 士兵站在瞭望台，注意是否有敵軍來襲。
❺ 大砲朝著敵軍發射。
❻ 城堡四周的護城河注滿了水。

軍事堡壘(2)

MP3 187

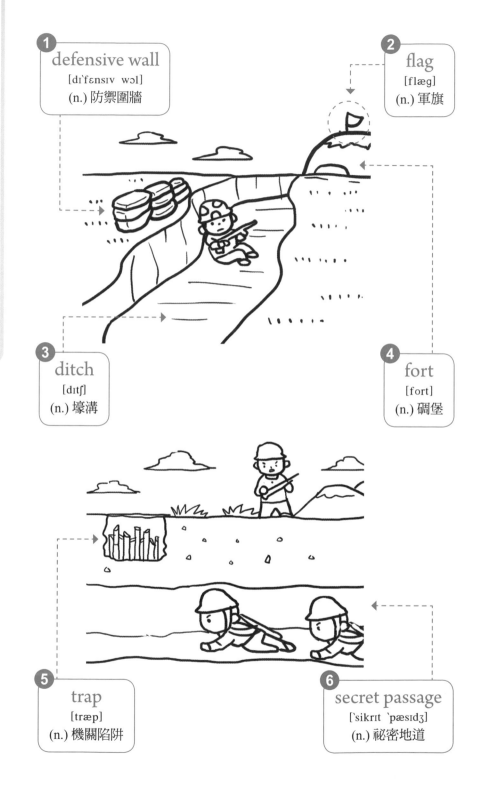

1 defensive wall
[dɪˋfɛnsɪv wɔl]
(n.) 防禦圍牆

2 flag
[flæg]
(n.) 軍旗

3 ditch
[dɪtʃ]
(n.) 壕溝

4 fort
[fort]
(n.) 碉堡

5 trap
[træp]
(n.) 機關陷阱

6 secret passage
[ˋsikrɪt ˋpæsɪdʒ]
(n.) 祕密地道

❶ 防禦圍牆
The defensive wall was designed to keep out enemy soldiers.
被設計為…用途

❷ 軍旗
Armies used to carry flags to show who they fought for.
他們為了誰而打仗

❸ 壕溝
The man didn't see the ditch, and he fell into it.

❹ 碉堡
Hundreds of soldiers live in the fort.

❺ 機關陷阱
The general set a trap to catch the enemies.
設置陷阱

❻ 祕密地道
The secret passage connected the president's office to a safe house.
連接總統府

學更多

❶ defensive〈防禦的〉・designed〈design（設計）的過去分詞〉・keep out〈不讓…進入〉
❷ army〈軍隊〉・used to...〈過去一向…〉・carry〈攜帶〉・fought〈fight（打仗）的過去式〉
❸ see〈看到〉・fell into〈fall into（掉入）的過去式〉
❹ hundreds of...〈數以百計的…〉・soldier〈士兵〉・live〈住〉
❺ general〈將軍〉・set〈set（設置）的過去式〉・catch〈抓住〉・enemy〈敵軍〉
❻ secret〈祕密的〉・passage〈通道〉・connected〈connect（連結）的過去式〉・president〈總統〉

中譯

❶ 防禦圍牆被設計來防範敵軍入侵。
❷ 軍隊一向以所攜帶的軍旗來顯示他們為誰而戰。
❸ 該名男子沒有看到壕溝，結果就掉進去了。
❹ 上百名士兵居住在碉堡裡。
❺ 將軍設置了機關陷阱來捕捉敵軍。
❻ 這條祕密地道連接總統府，通往一個安全的處所。

1 cordon
[ˋkɔrdn̩]
(n.) 封鎖線

2 evidence bag
[ˋɛvədəns ˏbæg]
(n.) 證物袋

3 dying message
[ˋdaɪɪŋ ˋmɛsɪdʒ]
(n.) 死前遺言

4 coroner
[ˋkɔrənɚ]
(n.) 法醫

5 murder weapon
[ˋmɝdɚ ˋwɛpən]
(n.) 凶器

6 corpse
[kɔrps]
(n.) 屍體

7 bloodstain
[ˋblʌdˏsten]
(n.) 血跡

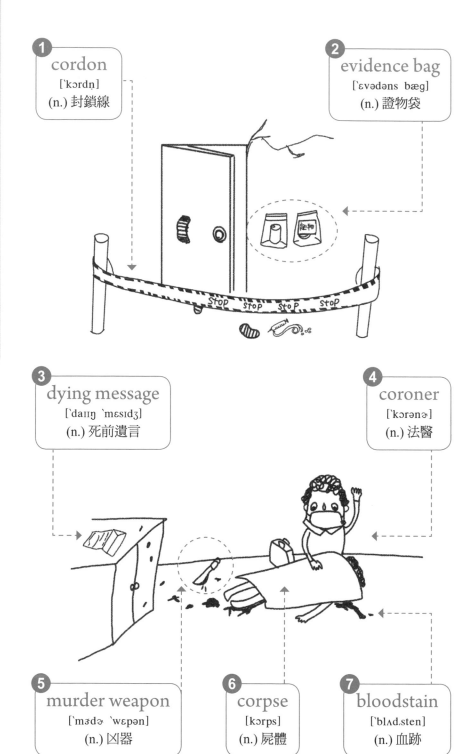

❶ 封鎖線

The police blocked off the area with a cordon.
封鎖了這個區域

❷ 證物袋

The police officer found some hair next to the body, so she put it into an evidence bag.
將它放入證物袋

❸ 死前遺言

The old man's dying message was to tell his wife he loved her.

❹ 法醫

The coroner said the man was killed by a knife wound.
男人被殺死　　　　　　刀傷

❺ 凶器

The police think the killer used a knife as his murder weapon.
當作他的凶器

❻ 屍體

After finding a dead body in the house, the police examined the corpse.
一具屍體

❼ 血跡

The police found bloodstains in the room, so they knew someone had
been attacked there.
有人被攻擊

學更多

❶ blocked off〈block off（封鎖）的過去式〉‧area〈區域〉
❷ found〈find（發現）的過去式〉‧hair〈毛髮〉‧body〈屍體〉‧evidence〈物證〉
❸ old〈老的〉‧dying〈垂死的〉‧message〈訊息〉‧wife〈太太〉
❹ said〈say（說）的過去式〉‧killed〈kill（殺死）的過去分詞〉‧wound〈傷口〉
❺ police〈警察〉‧killer〈兇手〉‧knife〈刀〉‧murder〈兇殺〉‧weapon〈武器〉
❻ dead〈死的〉‧examined〈examine（檢查）的過去式〉
❼ knew〈know（知道）的過去式〉‧attacked〈attack（襲擊）的過去分詞〉

中譯

❶ 警察以封鎖線封鎖了這個區域。
❷ 警察在屍體旁邊找到一些毛髮，所以她把那些毛髮放入證物袋。
❸ 老先生的死前遺言是告訴他的太太：他愛她。
❹ 法醫說該名男子是因刀傷而身亡。
❺ 警察認為兇手的凶器是一把刀子。
❻ 在屋內找到一具死屍之後，警察便對屍體展開調查。
❼ 警察在房間裡發現血跡，所以他們知道有人在那裡遭受到攻擊。

1 survivor
['sə`vaɪvə]
(n.) 倖存者

2 witness
['wɪtnɪs]
(n.) 目擊證人

3 police
[pə`lis]
(n.) 警察/警方

4 fingerprint
['fɪŋgə,prɪnt]
(n.) 指紋

5 shoeprint
['ʃu,prɪnt]
(n.) 鞋印

6 crime scene investigator
[kraɪm sin ɪn`vɛstə,getə]
(n.) 鑑識人員

❶ 倖存者
There were no survivors from the airplane crash. Everyone died.
飛機失事

❷ 目擊證人
She's a witness. She saw everything.

❸ 警察 / 警方
The police are trying to catch the criminal.

❹ 指紋
Whenever you touch something, your fingers leave fingerprints.
留下指紋

❺ 鞋印
The walker left shoeprints in the snow.

❻ 鑑識人員
Crime scene investigators look for evidence that will tell them what happened.
告訴他們當時發生了什麼事

學更多

❶ airplane〈飛機〉‧ crash〈墜毀〉‧ died〈die（死）的過去式〉
❷ saw〈see（看）的過去式〉‧ everything〈一切事物〉
❸ trying〈try（試圖）的 ing 型態〉‧ catch〈抓住〉‧ criminal〈罪犯〉
❹ whenever〈每當〉‧ touch〈觸摸〉‧ finger〈手指〉‧ leave〈留下〉
❺ walker〈行人〉‧ left〈leave（留下）的過去式〉‧ snow〈雪〉
❻ crime〈犯罪〉‧ scene〈現場〉‧ investigator〈調查者〉‧ evidence〈證據〉

中譯

❶ 這場空難沒有倖存者，所有人都身亡了。
❷ 她是目擊證人，目擊了一切。
❸ 警方試圖要抓到犯人。
❹ 每當你觸碰某個東西，你的手指都會留下指紋。
❺ 行人在雪中留下了鞋印。
❻ 鑑識人員會尋找證據，透過證據推斷當時發生了什麼事。

1 fresco
[ˈfrɛsko]
(n.) 壁畫

2 stained glass window
[stend glæs ˈwɪndo]
(n.) 彩繪玻璃窗

3 cross
[krɔs]
(n.) 十字架

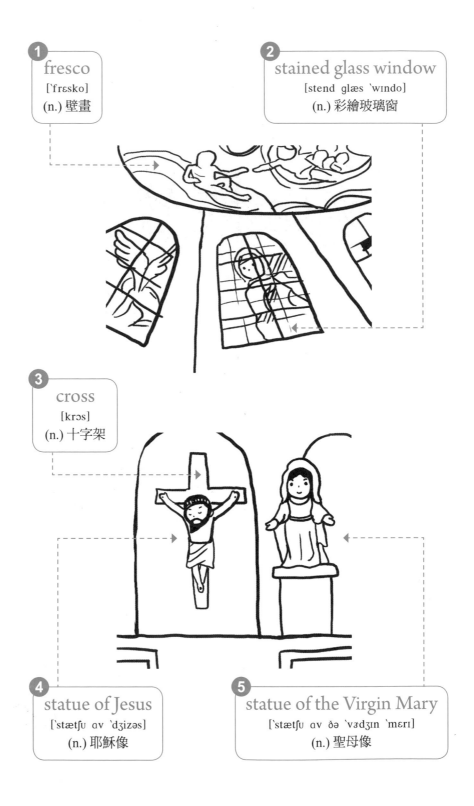

4 statue of Jesus
[ˈstætʃʊ ɑv ˈdʒizəs]
(n.) 耶穌像

5 statue of the Virgin Mary
[ˈstætʃʊ ɑv ðə ˈvɝdʒɪn ˈmɛrɪ]
(n.) 聖母像

❶ 壁畫

People always stop to look at the large fresco. It's a beautiful painting.
　　　　　　　　　　　　　　看著巨型壁畫

❷ 彩繪玻璃窗

The stained glass window is very colorful.

❸ 十字架

The cross reminds Christians of how Jesus died.
　　　　　提醒基督徒…

❹ 耶穌像

The statue of Jesus shows him talking to his followers.
　　　　　　　　　　和祂的信眾說話

❺ 聖母像

The statue of the Virgin Mary shows Jesus' mother smiling at her baby.
　　　　　　　　　　　　　　　　對…微笑

學更多

❶ always〈經常〉‧ stop〈停住〉‧ look at〈看〉‧ large〈大的〉‧ beautiful〈美麗的〉‧ painting〈繪畫〉

❷ stained〈著色的〉‧ glass〈玻璃〉‧ window〈窗戶〉‧ colorful〈色彩豐富的、鮮豔的〉

❸ remind〈提醒〉‧ Christian〈基督教徒〉‧ Jesus〈耶穌〉‧ died〈die（死）的過去式〉

❹ statue〈雕像〉‧ show〈顯示〉‧ talking〈talk（說話）的 ing 型態〉‧ follower〈信徒〉

❺ Virgin Mary〈聖母瑪利亞〉‧ smiling〈smile（微笑）的 ing 型態〉‧ baby〈嬰兒〉

中譯

❶ 人們經常駐足欣賞這幅巨型壁畫，它是一幅美麗的畫作。

❷ 這片彩繪玻璃窗的色彩豐富鮮豔。

❸ 十字架提醒著基督徒，耶穌是如何受難的。

❹ 這尊耶穌像是耶穌與信眾說話的模樣。

❺ 這尊聖母像是耶穌的母親對自己的嬰兒微笑的模樣。

191 教堂裡(2)

MP3 191

1 clergy
[ˋklɝdʒɪ]
(n.) 神職人員

天主教最高元首，長駐羅馬梵諦岡。

2 Pope
[pop]
(n.) 教宗

3 Bible
[ˋbaɪbl̩]
(n.) 聖經

4 nun
[nʌn]
(n.) 修女

5 confession room
[kənˋfɛʃən rum]
(n.) 告解室

天主教的神職人員，通常是一個教堂的管理者，並主持教堂的宗教活動。

6 priest
[prist]
(n.) 神父

❶ 神職人員

Hew surprised me when he said he wanted to join the clergy. I didn't know he wanted to become a priest.　　　成為神職人員的成員

❷ 教宗

The Pope is the leader of the Roman Catholic Church.
　　　　　　　　　　　　　　　　羅馬天主教會

❸ 聖經

Christians believe the Bible is the word of God.
　　　　　　　　　　　　　　上帝說的話

❹ 修女

Nuns are not allowed to marry. They devote themselves to God.
　　　　　　　　　　　　　　　　　奉獻她們自己

❺ 告解室

The man went into the confession room to say what bad things he had done.
　　　　　　　　　　　　　　　　　　　　　他做過的壞事

❻ 神父

The priest spoke to the people about the Bible.
　　　　向人們說

學更多

❶ surprised〈surprise（使驚訝）的過去式〉．join〈成為…的成員〉．become〈成為〉

❷ leader〈領袖〉．Roman〈羅馬的、羅馬人（的）〉．Catholic〈天主教的、天主教徒〉．church〈教會〉

❸ Christian〈基督教徒〉．believe〈相信〉．word〈言辭〉．God〈上帝〉

❹ allowed〈allow（允許）的過去分詞〉．marry〈結婚〉．devote〈奉獻〉．themselves〈她們自己〉

❺ went into〈go into（進入）的過去式〉．confession〈告解〉．done〈do（做）的過去分詞〉

❻ spoke〈speak（說）的過去式〉．people〈人們〉

中譯

❶ 當 Hew 告訴我他想要成為神職人員時，我感到很驚訝。我不知道他想要成為神父。

❷ 教宗是羅馬天主教會的領袖。

❸ 基督徒相信聖經是上帝之言。

❹ 修女不被允許結婚，她們將自己奉獻給上帝。

❺ 該男子進入告解室，說出他所做的壞事。

❻ 神父向眾人講授聖經。

192

教堂裡(3)

MP3 192

1 altar
[ˈɔltə]
(n.) 祭壇

2 statue of Jesus
[ˈstætʃu ɑv ˈdʒizəs]
(n.) 耶穌像

3 choir
[kwaɪr]
(n.) 唱詩班

4 mass
[mæs]
(n.) 彌撒/禮拜儀式

5 offering box
[ˈɔfərɪŋ bɑks]
(n.) 奉獻箱

6 believer
[bɪˈlivə]
(n.) 信徒

❶ 祭壇

The altar is in front of a huge statue of the god.
　　　　　　　　　　　　　一尊大型神像

❷ 耶穌像

My favorite statue of Jesus is located in Copenhagen.
　　　　　　　　　　　　　　　位於哥本哈根

❸ 唱詩班

The choir sang beautifully on Sunday morning.
　　　　　　　唱得很好聽

❹ 彌撒 / 禮拜儀式

Hundreds of people go to mass at this church on Sunday morning.

❺ 奉獻箱

People put money into the offering box.
　　　　　把錢放入

❻ 信徒

June never used to go to church, but she's a believer now.
　　以前從未

學更多

❶ in front of...〈在…的前面〉・huge〈巨大的〉・statue〈雕像〉・god〈男神〉

❷ favorite〈特別喜愛的〉・Jesus〈耶穌〉・located〈locate（坐落於…）的過去分詞〉・
　Copenhagen〈哥本哈根〉

❸ sang〈sing（唱）的過去式〉・beautifully〈出色地〉・Sunday〈星期日〉

❹ hundreds of...〈數以百計的…〉・church〈教堂〉

❺ put...into〈把…放進〉・money〈錢〉・offering〈捐獻〉・box〈箱子〉

❻ never〈從未〉・used to...〈過去一向…〉

中譯

❶ 祭壇設在一尊大型神像的前方。

❷ 我最敬愛的那尊耶穌像坐落於哥本哈根。

❸ 週日早晨的唱詩班唱得很動聽。

❹ 週日早晨會有上百名群眾到這間教堂參加彌撒。

❺ 人們將錢投入奉獻箱。

❻ June 以前從來不去教會，不過她現在是名信徒了。

193

寺廟裡 (1)

MP3 193

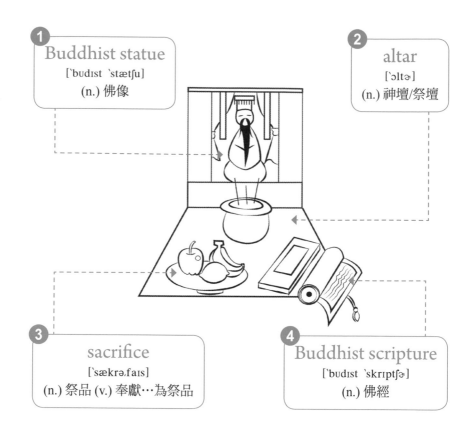

1 Buddhist statue
[ˋbʊdɪst ˋstætʃu]
(n.) 佛像

2 altar
[ˋɔltɚ]
(n.) 神壇/祭壇

3 sacrifice
[ˋsækrəˌfaɪs]
(n.) 祭品 (v.) 奉獻…為祭品

4 Buddhist scripture
[ˋbʊdɪst ˋskrɪptʃɚ]
(n.) 佛經

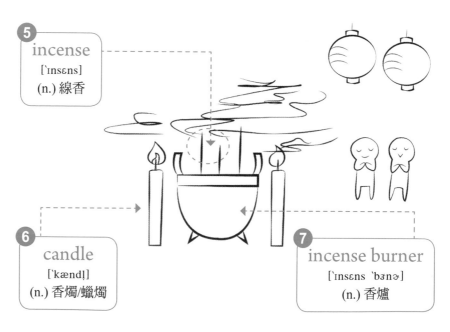

5 incense
[ˋɪnsɛns]
(n.) 線香

6 candle
[ˋkændl̩]
(n.) 香燭/蠟燭

7 incense burner
[ˋɪnsɛns ˋbɚnɚ]
(n.) 香爐

❶ 佛像

The Buddhist statue was carried into the temple.
<u>被搬進</u>

❷ 神壇 / 祭壇

The altar is in front of a huge statue of the god.
<u>在一尊大型雕像的前方</u>

❸ 祭品 / 奉獻…為祭品

People used to worship their gods by sacrificing animals.
<u>祭拜他們的神明</u>

❹ 佛經

The monk spent his day reading Buddhist scripture.
<u>花費他一天的時間</u>

❺ 線香

The burning incense creates a nice smell.

❻ 香燭 / 蠟燭

When the power in their home went off, the family lit candles to give themselves light.
<u>點蠟燭替他們自己照明</u>

❼ 香爐

People put their sticks of incense into the incense burner.
<u>他們手上長條狀的線香</u>

學更多

❶ Buddhist〈佛教的、佛陀的〉‧carried〈carry（搬運）的過去分詞〉‧temple〈寺廟〉
❷ in front of...〈在…的前面〉‧huge〈巨大的〉‧statue〈雕像〉‧god〈男神〉
❸ used to...〈過去一向…〉‧worship〈崇拜〉‧animal〈動物〉
❹ monk〈僧侶〉‧spent〈spend（度過）的過去式〉‧scripture〈經文〉
❺ burning〈燃燒的〉‧create〈產生〉‧nice〈好的〉‧smell〈香味〉
❻ power〈電力〉‧went off〈go off（熄滅）的過去式〉‧lit〈light（點燃）的過去式〉
❼ put〈放〉‧stick〈條狀物〉‧burner〈爐子〉

中譯

❶ 佛像被搬進寺廟裡。
❷ 神壇設在一尊大型神像的前方。
❸ 人們過去一向以動物作為祭品，來祭拜他們的神明。
❹ 僧侶整日朗誦佛經。
❺ 燃燒的線香飄散出宜人的香味。
❻ 當家裡停電時，他們點了蠟燭來照明。
❼ 人們將手上的線香插入香爐中。

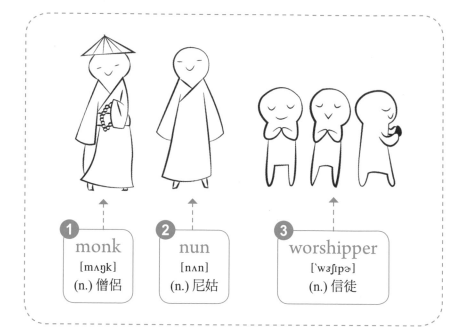

1 monk
[mʌŋk]
(n.) 僧侶

2 nun
[nʌn]
(n.) 尼姑

3 worshipper
[ˈwɝʃɪpɚ]
(n.) 信徒

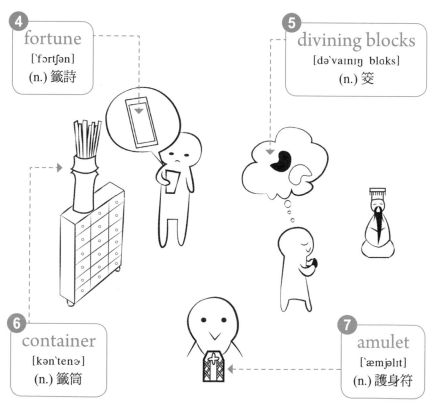

4 fortune
[ˈfɔrtʃən]
(n.) 籤詩

5 divining blocks
[dəˈvaɪnɪŋ blɑks]
(n.) 筊

6 container
[kənˈtenɚ]
(n.) 籤筒

7 amulet
[ˈæmjəlɪt]
(n.) 護身符

1 僧侶

The monk is not allowed to marry.
　　　　　　～～～～～～～～
　　　　　　不被允許

2 尼姑

The nun has to shave her head regularly.
　　　　　　～～～～～～～～～～～～
　　　　　　剃掉她頭上的毛髮

3 信徒

The worshippers held incense and gathered inside the temple.
　　　　　　　　　～～～～～～～　　　　　　～～～～～～～～～～
　　　　　　　　　拿著香　　　　　　　　　　聚集在寺廟裡

4 籤詩

Read out your fortune. What does it say?

5 筊

The woman threw the divining blocks into the air and looked at
how they landed on the floor.
～～～～～～～～～～～～～～
它們如何掉落在地上

6 籤筒

Take a long divining stick from the container.
　　～～～～～～～～～～～～～～～
　　一支長籤

7 護身符

He wears the amulet because he says it keeps him safe.
～～～～～～～～～　　　　　　　　　　～～～～～～～～～～
戴著護身符　　　　　　　　　　　　　　保佑他平安

學更多

1 allowed〈allow（允許）的過去分詞〉‧ marry〈結婚〉
2 shave〈剃毛髮〉‧ head〈頭〉‧ regularly〈定期地〉
3 held〈hold（拿著）的過去式〉‧ incense〈線香〉‧ gathered〈gather（集合）的過去式〉
4 read out〈宣讀〉‧ say〈顯示〉
5 divining〈神賜的〉‧ block〈積木〉‧ landed〈land（落下）的過去式〉
6 take〈拿〉‧ long〈長的〉‧ stick〈條狀物〉
7 wear〈戴著〉‧ keep〈使…保持在某一狀態〉‧ safe〈安全的〉

中譯

1 僧侶不被允許結婚。
2 尼姑必須定期剃髮。
3 信徒拿著香，聚集在寺廟裡。
4 唸一下你的籤詩。上面寫了什麼？
5 那名女子將筊拋向空中，然後看它們掉在地上後呈現什麼樣子。
6 從籤筒裡拿出一支長籤。
7 他戴著護身符，因為他說那能保佑他平安。

溫室裡

MP3 195

1 plant
[plænt]
(n.) 植物

2 soil
[sɔɪl]
(n.) 土壤

3 grass
[græs]
(n.) 草

4 sprinkler
[ˋsprɪŋklɚ]
(n.) 灑水設備

5 pesticide sprayer
[ˋpɛstɪˌsaɪd ˋspreɚ]
(n.) 農藥噴霧器

6 spade
[sped]
(n.) 鏟子

7 fertilizer
[ˋfɝtḷˌaɪzɚ]
(n.) 肥料

有機肥料

❶ 植物

Andy put his new plants in the garden.

❷ 土壤

The gardener put the plants into the soil.
　　　　　　　　　　把植物種入土壤

❸ 草

It hasn't rained for a long time, so the grass is turning brown.
　　已經很久沒有下雨　　　　　　　　　　　　變黃

❹ 灑水設備

The sprinkler sprays water all over the garden.
　　　　　　　　　　　　整個庭院

❺ 農藥噴霧器

The farmer walked through his fields with a pesticide sprayer.
　　　　步行穿梭於他的田地

❻ 鏟子

Fred used a spade to dig in his garden.
　　　用鏟子挖掘

❼ 肥料

Rich uses fertilizer to help his plants grow.
　　　　　　　　　　　幫助他的植物生長

學更多

❶ put〈擺放〉‧ new〈新的〉‧ garden〈庭院〉
❷ gardener〈園丁〉
❸ rained〈rain（下雨）的過去分詞〉‧ turning〈turn（變）的 ing 型態〉‧ brown〈褐色〉
❹ spray〈噴灑〉‧ all over〈到處〉
❺ through〈在⋯之中〉‧ field〈田地〉‧ pesticide〈殺蟲劑〉‧ sprayer〈噴霧器〉
❻ used〈use（使用）的過去式〉‧ dig〈挖掘〉
❼ help〈幫助〉‧ grow〈生長〉

中譯

❶ Andy 把新的植物擺在庭院裡。
❷ 園丁把植物種入土壤。
❸ 已經很久沒下雨了，草逐漸變黃。
❹ 灑水設備會將水噴灑在整個庭院。
❺ 農夫帶著農藥噴灑器在自己的田裡穿梭。
❻ Fred 用鏟子在庭院挖土。
❼ Rich 使用肥料幫助他的植物生長。

196

建築工地 (1)

MP3 196

1 helmet
[ˈhɛlmɪt]
(n.) 安全帽

2 reinforced concrete
[ˌriɪnˈfɔrst ˈkɑnkrit]
(n.) 鋼筋混凝土

3 scaffold
[ˈskæfḷd]
(n.) 鷹架

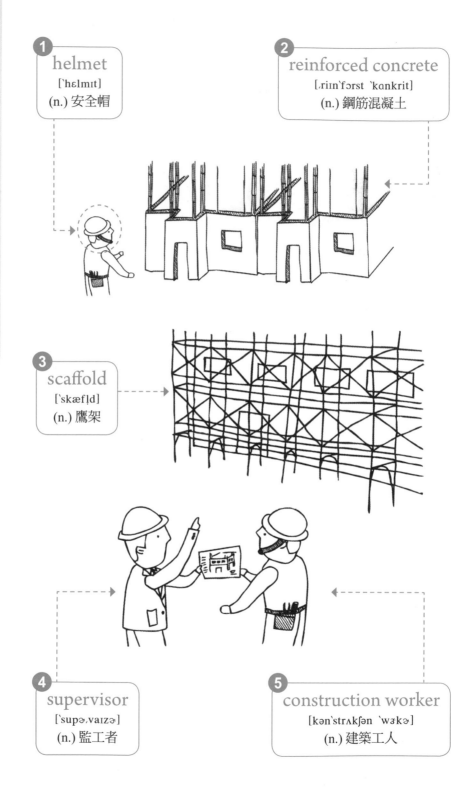

4 supervisor
[ˈsupɚˌvaɪzɚ]
(n.) 監工者

5 construction worker
[kənˈstrʌkʃən ˈwɝkɚ]
(n.) 建築工人

❶ 安全帽

A helmet will protect your head from falling stone.
<u>保護你的頭部避免…</u>

❷ 鋼筋混凝土

Reinforced concrete has steel inside it.

❸ 鷹架

Builders usually put a scaffold around buildings.
<u>在建築物的四周搭建鷹架</u>

❹ 監工者

The supervisor told his workers what to do.
<u>該做些什麼</u>

❺ 建築工人

There are 20 construction workers building the house.

學更多

❶ protect A from B〈保護 A 避免 B〉‧ falling〈落下的〉‧ stone〈石頭〉

❷ reinforced〈強化的〉‧ concrete〈混凝土〉‧ steel〈鋼鐵〉‧ inside〈在…的裡面〉

❸ builder〈建築工人〉‧ usually〈通常地〉‧ put〈放〉‧ around〈圍繞〉‧
building〈建築物〉

❹ told〈tell（告訴）的過去式〉‧ worker〈工人〉

❺ construction〈建造〉‧ building〈build（建築）的 ing 型態〉‧ house〈房子〉

中譯

❶ 安全帽會保護你的頭部避免落石砸傷。

❷ 鋼筋混擬土內含鋼鐵。

❸ 建築工人通常會在建築物四周搭建鷹架。

❹ 監工者告訴他的工人該做些什麼。

❺ 有 20 名建築工人在建造那棟房子。

建築工地 (2)

MP3 197

1
tower crane
[ˋtauɚ ˏkren]
(n.) 塔式起重機

2
crane
[kren]
(n.) 吊車

3
digger
[ˋdɪgɚ]
(n.) 挖土機

4
brick
[brɪk]
(n.) 磚塊

5
wheelbarrow
[ˋhwilˏbæro]
(n.) 手推車

❶ 起重機
Several tower cranes were used to build Taipei 101.
　　　　　　　　　　　　　　被用來建造台北 101 大樓
❷ 吊車
Cranes are used to lift materials up into the air.
　　　　　　　用來吊起物料
❸ 挖土機
The mechanical digger can dig up lots of ground quickly.
　　　　　　　　　　　　　　挖出大量土壤
❹ 磚塊
In Britain, most houses are made with red bricks.
　　　　　　　　　　　　　用紅磚建造的
❺ 手推車
The gardener put the plants and his tools in a wheelbarrow and
pushed it down the garden.
　　　推手推車到花園裡

學更多

❶ several〈數個的〉‧tower〈塔〉‧build〈建築〉
❷ be used to〈被用來〉‧lift up〈吊起〉‧material〈物料〉
❸ mechanical〈機械的〉‧dig up〈挖掘〉‧ground〈土壤〉‧quickly〈快速地〉
❹ Britain〈英國〉‧most〈大部分的〉‧made〈make（做）的過去分詞〉
❺ gardener〈園丁〉‧put〈put（放）的過去式〉‧plant〈植物〉‧tool〈工具〉‧
pushed〈push（推）的過去式〉‧down〈到〉‧garden〈花園〉

中譯

❶ 有好幾台起重機被使用來建造台北 101 大樓。
❷ 吊車是用來將建材吊至高空的。
❸ 機械挖土機可以迅速地挖出大量土壤。
❹ 在英國，大部分的房子是用紅色磚塊砌成的。
❺ 園丁將植物和他的工具放入手推車，並將它推到花園。

1 press conference
[prɛs ˈkɑnfərəns]
(n.) 記者會

2 photographer
[fəˈtɑgrəfə]
(n.) 攝影師

3 camera
[ˈkæmərə]
(n.) 攝影機/照相機

4 microphone
[ˈmaɪkrəˌfon]
(n.) 麥克風

5 reporter
[rɪˈportə]
(n.) 記者

❶ 記者會

The day that the representative held a press conference in the hotel,
<u>在飯店召開記者會</u>

almost every reporter from different newspapers came.

❷ 攝影師

The photographer took pictures of the movie star.

❸ 攝影機 / 照相機

The man took a picture of his girlfriend with his camera.

❹ 麥克風

The singer held a microphone in her hand.
<u>握著麥克風</u>

❺ 記者

The reporter asked the president some questions about his meeting.
<u>跟他的會議有關的問題</u>

學更多

❶ representative〈代表、代理人〉．held〈hold（舉行）的過去式〉．press〈記者們〉．
conference〈會議〉．almost〈幾乎〉．newspaper〈報社〉．came〈come（來）的過去式〉
❷ took pictures〈take pictures（照相）的過去式〉．movie〈電影〉．star〈明星〉
❸ girlfriend〈女朋友〉
❹ singer〈歌手〉．held〈hold（握著）的過去式〉．hand〈手〉
❺ asked〈ask（問）的過去式〉．president〈總統〉．question〈問題〉．meeting〈會議〉

中譯

❶ 發言人在飯店召開記者會的那天，幾乎各家報社的記者都來了。
❷ 攝影師拍了一些電影明星的照片。
❸ 男子用他的照相機幫女朋友拍照。
❹ 歌手將麥克風握在她手中。
❺ 記者詢問總統一些有關他所出席的會議的問題。

199

記者會(2)

MP3 199

1 lawyer
[ˋlɔjɚ]
(n.) 律師

2 victim
[ˋvɪktɪm]
(n.) 受害者

3 spokesperson
[ˋspoksˏpɝsn̩]
(n.) 發言人

4 conference table
[ˋkɑnfərəns ˋtebl̩]
(n.) 會議桌

5 champagne tower
[ʃæmˋpen ˋtauɚ]
(n.) 香檳酒杯塔

1 律師

The lawyer defended his client in court.
　　　　　替他的當事人辯護

2 受害者

The victim told the police about his attacker.
　　　　　　　　　　　　　襲擊他的人

3 發言人

The spokesperson gave a statement for her client.
　　　　　　　　　發表聲明

4 會議桌

The business people sat around the conference table for their meeting.
　　　　　　　　　　　　圍繞著會議桌入坐

5 香檳酒杯塔

John and Denise celebrated the occasion by pouring champagne over a stack of glasses. It was a champagne tower.　　　在疊起來的玻璃杯上倒香檳

學更多

1 defended〈defend（替⋯辯護）的過去式〉・client〈委託人、當事人〉・court〈法庭〉

2 told〈tell（告訴）的過去式〉・police〈警察〉・attacker〈攻擊者〉

3 gave〈give（給）的過去式〉・statement〈聲明〉

4 business people〈商人〉・sat〈sit（坐）的過去式〉・conference〈會議〉・meeting〈會議〉

5 celebrated〈celebrate（慶祝）的過去式〉・occasion〈時刻、場合〉・pouring〈pour（倒）的 ing 型態〉・champagne〈香檳酒〉・over〈在⋯上面〉・a stack of〈一堆、許多〉

中譯

1 在法庭上，律師替他的當事人進行辯護。

2 受害者將襲擊他的人的相關線索告訴了警方。

3 發言人替她的委託人發表了一份聲明。

4 商人圍坐著會議桌開會。

5 John 和 Denise 從層層疊起的玻璃杯上方傾倒香檳，藉以慶祝這特別的時刻。這是一個香檳酒杯塔。

MP3 200

1 security
[sɪˋkjʊrətɪ]
(n.) 警衛

2 celebrity
[sɪˋlɛbrətɪ]
(n.) 名人

3 satellite news gathering
[ˋsætl͵aɪt njuz ˋgæðərɪŋ]
(n.) 衛星連線

「satellite news gathering」可縮寫為
「SNG」。

（名人特寫圖）

4 paparazzi
[͵pɑpəˋrɑtsɪ]
(n.) 狗仔隊

（狗仔隊特寫圖）

5 bodyguard
[ˋbɑdɪ͵gɑrd]
(n.) 保鏢

❶ 警衛

The security guard stood outside the building to stop people from going inside. ~~阻止人們進入~~

❷ 名人

The celebrity has his picture taken everywhere he goes.
~~他被別人拍照~~

❸ 衛星連線

There are several SNG cars outside the president's home.
~~有好幾台 SNG 車~~

❹ 狗仔隊

The paparazzi follow the star everywhere and try to get interesting pictures.
~~狗仔到處跟著明星~~

❺ 保鑣

The star has a bodyguard to look after her.
~~照顧她~~

學更多

❶ guard〈守衛〉‧ stood〈stand（站）的過去式〉‧ outside〈在⋯外面〉‧ building〈建築物〉‧ stop...from〈阻止 A 避免 B〉‧ inside〈裡面〉

❷ picture〈照片〉‧ taken〈take（拍攝）的過去分詞〉‧ everywhere〈到處〉

❸ several〈數個的〉‧ satellite〈衛星〉‧ news〈新聞〉‧ gathering〈採集〉‧ president〈總統〉

❹ follow〈跟隨〉‧ star〈明星〉‧ try〈試圖〉‧ interesting〈引人關注的〉

❺ look after〈照顧〉

中譯

❶ 警衛站在建築物外面，阻止人們進入。

❷ 那個名人不論到哪，都會被人拍照。

❸ 總統家外面有好幾台 衛星連線（SNG） 車輛。

❹ 狗仔到處跟蹤明星，試圖拍些引人注目的照片。

❺ 那個明星有一名負責照顧她的保鑣。

1 court
[kort]
(n.) 法庭

2 judge
[dʒʌdʒ]
(n.) 法官

依法擔任審判工作，
代表國家行使審判權
的司法人員。

3 prosecutor
[ˋprɑsɪˌkjutɚ]
(n.) 檢察官

代表國家進行犯罪偵
察、提起公訴、指揮
刑事裁判執行的司法
人員。

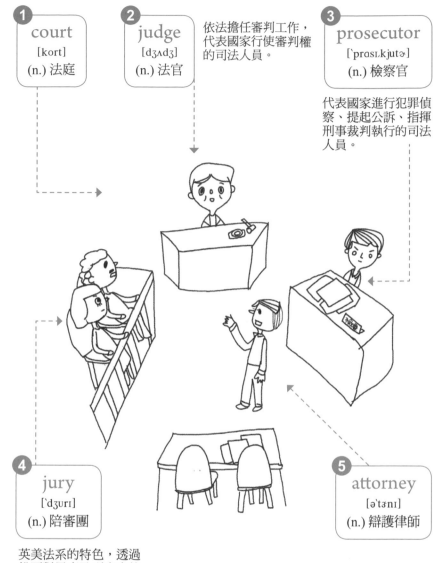

4 jury
[ˋdʒʊrɪ]
(n.) 陪審團

英美法系的特色，透過
投票對民事及刑事案件
表達意見。

5 attorney
[əˋtɝnɪ]
(n.) 辯護律師

6 public gallery
[ˋpʌblɪk ˋgælərɪ]
(n.) 旁聽席

❶ 法庭

Lots of people went to court to watch the trial.
　　　　　　　　　　　　　　旁聽審判

❷ 法官

The judge told the criminal he had to go to jail for three years.
　　　　　　　　　　　　　　他必須入監服刑

❸ 檢察官

The prosecutor said that the man should be locked up for a long time.
　　　　　　　　　　　　　　應該被關起來

❹ 陪審團

The jury decided that the man was not guilty.
　　　　　　　　　　　　　　無罪的

❺ 辯護律師

I have a good attorney, so I don't think I'll be going to jail.
　　　　　　　　　　　　　　我不覺得我會入獄

❻ 旁聽席

People gathered in the public gallery to watch the trial.
　　　　聚在旁聽席

學更多

❶ lots of〈很多〉‧ went〈go（去）的過去式〉‧ trial〈審判〉
❷ told〈tell（告訴）的過去式〉‧ criminal〈罪犯〉‧ jail〈監獄〉
❸ said〈say（說）的過去式〉‧ locked up〈lock up（關起來）的過去分詞〉
❹ decided〈decide（裁決）的過去式〉‧ guilty〈有罪的〉
❺ have〈有〉‧ good〈好的〉‧ think〈想〉
❻ gathered〈gather（聚集）的過去式〉‧ public〈公開的〉‧ gallery〈旁聽席〉

中譯

❶ 許多人到法庭旁聽審判過程。
❷ 法官告訴罪犯，他必須入監服刑三年。
❸ 檢察官說那名男子應該要被關很久。
❹ 陪審團裁決該名男子無罪。
❺ 我有一個很好的辯護律師，所以我想我應該不會入獄。
❻ 人們聚集在旁聽席，旁聽審判過程。

法庭上(2)

MP3 202

1 defendant
[dɪˋfɛndənt]
(n.) 被告

2 witness
[ˋwɪtnɪs]
(n.) 證人

3 plaintiff
[ˋplentɪf]
(n.) 原告

4 handcuff
[ˋhænd͵kʌf]
(n.) 手銬

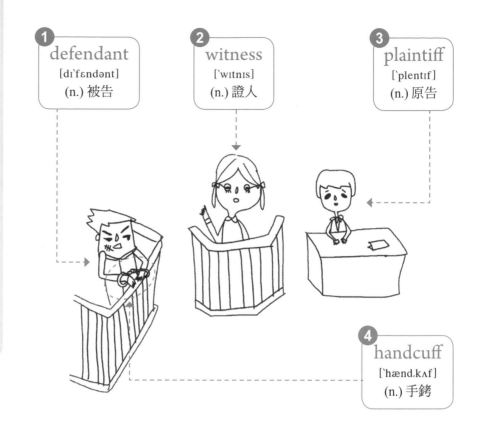

5 verdict
[ˋvɝdɪkt]
(n.) 判決

❶ 被告

The defendant in the court case said he had done nothing wrong.
　　　　　　　　訴訟案件

❷ 證人

Several witnesses told the judge and jury what they knew.
　　　　　　　　　　　　　　　　他們知道的事

❸ 原告

The plaintiff was trying to sue the defendant for $3,000,000 NT.
　　　　　　　　　　　　對被告提出訴訟而要求…

❹ 手銬

The criminal had to wear handcuffs on his wrists during the trial.
　　　　　　　　　　　　　　　　　　　　　　進行審判的過程中

❺ 判決

The verdict of the case was that the man was not guilty.
　　這件案子的判決結果是…　　　　　　　　　　　　無罪的

學更多

❶ court〈法庭〉・case〈案件〉・done〈do（做）的過去分詞〉・wrong〈錯誤的〉
❷ several〈數個的〉・judge〈法官〉・jury〈陪審團〉・knew〈know（知道）的過去式〉
❸ trying〈try（試圖）的 ing 型態〉・sue〈提出訴訟〉
❹ wear〈戴著〉・wrist〈手腕〉・during〈在…的整個期間〉・trial〈審判〉
❺ guilty〈有罪的〉

中譯

❶ 這件訴訟案中的被告說他沒有做錯任何事。
❷ 數名證人向法官和陪審團陳述他們所知道的事。
❸ 原告試圖對被告提出訴訟，要求台幣三百萬元的賠償。
❹ 審判過程中，罪犯必須在手腕上銬著手銬。
❺ 這件案子的判決結果，裁定那個男人是無罪的。

附錄

詞性分類 × 字母排序

詞性分類 × 字母排序

詞性分類 × 字母排序

詞性分類 × 字母排序

詞性分類 × 字母排序

詞性分類 × 字母排序

詞性分類 × 字母排序

詞性分類 × 字母排序

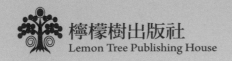

Fly 飛系列 09

圖解生活實用英語：舉目所及的人事物（附 1MP3）

初版一刷　2015 年 8 月 7 日
初版二刷　2015 年10月21日

作者	檸檬樹英語教學團隊
英語例句	Stephanie Buckley、張馨勻
插畫	許仲綺、陳博深、陳琬瑜、吳怡萱、鄭菀書、周奕伶、葉依婷、朱珮瑩、沈諭、巫秉旂、王筑儀
封面設計	陳文德
版型設計	洪素貞
英語錄音	Stephanie Buckley
責任編輯	沈祐禎、黃冠禎
發行人	江媛珍
社長‧總編輯	何聖心
出版者	檸檬樹國際書版有限公司 檸檬樹出版社
	E-mail：lemontree@booknews.com.tw
	地址：新北市235中和區中安街80號3樓
	電話‧傳真：02-29271121‧02-29272336
會計‧客服	方靖淳
法律顧問	第一國際法律事務所 余淑杏律師
	北辰著作權事務所 蕭雄淋律師
全球總經銷‧印務代理	知遠文化事業有限公司
網路書城	http://www.booknews.com.tw 博訊書網
	電話：02-26648800　傳真：02-26648801
	地址：新北市222深坑區北深路三段155巷25號5樓
港澳地區經銷	和平圖書有限公司
	電話：852-28046687　傳真：850-28046409
	地址：香港柴灣嘉業街12號百樂門大廈17樓
定價	台幣399元／港幣133元
劃撥帳號	戶名：19726702‧檸檬樹國際書版有限公司
	‧單次購書金額未達300元，請另付40元郵資
	‧信用卡‧劃撥購書需7-10個工作天

圖解生活實用英語：舉目所及的人事物 /
檸檬樹英語教學團隊著. -- 初版. -- 新北市：
檸檬樹, 2015.08
面；　公分. --（Fly 飛系列；9）
ISBN 978-986-6703-78-2（平裝附光碟片）

1.英語　2.詞彙

805.12　　　　　　　　　　　104009314